UNBREAKABLE

SPECIAL EDITION

TEXAS HEARTS
BOOK THREE

ERIN ROSE

For the ones fighting a silent battle in their minds,
and the ones who love them through it all.

ISBN: 979-8-950404-01-6

This book is a work of fiction. Any references to historical events, popular culture, corporations, real people, or real places are used fictitiously. Other names, characters, places, and events are products of the author's imagination, and any resemblance to actual events or places or persons, living or dead, is entirely coincidental. Stella, however, is based on an actual goat.

No part of this book has been created using AI-generated images or narrative. The author supports the rights of humans to control their artistic works.

Written by Erin Rose
Edited by Mad Hatter Edits
Sensitivity Edited by Dee Lamarr

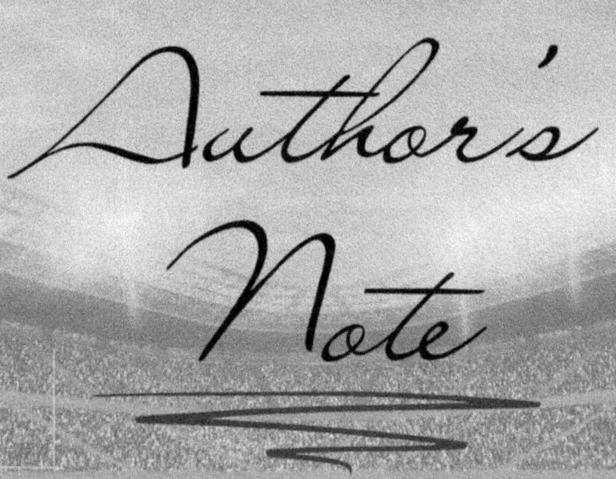

FOREWORD

This book deals with some heavy mental health topics that I tried to handle with the utmost care and respect. Theo's mental illness is an amalgam from my training and experience as a licensed therapist, inspiration from past clients, research, and firsthand accounts from individuals diagnosed with the same condition as the MMC.

Any views of/attitudes towards mental health conditions, medication, and symptoms do ***not*** reflect the personal opinions of the author, but those of the characters based on their experiences and biases. The mentions and depictions of suicidal thoughts and urges are those of the character **only**.

Theo's journey with mental illness is completely his own. His experience was made as accurate as possible, but artistic license was still taken. Everyone's journey with mental health is different—no two stories are alike. My hope is that Theo's story breeds empathy, understanding, and awareness for those living with a mental illness, their families, and their partners.

If you or a loved one is struggling with mental health or in crisis, help is always available. Your mental health matters, so please do not hesitate to utilize the resources below:

Suicide & Crisis Lifeline: Call or text 988

Live Crisis Counselor Text Line: text HOME to 741741

Content Warnings

This book is intended for mature audiences only (18+). All scenes between the two main characters ARE consensual. This book includes explicit sex scenes.

This book contains scenes that some might find triggering. One character's struggles with mental illness and neurodivergence is detailed in this book. This includes manic episodes, depressive episodes, depictions of suicidal ideation, aborted suicide attempts, and intrusive thoughts encouraging suicide.

There is a brief scene of dubious-consent regarding sexual activity due to recreational drug use by the characters involved. One of the MMCs also engages in sexual activity before he's involved with the other MMC. There is no cheating in this book. Brief mention of car accident occurring due to intoxication. No one was injured.

Please practice self-care and take care of yourself before reading this book. Your mental health is most important!
Content Warnings: Manic and Depressive Episodes depicted, Suicidal Thoughts and Suicidal Ideation depicted, Drug Usage to Self Medicate, Alcohol Use Disorder, Driving Under the Influence.

Dawson & Theo's Second Chance Playlist

1h 13m

Dancing On My Own — Calum Scott
Somebody To Love — Queen/Paul Canning
Somewhere Only We Know— Keane/Boyce Avenue
Viva La Vida — Robert R
Faithfully — Piano Tribute Players
Iris — Boyce Avenue
Song for the Waiting — Aron Wright
Chasing Cars — Snow Patrol
Only You— Jake Wesley Rogers
Head Above Water -- Avril Lavigne
Carry You Home — Alex Warren
I Don't Want To Miss A Thing — Aerosmith
Rescue My Heart — Liz Longley
Flaws — Calum Scott
Unbreakable — Jamie Scott
Runaway — The Blue Notes
Unwell - Taylor Acorn
Don't Give Up On Me — Andy Grammer
Who Knew - P!nk
Zombie — YUNGBLUD

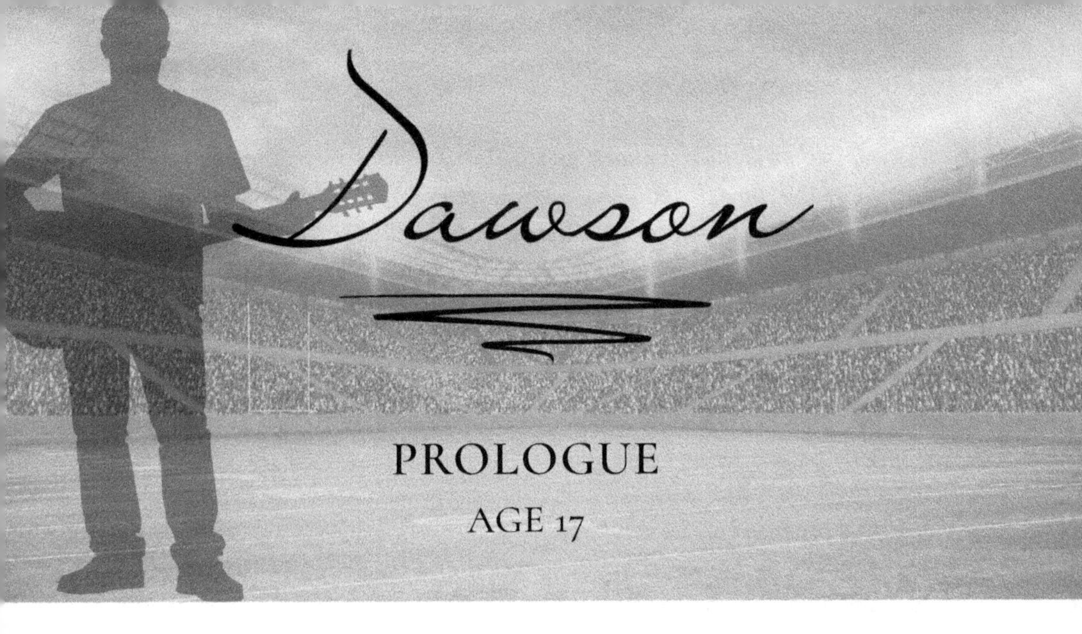

PROLOGUE

AGE 17

Cold.

That's all I feel sitting here on the ground at our place. Our hideout.

Our Neverland.

He always thought it was a clever name for this place when we were kids. It was the one place we didn't have to worry about the outside world or growing up, which was ironic since we probably did the most growing up in this very spot together.

But he's not here.

He's not anywhere.

I look down at my tux, remembering how excited I was for him to see me in it. I had hoped he'd peel it off me when we snuck back to Neverland later tonight. I knew without a doubt he'd look beautiful in his.

Homecoming was supposed to be our big moment. After years of hiding, we were finally going to walk into that gym, hand in hand, and show everyone the truth of us and what we were to each other. Not just best friends, but soulmates.

So where the hell is he?

Maybe I didn't wait back at the house long enough? He's never been a punctual person, so maybe he just lost track of time or fell asleep? Or maybe he went to get one of those flower things for my tux and he's running late? It would be just the kind of cheesy, romantic thing he'd think of.

I numbly pull out my phone and call him again. I can't remember how many times I've done this tonight. Eight? Fifteen?

It goes straight to voicemail this time without even ringing.

Damn it! I don't fucking understand. Where is he? Why isn't he here with me where he belongs?

He's been acting so weird the last two weeks, but I didn't think anything of it. He goes through strange moods all the time. What if he was having second thoughts about coming out? I mean, that can't be it. After the football game last night, he was excited and told me he couldn't wait for the dance. He'd gone a little overboard with the drinking at the afterparty, but he still seemed happy! He promised me he was okay.

Oh god, what if he isn't? Why the fuck didn't I try harder to find out what was going on with him?

I scramble to my feet, making a beeline for his house. As soon as I'm clear of the woods at the back of the property, I sprint towards his house. My gut is telling me that something is wrong, otherwise he would have picked me up like he promised to do. Like we planned.

I bang on his front door relentlessly. I try to catch my breath as I wait for him.

He's okay. He has to be okay.

The door opens and I want to collapse in relief until I get a better view of who opened it.

"Mr. Bishop? Is Theo home? He didn't come to meet me for the dance and he's not answering his phone."

I sound breathless and hoarse, sweat making a slow journey down the back of my neck, but I don't care. I just need to see him.

Mr. Bishop seems...off. He looks disheveled and upset, and he's giving me a weird look. Why is he looking at me like that? My stomach is cramping painfully.

"He's not here, Dawson," he tells me, but it takes me a bit to process what he said.

"What do you mean? Where is he then?" I ask frantically. I feel seconds away from breaking down into tears or screams or God knows what. This is too much.

"He's going to stay with his mother."

"What? That doesn't make sense. His mom is out in Huntsville or something. Why would he be there? I don't—"

My throat is closing. I can barely force the words out.

Fuck, I feel sick.

"It's for the best. Trust me."

For the best? What the fuck does that mean? What's best for Theo is being with me!

"Sir, please, I just need to talk to him..."

"I'll let him know and he can reach out when he's ready," Mr. Bishop says.

"Wait, just—you don't understand. I need—"

"He can't talk right now, Dawson," he cuts me off. "But he's safe and where he needs to be. I'm sorry, but that's all I can tell you."

"P-please...it's Homecoming. W-we had plans...we—"

"Dawson..."

Everything is falling apart. My chest is caving in, breathing hurts. My face is wet with tears, making my eyes blur. My brain and heart are screaming, I can't do this. I can't...I need Theo. I just want Theo.

But Theo is gone.

"C-can you...at least tell h-him that I...that I love him?"

The look Mr. Bishop is giving me is a kick to the gut. He's always been kind to me, treated me like a son. But all I can see on his face now is...pity.

"I'll give him your message." I turn to walk away but he calls to me. "Dawson?"

I can't help the wave of hope that hits me before his next words shatter it.

"I don't say this to be cruel, but you need to let him go...and find a way to move on."

The door closes gently in my face. It feels like the final nail in my coffin as I'm buried alive. I'm trapped, unable to breathe, or think, or do anything, but slowly die inside.

Let him go?

He's already done that.

Theo left me and I have no choice but to move on. But I can't. I'm left here.

Broken.

Alone.

Cold.

CHAPTER ONE

Time heals all wounds. That's what we're told as children from the moment pain touches us. It's meant to give us solace and remind us that whatever heartache we're experiencing will pass and we'll eventually feel better.

I've never heard bigger bullshit in my entire life.

Time healed nothing for me. That fact was made damn clear the second I saw *him* again last weekend. I had been there to help out my best friend Bash move his boyfriend Micah into their new apartment. Suddenly, there he was. And he hadn't been alone.

He had been sucking face with some guy, oblivious to everything around them as they were saying goodbye after what I'm sure had been an eventful night. When they'd finally come up for air he had seen me across the lobby.

I know pain. I've had bones broken, my shoulder dislocated. I've been tackled more times than I can fathom on the football field. Yet none of that pain could even touch what I felt seeing Theo Bishop again after nearly four years.

Like I said. Time heals shit.

Now I was sitting there in a bar listening to godawful karaoke, surrounded by my friends, trying to have fun after a grueling end to the semester. Needless to say, fun was the farthest thing from my mind. Theo made it impossible. It seemed like he was everywhere. First, the apartment where my best friends lived, and now the bar where we came to hang out. It felt like he was invading my space and killing my peace of mind as I watched him with his shiny new toy for the evening. He wasn't the same man from the apartment building, which somehow hurt worse than if he'd been Theo's boyfriend. How many other guys were there?

The Theo I used to know wasn't a player. A flirt, sure, but he was ruthlessly loyal and a hopeless romantic. You wouldn't know that from how he was hanging all over his "date" while also checking out any person near him that caught his interest. Every few minutes, the guy yanked his face down for a messy, heated kiss that Theo returned so enthusiastically it made the beer I'd been drinking bubble and churn in my stomach.

This wasn't supposed to hurt so much. Years had passed. I thought I'd moved on like I was told to, but every nerve ending was on fire. My brain conjured images of me stomping over, ripping Theo away from that handsy fucker, and reclaiming those sinful lips as mine.

But even as I thought it, I knew it wasn't possible. He was no longer mine and hadn't been for a long time. A bone-deep sadness sunk in, blanketing me in a heaviness that felt inescapable.

My friends were going on about summer plans and other things, but I couldn't make myself focus on them. Breathing was taking all of my energy. My fingers twitched out a rhythm, dying for a release on ivory keys as they always did when I was stressed or overwhelmed. My gaze caught on a keyboard on stage, my mind made up in a split second.

I slid out of my chair and made my way up to the karaoke master, whispering in his ear what my plan was and fully prepared to beg for the chance. I didn't know if he was a Longhorns football fan who recognized me or if he could sense my desperation, but he let me skip the lineup without a fuss. I settled behind the rather impressive keyboard and set up the microphone how I needed it.

"Hey guys, um...I'm hoping y'all don't mind if I change things up a bit for karaoke night," I murmured into the mic. The crowd gave an eager round of applause, which helped settle some of the nerves rioting in my gut. I had a flicker of doubt that it was a mistake to do this right then, knowing what I'd be revealing to him if I did.

Like a magnet drawing me in, my eyes drifted up and connected with those striking blue ones that I used to get so lost in. My chest felt like it was caving in under the tension building between us and I knew he felt it too. I could see it carved into every line on his beautiful face. Our tether of fate couldn't be cut, no matter how hard he had tried to sever it.

I filled my lungs with a steadying breath and then started to play. I'd played the Calum Scott song so many times since I'd first heard it that it was now ingrained in me. The words poured out of me as I flayed myself alive on the stage, my wounds exposed for all to see.

For him to see.

Lyrics of watching your former love kiss someone else while standing helpless and invisible in the corner dug into my skin like splinters. My sight once again snagged on Theo's and this time, I didn't look away. Some part of me wanted him to see my pain, my anger. He should know what he's done to me.

That flawless jaw ticked repeatedly and his brows drew together as he held my gaze. So many unanswered questions raced through my head and I could almost fool myself that he heard them.

I sang of the distance between us, him being so far away while still near. The music was no longer my own. It came from a part of me clawing its way up through layers of resentment, hurt, and longing. I couldn't control it. I was shocked I'd still been able to steady my voice and not miss a beat. Theo's eyes were penetrating, and I felt the force of them through the haze of pain that was swirling between us. It was like a knife being wedged between my ribs.

My voice cracked on the last refrain, the truth of our reality crashing into me suddenly. Just like the song said, all I could do was say goodbye. This wasn't a "hello again" or a sweet reunion. This wasn't two lovers finding their way back to each other. This was a blip on our timeline, a passing moment I couldn't hold onto.

I saw the moment he recognized the shift in me and his hand went to a chain around his neck, wrapping it around the object hanging there. My heart was pounding, breaking, shattering in the last chorus as I gave everything into the song. Years of memories flooded me in a beautiful, destructive tidal wave as I crooned the final notes before it all stopped.

It was as if time had paused to let the dust settle around us, like dueling pistols fired into the stillness and we were waiting to see the damage. Who drew first? Who was the first to fall?

People rose to their feet, claps and cheers filtering through the sound of blood rushing in my ears. All the while our gazes were still locked and I silently pleaded for him to hold on. To not let go.

Not again.

But he looked away and I was left bleeding out on the stage.

I shook myself out of my stupor and gave a small smile to the audience, barely aware of anything other than my urgent need for an escape. Everything was too much. The lights, the sounds, the stifling air. It saturated my veins and suffocated me.

I jumped off the stage and quickly headed for the back exit. I vaguely registered people's praises and back slaps as I passed them, but all I could focus on was getting out before I broke completely.

I burst out onto a dimly lit backstreet that was thankfully empty save for a couple of parked cars. I fought to bring air into my lungs, feeling every thump of my heart against my ribs like a cannon shot. My fingernails bit into my palms, the sharp sting helping to ground me.

"Nice song, Mercury."

My head fell back on a resigned sigh as the raspy timbre of his voice washed over me. His old nickname for me was both a caress and a slap in the same measure. He always did have a knack for sneaking up on me.

"Guess I should have expected the cold shoulder," he mumbled when I didn't respond.

A bitter laugh escaped me before I could force it back. Emotions warred within me, all fighting to the surface to break free. I spun on my heel to face him and fuck, it was a mistake. My mind whited out as my eyes crashed with those crystalline blues, so different from my own pale shade. The stubble on his jaw sparked memories of how it used to feel against my flesh. The lean muscles in his arms reminded me of how I used to belong wrapped in them.

But that was then.

"Why?" I croaked out. Of all the questions and retorts and scathing accusations that clashed inside me, that one word slipped free, weighted down with all the pain I still carried.

Theo's face contorted ever so slightly and his guilt was easy to read. He knew what I was really asking.

Why did you leave me?

His fingers twitched restlessly at his side, like he was reaching for something he couldn't quite grasp. His Adam's apple rippled with a rough swallow.

“I had no choice,” he said barely above a whisper.

“No choice?” I asked incredulously. He didn’t respond or even look me in the eye. All this time waiting for those four words that did nothing to mollify me. If anything, they ignited my rarely seen temper and it was all I could do to keep from decking him in the face.

The silence stretched and twisted around us, and it made my skin itch just under the surface.

“You say you didn’t have a choice,” I grated out, “but you stole mine away from me. I didn’t get a choice to say goodbye or know what went wrong. You just disappeared without a word and it—”

It broke me.

I managed to bite back the admission before it left my lips. He’d seen enough of my vulnerability and scars for one evening. I’d never been good with words or expressing myself. Music had always helped me speak from the heart when my words failed me. My song tonight said more than I could ever hope to get out amidst the storm of turmoil inside me.

“Forget it. It doesn’t matter anymore,” I intoned, shaking my head at the absurd expectations I had for any answers. I went to move around him, but his hand darted out and gripped my bicep firmly.

I was whipped around and shoved against the wall, his hand cradling the back of my head as his lips crashed into mine. The world tilted under my feet at the familiar taste of him. His tongue invaded my mouth and all I could do was surrender to him. All the thoughts racing through my head were silenced as he devoured me like he had the right to.

I felt his thigh shove between my legs, my cock hardening so fast I got a little lightheaded. He tangled his fingers in my hair and I fed him my moan at the delicious sting when he tugged it just like he used to. He still played my body better than I played that piano.

It infuriated me. I needed to tear myself away, to shove him back and demand he explain himself. I wanted to rage at him and ask how he dared to kiss me like he still loved me, like he’d never left.

But I couldn’t. No part of me could bear to lose even the tiniest fraction of him that I could get.

Before I could get my bearings, he ripped away from me, his panting breaths mingling with mine in the few inches that separated us. I was trembling, clutching at his waist as though I could anchor us to this moment so it couldn't be over.

"Dawson," he rumbled. I clamped my eyes shut. I couldn't look at him. Not when I heard the warning loud and clear in his voice.

"I'm not the Theo you remember. I'm not him. You need to grieve him and move on because he's gone. Don't keep holding on to a ghost."

My mangled heart shredded even further and I didn't think that was possible. The last ember of hope within me extinguished and I went numb. I slowly opened my eyes only for them to catch on the chain that dangled in front of his chest, threaded through a silver high school class ring.

My breath hitched and the numbness splintered at the sight. Tears welled along my lash line and I fought to hold them back. An aching lump formed in my throat and lodged there. I reached for the ring, gingerly fingering the metal and the initials I knew to be inscribed on the inner edge.

My initials.

"Yet you still kept this," I whispered hoarsely.

"I made you a promise," he said, low and rough.

"Then it's the only one you didn't break." I glanced up at him and remorse flashed in his eyes before they shuttered quickly. Theo stepped back, taking all the warmth in my body with him. I shivered when the coldness I felt was reflected in his stare.

"Like I said, I'm not him anymore," he said coolly. I was frozen in place as he disappeared back into the bar, reeling from our disorienting encounter. I was shaken up and left on edge with far more questions than I had before.

I made my way back inside and crumpled into my seat, gaze trained on the tabletop so I didn't see the pity or apprehension on my friends' faces.

"Hey D...what do you need from us right now?" Bash asked. I barely felt the hand he laid comfortingly on my shoulder.

"I just..." I broke off, not knowing how to answer him. I didn't want to talk. I didn't want to explain. There was only one thing that came to mind. "I need to forget..."

No explanation needed, they all jumped into action. Shots were lined up in front of me, stories were told to distract me, and one of

Micah's friends, Fin, stole my hand for some kind of massage that nearly put me in a coma of bliss.

I could sense everyone's curious stares and the pity they undoubtedly felt for me. As hard as I struggled to keep my gaze pinned to the table, it was pulled in Theo's direction. I immediately wished I hadn't looked. He grabbed his date's hand with a look of grim determination on his face as he pulled the grinning man behind him and strode out the front door.

My stomach rolled violently and I downed the nearest shot glass, praying to whatever deity happened to be listening that I could get trashed enough to forget every second of the night. It might have been a fool's errand, but fuck if I wasn't going to try.

Eventually, I settled into a foggy state as the alcohol permeated my blood. Griffin, a lacrosse player who was friends with some of the guys at the table, had us cracking up over this story of tragically timed food poisoning the lacrosse team had gotten coming back from an away game. As one who had often endured very long bus rides with the football team, I couldn't even imagine being trapped in a vehicle with the smells and sounds of my suffering teammates like that.

The story had done its job for a little while, but it wasn't long before the memories of me and Theo seeped back into my consciousness. Once everyone's attention was on the conversation and off of me, Aly sidled up next to me. She'd been eyeing me all night, but once I had noticed Theo, she'd faded into the background with everyone else.

She was Fin's best friend whom I hadn't met before that evening, but he had brought her along to integrate into the group. From what I had heard and seen so far, she seemed really nice. Funny, sweet, beautiful. Everything I should have wanted instead of being hung up on the guy who left me behind. She gave me a look I couldn't quite interpret with the alcohol buzzing through me. Her hand landed on my knee, squeezing it gently. Through my slightly blurry vision, I saw her lips tug into a soft smile.

"Want some company tonight?" She asked quietly. I felt myself nodding without really knowing what I was saying yes to. She linked her fingers with mine, said a quick round of goodbyes to our friends and promised them she'd get me home safely.

We made it outside and the muggy Texas air did nothing to cool my sweaty skin. I stumbled behind her as she started down the sidewalk, but she only squeezed my hand tighter.

"It'll be okay, Dawson. I've got you," she reassured me. I mumbled out the directions to my apartment, trusting her to steer us the right way. I didn't know what she wanted from me or if I could even give it to her, but I did know one thing. I didn't want to be alone.

With one devastating kiss and my ring around his neck, Theo destroyed me all over again and I was scared of what would be left of me in the morning.

CHAPTER TWO

"I hope you realize I'm still salty about you abandoning me for the rest of the summer," Aly griped from my bed, twirling my plush football pillow in her hands. "Who am I supposed to hang out with now? Fin works most days and my other friends all went home in May."

"It's just a few weeks. You're also welcome to come hang out anytime you want, Al. My parent's house isn't that far."

"Oh gee, you know I'd love to, but some of us work for a living, Hayes," she sassed. She stuck her tongue out and threw the pillow at my head, missing by several inches.

"Very classy. Temper tantrums are a good look on you," I teased. Aly gasped loudly, her hand flying to her chest.

"That was the most romantic thing you've ever said to me," she said dramatically. "Now see? Where am I going to get that kind of devoted affection until school starts again?"

"Tinder," I deadpanned, earning me both her middle fingers even as she smirked, kissing the tip of one and blowing it at me. I grabbed and stuck it in my pocket before I headed into the bathroom to gather my toiletries as Aly went off about her summer work schedule and some problem with a bitchy coworker.

Aly and I had become close in the last five weeks after karaoke night. She didn't mind that I wasn't a big talker and would rather be at home than out partying, whereas she lived for the Austin nightlife and really only stopped talking to eat or sleep.

That night at the bar, I had figured she'd wanted to hook up and I'd been fully prepared for her to freak out or get angry at me for leading her on when I couldn't go through with it. I had thought about it the entire walk to my place, determined and desperate to feel anything other than the fierce ache that had started the moment I laid eyes on Theo and his date.

By the time we'd walked through my door, the thought of touching anyone but him made me sick to my stomach. Surprisingly, Aly hadn't been offended in the slightest. Instead, she threw herself on my couch, pulled up some cheesy action movie, and had me laughing most of the night with her insane commentary.

Somehow she picked up on exactly what I had needed. She never pressed me for information on Theo past his name or what had happened to tank my mood before I rejoined the group. I didn't know if she sensed that I wasn't emotionally able to talk about it or she just wasn't the prying type, but I got to live happily in denial when she was around. No pressure, no expectations, no questions asked.

"Well, it's an open invitation if you get some time off. We've got a guest room with your name on it," I told her as I sauntered back into my room and zipped up all my stuff.

"What about football practice?" She asked curiously. "Aren't you muscly jock types supposed to be practicing twenty-four seven to keep your bodies from exploding with all that testosterone?"

My gut clenched uncomfortably at the question. It had become a bit of a sore subject for me lately.

"I went to the two required camps in June, but the rest of them are optional up until August. The sport steals most of my time during the fall as it is. I didn't want it to steal my whole summer too, you know?"

In truth, I probably should have been staying on campus and going to practices and workouts with the team. However, with certain decisions I'd recently made for myself, the sport just wasn't as important as it used to be. That was a conversation I needed to have with my dad sooner rather than later, but I hadn't really worked up to that yet.

"Uuughh, but why are you going home? No one actually wants to spend their summer break with their parents, unless they're being forced," Aly sulked. "Wait. Is that it? Are you being coerced into this? Is this against your will? Blink twice if you're under duress!"

"Of course it couldn't possibly be because I actually *like* seeing my family?" I shot her an unimpressed look. She stared back, horrified by the notion.

"You mean there are actually people who *enjoy* their family? I thought that only happened in really cheesy sitcoms," she shuddered.

"It's been known to happen on occasion," I responded dryly.

"Sounds like my personal nightmare, but what the fuck do I know? My mom gets boozy with the pool boy and my dad is an emotionally stunted, workaholic mess, hence why I chose a school hundreds of blessed miles away from them," she snickered.

"What about a boozy mess?" Nate burst into my room and threw himself on the bed next to Aly, loudly crunching on an apple in his hand. "Sounds like a good time to me."

Nathaniel had a habit of crashing into my room unexpectedly and I had long ago given up trying to break him of the habit. I'd have better luck potty training a squirrel. Rooming with your best friend definitely has its drawbacks at times.

"We were talking about how my parents are an unmitigated disaster compared to Dawson's own Brady Bunch," Aly explained with a deceptively sweet smile.

"That's a little bit of a stretch—"

"Nah, that's not quite right. His parents give more *Friday Night Lights*. His dad always reminded me of Coach Taylor. Did you know he was in the NFL? Daddy Hayes was one of the best QB's in his day. That dude's arm was golden!" Nate relayed excitedly.

"Christ, please never call him Daddy Hayes again, I beg you," I groaned. Nate just cackled and blew me a kiss.

"Oooh, Coach Taylor was hot. With how gorgeous Dawson is, I can see his dad being that way too. Is he a total silver fox?" Aly chirped gleefully.

"Well, he's not so silver, but I'd say he's a solid 8.5. Here, check it out!" Nate yanked out his phone, presumably to either Google my dad or stalk my Instagram for pictures of him.

"Great. Cool. So y'all freaks do that and I'm just gonna go vomit real fast and hit the road," I grouched, grabbing my duffle up before trudging into our living room.

"Hot damn!" Aly shouted from my bedroom. "Dawson, on a scale of one to ten, how open is your dad to having a sugar baby? Please say ten!"

"If he does and your mom gets lonely, I'd be happy to step in and comfort her!" Nate yelled out. "Hey D, that means I'll be your new daddy!"

"God, I need so much therapy," I grumbled to myself as their laughter carried down the hall.

I grabbed my car keys and intended to hightail it out of there, but was intercepted before I made it to the door.

"Aw, were you seriously trying to leave without a goodbye? Not cool, bro," Nate complained from the hallway. "I was just teasing you, D. I didn't mean anything by it..."

Regret swamped me at seeing the worry on his face. "Don't sweat it, man. We're all good," I reassured him. "I just promised my mom I'd be there before noon, is all."

The little white lie didn't make me feel great, but I couldn't easily explain my desperate need for space when I was feeling overstimulated, and I didn't want Nate to take it personally. I loved my close knit group of friends, but their personalities were so different from mine that I often needed alone time to regroup after hanging out with them. Even Bash, who was the closest to my temperament, was still subjected to me only being able to take him in small doses. That was pretty much everyone. I didn't *people* very well. The only person who'd ever been an exception to that rule was—

Fuck. No. We're not thinking about him. Erase the hard drive and move the hell on, like he told you to.

If only life worked that way. I was slowly becoming convinced nothing would completely erase Theo from my memory.

Or my heart.

I shut the door on that thought fast and hard. I needed to get home, away from UT, away from where *he* was now. This last month, I had managed to avoid him after our run-in at the bar, only going from my apartment to the athletic facility and back as much as I could. I also avoided hanging out with Bash and Micah at their new place since we'd discovered Theo was evidently their neighbor now. Knowing he was on the same campus as me after all these years was screwing with my head. Thankfully it was summer and I hadn't run into him around campus or, God forbid, one of my classes.

And then there was the kiss. One damn kiss that stole my sanity and haunted every hour of thought. It infuriated me as much as it consumed me. He kissed me, then in the same breath told me to forget him. What the hell was I supposed to do with that?

"Dawson? You alright?"

Aly's voice snapped me out of it. I realized a beat too late that she had emerged from my room and been trying to get my attention.

"Yeah, sorry. What did you say?"

She bit her lip and cocked her head at me. I ignored the question I saw on her face. It was getting harder to keep everything I'd been struggling with bottled up and locked away from those closest to me. But I wasn't ready to deal with it.

"She asked if you're still throwing your big Fourth of July party. Your parents are out of town that weekend, yeah?" Nate supplied.

Truthfully, I had forgotten that I volunteered my parents' place for the holiday a few months back. I couldn't even tell you how Nate and Bash coerced me into it, but somehow those fuckers managed it.

"Yep. Dad gave us the green light as long as I promised him we wouldn't trash the house and the pool."

Nate whooped at the news and started brainstorming all the different types of fireworks he and our friends could buy for the occasion. All the while, Aly pinned me with her inquisitive gaze, making it feel like she could see straight through me to all the anxiety and unease that plagued me. About football, about Theo, about this unrelenting sense of dread that everything was about to change.

"Yeah, that sounds great," I tried not to sigh. "I really need to get going. I'll see you in a few days. Text me later, ok?"

I didn't stick around to hear their response. I snatched my bag and fled out the door, wishing I could just as easily flee from my problems.

CHAPTER THREE

I zoned out for the half hour it took to drive to my house, muscle memory leading me back while my mind spun out. I couldn't seem to force away the anxiety about Theo being back and the talk I needed to have with my dad.

Once I turned onto the long driveway to my childhood home, I was thankfully distracted by the sight of my sister Danielle attempting to wrangle her pet goat Stella in the front yard. Back in high school, she had rescued the scraggly creature from one of the neighbors down the road who had sold their land and left her behind.

I can fucking relate...

She'd cracked my dad in under a minute to let her keep it. Mom was the tougher sell, but even she broke and let her keep the wretched thing. It was definitely on brand for my sister. Not many people said no to her. Once Dani left for Baylor two years ago, it came down to my parents to take care of the animal, but even they fell in love with her before long. As for me, I gave goatzilla a wide berth after the furry demon nearly took my balls off during feeding time the first month we had her.

I heard Dani shrieking at the fast little fucker as I pulled up and climbed out of my truck, the goat darting around her quicker than she could keep up.

"You come here right now! Don't you—oh for the love of...I swear, if you think I'm feeding you after this—agh, *stop* it! STELLAAA!"

The goat screamed in response, the sound drowning out Dani's frustrated ranting. Dani let out an indignant squawk and stomped her foot like a child instead of the twenty-year-old she was.

"Don't you scream at me! I haven't seen you in months and *this* is the welcome I get?"

"That's because she's a Longhorns fan. We'll have to cleanse the house now that you've tainted it with your Baylor stench," I called out.

Dani whipped around and flipped me the bird. "Cleanse this, bitch!"

"Language," I grasped my metaphorical pearls. "Do you kiss our mother with that mouth?"

She rolled her eyes even as she broke into a grin and charged, my arms wide open to catch her as she barreled into me.

"I missed you, loser! It's about time you showed your ugly face," She said, hugging me with a stranglehold around my neck while her five foot three frame had me bending down uncomfortably.

"Yeah yeah, I missed you too, gremlin," I said affectionately. I ruffled her hair before playfully shoving her away. "Also FYI, Stella is making a break for the back acre over there."

Dani cursed before chasing after the animal yet again. I took a second to drink in the view of my family home. It sat on fifteen acres mostly made up of dense woods that were common around the Barton Creek Greenbelt outside Austin. It had been the main selling point for Dad when he and Mom bought it.

I had practically grown up in those woods. They were the landscape of most of my childhood adventures after moving here. I'd lose myself for hours in the foliage, hiding from the world and enjoying the solitude it provided. It was also within those woods that I first met the curious, kind boy who became my best friend.

The boy who became my everything.

In my frantic desire to escape the city and where I knew he would be, I hadn't thought about how much of our shared history was on this very land. Pieces of us were sunk into the earth, carved into the trees, floating on the wind. There was no place I could go where memories of us couldn't reach me.

I shook off the painful nostalgia, unwilling to let more thoughts of him invade and headed inside. The smell of my mom's barbecue greeted me and my stomach gurgled on cue. Coleslaw and baked beans were laid out on the island as I rounded the corner into the empty kitchen.

"Uhh, hello? Mom? Dad?" I called out into the house.

A flash of brown and white flew out at me, tangling in between my legs. I dropped to my knees and was immediately assaulted by a wet tongue and needy whines.

"There's my Penny girl! How are you, sweet baby? I missed you so much. Did you miss me?" I cooed at our Springer Spaniel. The dog relentlessly tried to fit all sixty pounds of her lean body onto my lap to no avail.

"Ah, I see where your priorities are. The dog gets top billing over your mother."

I stood and made my way over to Mom, giving her an indulgent smile. She pulled me into a long hug, her familiar cloves and honey scent hitting my nose. When she pulled back, she looked me over as she always did, as if to check I was still in one piece.

"Well, you don't look any worse for wear. You have my good genes to thank for that," she winked at me.

The back door swung open with a *thunk* and Dani strode in with twigs in her hair and grass stains up and down her front.

"Too bad you can't say the same for her," I smirked. Dani smacked me on the back of the head as she plodded into the kitchen with us.

"I almost took an eye out trying to get Stella back in her pen. It was like corralling the Flash," she growled. "What the hell have you been feeding her, Mom?"

"Nothing but the usual, sweetie. Her pellets, some hay, a little cocaine to give her some pep. Why? Was that not right?" Mom blinked innocently.

"Okay, the sarcasm can go take a long walk off a short cliff, thank you," Dani groused. "Next time you give me grief about my sass, I'll remind you of this moment, woman."

She narrowed her eyes and stole a dinner roll off the island before turning on her heel to head to her room.

"I forgot how fun it is to rile her up," Mom chuckled. "Honey, would you mind grabbing your dad for lunch? He should be in his office."

I gave her a quick nod and bounded up the stairs. I peeked into the first room in the hall and saw Dad lounging back in his massive leather chair, reading through a sheaf of papers. Hanging above his head were two NFL jerseys, one from his tenure with the Bears and the other from his time with the Cowboys.

We'd moved to Dallas from Chicago when I was too little to remember it, but we'd landed in Austin when a torn rotator cuff forced Dad to retire when I was about nine. He always said the silver lining of his injury was more time with us, but we all knew how much he missed it. It was one of the reasons it was so hard to find a way to tell him that I wouldn't be following in his steps.

Dad glanced up and grinned when he saw me come in. His sandy brown hair that matched my own had a few flecks of gray barely visible in the light with faint laugh lines around his eyes. Nate's and Aly's disturbing comments from earlier popped into my head and I inwardly groaned.

Note to self: Google nearby therapists tonight.

I wasn't a stranger to people drooling over both my parents. It just wasn't something I wanted to hear about...ever. Especially from my friends.

"Hey champ, how's it going?" Dad asked, rounding the desk and engulfing me in his arms.

"Can't complain. I'm just livin' the dream," I lied cheerfully.

"Excited for your last year at UT?" he smiled widely. He leaned back against his desk, picking up the photo of me in my Longhorn football gear that he kept next to his computer. "Those were some of the best years of my life playing for the Horns. And now you're about to be a senior and graduate soon. Damn, it goes by so fast," he sighed wistfully. "By this time next year, you'll be signed to a pro team and really living out that dream of yours."

The ever-present knot in my stomach tightened even more. It would have been the perfect segue to tell him what I'd known for over a year, that my dreams lay outside the professional sports world.

Come on, just say it. Don't be a pansy about this, Hayes. Rip off the band aid and tell him already.

"You bet," I choked out with a tight smile.

You cowardly liar who lies like a lying coward...

"I only hope your decision to duck out on conditioning and practice this summer doesn't hurt your chances. I'm still shocked you even got Coach Walker's approval for this as the team captain." His tone was laced with disapproval and I couldn't meet his eyes.

Admittedly, Coach wasn't my biggest fan after I pressed the issue to leave campus a few weeks ago, but I couldn't find it in me to care much.

I had spent the last seven years giving everything I had to football, summers included, trying to live up to the quarterback legacy left by my dad and my grandpa.

The truth was I wasn't as invested anymore. It wasn't what I wanted for my life. For years, Dad has held onto the dream that I would pick up his NFL mantle and get drafted after graduation. Every football season was spent pushing me to be the best, look good for scouts, keep my "eye on the prize".

It was all too much, it was becoming suffocating. I hated disappointing him. He was hard on me, but he loved me and truly believed I could go all the way. I just wished his dream wasn't at the expense of mine.

I shoved my hands in my pockets so that dad didn't see them shaking.

"I promise, it's not gonna be a problem. Coach understood and I'll keep up my conditioning here," I assured him, feeling like a piece of shit for not coming clean. "Uh, Mom says lunch is ready for us by the way. We should head down."

I tried to make it to the door, but Dad called my name and I reluctantly turned back to him. The look on his face was indecipherable and I worried he'd seen through my lies.

"You, uh...you happen to see anyone over at the Bishops' house when you pulled up?" Dad inquired casually, throwing me off at the change in topic.

Pathetic didn't even begin to describe how my pulse raced at the sound of Theo's last name. I instinctively looked out the window to the house next door, remembering how I'd spent the better half of my teenage years sneaking over there. I could practically sketch from memory the layout of the backyard, the limestone pool, and the gnarled oak tree that could be scaled up to the last room on the top floor. A room I knew better than my own.

"N-no, I didn't," I stammered.

"Gotcha," Dad quickly responded. "I just wondered if, um, Grady was home yet. I had a question to ask him about some boat repairs I'm doing, but I'll call him later. No big deal. So, lunch?"

I gave him a bewildered look, wondering why he was nervously rambling and seemed uncomfortable. My Dad didn't ramble. He was one of the most put-together and eloquent people I knew. Something told me there was more to his question, but I also didn't want to prolong the conversation. Even hearing about Grady, Theo's dad, had me flashing back to the last time I talked to the man three and a half years ago. And that was a night I had zero fucking interest in revisiting.

At lunch, I made it a point to keep my mouth full so I was less likely to be interrogated about what was going on in my life per the Hayes family tradition. Dani prattled on at length about her time at Baylor while Mom pressed for information on her dating life. That set Dad off on a story about some crazy clients he'd shown around this lakefront property last month just to avoid the topic of Dani dating or doing anything dating-adjacent. I almost cried in gratitude since I'd heard details from her before that I was still trying to scrub from my brain.

I kept my answers short and easy, sticking to news about my friends, my fall schedule, and talking offensive strategies with Dad. But I was distracted, unable to keep my mind from straying to the house next door. More specifically, the boy who used to live there. The past hung over my head like a damn raincloud, keeping me in its shadow and threatening to open up and drown me at a second's notice.

"I'm gonna head upstairs," I announced abruptly. Varying looks of confusion or concern were aimed my way as I pushed back from the table. "Thanks for lunch, Mom."

I hightailed it to my room, not leaving them any time to question my odd behavior. Besides a new bedspread and the closet emptied of my clothes, my bedroom hadn't changed much. It gave me a measure of comfort to see my old trophies and knickknacks cluttering the shelves.

I ran my fingers over the digital piano that sat in the corner, the one I had begged my parents for in high school. We had a baby grand piano in the den, but I'd been confined to playing certain hours due to the uncontrollable volume. However, the convenient headphone jack on the digital one gave me the freedom to play all hours of the day or night.

I plopped down on the edge of my bed, memories of rumpled sheets, sweaty skin, and breathy moans assailing me. My eyes drifted close as I trailed my hand over the mattress slowly, as though I could still feel the warm body that used to lay there next to me, curled around my sated frame.

My eye then caught on the mahogany Gibson gracefully set on its stand next to my window. It had been a birthday present when I'd turned eleven. I couldn't count the times I'd made myself bleed from the hours I spent strumming those strings. My throat tightened at the sight of the guitar pick stuck underneath the strings of the top fret. I pulled the sliver of blue free, the edges and pieces of the logo faded from years of use.

I ran my thumb over it reverently as though afraid it would crumble in my hand. Something cold and wet slid down my cheek and irritation struck me as my eyes stung. I had the irresistible urge to toss it out the window and at the same time cradle it to my chest. It was fucking stupid how a quarter-sized piece of plastic could evoke such a fury of emotion.

I grabbed the guitar from its mount and slung it around my back by the strap, creeping back down the stairs. I hoped like hell that my family were either all still at the dining table or otherwise busy so they wouldn't notice me slipping out of the house. I tried to tiptoe past the living room and had the back door in my sights before an annoyingly smug voice stopped me.

"You know, you'd have better luck sneaking out if you didn't clomp around like a Clydesdale," Dani piped up behind me.

And that plan died a very quick death.

"I'd have even better luck if I was an only child," I snarked. She was unperturbed, leaning against the wall with a knowing smirk.

"So tell me. What's wrong?" Her hazel eyes that looked so much like Mom's had me squirming as she studied me carefully.

"What makes you think anything's wrong?"

"Uh, hi, who do you think you're talking to?" she sassed, one eyebrow raised at me. "One, I've known you my whole life, genius. Two, you just tried to sneak out of the house all stealthy even though you suck at it. Three, you've got your guitar and that usually means you're off to be all mopey and work through whatever emotions are trying to break through that perfect, Texas golden boy exterior you fight so hard to keep up. The defense rests, your Honor."

Yeah, I am so wishing I was an only child at the moment. I've got fifteen acres and a shovel...it could still happen.

"I think I'm gonna plead the fifth, counselor. Later," I replied. I tried again to make a quick exit, but my feet rooted in place at her next words.

"He's here, by the way..."

I didn't need to ask her who she meant. The soft, sad lilt to her voice told me everything I needed to know.

"Do Mom and Dad know?" I was pretty sure I knew the answer already. The pieces clicked in place why Dad had been so sketchy earlier, asking me if I'd seen anyone next door. I didn't know whether to be pissed off he hadn't outright told me or grateful for a few more hours of blissful ignorance.

"We all saw him arrive a couple weeks ago," she said quietly. "I don't know if he's only staying with his dad for the summer or..."

"Nah, he's back," I told her. A loud breath escaped me and I turned back to her. "I saw him a couple times back in May. He's either going to UT or just living near campus, I don't know."

Dani's brows furrowed as she gave me a regretful look. "How did it go when you saw him?"

I laughed humorlessly, dragging a hand down my face. "It, uh..."

God, I didn't even know how to answer that. How did I make sense of the fact that it was like being ripped in half and becoming whole again simultaneously? Seeing Theo had been crushing and painful, yet it also felt like the first full breath I'd taken since the night I learned he left.

Dani didn't ask me to explain, closing the distance between us and wrapping her arms around my waist tightly. She didn't say anything and neither did I because what was the point? She understood better than anyone what Theo leaving did to me. I was half the person I used to be, hiding behind the smiling, congenial façade everyone expected of Dawson Hayes.

She released me and I hastily dove out the back door. I hopped in the golf cart that stayed gassed up behind the shed and took off toward the back of the property.

I took the path that cut through the woods and soon came up on the old, abandoned barn nestled in a small clearing surrounded by the thicket of trees. It was open and three-sided like it had been cut in half, timeworn and battered but still standing. It was a remnant of when the land was used for farming, splitting the border of our property and *his*.

Which had made it *ours*.

I took in the derelict ladder that led up to the loft that looked new and out of place with the rest of the structure. After one of the boards broke and nearly dropped out from under me when I was sixteen, Theo and I spent that summer rebuilding it with his father. The bones of the barn were stronger than they looked, but we would've built it up ten times over if needed.

It had become our refuge, our home away from home. We spent hundreds of nights in sleeping bags right under the half-roof, talking about everything and nothing. I'd bring my guitar and play for hours until my hands cramped while Theo sang along, usually out of tune.

This was where we grew up together while fighting to hold onto our youth, just so we could stay in those happy moments even a little longer. It was why Theo had named it Neverland.

I climbed out of the cart and settled in my old chair in a corner of the barn. I nested the guitar on my lap and the pick glided across the strings without conscious effort, the rich and resonant sound warming me from the inside. I let myself go as the melody of a long forgotten song flowed from my fingertips and vibrated around me. I hadn't played it in ages, but the chords came back as though they were burned into the muscles and tendons of my hand.

Memories stirred, blending together in an endless sequence that dragged me under and blurred the lines of reality. I was here and there, feet in two separate worlds where time had no rules. The music pulled me in as I got lost in the past, only to be ripped back to the present by a voice that inexplicably still held the power to stop my world.

"I've got to say, Mercury, I did miss hearing you play for me."

CHAPTER FOUR

AGE 11

"What's that you're playing?"

The unexpected voice made me jump and I fumbled my guitar. It was still a little on the bigger side for me, but Mom promised I'd grow into it. I whipped my head toward my best friend as he came ambling up the path to our hideout. He always knew to find me in Neverland.

He smiled as he dropped down next to me on the hay, criss-cross applesauce style. His skin was a little pink from the sun and his blond hair was tangled like he got caught in a tornado, but that's kind of how he always looked. Theo had a wild look to him that I'd liked since the day I met him two years ago, right in this spot.

I remember the first time he snuck up on me, I had been playing then too. He kept badgering me for my name and why I was there. I'd been so upset and angry that we'd moved to Austin that I hadn't really talked to anyone that first week, so I hadn't answered him at first. He hadn't seemed to care since he just kept talking, telling me his name was Theo, that he liked my music, that he was my neighbor, and he just knew we would be best friends.

Guess he'd been right.

"It's a Queen song," I told him, tucking my head down so he couldn't see my embarrassment. "I know it doesn't sound that good right now."

"Shut up, you sound awesome! Is that the guitar you got at your birthday party last week? I still can't believe your parents got you one! I can't wait until

I turn eleven soon. Is it hard to play?" Theo asked, talking a mile a minute like he normally did.

"Kinda. It's a little hard to hold, but I'm getting used to it," I mumbled. I plucked at the strings, trying the chorus again to see if I could play it smoother that time. Mom had been teaching me to play since I was seven, then I started guitar lessons. I was getting pretty good, but I still struggled when learning a new song though.

"Hey, I think I know this one! It's, uh...love something..." he said as he listened to me carefully. I couldn't help but smile when he made an "aha!" noise then quickly backtracked when he didn't guess it right.

"It's 'Somebody to Love'. It's one of my favorites. I'm trying to learn it for my guitar class recital," I shared with him.

Theo's smile widened, showing off his slightly crooked teeth. "Dude, that's so cool! Oh! You should dress up like that lead singer guy from the band when you play it! I can draw you a fake mustache and everything!"

"No way are you drawing a Freddie Mercury mustache on me!" I laughed off his suggestion. "I don't want to dress up. That's so embarrassing. I'm already gonna mess it up 'cause I'm so nervous. I don't need to look crazy too."

"You're gonna do amazing, Daws," he promised. I looked up at him and he smiled at me all soft. I didn't know why, but I felt all warm and calm whenever he showed me that kind of smile. It made him look...pretty. Could boys be pretty? If so, Theo definitely was. Really pretty.

I squirmed a bit and started up the song again. I messed up some of the chords and my voice was a little shaky with Theo paying so close attention to me, but I was getting better.

Theo interrupted with a loud yell halfway through the song and I stared at him with wide eyes as he leapt to his feet.

"Holy crud, I forgot I had something to give you! Stay right here, I'll be right back!" Theo took off running toward his house before I could say anything else. I hadn't been planning to go anywhere anyway, but okay.

It only took him about ten minutes, and he was panting and sweaty from running up to his house and back. He crashed onto his knees in front of me, holding out a guitar pick inches from my face. It took me a second, but I finally recognized the picture on the front of it.

The Queen logo was printed on the swirly blue pick with the lions, phoenix, and crown inside the Q. I took it from him carefully, flipping it around to see the band name on the back.

"I found this at a town market thing Mom dragged me to when I saw her

last weekend, and it made me think of you. I know they're your favorite. I kept forgetting to give it to you," Theo explained with another big grin on his face. "It's nothing special, but maybe it'll bring you luck when you play at your recital."

I had a bunch of guitar picks at home. I sometimes took Mom's picks to use and I almost always got a new one whenever she took me to the music store. None of them came close to how much I loved this pick Theo gave me. I loved that he picked it out for me, knowing it was my favorite band and because it made him think of me.

I didn't know what to say. When I got overwhelmed, I couldn't make any words come out. Theo didn't try to force me to say anything. He never did. He talked all the time, and he didn't care that I didn't talk a lot or didn't always know what to say.

I silently set my guitar down and leaned forward to grab Theo for a hug. He wrapped his thin arms around my back and let me show him how much I loved the gift instead of saying it. Mom always said actions speak louder than words anyway. When I let go, he just smiled at me again and nodded at the guitar.

"Alright Mercury, let's see what you've got!"

I BEGAN to wonder if I had somehow royally fucked up in a past life to deserve what was happening to me. It was the only valid reason I could think of to explain why I was being subjected to this torture.

"You done playing or did I throw off your groove?" Theo called from his hidden place up in the barn loft. My fingers might as well have been glued onto the stringers for as useless as they were then.

My mind was screaming at me to get the hell up and out of there, but my throat went dry and every joint in my body felt cemented in place. All my brain cells died an epic death the instant I heard Theo's voice.

Loud sounds of scuffling on the wood above me finally spurred me into action and I shot up off the chair. I didn't make it three steps before Theo dropped down from the planks a foot away from me. His eyes connected with mine and struck me like a bolt to the chest. I stumbled back a step as though physically moved by the magnitude of it.

"What are you doing here?" I snapped.

"Well, I was enjoying the free concert, but then you had to go all diva and walk off stage before the encore," Theo teased.

"Are you following me?" I asked, anger warming my blood. At least that's what I convinced myself it was.

Theo looked around exaggeratedly like the answer was obvious. "Um, pretty sure I wasn't the follower if I got here first. You're the one who interrupted *my* quiet time being all Kurt Cobain-y."

"It wasn't a Nirvana song," I grumbled under my breath.

Yes, because that's what's important right now. Way to sound as dumb as a sack of dicks, Hayes. Good job. I'm proud of you.

"I'm aware," Theo said simply. "How could I forget one of your favorite songs to play for me?"

"I wasn't playing it for you," I muttered petulantly. "Now or then."

"That's not quite how I remember it, Mercury," Theo tsked, circling me slowly like I was prey caught in a trap. His presence was heavy and oppressive, robbing me of breath and coherent thought.

"Stop calling me that," I bit out through my tightly clenched jaw. I breathed deeply through my nose, holding myself back from flying off the handle and wiping that impish look off his face with my fist.

Right, like punching him is what you've fantasized about doing to him lately. Show of hands for anyone who buys that?

"Now why would I do that when it puts that sexy blush on your face?" he smirked, stopping right in front of me and sinking his teeth into his full bottom lip. I felt another flash of heat bleed onto my cheeks, his eyes flaring when he noticed.

What was wrong with me that he still had this much control over me? My body wasn't his anymore, yet he was still able to influence the blood to rush straight to my face...or down to other places.

I inhaled shakily and wet my chapped lips. Theo's gaze drifted down to my mouth and the air evaporated in my lungs. Heat suffused every limb and my heart rate spiked dangerously while we were caught in this tense standoff. I was vaguely aware that I could now see each individual lash on his mesmerizing eyes and the small, pale birthmark on the outer corner of his left brow. The urge to trace my finger over it like I used to hit me hard and my hand twitched at my side.

When did he get so close? Or did I get closer to him?

His warm breath fanned across my lips and I jolted out of the spell he'd put me under. I jerked back, nearly tripping over my own feet in my desperation to create space between us. Theo's hand darted out to steady me, but I pulled away from him as though he would burn me. He'd already done enough damage without even laying a finger on me.

"No, just—stop," I begged, dragging in oxygen greedily and distancing myself a bit more. When I felt more in control, I turned back to see him watching me warily.

"What...I mean...you just...I don't..."

"I think I'm gonna need a few more syllables there," Theo replied awkwardly as I sputtered like my brain was skipping.

"What the fuck is your deal?" I barked out. "Almost four years you've been gone without a damn word and now all I get are mixed signals? First, you ran away that day at your apartment, then you kissed me in that alleyway. Right after that, you told me to move on and forget you, but then you call me sexy and try to kiss me again now? What the hell do you want from me, Theo?"

He stared impassively at me while I struggled to keep my cool. He was like a sadistic seesaw, going up then down, hot then cold, my old Theo then...whoever he was now. I didn't have the capacity to keep going back and forth with him. I wasn't strong enough.

When he just stood there, unwilling or unable to answer me, I headed back to the golf cart.

"I'm sorry, okay?" he called out just as I loaded my guitar onto the seat. I waited and listened with my back still to him.

"You're right. I've been an asshole to you," he started. I turned to look at him and saw regret and sincerity in his gaze. "That first day I saw you in my building, I kind of freaked out. I obviously hadn't expected to see you five fucking feet from me while I—"

He trailed off uncomfortably, looking anywhere but at me. "While you made out with your boyfriend?" I couldn't help but add.

"He's not my boyfriend," Theo scoffed, but it did nothing to tamp down the acidic envy I felt remembering how he'd kissed and looked at the other man.

"Don't care," I lied flatly. Theo's brows pinched and his lips turned down before he nodded tightly.

"Right," he muttered. "Anyway, I wasn't prepared for that first time, and I figured when I saw you again, I'd be ready to actually talk to you and...explain things maybe."

The last part kicked up at the end like a question and he looked unsure of himself. It was so unusual to see Theo be apprehensive and nervous that I wondered if his warning really was true. Maybe he wasn't the same Theo I used to know.

"So that crap you pulled in the alley? Was that your idea of "explaining" things to me? If so, you might want to work on your execution a bit because I'm still confused as fuck and—"

"Jesus Christ, Dawson, it wasn't like I planned for it to happen that way!" Theo snapped sharply. "I was there minding my own business on a damn date when you hopped up onstage and serenaded me with a fucking swan song in front of everyone. Excuse me if it messed with my head just a goddamn bit because I thought—"

He broke off with a frustrated growl, dragging his long fingers through his mess of golden blond hair. I despised that my fingers flexed instinctively from the memory of it sifting through my hands. I crossed my arms to keep from doing something insane, like reaching for him and taming those wild locks myself.

"You thought what?" I croaked. "Thought I was over you and what you did to me?"

"No, I thought I damn well was!" he barked.

I caught his gaze and a sharp pain lanced through me at the anguish on his face. Of course he was over it...over me. He was the one who'd left and blocked all my attempts to contact him after Homecoming night.

But he wasn't the one who didn't say a word to another person for days on end, playing until his fingers bled on the guitar and tears soaked the piano keys. He wasn't the one who'd dragged his sorry ass back to Neverland every night for two weeks with a juvenile belief that he'd come back for me and I'd somehow find him waiting there.

Then I'd come along with my asinine impromptu performance in the hopes that he'd, what? See what he left behind and realize he'd made a mistake throwing us away? If I was honest with myself, that's exactly what I'd imagined. Yet he'd still warned me off him, he'd still told me to move on, and he'd still taken another man home while once again leaving behind the one he didn't want.

"Then why did you kiss me?" I blurted quietly.

Theo looked away, his jaw ticking rapidly in a familiar show of his frustration. When he finally drew his gaze back up to mine, something like resignation settled across his features.

"We never got to say goodbye," he said, so softly I almost hadn't heard him.

Somehow that answer speared me deeper than anything else he could have said. The knowledge that he'd pitied me enough to give me the kiss-off made my heart desiccate in my chest.

"And whose fault was that?" I whispered hoarsely through the aching knot in my throat.

Theo's eyes flamed and his nostrils flared. "You don't fucking know what really happened that night, what I went through."

"Because you didn't tell me!"

"I told you I *didn't have a choice*. I didn't choose to leave you."

"You know what, that's bullshit! What about the three months of my missed calls and texts? What about blocking my number? Are you saying you didn't choose that?"

"It's not as simple as you're trying to make it!" he gritted through his teeth.

"That's not a no, Theo. Did you or did you not choose to ignore my messages and cut me off after you left?"

His attention fixed on a point somewhere beyond my shoulder and it was answer enough for me. I was at the end of my patience, my nerves frayed and raw. It felt wrong for us to be shouting and hurling blame at each other, especially in this place.

This was where we'd met, where everything for us began. Our friendship grew here from innocent connections into a love that rooted in our bones and blood. I didn't want to desecrate every beautiful memory we'd built there with our bitterness and pain.

I turned back toward the golf cart, wanting to get away before any more damage was dealt between us. I jumped on the seat and turned it on, glancing back at Theo to see him fiddling with my ring around his neck.

Something about seeing it there, watching him run his fingers over it as though it were special, like it actually meant something to him, made anger coil in my chest.

"Give it back," I growled, jumping out of the cart and stalking towards him, my eyes dropping to the ring. His head reared back, hurt and shock splashed across his features as he realized what I meant. I glared at him until his chin dropped to his chest, shoulders slumping. As though reluctant to part with it, Theo slowly unlatched his silver chain and slid the ring from it, holding it out to me with trembling fingers.

I snatched it back, making him flinch. I shoved it into my pocket and tried to ignore the sting of regret from my action.

"Dawson?" Theo asked quietly.

I closed my eyes and blew out a harsh breath through my nostrils, trying to stay unaffected until I could escape. When he didn't continue, I glanced up and the lost look on his face almost brought me to my knees.

He said nothing as he held my gaze, an uncomfortable pressure building up behind my ribs from the breath I had yet to release. The air hung heavy with so much left to say between us though we stayed silent.

His eyes pleaded with me to understand.

Mine begged him to let me go.

Finally, he took a stuttering breath and a hint of a smile tugged at his lips.

"I'll see you around?" he asked, a tinge of hope in his words. His face fell a bit when all I gave him was stony silence. I cleared my throat and went back to the golf cart. Without another look, I took off without answering him.

I had come home to get away and avoid all the shit in my life that was weighing down on me, but within a few hours Theo had managed to wreck it with his inescapable presence. My stomach sank with every inch of distance I put between us as an uneasy feeling burrowed into my gut that I'd just left my heart back at that barn, bleeding out in his hands.

CHAPTER FIVE

The door slammed shut behind me and the sound echoed sharply through the cavernous foyer. I kicked off my shoes with more force than necessary, both clunking against the wall loudly as I went in search of a drink.

My hand crept up to my chest, hating the cold feel of my skin without the comforting weight that had been there for years. My stomach soured recalling how Dawson had all but yanked his ring from my grasp. I had come dangerously close to begging him to take money, my car, even my arm in exchange. He'd ripped a lifeline from me without even blinking, without realizing what he was truly taking, and dread sank into my gut that I'd never get it back.

That was as impossible as winning back Dawson himself. That bridge burned long ago and I'd lit the match before I even realized what I had done.

Before I could reach the den and the whiskey cart that called to me like a Siren, I heard Dad's low, throaty voice come around the corner.

"Hey kiddo, everything alright?"

"Sure," I muttered. "Life is a fucking cabaret."

"Did something happen? You seemed okay when you left the house earlier." Dad's brows knitted in concern and for some reason it only pulled another thread of my fraying patience.

"Well, that's because I was high," I responded flippantly with a cheeky grin. "Ahh, weed. The wonder of wonders, right?"

I turned to walk out to the back patio, hearing my name on a deep sigh of disappointment. I didn't need to see the judgment smattered across his face to know it was there. It was all I was capable of provoking in others nowadays, along with healthy doses of cynicism and exasperation.

Every other thought that drilled into my stream of consciousness reminded me how much of a fuckup I was now, how difficult I had become to even exist around. I was always too much or not enough. No matter what I did to distract or numb myself, those thoughts felt like tiny shards embedding themselves in my head.

"Theo, please talk to me," Dad implored as he followed me outside like I knew he would. Despite all the shit I'd put him through, he still cared and tried to be there for me. It was more than I could say for Mom. I still hadn't heard from her since December when she banished me back to Austin. I'd even become too much for the woman who gave me life, but Dad still held on.

I wonder how much longer it'll be before he loses faith in me too. What line will I inevitably cross that pushes him away with everyone else who gave up on me?

"Don't wanna," I grumbled, dropping onto a pool lounger. He took the one next to me, his body angled towards me with his forearms resting on his knees.

"Look, I know you only came to stay with me this summer because I asked you to—"

Yeah, because even after moving out, you still don't trust me to be alone...

"—and I don't want to force you to talk to me, but I wish you would. You know I'd never judge you."

You say that now, but if I let you in, you'll see every bit of my chaos and I'll lose you too...

"I know, Dad. There's just not much to talk about. I'm in a shitty mood, that's all."

"Are you still feeling okay after going back on your medication? You haven't missed any, right?"

"Nope, I'm on it. I think I'm still adjusting to them. It takes a while, you know?" I lied as convincingly as I could. It had taken several months to get him to trust me and stop counting my pills when I moved back. That was a fucking headache I had no interest returning to.

"Yeah, I get it. And I know you've been doing well the last few months. I just worry about you," he said softly. "Are you sure you'll be okay while I'm gone this week? I'd cancel the trip if I could, but we've had this conference scheduled for months and I couldn't get out of it."

"No worries. I'm chill. I mean, what kind of trouble can I get into in a week?" I replied, shooting him a charming grin.

"God, let's not answer that question, please. I'm too old for that level of stress," he groaned, but I saw the smirk fighting to get through.

"Those forties really hit like a bitch, don't they?" I joked. He rolled his eyes before studying my face intently.

"Promise me that you'll call if you need me? You won't hide it if it... gets bad again, right?"

More guilt bubbled up in my core. Dad was so trusting, even in the face of all my problems, and I took full advantage to hide behind my lies. I was a real piece of shit, but he just wouldn't understand. No one ever did.

"I promise."

After a beat, he looked placated and stood to leave. The tension in my body eased as the metaphorical bullet I'd just dodged whizzed right by me and back into the house along with Dad's meddling.

"One thing though..." he started.

Fuck. So close.

"Maybe you should steer clear of the barn and the Hayes' side of the property while you're here. I saw Dawson's truck over there, so I thought..."

"Thought what?" I asked cautiously. That innate protectiveness of Dawson sizzled under my skin and I subdued the urge to lash out.

"I thought it would be best if you didn't run into him."

"Why?" I asked angrily, swiveling to stare him down. "Why should I avoid my best friend?"

"Are you sure he'd still consider you his best friend?" Dad questioned and a lead weight dropped into my gut. "You've been back since winter break and to my knowledge, you haven't reached out or talked to him since your...accident senior year. Isn't that what you told me?"

The mention of the night that started us down this fucked up road squeezed my chest in an unforgiving vice. Guilt wracked me at the memory of waking up in that hospital bed and realizing what I had done...and what I had lost. Oblivious to my tormented thoughts, Dad pressed on.

"From what his parents told me recently, Dawson's doing really well. He's seemed to have moved on and so have you, so maybe it's better for you both to continue on separate paths," he said, and I could tell he was gearing up to impart some patented parental wisdom. "Now, you know I love Dawson. He's a great kid, but I don't want you getting wrapped up in him right now and neglect your health. You need to focus on yourself and doing well in school, not rekindling a relationship, even as friends. I know your mom and I didn't give you much of a choice after what happened, but Dawson was really affected when you left. If he's happy now, then perhaps the kindest thing is to leave him be."

I sat stone-faced until he finally retreated back inside, leaving me to stew in silence. His words poured salt into the open wounds that littered my fucked up soul, dredging up every bit of self-loathing and regret that had built up over the last three and a half years. I had no one to blame but myself for losing Dawson, but the thought of him moving on from me and what we had shared made me equal parts nauseous and furious.

Even though I could tell he'd been lying back at the barn, it still stung to hear him be so apathetic about me being with other people. His song at the bar had proven that he still felt something for me. I'd seen it in those soulful eyes that were never able to hide the truth from me. The twisted part of me wanted his jealousy, if for nothing more than proof he hadn't gotten over me.

I only wish my own outburst had been true, that I'd somehow gotten over what I'd done to him. That I'd somehow been able to wash my hands of the guilt I felt at leaving him the way I did and forgive myself.

As if I were capable of that. That would happen the day I moved on from Dawson, and that would only happen when my heart stopped beating.

It didn't matter what I did, what I smoked, what I drank, or who I fucked, Dawson still invaded every thought and dream of mine since the day I left. I had managed to avoid him for damn near six months once I transferred to UT thanks to my temporary living arrangement with Dad. It had been rough as hell knowing that Dawson was so close to me again, yet I hadn't been anywhere near ready to face him. Running into him that day at my apartment shocked the hell out of me.

Of all the sin joints in all the campuses in all the world, he had to walk into mine.

The last thing I had expected was for that blast from the past. I had only moved into that space a couple months before that after finally gaining Dad's trust enough to move out of his house. I had relished in the freedom and solitude it brought me, both dreading and yearning for the moment I saw Dawson again. I could have contacted him, but I was stopped every time by the simple fact I couldn't tell him the truth about why I had left. He'd never come near me again if he knew everything.

It wasn't anything new. I'd accepted that I was better off alone. Losing the few friends I'd made in Huntsville had shown me that. The moment they had learned about the devil on my back, everything had changed. Daily texts dwindled to once a week, usual hangouts were cancelled, my calls were ignored, and discomfort bled into every look aimed my way. Then they disappeared altogether.

It didn't take long for me to spiral out of control once I'd lost them all. Grades, social life, sanity. All of it went down in a headlong rush until I crashed.

Literally.

A nifty little equation of pain pills and insomnia with a tequila chaser was the perfect recipe for my unintended physics lesson involving my Audi and a big ass tree. The same Audi that had been gifted to me for my birthday a few months earlier by my mom and step-dad. That hadn't been the first or even fifth time that they had to deal with the disastrous effects of my...condition.

In exchange for them keeping Dad in the dark about the incident, I moved back to Austin quickly and quietly with the promise that I'd start taking my medication again after the doctor they forced on me upped my dosage for the third time. They'd recruited Dad in their scheme to keep me "on track" which meant counted pills and a supervised living situation until I had proven I was back in control of myself.

It didn't make a difference that I told them repeatedly I hated how the meds made me feel and that they didn't really help. They didn't give me control, they stole it from me. I loathed the side effects. Being on them, I was muted and dull to the point I didn't recognize myself.

Shit, maybe that was a good thing. Who I had become wasn't

enough to keep people from leaving me. In some ways, I was thankful I had been the one to leave Dawson before he could do it himself. And I had no doubt in my mind he would have.

Dawson was better off without me. Once he understood the reality I lived with, he'd only see me as a sickness that couldn't be cured.

I SHOOK out the small pink pill onto my palm, despising the sight of it. It was a fickle friend who left me with as many problems as it solved. I dropped it in the toilet and flushed it down, instantly breathing a little easier. I hadn't been so lucky yesterday morning when Dad had caught me with a pill in hand before he left for his flight, so down the hatch it went. I'd had half a mind to throw it back up the minute he left, but I couldn't stand vomiting.

Two days later and I still had to remind myself that one pill wouldn't screw me up, but I knew the dangers of messing with my meds, so I mentally scanned my body to reassure myself I was okay.

My mouth isn't dry, my stomach is calm, my hands aren't shaking or twitching...I'm fine. Everything is fine.

Except everything was *not* fucking fine. I was on edge and anxious, wanting to do everything and nothing at the same time. My thoughts were being tossed into a blender, spraying random words and ideas around my head until I couldn't distinguish one thing from another.

I reached up more than once to grasp Dawson's ring when it overwhelmed me, continually forgetting that it was no longer mine to hold. Being without the token that had been my grounding force for years, my talisman, left me feeling unbalanced and so...alone.

For the rest of the day, I was constantly in motion to keep my mind focused, a steady buzz thrumming in my veins. I was running on a handful of hours of sleep over the last few days, but I had to stay active to keep my thoughts from creeping into darker territory. It was in the quiet moments where I was most vulnerable.

By late afternoon, I'd reorganized my room, scoured the attic for old family heirlooms I was positive had to exist, rage-wrote letters to my old friends relaying all the betrayal and hurt I'd felt at them ghosting me, went for a jog, started a puzzle Dad had stashed in the hallway closet, and jacked off at least three times which did nothing to kill the underlying buzz that was still there. Ultimately I decided a swim was the perfect way to relax my frazzled brain.

The sun-warmed water was as decadent as liquid silver being poured over me as I dove in. I envisioned it washing away all my worries from the last few days, cleansing me of everything but peace. I let my mind conjure up memories of corded muscle, soft skin, heat around my cock, and cornflower blue eyes that stirred my blood with a single look.

I lost track of how long I'd been floating there when voices from across the yard pulled me out of my lusty reveries. I hauled myself out of the pool and crossed over to the low white fence that separated the Hayes and Bishop land. The higher of the voices was animated and pleading, but not one I recognized. But the soft baritone that answered her struck me in the chest with the force of a nine pound hammer. That same voice had begged and moaned my name in my subconscious not even five minutes ago.

Dawson came into view around the side of his house being trailed by a short, pink-haired girl whom he seemed to be unsuccessfully evading. Neither of them noticed me as I hopped the fence and strolled over, increasingly curious about the newcomer. She gripped his arm in both her hands, dragging him to a halt and flashing him huge puppy eyes I could see from here. I desperately hoped she was a friend of Dani's or maybe a cousin I'd never met, anything but what I feared she could be.

As I drew closer, I saw Dawson's eyes roll and a smirk grace his pillowy lips as the girl squealed in thanks, jumping into his arms and smacking a kiss to his lightly stubbled cheek. The affectionate smile he gave her churned my stomach and bile climbed my throat when I realized she was exactly what I was afraid of.

She was his.

As she landed back on her feet, Dawson turned and caught sight of me, the smile dropping off his face. Cold slithered down my spine at the reminder that his smiles didn't belong to me anymore. Now they were someone else's. And that someone was now looking at me with vague recognition and open curiosity.

"We've got to stop meeting like this, Mercury," I teased, attempting to break the uncomfortable silence. He glared at me, staying stubbornly mute as I stood there dripping wet like a jackass.

"Well, this is nice and awkward. Sorry if this one's a little crabby. That's probably my fault," the perky interloper piped up, jerking her thumb in Dawson's direction. "I tend to have that effect on him. I'm Aly, and you are?"

I'm the guy who has fucked your boyfriend in so many positions that we made the Kama Sutra look like a junior high sex ed class.

I dragged my attention over to her and pasted on a tight smile. "Theo. Nice to meet you," I replied, shaking her outstretched hand a little harder than necessary. Intrusive images of her touching Dawson with those too-soft hands popped up and I pushed back the impulse to crush her hand in mine. That would win me no points with Dawson and I was already batting in the negatives.

"You look kind of familiar. Do you go to UT?" the girl asked.

"Yep. Transferred in January from Sam Houston State," I shared, noticing Dawson regarding me warily out of the corner of my eye.

"Oh awesome! So how do you and Dawson know each other?"

"We were—"

"Neighbors," Dawson interrupted. "We used to be neighbors." His features remained neutral, unbothered, as though he hadn't just wiped away all our history with one word. Betrayal sliced through me at how easily he dismissed me. Us. Everything we meant to each other.

Am I not even good enough of a memory for you to hold onto?

Aly's shrewd gaze lingered on Dawson for several beats as he avoided my own. The silence beared down on us until I physically felt the pressure of it on my chest.

"We gotta get going. We have friends who will be here soon," Dawson mumbled, shifting from foot to foot nervously. I nodded, unable to speak past the tightness in my throat. Avoiding Dawson had seemed like a good plan when I came back home, but seeing how eager he was to get away from me made me want to rip my hair out.

"That reminds me!" Aly chimed in. "We're having a party tonight for the Fourth! A ton of people will be there. You should come over if you're not doing anything. It could give you and Dawson a chance to catch up! I'm sure you have a lot to talk about now that you're back."

I peered at her, wondering what the hell her game was. Did she know more about our past than she let on? I supposed it could be a test to see how I acted around him again now I knew he was taken. Did she know about our kiss at the bar? The song he played for me? I entertained the thought that she could be inviting me for some fucked up prank, a way to assert her dominance as Dawson's girlfriend. But there was no malice on her features. The smile she aimed my way seemed genuine enough.

A rejection sat on the tip of my tongue, but I swallowed it at the dismay written on Dawson's face. The petty bitch in me wanted to mess with him for denying our history together. For making us out to be less than what we were, especially in front of his new bedwarmer.

"Sure, why not? Sounds like fun," I agreed. His eyes flashed a warning at me, but I refused to back down. If Dawson thought he could brush me off and pretend we meant nothing to one another, then I'd make damn sure he couldn't ignore me.

Game on, Mercury. Game-fucking-on.

CHAPTER SIX

The boisterous crowd that swarmed Dawson's house made me burn with irrational anger. For years, the Hayes house had been as much a home to me as my own. The laughter, the music, and the energy that pulsated from the party all served as a reminder that I was no longer part of Dawson's world. Others had been welcomed with open arms into his home and his life when I had been forced to leave him behind.

But I was a selfish motherfucker who couldn't resist being lured back into his orbit. The restraint that had helped me keep my distance the last few months was stretched beyond its limit. I just wanted to see him. And honestly, fuck those insidious thoughts that tried to convince me I didn't belong anymore. This was my home, even if I never thought it would be again.

That bravado lasted for exactly three seconds as I wove my way through the partygoers. My anxiety cranked up and I dreaded running into Dawson and his new squeeze around every corner. I had no idea how I'd handle it if I saw them wrapped up in each other, all lovey and shit. The images flashed through my mind as though I had an advanced fucking screening to prepare me for what I'd eventually stumble across.

Paranoia speared through me wondering how much she meant to him. Had she won his heart yet? Had he given her pieces of himself that were meant to be mine? That would *always* be mine?

I owned his heart once and I never agreed to give it back. It didn't belong to her. None of him belonged to her.

Even as I thought it, fresh fears flooded my brain. A slew of intrusive thoughts assaulted me as every face was suddenly a potential threat. Were any of them his best friends now? Had any of them fallen into his bed? How many were there after me? Did any of them know what his cum tasted like or left their marks on his skin?

Dawson had always been popular and I was positive there was no shortage of people who would happily hop on his dick. Of course, he never gave anyone else a second glance when we were together, loyal to his core. But we were no longer dating and he hated my fucking guts.

It's no better than you deserve...you did this. He'll find someone else and you'll be forgotten.

Electricity flickered under my skin the higher my anxiety climbed. I recognized the itch, the undeniable craving for something to help me let go. I needed something to take off this godforsaken edge I hadn't been able to shake the last couple of days. Thinking of Dawson being with other people spiked my blood with fury, fear, and frustration.

I scratched compulsively at my collarbone, still feeling the phantom weight of his ring. The further into the party I ventured, the more intense everything felt. Every emotion felt heightened and teetered on the edge of my control. The chaotic thoughts that ran rampant all day surged again, a high speed train flying through my brain with no hope of stopping.

I ran smack into a wall of muscle, not paying attention to anything around me as I got lost in my own head.

"Oh shit! My bad," I sputtered as hands gripped my biceps to steady me.

"Hey, no worries! No harm, no foul, man." The guy flashed me an easy smile and gave me a quick once over, and there was no mistaking the spark of interest in his perusal. I could almost smell it on him and... *yep, there's that ping on the gaydar. Or bi-dar? Either way, bro's throwing vibes.*

"Wish I could at least blame it on a good buzz, but I'm tragically sober," I joked, pulling back subtly until his hands fell away.

"Ouch. Sounds like you have some catching up to do," he smirked. "I'm Corvin, by the way."

"Theo," I up-nodded, scanning the sea of bodies for the only reason I came in the first place.

"How about I show you where you can grab a drink? I've heard I'm not terrible company to have," he flirted.

"Thanks, but I'm actually looking for someone. You know Dawson Hayes?"

"You mean, the quarterback on my team, whose house I'm currently at, attending a party he happens to be throwing? Nah, never heard of him."

A snort escaped me at his sarcastic reply. "So you're useless to me then?"

"Eh, I can think of a few other ways I could be pretty damn useful to you." His heated gaze trailed down my body slower than before. Shame welled in my chest when his blatant interest made my cock twitch behind my zipper. I didn't really want him, but that hadn't necessarily stopped me before. I couldn't always shake off the need that sometimes grew in tandem with the energy buzzing under my skin.

"Do you know where he is around here?" I asked politely. Corvin breathed out a chuckle, shaking his head at the way I'd bypassed his lewd invitation.

"I think he's out by the pool. Come on, I'll show you," he said, gesturing for me to follow him. That earlier irritation simmered as I thought of how fucking ironic it was he thought he had to usher me around the house I knew like the back of my hand. Little did he know, I had been the one who helped Dawson clean that pool as part of his chores every summer. I had almost busted my skull open trying to back-flip off their diving board at sixteen. I'd attended every birthday pool party that Dani threw since the year I met Dawson.

My unsolicited tour guide led me outside and over to a large group of people congregating around a beer pong table set up on the far side of the deck. My irritation reached nuclear levels at the sight of Dawson with his girlfriend right by his side while he laughed at something a hot blond dude was saying to him. He shoved playfully at Dawson who only laughed harder, his eyes crinkling at the corners and cheeks flushing pink, either from laughter or the drink in his hand. Their interaction betrayed an easy familiarity that had green envy digging claws into my chest.

I used to be the blond guy in his life who made him laugh, who made his eyes dance, who brought out that joy on his face. I never had to compete with anyone for his attention before because we used to be everything to each other. Best friends, family, neighbors, confidants, boyfriends, soulmates. There were never enough labels that encompassed all that we were. And I'd lost every single one of them.

Beyond the jealousy, I couldn't help noticing how damn sexy Dawson looked. The low slung jeans sitting just right on his hips, the tight navy V-neck showcasing all those quarterback muscles, the chunky watch that drew the eye to his delicious forearms, his soft hair that was perfectly tousled.

All of it was working for me. No surprise there. Dawson had been my walking wet dream since I'd first understood what it was to desire someone. I had also been horny as fuck the last few days and jacking off wasn't quelling the thirst. It was getting worse every day, but one drink of him was all I'd need. My dick had only twitched from Corvin's innuendo, but a single look at Dawson and it was doing a full-on gymnastics routine in my damn pants.

"Yo, QB!" Corvin called out and Dawson's head swung in our direction. Just like earlier, his smile vanished at the sight of me. It hurt even worse if that was fucking possible.

They greeted each other with clasped hands smushed between one of those stupid bro-hugs. I hated how even their friendship had my teeth grinding together.

"What's up, man? Glad you could make it," Dawson said. "Guys, this is Corvin, one of our running backs. And that's Theo." He addressed the group around him, waving a hand toward me and Corvin. My stomach curdled at how he'd thrown my name out there like an afterthought, like I was just another body in the crowd.

A chorus of "hey" and "what's up" came from his circle of friends.

"This is Micah and Bash," Dawson continued, pointing to an attractive couple of guys with their arms wrapped around each other. "And that's Cal, Rhys, Fin..."

He went around the circle continuing to introduce everyone, but I barely heard him over the dark thoughts stirring in my head. They were becoming harder to block out. Destructive impulses were pushing to the surface, mutinous voices screaming how truly worthless I was to him. I blinked hard to clear them away and my eyes met Aly's. Her smile turned softer and more...knowing. As though she knew how close I was to tearing apart at the seams.

I didn't want her goddamn pity. I didn't want anything from her except Dawson's love returned to me. But I couldn't deny it was nice to be seen for a change. Even if it wasn't by the person I wanted.

"You gents care to play a round? D-man and I are up, but every one of these assholes has bowed out," Blondie slurred with a teasing grin obviously brought to us by his sponsor, Fireball.

"They only cut out because you somehow defy the laws of nature and get better the drunker you are, fucker," Dawson snickered at him.

"Hey! You're about to benefit from my mad skills, so I'd show some respect, asshole" he scoffed. "So you two in?"

Corvin looked at me expectantly. "What do you think? You and me against Hayes and Nate?"

Ah, that's the dickwad's name. Good to know. Can't make a decent voodoo doll without it.

A quick glance at a tense-as-fuck Dawson made my agreement all too easy. "Why not? I'm a pro at sinking balls into small, tight places," I replied, gaze locked on Dawson's. He froze, fire flaming in his cheeks as Nate choked on his beer with laughter.

"Seems I chose the right partner," Corvin chortled, his smirk as suggestive as my words. My gaze slid back to Dawson's and the fire in his face spread to his eyes, flames of anger licking at his irises. Excitement lit inside me at the jealousy I saw there.

That's it, babe, don't hide from me. If you're jealous, that means you care. If you care, that means I haven't completely lost you...

The game started out friendly with his crew of friends cheering both teams on. Their banter and warmth made an ache sprout in my chest, a yearning to know what it would have been like had I stayed and become a part of this new family Dawson seemed to have found.

By the second round of the game, I was fast approaching the point of no return. Dawson hadn't been lying about Nate and his infuriating abilities as he sank yet another shot flawlessly. I cursed loudly, downing my ninth cup of beer while Corvin groaned beside me. They'd been filled a bit more than was traditional, but as my temper simmered more and more with every smile, laugh, or friendly touch Nate and Dawson shared, I welcomed inebriation as sweet relief.

"I swear, y'all suckers are getting hustled. Nate gets lost getting to a point, but somehow he's sinking all the balls when his blood is probably 80 proof by now," Bash joked, eliciting laughs from the others.

"Fuck you very much, Dupont." Nate flipped him off with that same goofy smile of his.

"Why do you think I chose to be on his team instead of against him?" Dawson tossed out, concentrating on his shot.

"Please, like Nate would let his Dawby-Bear be on anyone else's team but his?" The guy clinging to Bash, maybe Micah, teased. Annoyance lanced through me at yet another reminder of how close Nate and Dawson were. *Just how fucking close are they?*

"Gross. Say that name again and you're going in the pool, and Bash won't be able to save you," Dawson threatened him, but the guy only cackled and shot him a wink.

"And Dawson's got another nickname for the collection," I muttered, not meaning to say it aloud. I felt eyes on me, but kept my focus on the game.

"So Theo, how do you know Dawson?" Nate asked me as I stepped back to let Corvin take his next shot.

"We knew each other as kids when he lived next door," Dawson answered before I could speak. The shard of betrayal he'd left in my heart when he'd denied our relationship to Aly earlier wedged even deeper. He shifted his nervous eyes to mine and anger bubbled up and loosened my lips. *Could also be the lukewarm beer I'm drowning in, but fuck it.*

"Yep. We go way back," I interjected enthusiastically. "You know how it goes. Childhood besties, attached at the hip, real Goonies-level shit. Our families were really close too."

Dawson's shoulders sagged and some of the tension left his frame at my answer. Until my mouth Usain Bolt-ed without my brain, fueled by my indignation.

"He also sucked my dick a few times, but what's a BJ between friends, right?" I added cheekily. That wasn't even two percent of what we'd done with each other, so I thought only letting that one thing slip was great restraint on my part. Dawson clearly didn't agree.

All the color drained from his face as silence descended on us. The atmosphere was stifling despite being outside, everyone nervously shuffling around us.

Ice quickly replaced the fire that had sparked in his eyes as he stared me down. "Well...we all experiment from time to time, don't we?"

"Must have been a hell of an experiment for you to keep coming back for more," I taunted as I sensed my control slipping further away. I saw the faintest tinge of sadness shadow his features, but it disappeared just as quickly as it came.

"I'm a slower learner, I guess. But thank fuck I'm past that phase and on to better things." He looped his arm around Aly's waist and hauled her to his side as though proving his point.

My heart sank to the pits of my stomach while fury rose up hot and sharp in its place. The heat of it melted through the pain that threatened to consume me and I clung to it desperately. Grabbing one of the full cups off the table, I tossed it back in one go and dropped it carelessly with a clatter.

"You know, this cheap shit isn't quite doing it for me. I'm gonna head inside and find a cold drink." *Or a room-temperature Xanny to calm the fuck down. I'm not picky.* "You coming?" I raised an eyebrow at Corvin in question.

He looked a bit uncomfortable at the obvious friction between me and Dawson, but he nodded and followed me back into the house.

"You okay? Seems like a lot of history there with Hayes. What's the deal with you two?" Corvin asked cautiously. I swallowed down the scathing retort that reflexively came up since I couldn't afford to alienate the one person who might help me find what I needed. What I craved.

"I'm fine and there's no deal with us. I'm gonna need something stronger than a fucking drink though."

"What were you thinking?"

Indecision warred within me. I had worked so hard to prove to myself that I could handle this...this curse that eroded every good intention and bit of light inside me. But then again, maybe this was just me. I was made of pain and bad decisions like they were the building blocks of my DNA. Why should I fight it if it got me nowhere?

"I just need to get out of my head..."

The words came out brittle, and I pinned him with a loaded look. Understanding dawned on his face and his smile turned impish.

"I think I can help with that."

Corvin grabbed my hand and dragged me along through the house.

His head was on a swivel, hunting out someone in the waves of dancing, humping people. He finally found who he was looking for and yanked me over to the pool table in the den.

We approached one of the guys playing in tight chinos and a light blue polo, lining up a shot. He popped the cue forward, sending the balls clacking loudly across the green felt. He caught sight of us and greeted Corvin, fistbumping him before settling his gaze on me.

"'Sup, Aaron. Listen, I got a friend who's not feeling too great. Might be a headache," he lied, nodding towards me. "You got anything that might help?"

Mr. Chinos scrutinized me with an unreadable expression. "Your friend looks a little pale. A little dose of Vitamin C might do the trick. Maybe some Vitamin E if that's more your bag?"

Sweat beaded at my hairline, promises I had made my mom, my Dad, even myself echoing in my mind. I'd broken them before and I hated myself more each time. Deep down, I didn't want to be this person. I didn't want to be weak and give in to this disease.

But I also didn't give a single fuck. I didn't care about risk or consequence. I didn't want to feel or think or hurt. I wanted escape.

"Both" I answered, all caution gone as the voices invaded louder than before, overtaking all sense. Aaron's brows shot up in amusement while Corvin's drew down slightly in concern.

"Ahh, we're bumping up, huh? It'll cost you a bit more though." I nodded in agreement and he set his pool cue down.

"Right this way."

They led me over to the bathroom, closing us inside. Once we were locked away, I passed him some cash and Aaron quickly set up a neat, white line on a decorative glass tray. The promises I had once made fractured, but it was too easy to justify the guilt away.

Damn it, it's not that bad.

It's not Oxy.

It's not like last time.

I haven't fallen that far again...

Rolled up paper was pressed to my nostril and I breathed in the line, the drugs sweeping through my body, burning away all the pain and guilt I carried and taking me higher.

And higher.

And higher, until nothing mattered. Until I never wanted to come back down.

STARDUST WAS SWIMMING through my veins. My nerves were sparking enough to start a fire. My head felt like it was in the clouds…or no, more like the clouds were overtaking my brain. They were pushing out the darkness that constantly hung over me and clogged my thoughts.

This was what I needed. This was my escape, the drugs drawing me up to the surface and allowing me to breathe again. The quick high of the cocaine had worn off, but the X had kicked in, making the world fuzzy around the edges as I danced in the middle of a hot, sweaty press of people.

Strong, rough hands grabbed at my waist and it set off explosions under my skin. *Dawson…*

My head fell back and my lids drifted close as Dawson's hands caressed my skin, tugging me back into his body. Something pinched at my memory, an unfamiliar sensation that I'd never had with him. His body felt a bit bigger, more muscled than I remembered. His hands gripped me more forcefully than he used to. But I guess that made sense. The years had changed him, hardened him like they had me.

Except where Dawson was hardened like a diamond, beautiful and pure and too good for this world, I became hard like coal. A cold, dark, shriveled version of the boy I used to be. A barely functioning husk that narrowly survived the deepest lows that came after the insurmountable highs.

The hard thickness pressing against my ass made me shudder. I missed his closeness. I wanted him inside me, filling me, owning me like no one else ever had. My hand crept back around, cupping Dawson's length while I vibrated with need. A loud groan rumbled in my ear and my muscles froze in place.

"Fuck Theo, keep going," Corvin begged in a low whine, nothing like the breathy, velvet whimper that I used to pull from Dawson so effortlessly. My stomach turned both in disgust at myself and crushing disappointment that he wasn't the man I wanted.

"Wait, I-I can't…"

I stumbled out of Corvin's grasp. I shouldered through the dense crowd, the haze of drugs still heavy. My attention caught on something across the room and my mind steeped in pleasure at seeing Dawson's face. His gaze connected with mine and even with his brows furrowed and mouth pulled in a tight line, he was still so damn beautiful.

My hand reached out toward him without conscious thought. I could almost trick myself into believing that he reached for me too. Noises faded, lights dimmed, and the world paused. The pull between us was infinite, stretching beyond time and reason, connecting us through all the devastation, loss, and anger.

All at once, the world rushed back in and I saw Aly saunter up to Dawson, her forehead lined in worry as she spoke to him. Her hand caressed his arm, breaking our contact as he dropped his attention to her. I wished I could read their lips, but in the next second I wanted to rip them off when Aly's lips brushed the corner of Dawson's mouth.

Red clouded my vision and pain rippled through me despite the drugs in my system. Watching them set off every instinct in my body to claim him, to remind him who he truly belonged to. And it would never be her. As long as I drew breath, Dawson was mine.

I reached for my ring, needing the steady weight to help me feel the smallest semblance of control. Panic flooded me when I couldn't feel it, but just as quick I remembered where it had gone. Disjointed thoughts hit my brain like electric pulses, sharp and fast.

He took it—beg for it—not her—find it—get it back—it hurts—can't do it—steal it—need it—

I blinked hard to clear the litany blaring in my head. I was upstairs in front of a too-familiar door, unsure of how I got up here. A singular focus had taken root and I couldn't think of anything else but finding the ring. I tore through Dawson's room, checking his drawers, desk, closet, anywhere he might have stashed it.

The door opened behind me and a split second of euphoria hit that he'd come for me, that he was there with me and not her.

Choose me—take me—don't leave—

"Theo, you alright? Why are you in here?" Corvin's voice reached me through my rapidly depleting high. Either those drugs Aaron gave me must have been shit or they were no match for the deluge of desperation and hurt that were burying me.

"Looking for something," I mumbled, darting glances around the room to see if I had missed any hiding spots. Corvin's warm hand ran down my back before he pulled me around to face him.

"Hey, look at me," he commanded softly, lifting my chin until I met his gaze. "You don't seem okay. Is Aaron's cocktail hitting you weird? Do you feel sick or anything?"

I ripped out of his grasp, feeling too hot, too stifled, too...everything. Every synapse was firing and my brain was broken morse code, lines and dots out of order. Dots of words swimming between lines of coke that hit me too fast.

Dawson doesn't care. Not enough. He is hers—get him back—get back at him. Show him. Make him hurt—I hurt—too much. Want him here—come back—fuck you! Fuck me—need to fuck—need to feel—him. Him. Always him.

Dawson—

Come back—

Please...

Lips pressed against mine, hungry and urgent. Hands tugged my hair and sent jolts of electricity straight to my cock. Skin clashed with skin and streaks of blissful pain followed nails down my back. A buckle clinked and a rush of cool air hit my legs as warmth engulfed my dick, and I surrendered to it.

I knew. The truth slithered through the lust and drugs and pain, and I knew. This wasn't Dawson. God, how I fucking wanted it to be. But I knew his touch, his kiss, his scent better than my own name and none of this was right.

It wasn't right. But I didn't care.

I couldn't.

I wish I was in control. But I wasn't.

I wish I was Dawson's. But I wasn't.

And after this?

I never would be.

CHAPTER SEVEN

The sight of Theo walking off with Corvin was hell. Out of sheer strength of will, I stayed put and managed to contain the fury and jealousy that stirred in my chest. It wasn't anger at Theo for outing us to my friends because I didn't really give a shit, but anger at myself for letting him get to me. I was a complete dick to insinuate that he was nothing more than an easy way to work through some confused sexuality or to even hint that Aly had taken his place. The hurt I'd seen on his face cut deep and knotted my chest painfully.

I couldn't help it. Watching him arrive with Corvin, out of all the fucking people he could have met, had soured my mood fast. It wasn't that my teammate wasn't a good guy, but he was a major flirt and one of the only openly queer players on our team. He'd even tried his luck with me a year ago, but I'd turned him down. He was attractive, nice, and probably would have been a fun date and a great lay, but just like with anyone else that came after Theo, not a single ounce of desire had sparked.

"Okaaay, this awkward silence is great and all, but it's clogging my pores," Fin spouted. The sassy spitfire that Micah and his best friend Rhys had brought into the fold last year had fit in seamlessly with our motley crew, so his lack of filter was nothing new to us.

"Yeah, and pointing it out is always a great way to clear the air. Good thinking," Aly sarcastically replied.

"Uh, yeah? It's like a verbal exfoliator, slutcakes. See? Awkward silence gone!" Fin snarked before she smacked him on the arm.

Their teasing squabble drew everyone else into the conversation, but my head wasn't in it. I was wrestling with the urge to track Theo down and apologize, but that would only lead to me spilling my guts about things I wasn't ready to say. About how confused and conflicted I really was, how damn hard it was being around him again, how it ate me up inside seeing him with someone else, how all the anger, regret, and resentment didn't hold a fucking candle to how much I just wanted to kiss him again. To hold him.

To never let go.

"Are you okay?" Aly asked softly, drawing me back. "I know you're probably ticked at him, but I really think you should go talk to him."

I had a feeling this would happen once I came clean to her after we ran into Theo several hours earlier. Her face had practically turned red from holding in her barrage of questions and I'd cracked. She'd been sharp enough to put together the basics once she recognized him from karaoke night, so I just filled in the blanks. Now she was firmly "Team Thawson" as she put it.

"What would be the point?" I scoffed, still fighting the pull towards him that was ever present. "You heard him. He did nothing but antagonize me from the second he stepped out here. What would it help?"

"Dawson, you know him better than anyone. That's what you told me, right? Don't tell me you didn't see right through that little performance of his."

"What do you mean?"

"He's hurting!" Aly cried. "The way he looks at you says it all. He misses you and he's hurt that there doesn't seem to be a place for him anymore. You proved as much when you didn't even introduce him as a *friend*. Just a neighbor, some kid you used to know. And when you implied that we were together and you've moved on—dick move, by the way—he was crushed. You can't tell me you didn't see that."

Bile rose hot and thick in my throat, shame coating me from the inside out. I didn't want her to be fucking right, but of course I'd seen it. I could read every speck of emotion that ran across his face. Those bright eyes of his held every ounce of pain and longing that I felt in return. His hurt reverberated in my bones as my own. Years of distance couldn't change that.

“Maybe you’re right,” I admitted quietly.

“It’s a common occurrence, or so I’m told.”

I rolled my eyes at her teasing and ventured inside to find Theo with Aly on my heels. It seemed to take ages just to make it back to my kitchen with all the people trying to talk or get me to dance. Even with years of being in the spotlight of most crowds, the attention still made me antsy and uncomfortable in my own skin. The extroverted mask I hid behind became suffocating quicker than most would believe.

Awareness thrummed through me, the sensation was one I’d know anywhere. A single glance was all it took to find Theo nestled in the mass of people, and the instant his gaze connected with mine, my heart seized.

Christ, he was still so beautiful. His muscles had filled out a bit with age, but were still lean and sinewy. He now sported a small diamond stud on his right earlobe and tattoos dotted his body when there’d previously only been one. The same one I had inked into my flesh to match.

His lips tugged into a breathtaking grin that short-circuited my brain, but there was something off about him. Even from where I stood, I could see the glassiness in his eyes and the slight sway in his body.

I grimaced when I noticed Corvin right behind him, trying to get his attention that was riveted on me. Theo seemed oblivious to Corvin’s hand on his arm while his own stretched out in my direction. Fuck, I could almost feel the brush of his fingers on my skin. I couldn’t stop my own hand from rising and seeking out his touch, like a magnet drawing me in. I quickly dropped my arm when I realized what I was doing, and a gentle tug on it stole my attention. My gaze swung to Aly’s concerned face.

“Hey, what’s wrong?” She looked over in Theo’s direction, her eyebrows crinkling even more as she studied him. “Um, maybe you should talk to him later actually. I think...honestly, it kind of looks like he’s on something. Corvin too.”

Hearing my worries more or less confirmed made breathing difficult. My breaths came in choppy as I worked to calm down, trying not to draw conclusions that made me want to rip my hair out at the root.

“I don’t—I don’t know if I can do this,” I whispered, my voice grated and hoarse.

Aly just gave me a sympathetic look and leaned up to press a small, chaste kiss to the outer corner of my mouth. "Only do what you feel is right, Daws. It'll all work out. I have faith."

Her words did little to soothe me. I understood better than anyone that fate was a cold bitch who turned hopes to ash and stole the things that mattered to you most.

"I need a minute. I'll be back," I told her and pulled her into a quick hug.

I darted up the stairs to my parents' room on the third floor. Up here the thumping stereo and ambient party noise wasn't as overwhelming. I burst into their bathroom and went straight for the sink, splashing cold water on my face and sucking in deep breaths. It did nothing to clear my mind, warring thoughts resounding in my head like dissonant chords.

I was angry at Theo, but I wanted him. It terrified me that he was back, but I was relieved to have him close again. I couldn't handle the truth of what happened back then, but I needed answers all the same. I hated him, but I loved him even more.

Had I really ever stopped? Was that even possible?

Sometimes I could pretend that I was really happy, that nothing was wrong or missing in my life. But maybe the real measure of happiness is our ability to pretend. How well are we able to pretend that our lives are what we want them to be? How good of an actor am I that people couldn't see that I was half a person?

The other half of me was torn away years ago before I even knew it had happened. The hole Theo left behind was irreparable, a sinkhole that only grew deeper and wider each day he was gone until there was nothing that remained of who I was before.

He told me he wasn't the same person anymore, but neither was I. The boy from before, the one who thought he was truly happy, who believed he'd found his soulmate, who trusted fate to keep them together? He disappeared the same night Theo did and I was all that was left in his place.

After using the bathroom and washing my hands, I braced myself to go back downstairs and pull Theo away to talk. I still wasn't sure what the hell I'd even say. If nothing else, I needed to make sure he was okay if Aly was right and he was high on something. I'd always taken care of him before. It seemed those old instincts didn't die easily.

I hit the second floor landing and headed for the next flight of stairs when unmistakable sounds coming from my room stopped me. I cursed under my breath, pissed that some wasted asshats seemed to be using my space like a room at the BunnyRanch.

I reached out to push open the cracked door, but the deep groan I heard next shattered everything inside me.

"Fuuuck, that's it. Suck me down..."

My gut cramped fiercely and I slapped a hand over my mouth to stop myself from losing the contents of my stomach. A violent shudder tore through me, but it didn't stop as more sounds poured from the room.

Everything reached me as though through a tunnel. Muffled and distant, but the pain was as sharp as a blade piercing my skin. It cut through muscle and sinew, organ and bone. I was frozen, stuck in that moment of purgatory as I listened to Theo's pleasure climb.

"Shit...I'm close. Ngh, yeah...faster. There—oh, fuck!"

My eyes slammed shut against the next roll of nausea. I couldn't stop the shaking that rattled me from head to toe, but cold rage shot down my limbs and propelled me forward.

I swung the door in fast, the abrupt move causing Corvin to jump away from where Theo was panting on the bed, pants undone and his cock limp and glistening with saliva. My gut spasmed and churned, and I breathed through my nose in a desperate attempt to stifle it.

"Fuck Hayes, you scared the shit out of me. Dude, I'm sorry—he just kissed me, and then I—" Corvin stammered.

"Get the *fuck* out of my room," I growled, casting him a venomous glare. I was quaking, grasping at every bit of animosity I could latch onto to keep the despair from drowning me.

Corvin's face turned crimson in embarrassment, but he wisely said nothing and rushed out the door, leaving Theo and I in strained silence. I couldn't look at him, keeping my gaze trained on the floor in front of me. In my periphery, I noticed Theo sitting up and tucking himself back into his jeans. His movements were clumsy and uncoordinated as he stood, running a hand through his disheveled locks.

"Mercury—"

"Don't." The word came out shredded and raw. I chanced a look up at Theo and it nearly collapsed my lungs. He looked flushed and crazed, his pupils dilated and darting across my face. His fingers fidgeted restlessly at his side.

"I didn't...mean to," he rasped brokenly.

"What is wrong with you?" I blurted out, my voice breaking. "How could you do something so fucked up?"

"I don't know. It just h-happened, and...I only wanted—Dawson, please..." he pleaded, stepping closer to me.

"Don't fucking touch me!" I shouted, backing away from him. I couldn't bear the thought of his touch on me. Not now. Theo's face paled and he wrapped his arms around himself, shivering visibly.

"I didn't really want him. I didn't...it wasn't what...I wanted you." Theo's voice shook in time with his body.

"Are you kidding me?" I hissed. "You disgust me. Why would I ever let you touch me after *that*?"

Theo shook his head frantically, his breaths coming in rapid pants. "No, no. You don't mean that..."

"The fuck I don't! If you think this is the way to get me back in your life, you're crazy."

His whole demeanor shifted on a dime, poison drenching his gaze.

"Don't fucking say that!" He exploded. "Don't call me that! I'm not crazy!"

"What the hell would you call the stunt you just pulled?"

"I didn't plan it! I just...it's not what you think."

"You brought that asshole up here to hook up in my room, Theo! On my bed!"

"That's not—"

"You took my virginity on that bed!" I thundered, my tears rising hot and fast. "We made love right there, in that very fucking spot, and you—"

I broke off, my hand clamping over my mouth as a sob forced its way up my throat. I turned my back on him, my abs clenching from the effort it took to keep from screaming in frustration, in misery. My world imploded, the weight of it crushing me as I struggled to hold myself together.

"God, I can't do this. Just get out," I begged, rubbing at the headache blooming behind my eyes.

"No, please! I need...*fuck*," Theo cried, and I heard him grunt painfully. I looked over and saw him yanking at his hair, pacing like a caged animal. "I need it back. The ring. Please, that's why I came up here. I can't—I can't lose it."

He continued to look around the room, as if forgetting I was there. A mirthless, wet laugh burst from my lips. That's what started this shit? That fucking ring? I didn't know what the hell happened to him to make him do something like this, but I barely recognized the man in front of me.

I'm not the Theo you remember. I'm not him. You need to grieve him and move on because he's gone. Don't keep holding on to a ghost.

His warning that night in the alley hit me, and in that instant, I knew what he meant. And I was done. I didn't have it in me to hold on any longer.

I dug into my pocket and pulled out the ring, his attention snagging on it the second I held it up. I threw it at him and Theo fumbled to catch it as it bounced off his chest. His glassy eyes caught mine and the relief I saw in them was devastating. My knees almost buckled at the loss of what I was giving up.

My last connection to him, to what we once were.

"Take it," I bit out coldly. "It means nothing to me now. Just like you. You should have stayed gone."

Theo's harsh gasp lanced through me, but I shoved down everything I was feeling, burying myself in apathy.

"Don't say that, Mercury...please, don't leave me..." he whimpered.

"I'm not leaving you, I'm kicking you out," I snarled. "Get the hell out of my house and don't come back here. Ever."

Theo's face crumpled, fingers clawing at his hair and his chest. He repeatedly mumbled under his breath, fragments of "sorry" and "no" barely discernible. A brutal wave of helplessness washed over me as I saw him break down. His cries stabbed at my ears and I crossed my arms to stop myself from clutching him to me.

I didn't want to feel sorry for him. He didn't deserve a shred of my sympathy or care. I hadn't wanted to admit it to myself, but from the second Theo walked back into my life, hope had reignited. I had stupidly believed that something good could come from his return, that maybe he'd found his way back to me after all.

But his filthy pleas to Corvin cut away the last remnants of faith I had in him. His moans played on hellish repeat in my head and the memory of his sated face made me want to gouge my eyes out.

After several minutes, Theo's sobs subsided and his eyes slid up to meet mine. They were hollow and vacant, and a current of guilt ran through me knowing I was the cause.

He didn't say a word. We stared at each other so long that I lost all sense of time. Part of me didn't want the moment to end because on the other side of it was a life I never wanted. A life without him.

Theo finally broke the contact, nodding absently as he moved to leave. He paused with his hand on the doorknob and threw me a helpless look.

"I know you won't believe me, but I'm so sorry, Dawson," he whispered roughly. "You might hate me, but it'll never be as much as I hate myself."

He was out the door before I could blink. I sighed heavily, exhaustion blanketing me like a shroud. My nose wrinkled at the sight of my bed, the comforter bearing the imprint left behind by Theo. I ripped it off the mattress, tearing at the sheets until they were a rumpled mess on the floor.

I crawled onto the bed and curled into myself. Warm tears cascaded down my cheeks, soaking the pillow beneath me and my lids slammed shut against the images of Theo and Corvin that assaulted me.

That was the third time I'd seen him with another man, and each time a little piece of me had died. How much more of me was possibly left to break? I hadn't thought there was anything more he could do to hurt me.

I was so fucking wrong.

Just as I once believed my love for Theo was infinite, so too was the damage he could inflict on my ruined heart. But that was my cross to bear. I'd given Theo my heart a long time ago, and it was his to do with as he pleased.

His to love.

His to protect.

His to destroy.

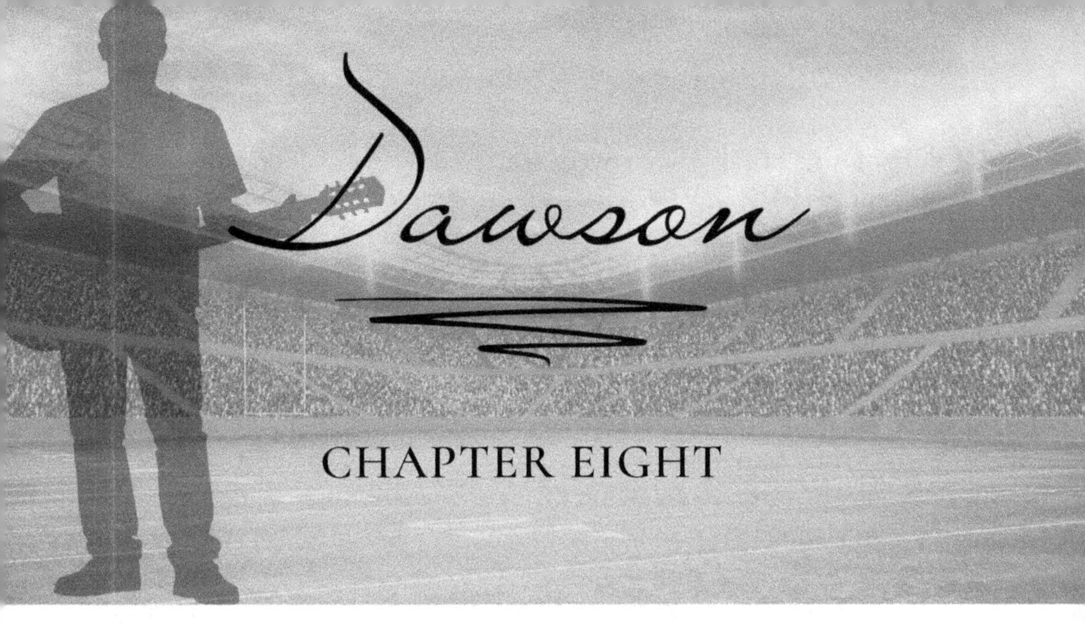

CHAPTER EIGHT

Warped voices echoed in my head as consciousness crept in slowly. I fought to stay in the dark where painful reality couldn't reach me, but it was useless.

"You think he's dead? He looks dead."

"We could always check his pulse. We just jam our finger against his neck, right? Or is it the wrist?

"Oh! I see him breathing! Nate, wake him up. Go sit on his face or something."

"If he's still into 'experimenting', he might get a kick out of that."

"You're right, I forgot about that! Whoo! Another one for the butt club!"

"Sweet Jesus, we are *not* calling ourselves that, Fin. It's too early for this shit. Restrain yourself."

"Ooo, kinky. You do it for me, Daddy. Rhys tells me you're so good when you're rough. Now, is anyone gonna wake him so we can eat pancakes?"

"Oh for the love of...never send men to do a lady's job. Move over, morons."

"Wow! So rude..."

Fuck, I think I might prefer being dead.

There was a swish of fabric and light pierced through the slits in my eyes. I squinted against the harsh glare, grumbling my displeasure.

Fuzzy forms of my friends were scattered near my door, coming into focus as the last of my sleep faded.

"You assholes are the worst, you know that?" I growled, rubbing at my eyes and trying to ignore the soft pounding in my temple.

Fin gasped loudly and Nate protested, but the others seemed unfazed. Bash, Cal, and Aly just stood there looking amused and their smirks were kindling to my already horrible mood.

"Whatever, just get out. What the hell are y'all even doing here this early?" Their smirks fell into varying looks of worry and hurt.

"Woah...sorry, D. We didn't mean to bug you," Bash said sheepishly. "We all planned to crash here last night, remember? Micah and Rhys are downstairs making breakfast for all of us."

Guilt turned my stomach and I felt like a huge dick. I wasn't normally like this, but after last night...

Damn it, *no*. I wasn't thinking about that. I didn't want to think about him ever again.

Good luck with that one, you pathetic bastard.

"Oh, right." I tried to focus on my friends and not what a shit show last night had ended up being. "Shit, I'm sorry for being an ass. I had a bit of a rough night."

Aly's inquisitive stare felt hot on the side of my face, but I ignored her as best I could while I got out of bed and trudged into my bathroom. I was still in last night's sweaty, wrinkled clothes and it hurt like a bitch to remove my contacts since my eyes were so gritty and swollen from crying myself to sleep. God, I was a mess.

I lumbered over to my dresser to pull out some fresh clothing, ignoring the five pairs of eyes that were tracking my every move. I started to pull my shirt off, but paused and turned to glare at my friends who continued to stand there watching me.

"Usually I charge for the show, so either cough up twenty bucks or get out so I can change," I grumbled.

"I've got a five!" Fin piped up. "You guys got any cash on you?"

"Alright, you horny mess, let's get some food in that mouth so nothing else comes out of it," Aly snickered as she shoved him out of my room and down the hall.

"Hey, everyone in this house appreciates a yummy-ass man. I was doing us all a favor!"

"Well, I hope you've learned your lesson, Hayes," Cal smacked his lips in mock disapproval.

"That I should change the locks?"

"No, that you should start charging more," he replied, looking at me like I was an idiot. "Twenty bucks is chump change. People are gonna start thinking you're Zach Galifianakis under there. I mean, no judgment if you've gone soft, QB. I know it's not as easy for you gridiron boys to stay hot and in shape like we do in lacrosse."

"Shut the fuck up, man," I snorted, hauling my dirty shirt off and throwing it at his face. He caught it in the air laughing, his dual colored eyes shining with mirth.

"I'll be damned. See, you could easily pull Magic Mike money with those abs. And you've got a built-in customer base with Fin down there. I'm only seeing positives here."

"And I'm positive your ass will be looking for breakfast elsewhere if you don't get out of my room," I smirked.

"See ya down there," Cal blurted as he strode quickly out the door.

"Masterfully handled," Bash chuckled before pinning me with a concerned stare. "Are you okay?"

"Yeah B, just tired," I lied, giving him a half-assed smile. "Let's go eat before Nate pilfers all our food."

"Speak for yourself. My baby has a giant plate squirreled away just for me, so I'm all good," Bash grinned smugly.

"Way to cheat the system."

"Don't blame me because you don't have an inside man."

"Didn't think I'd need one seeing as it's my damn house. I'm the inside-ist man you can get," I mumbled.

We made our way down to the kitchen and drool filled my mouth at the smell of waffles and bacon. The kitchen was filled with our small, but growing crew and my pissy mood mostly dissipated at the sight. Micah and Rhys were busy at the stove while Cal, Aly, Nate and Fin had sat down with Cal's friends Griffin and Kenji at the long island bar top. Bash and I joined the eight of them while they all chatted together and wolfed down breakfast.

I'd met most of them through a weird domino effect. Once Bash introduced Micah to me and Nate, the rest snowballed from there. It was a big "friend of a friend" type deal all around, but we'd all pretty much settled into genuine friendships in one way or another. It was an unusual phenomenon for me that I was still getting used to.

Growing up, I'd never had a ton of friends, preferring to spend my time playing music or reading. I had been the quiet, aloof kid always humming songs or playing air piano in class. Football eventually changed that, along with kids learning my dad was *the* Lincoln Hayes, but I was still that same quiet kid inside. Being popular meant nothing to me because no one really cared about knowing the real me. They ignored my quirks instead of accepting them, and they only cared about my name being attached to them in some way.

The only one who had ever truly cared about me was Theo. He didn't care about my dad's status or money. He didn't think I was weird. He just appreciated me for who I was, flaws and all.

After I lost him, I pretty much limited my circle to Nate and Bash once I met them at UT. Even when most of the campus knew me thanks to my quarterback status, I mostly kept to myself. Sure, I went to parties and occasionally hung out with guys from the team, but I never shared anything about myself beyond a smile and inane small talk. I was window dressing, a pretty face that people thought of as a friend merely because I was friendly.

It made me thankful for this ragtag group who was quickly becoming a support system I didn't realize I needed. My breakdown at the karaoke bar was one of many times now that these guys had shown care and interest in me beyond the Hayes name and my jersey number. They reminded me that Theo wasn't the only one who would embrace and appreciate the real Dawson.

Still, they would never know me as deeply and intrinsically as Theo had, but that was the price I paid when one person owned my soul. I had pieces of myself to give to others, but I'd never feel whole without him.

Clattering plates and arguing snapped me out of the miserable musings.

"Ouch! Look, I'm starving, I just wanted seconds!" Nate complained, raising his hands to fend off Rhys who held a plate out of his reach with one hand and smacking Nate with the spatula he held in the other.

"You already had seconds and this is Dawson's! If you want more pancakes, then *you* go make them!" Rhys chided.

"But but but—that's so much work," Nate whined. "And you and Micah were the ones who offered to cook for us in the first place!"

"I'm sorry, do I have IHOP stamped on my ass?" Micah sassed from the stove where he finished up the last strips of bacon.

"How am I supposed to know? If your boyfrestie over there is into sharing now, I'd be happy to check," Nate teased with a wide grin. Bash popped him on the back of the head as he walked by.

"Excuse you, but the term is 'bestie-boyfriend'. Also this is not made-to-order and my ass isn't on the menu."

"Nope! Don't you say it," Rhys warned, pointing an accusatory finger at Cal from across the kitchen island.

"Oh be fair now, Sweetness. He teed it up for me," Cal complained. Rhys only huffed and handed me my plate, which I took gratefully and thanked him for. He ambled over to Cal who hooked him around the waist, pulling him onto his lap. I swear, they were as sickeningly sweet as Micah and Bash most days.

You're only jealous because you used to have that with someone else...

And just like that, my mood soured once again as I told my inner voice to fuck right off with the unwelcome reminders. It was already a losing battle to shove down the memories from last night when everything went to shit.

The masochistic part of me couldn't help but wonder if Theo was okay this morning. He'd definitely been high last night and I had been particularly cruel to him...not that he didn't deserve at least some of it.

Whatever, it wasn't my business anymore.

"So how did the rest of the party go?" I asked a little too loudly. Wide eyes snapped to me, but Griffin happily took the opening. I'd learned fast that the brash auburn-haired lacrosser was always ready with an outrageous story...or three.

"Man, you missed the best part! These two chicks were apparently doing the same dude on the baseball team, and when one of the girls ran into him and the other girl was grinding all up on each other, she *lost* it. Grabbed the other girl's hair, ripped her off the guy, and started smacking the hell out of her! While those two were fighting on the floor, the dude snuck off with *another* chick dancing nearby and ended up making out with her in the pool!"

"Is that it? If that's all you've got for us, I'm changing the channel. I've seen juicier stuff on reruns of *Jersey Shore*," Fin said with an arched brow. Griffin narrowed his eyes at him and I could've sworn I heard him growl.

"Pipe down and let me finish before I come over there and hit your mute button."

"Babycakes, you couldn't find my button with a compass and a prayer. Even if you did, I doubt you'd know what to do with it," he snapped with an impish grin.

I didn't want to know if that was irritation or heat I saw in Griffin's gaze. Ever since he and Fin had met this year, they lived to fuck with each other, but there was always an undercurrent of something more. That was so far beyond what I had the mental capacity for right now.

"Anyway, what I was about to say," Griffin continued sharply, "was after the two chicks had stopped fighting long enough to find baseball bro in the pool, they ended up jumping in and trying to fight the other girl he was making out with. But after about two minutes of the crowd egging them on, they all started making out with each other and went off to hook up somewhere and left poor baseball guy all by himself. But as they were leaving, they all threw out that he apparently swings with a "little bat" and he'd have better luck scoring a homerun on the field because he couldn't get one out of them!"

Laughter broke out at Griff's enthusiastic ending, and even Fin's lips twitched at hearing the misfortune of the hapless playboy. But I barely cracked a smile. Hearing about party hookups dropped my mind back down a rabbit hole I was desperate to avoid. I was floating between feeling nothing at all and drowning in despair after what happened with Theo.

A hand gripped my shoulder and shook me hard, and Nate's face came into view. "Dude, what's up with you? You don't look so good."

I looked around to see everyone else's eyes on me, scrutinizing me carefully. My neck heated under the collar of my shirt.

"Nothing," I replied quickly, but every face in the room twisted with skepticism and disbelief.

It wasn't my nature to talk about myself or my problems. I pushed things down, buried them until I could release them back into the world as notes and chords. I was always willing to let others unburden themselves with me, help them carry whatever weighed them down. Theo had been the only one I trusted enough with my vulnerabilities, but after he left, my walls came up and everything I felt was barricaded behind them.

"Really, it's nothing. The party just ended up sucking for me, that's all," I murmured reluctantly. The last thing I needed was to trauma-dump on my friends over breakfast.

"I'm guessing it has something to do with the *Dawson's Creek* episode that awkwardly played out during beer pong?" Fin asked curiously.

"Hah! I get it," Nate barked out happily.

"Oh my God, Finny..." Aly mumbled, biting back a smile.

"For why?" Rhys chastised.

"Can I add a splash of tact to your juice there, babe?" Micah smirked.

"OMGeez, what did I do wrong this time?" Fin complained with wide doe eyes.

"Nothing, you're fine. I know we were a bit...dramatic last night. The thing is Theo and I have, uh, history."

"Yeah, we caught onto that after the first thirty seconds of angry sexual tension," Cal interjected, grunting in discomfort when Rhys elbowed him in the ribs to silence him.

I flushed at his comment. "We did *not* have sexual tension..."

"So you're saying you weren't thinking about jumping his bones again?" Griffin asked.

"What? No, why—didn't you notice we were at each other's throats last night?" I argued.

"Only because you couldn't go at each other's naughty bits instead," Fin added unhelpfully. "You two were throwing major vibes, just sayin'."

"That's *not* what was happening."

"Aw, it's cute you think that, but it really was," Micah confirmed with faux sympathy. "Did he actually look a little pissed at Nate for some reason, or was that just me?"

"No, I totally caught that! I think he was jealous," Fin agreed.

Nate grinned and slung his arm over my shoulder. "I mean, who can blame him? I'm a straight catch. And Dawson and I do have a love that can't be contained...isn't that right, boo?"

He leaned up and planted a loud kiss on my cheek. I detached myself from him and wiped my face off as he laughed.

"Why the hell would he be jealous of Nate when he thinks Aly and I are dating?"

"Wait, you and Aly are dating? Since when? How did I not know about this?" Nate threw me an accusatory look.

"We're not, but Dawson heavily implied we were…twice."

I glared at Aly, the judgmental tone in her voice unmistakable. "Look, I'm not proud of lying about it, but I only did it because…"

Their expectant gazes were pinned on me, but I wasn't sure how to explain why I'd wanted Theo to believe I was taken so he didn't think I'd just been pining after him for nearly four years while he'd clearly been off screwing anyone he wanted and ignoring my existence. I didn't want to come across jealous and petty.

Even though I was. Hard core. Like an asshole.

"It was because…we—I mean, he…that is…"

"I'd like to buy a vowel please, Vanna," Micah muttered when I failed to string together a coherent sentence.

I growled in frustration. "Yeah, no. I'm not talking about this. Thought I could, but I can't. Experiment over."

"You sure do like to experiment a lot, huh?" Fin mumbled and I could hear the amusement in his voice. I glared at him as he scrambled to shovel a forkful of pancakes into his mouth, peering at me innocently.

"You can't give us anything? I mean, you kind of left us on a cliffhanger there, D," Nate remarked through a mouthful of food.

"Fine, whatever. Theo and I used to be a thing. We were together for a long time and then he left without a word our senior year and yeah, it majorly sucked. I hadn't heard from him since, but he recently moved back and it's fucking with me a bit because I didn't think I'd ever see him again. Now he's being all cagey and weird, so there's no chance in hell of us ever getting back together. I just want to forget about everything and move on with my life. Can we please drop it now?"

My confession sucked the oxygen straight from the room. I concentrated on scarfing down my unfortunately cold breakfast instead of entertaining any other questions from them. I had no more mental or emotional bandwidth, so I was determined to move on from the subject of my pitiful love life.

"Dawson?…"

"Please don't ask me anything else about it. It's…a lot," I pleaded gently.

"Why can't any of us go one semester without drama in our love lives? Honestly, it's becoming a concerning pattern," Micah sighed loudly.

"Because life sucks ass sometimes," Cal grunted in agreement.

"That is a truly terrible saying," Fin retorted. "Half of the people at this table know the joy of sucking ass. It's like in the top ten things to try in life. Hardly a negative."

"Micah sure is a big fan," Bash chuckled before his boyfriend thwacked him hard on the shoulder.

"Even I'm not opposed to it from time to time," Aly weighed in.

Nate's eyes seemed to dislodge from his skull. "Wait, chicks like that too? Like, it's the same feeling for you...back there?"

"Uhh, yeah? Why wouldn't it be? My ass is just like yours."

"This is the weirdest fucking breakfast I've ever had," Kenji muttered.

"You know, we can just stop talking about—"

"Maybe life's just really bad at sucking ass?" Nate cut me off. "That seems more accurate, though I wouldn't personally know. I'm assuming there's a wrong way to do it, right?"

"Well, wrong is a bad word for it. It does take a certain finesse to do it properly, and sometimes if they—"

"For fuck's sake, please don't finish that thought, Fin. I'm eating," Aly whined.

"Well, excuse me sassy pants, but you jumped into this first!"

"Anyway, don't lose faith, D-man," Nate smiled, ignoring Fin and Aly. "Things will work out with Theo the way they're meant to, maybe even better than you're expecting."

"Thanks, man." I couldn't hate his endless optimism, even if I disagreed with him. I wasn't sure there was anything for Theo and I to work out anymore, no matter how much I had wanted it to.

"For sure! Life's anal oral skills are bound to improve this year and then you'll reap the benefits!"

A chorus of groans and laughs came from the group as Nate continued to argue his point, the bizarre debate growing in volume and enthusiasm from everyone except me and Kenji.

"Hey Nate, you know who'd be *delighted* to give you a personal lesson on rimming?"

Nate glared at Micah's mischievous face. "Do not go there, Russo.

I'm not letting you ruin my appetite if you are going to be talking about *him*."

"Oooh, yeah," Cal grinned. "I forgot you and my boy Mateo have this weird thing between you. Want me to text him that you miss him?"

"Hell no! This is a text-free zone! In fact, all of you are in violation of Breakfast Code 17.4 and I'm going to have to confiscate all your devices. Hand them over."

"But then how will I know what he texted back?" Cal waved his phone tauntingly. "Hey hey! I see text bubbles!"

"NO! Pop those damn bubbles, Hawkins!" Nate jumped up and launched across the room towards Cal, who took off with his phone in hand out the back door. Even I couldn't help choking out a laugh with the others as we watched through the windows as Nate chased Cal in zig zags across the lawn with Stella the goat now in hot pursuit. I wasn't sure how she got out of her enclosure again, but seeing their horrified faces and hearing their distant shrieks as she charged them made it worth it.

"Mmm, I can already smell the fresh drama coming," Fin announced brightly. "Welcome to the 75th annual Hunger Games, everyone."

I finished my food while my friends talked and enjoyed the morning once the guys came back inside, panting and sweaty. I smiled to myself as I thought how lucky I was to have these people in my life now, weird as they were. When my gaze drifted out the window to the Bishop's house, my smile faded. My friends had managed to distract me for a small time, but even that hadn't been enough to bury the memories of last night.

I excused myself from the table to go shower, telling them all to hang out and make themselves at home. Truthfully, I just needed some space to decompress after the last twenty-four hours. I made it to my room, locking the door behind me to avoid any more good-intentioned, but unwanted intruders.

Coming home hadn't exactly been the peaceful getaway that I'd been hoping for. My peace of mind had been stolen the first day I arrived and it had only gotten worse with every encounter with Theo. I promised my parents I'd be here when they got back from their short holiday trip, but the second they were home, I was heading back to campus. I needed to get back to my life the way it was before Theo stormed back into it. It may not have been everything I wanted it to be, but it was perfectly fine.

I whipped off my shirt and headed for the bathroom, but movement out the window caught my eye. Across the way, I noticed a sleek red sedan pulling up the Bishop's driveway. I watched a man climb out and though I couldn't quite see his face, his build was faintly recognizable. He trudged up to the porch and knocked, throwing a sweeping glance over his shoulder and I saw it was Corvin.

I hated the way my chest clenched and my stomach churned as I saw the door open. Corvin waltzed inside after a few seconds, not even allowing me a glimpse of Theo before it shut again.

I didn't want to think of why he was there at ten in the morning or what they were doing. I only had so much sanity left. It made no sense to me that Theo had seemed so wrecked at our falling out last night, only to turn around and invite Corvin into his home, possibly into his bed, hours later.

The realization ripped the breath from my lungs. Theo might have still wanted me on some level, but I clearly wasn't the only one he wanted. To know the love of my life no longer saw me as the love of his shredded something inside me. I shuffled into my shower on autopilot, adjusting the temperature until the water scorched my back and gave me a different pain to fixate on.

I couldn't keep doing this, grappling with betrayal and hurt I had no right to feel. And if I was honest with myself, I was tired of being angry and bitter. I couldn't hate Theo if I wanted to and the resentment I felt was eating me up inside. This wasn't who I was.

Maybe the only way forward was to forgive Theo and put everything behind us. Not just the bad, but the good as well. Wipe our slate clean and start over. I didn't think we could start as friends, but perhaps with time we'd get there. Even as I thought it, I knew it wouldn't be that simple.

How do you erase a lifetime of memories? Was it even possible to forget every laugh or word of love between us? Could we sweep every smile, kiss, and intimate touch under the rug like they never happened?

I hoped the answer was yes because I couldn't keep living this half-life. If Theo had any mercy left for me, he'd give me back my heart so I at least stood a chance at piecing it back together.

Theo

CHAPTER NINE

My body ached like a motherfucker and my jaw was sore like I'd been clenching for hours. I tried to open my eyes, but it was as useless as if they'd been glued shut. I always forgot how much cocaine fucked me up the next day.

Wait, is it the next day or later? Where the hell am I?

"We're at your place. You've been crashed out for almost ten hours now."

My lids shot open at the deep rumble and I instantly regretted it when the UV rays burned like a bitch. I guess I'd voiced my thoughts out loud, but who even answered me?

I swiveled my head around and saw Corvin lounging back in the recliner across from me. His eyes were bloodshot as he rubbed at them and yawned, looking a bit worse for wear. Confusion swamped me as I tried to recall why he was sitting in my living room.

"The fuck happened?" I grated out, wincing. Swallowing a Brillo pad would have hurt less.

"I'm not surprised you don't remember. You were pretty fucked up."

A sense of unease settled over me at his tone. My stomach soured as I looked down at my naked chest and legs clad only in boxer briefs. Fuck, did we hook up again? I couldn't remember. It was like crawling back into my mind after being forced out of it, unaware of what my body had done while I was gone.

I didn't want to know what I did while I was fucked up. It would only make me loathe myself more.

"Not to be rude, but what are you doing here?" I asked. My head was pounding and it took immense willpower to concentrate.

Corvin slouched forward to rest his elbows on his knees, furrowing his brows as he looked me over.

"I caught up to you when I saw you leaving the party. You were still kind of out of it and when you said you lived next door, I walked you back home to make sure you got inside okay. But you seemed really upset, so I showed up yesterday morning to check on you. I just felt like some of that might have been my fault..."

I waited for his words to trigger some memory of what had happened following the party until now, but it was still a murky blur. Since I was too cowardly to ask what might have gone down between us, I asked the next most important question.

"How did I get high again? Did you bring shit with you?"

Corvin cleared his throat and he fidgeted with his hands. "No, but when I came by to talk to you, you were kinda irritable and kept mumbling to yourself about something. You wouldn't tell me what was wrong. You just asked me to call Aaron for some more party favors. I mean, I fought you on it at first but you wouldn't let it go, so I texted him to come hang out."

Shit, that definitely sounded like me after a coke high. The come-down sucked ass and always put me in the worst mood. I rubbed at my throbbing temple and breathed deeply through my nostrils.

"What exactly did I take?"

"Uhh well, we all drank on and off all day, but he still had some coke left so you guys rolled some dirty joints and hit about two or three of those. Then you grabbed a couple Xanax from your room and eventually passed out on the couch around three in the morning. He headed out after that. I made sure to flip you on your side just in case you...you know, got sick or something."

"Fuck me," I breathed. It wasn't the first time I had used a Xanny to smooth out the ride down from mixing weed and coke. I had sworn to myself I was past this shit, but one disastrous night with Dawson and all my good intentions came crashing down.

I was lucky I didn't fucking OD, though part of me didn't entirely care if I had.

It's not like you haven't been there before...

Corvin's forehead was etched with worry lines as he abused his bottom lip. I wasn't sure if he expected me to keel over right there or was waiting for me to talk to him, but I just wanted to be alone. I gingerly stood and stretched, the movement rippling through my muscles like fire.

"Wait, what time is it? Hell, what *day* is it?"

Corvin grabbed his phone off the side table before answering. "It's about one thirty in the afternoon on the sixth."

Over a day lost on a stupid bender. Fuck...

"I'm sorry about all that, man. I'm not sure what got into me," I muttered, averting my gaze.

Except I knew exactly why I'd gone off the rails. The missing hours since Corvin had come over might have been fuzzy, but my fight with Dawson was still crystal fucking clear. I had wanted to forget, to be able to breathe again, but even my mini spiral hadn't been enough to drown it all out.

It all still rang in my head, sadistic and loud. Dawson's feral words that I meant nothing to him, that he was finally done with me made me want to fall at his feet and beg him not to give up on me. It was though my chest had been set ablaze, incinerating the last threads of hope I had for us.

The voices were getting stronger and I didn't want to fight them anymore. I was so damn tired. Tired of being strong, of keeping it all together, of just...fucking existing.

What was the point when my soul no longer had its other half? Why work so hard to get through each day when my heart was living outside of my chest and wanted nothing to do with me anymore?

"Nah, it's all good," Corvin assured me sheepishly. "I figured you must have been dealing with something really rough, is all. It's just crazy you don't really remember anything."

"Yeah, that happens when you chase benzos with booze," I croaked out, rubbing at my eyes and exhausted to my damn bones.

"Oh shit," he murmured with wide eyes. "I didn't know that. No wonder you're hungover as fuck."

I waved my hand dismissively, but froze when I saw him stand to slip on his sweatpants and pull on his shirt. I hadn't noticed he'd also been half naked when we were talking, but now it was all I could focus on. Nausea swirled in my gut. I hadn't wanted my shameful actions confirmed, but the possibility seemed too big to ignore.

"Uh, did we..."

I trailed off, unable to finish because I still wasn't sure I wanted to know the answer. Corvin quirked a brow at me in question. I gestured awkwardly between the two of us and the lightbulb went off in his head.

"You mean, did we fuck?"

Bile surged in my throat and all I could manage was a quick nod. Corvin's cheeks reddened darker than before and he let out a nervous laugh.

"Nah, we didn't. I-I mean, I...tried to throw hints and went in to kiss you once, but when I noticed you were too out of it, I stopped. After that, we all just got more hammered, so it wouldn't have happened anyway."

Relief hit me hard and fast. I shouldn't have been as shocked as I was, but it was just another side effect of what I lived with. Two sides of me constantly at war with each other, pulling me up then dragging me down in a vicious tug of war that I would never win. This side always felt preferable than the alternative, but it robbed me of all impulse control and self preservation. What went down with Corvin at the party was proof of that. I was just fucking glad it hadn't happened twice.

Not that it mattered. Dawson despised me now and wouldn't touch me again. I could shave my head and live as a celibate monk and it wouldn't change that fact.

The thought soured my stomach further and I rushed off to the downstairs bathroom. I splashed cold water on my face, breathing through the sick feeling until it had passed. I relieved myself and washed my hands, and when I came out Corvin was standing there with his hands shoved in his pockets.

"You alright?"

"I'm good," I murmured. "Look, I appreciate you coming over to check on me and for..."

"Helping you get loaded for sixteen hours straight?" he smirked shyly.

"Yeah, that," I breathed out on a chuckle. "It was also cool of you to make sure I was safe after. Thanks for that. And just so you know, you weren't the reason I was upset. That was all on me."

He nodded and let out a relieved sigh. "Cool. Well, in that case, would you...I don't know, wanna grab dinner or something next weekend?"

I could only blink at him as I processed his words. "Like a...date?"

"Sure," he smiled. "I know we kinda went zero to sixty since we met, what with the BJ and impromptu pharm party, but I'd like to get to know you if you'd let me. I'll be a perfect gentleman, I swear!"

My heart twisted at the offer. If we'd met before Dawson's party or even before May, I would have said yes. I would have been up for anything and relished in my disinhibition. I would have fucked him and used him however I wanted because I wouldn't have cared. I didn't truly need drugs to be high. My mind took me up and down without my knowledge or cooperation, and when I was up I had no walls or filters. No boundaries. No fear.

But things had changed. I could feel it. I was being dragged back down, swamped with shame, guilt, and disgust. It was a mental clarity that should have been relieving, but was instead biting and caustic. Things I'd said and done over the last several weeks pommeled my brain as I spun out internally over what I'd done.

Why did I ever think I could handle this? Control it? What does it say about me that my own mind turns against me and all I do is give into it?

"Theo?"

I snapped my head up at the sound of my name. I couldn't handle this right now. It was too much.

"Oh, I...I'm seriously flattered, but I'm not quite ready for that right now. I'm sorry," I replied. His face fell a bit, but he shot me a small smile anyway.

"Hey, no worries, I get it. Can I at least get your number? It couldn't hurt to have another friend, right?" he said good-naturedly.

I nodded my agreement and went to grab my phone off the sofa. The screen lit up and I saw a notification from PayPal that I'd sent Aaron a sizable chunk of change for his merchandise. I grunted in annoyance at the reminder of my stupidity, but unlocked my phone and handed it to Corvin. Once he'd texted himself from my number and saved his info on my phone, I walked him to the door.

"So I'll text you and maybe we can meet up for coffee or studying sometime?" Corvin asked, hovering at the threshold expectantly.

"Yeah, maybe," I said noncommittally. "Uh, drive safe, okay?"

He smiled and shifted on his feet a bit before closing the distance between us, planting a kiss on my cheek. I was stunned and frozen as he walked out to his car and took off. I ambled back into the house, my head a mess of thoughts I couldn't begin to decipher.

I knew from experience that this was the start of a slow slide that I always dreaded. Unless I wanted to flood my body with narcotics, there was no way out of it but through it.

God, I hated this part so fucking much. I felt panic start to well up in my chest thinking about the abyss that waited for me now that the high was over. It was a shift that was subtle, but also like a wrecking ball to my system. Maybe Dad had been right to keep me on my meds.

My hand floated up to my chest as it always did in stressful moments, but the ring wasn't there. My breath hitched at the memory of Dawson throwing it at me in his room. He gave it back. I didn't want to think about the cruel words he spewed as he did it, so I only focused on the fact that *he gave it back.*

Where the fuck is it then?!

I dove for the couch, spastically searching the cushions and the floor surrounding it but coming up empty. I spun around, eyes searching without really seeing as my breathing sped up and I fought to stay grounded.

A glint of silver snagged my attention on the mantle and I froze. I didn't know why it was there, but I didn't care. I snatched it up quickly, hugging it to my chest. My breath left me in a rush and I squeezed my eyes shut against the tears that sprang up. I wanted to curl up in a ball like fucking Gollum and never let it out of my sight again.

Christ, I was such a mess.

A timid knock at the door startled me. I shoved down my irritation at the interruption, assuming Corvin had forgotten something and come back. I trudged over to open the door and my heart stuttered at the sight of the man on my porch.

Dawson's freckled cheeks stained the lightest pink as I stared wide-eyed at him, almost positive he was a figment of my drug-addled imagination. His brows pinched and his mouth flattened into a line as his gaze swept over me head to toe.

"You look like shit," he stated.

I just continued to gape at him. I couldn't fathom why he was here when he'd basically told me I was dead to him. Some tiny flickering hope in the back of my brain said maybe he was there because he still wanted me, that he couldn't let me go.

"Can I come in?" Dawson asked. The request was soft and shaky and so unlike him that it threw me off guard. I nodded mutely and stepped aside to let him in.

He glanced around the open room anxiously. When he caught sight of the burned down joints on the living room table and the beer bottles scattered about, disappointment and worry lined his features.

"I wanted to come talk to you yesterday, but you...had company," he finished uncomfortably. Acid bubbled in my stomach at the thought that Dawson most likely assumed I'd been shacking up with someone for two days.

"Anyway, I wanted to come by and maybe clear the air between us if you're free to talk...or if you want to, that is."

My heart wrenched behind my ribs as his gaze connected with mine. I didn't deserve his time or his words, but he was willing to give me both. I wasn't strong enough to turn him down. It felt like I was on borrowed time with Dawson, so I was going to take every morsel of his attention that I could get.

"Of course I do," I rushed to accept. "Let's go sit outside though. I could use some air."

I snuck his ring onto my finger as I led him out past the pool and to the fire pit close to the tree line. He dropped gracefully into one of the Adirondacks situated around it as I took the one beside him, taking a fortifying breath as I waited for him to speak.

After a couple of minutes of silence, I chanced a look over at him and the agonized expression on his gorgeous face triggered painful spasms in my chest.

"I've thought about this a lot the last couple days. I hoped we could hash things out and try to find a way past everything...but I've just been so goddamn angry with you." Dawson's voice was tight and strained, his knuckles flexing on the armrest next to me.

"Dawson..."

"Why was he here?"

"What?"

He shot me a cold glare and his jaw twitched. "Corvin. His car has been in your driveway since Wednesday morning."

I squirmed in my seat. "He just came by to talk and apologize after the...incident at the party. But I was kind of having a rough comedown, so he texted a friend of his to come over and hook me up with some stuff."

Dawson cursed under his breath and ran his fingers through his thick hair. "So you decided to get high and party again not even twelve hours later? Jesus, did you hook up with him again too?"

Anger suffused my veins at his question, hitting too close to my anxiety from earlier. "No, I fucking didn't. And you have no right to ask me about who I choose to fuck or not."

The words hit their intended target as I watched Dawson wince and visibly deflate. He turned his head away from me, but I saw his Adam's apple bob repeatedly as though struggling to swallow. I immediately regretted my comment, but I was too on edge to take it back.

"Fair enough," he said roughly. "Contrary to what you might think, I didn't come over to make you feel like shit. I just wanted to get some answers and see if we could put all this crap behind us."

That tiny spark of hope flared a bit brighter, but dimmed just as quickly since there was no way I could tell him everything. I knew Dawson better than I knew myself. He wouldn't be satisfied with a half-truth, yet that was all I could give him.

"I'm so sorr—"

"Stop," he demanded sharply. "I don't want to hear any lame excuses or half-assed apologies. What I want is a reason why."

"Why what?" I rasped out.

"Fuck, Theo. Where do I even begin?" he snapped. "Why did you screw Corvin in my room? Why did you act like a crude jackass in front of my friends? Why did you not tell me you were moving back? Why did you ignore me for fucking three and a half years? Why did you... leave me?"

The last question left him in a low, broken whisper, and it ripped through my insides. How could I give him the answers when they were all intertwined, stemming from the one problem I couldn't burden him with?

"Damn it, say something!"

"I don't fucking know!" I jumped up, pacing agitatedly. "I don't know why I'm like this! I don't get why the fuck my brain is wired wrong or why I do the stupidest shit."

At least that part was the truth. I still don't know what I'd done wrong in my life to deserve this curse.

"That's all you have to say to me? You don't know?"

"You don't understand," I ground out, clutching at my hair. "I can't tell you..."

"Why not?" Dawson asked desperately as he stood to face me. "We never used to keep secrets from each other. Never. That's not like you. But then neither is abandoning me without an explanation or goodbye, so why am I surprised?"

"I didn't do it to hurt you, Dawson."

"I'd believe that if it didn't seem like every time we've run into each other since May, you've been determined to hurt me however you can."

"Like what you did last night didn't hurt me?" I bit back. "You treated me like I was a stranger. Like we haven't known each other almost our entire damn lives."

"It's no different than how you've treated me! You ghosted me for years and have done nothing but give me whiplash since the second I saw you again."

"Because I thought it would be easier for both of us to stay away!"

"And then you got blown by one of my *fucking teammates* in my bedroom of all places, and you were so high that you didn't even care."

"That's not true! I did fucking care! I never meant—"

"I didn't do anything to deserve that, Theo! I loved you!" His voice cracked and it was all I could do to remain standing. I forced myself to ignore the past tense of those three words. If I focused on that, I'd shatter.

We stared each other down, grief and heartbreak volleyed between us like cannon fire. His eyes shimmered with tears and I wanted to tear my heart out and offer it to him, anything to make up for the pain I'd caused. I didn't want to keep doing this with him. I fucking despised hurting him and I knew that was all I'd done since coming home.

"I'm so sorry, Mercury," I apologized thickly. "You're right. You don't deserve any of this. I'll explain as much as I can, but please understand there's some things I'm not ready to talk about."

He seemed ready to argue with me, but eventually conceded with a small nod and sat back down. I blew out a heavy breath and sat on the edge of the fire pit in front of him. I kept my eyes trained on his shoes so I wouldn't have to see the effects of my confession.

"How much do you know about why I moved away?"

"Not much," he murmured. "I went to your house when you didn't show up for Homecoming. Your dad only told me you were going to live with your mom and that I should...let you g-go."

The hitch in his voice pierced right through me. Images of a confused, distraught Dawson waiting for me at Neverland permeated my thoughts and pain pulsed through my ribcage. I wanted to reach for him and comfort him however I could.

"I'm sor—"

"Just get on with it," he pleaded quietly.

I cleared my throat and tried to speak past the solid lump wedged there. "I asked my dad not to tell you why he sent me to Huntsville. The reason I wasn't there to meet you that night was because I was in the hospital."

I paused at Dawon's sharp intake of breath. "What do you mean you were in the hospital? Are you okay? Oh my god, are you sick? Are you—"

"I'm fine now, and no, I'm not sick. I mean, I was in a way, but it's complicated," I rushed out.

"How is it complicated? What the hell happened? Why didn't either of you just tell me?" he asked frantically.

"Because you wouldn't have understood."

"Then make me understand now! I deserve to know what happened to you."

"Damn it, Dawson, I overdosed!"

I sensed his body go rigid in front of me, like even the air around him solidified. "You what?..."

"I never wanted you to know. It happened when I got back from that party we went to after the Homecoming game. I was already pretty trashed by the time you brought me home, but I was really stressing about something. I was having a hard time handling it, so I popped some Oxy I bought a few days before that."

"Wha—that doesn't make sense. You had never taken drugs before," he sputtered.

"That was the first time," I admitted gruffly. "I didn't know how bad it could be to take Oxy while wasted. Or at least, I didn't think anything that bad would happen."

Dawson made a muffled sound of distress and I reached for his hand before I could think better of it. To my shock, he didn't withdraw from my touch and God, I wanted to do a fucking cartwheel.

"Do you remember anything about it?"

"I remember feeling extremely tired and confused. I thought it was just the alcohol, but then I got really cold and clammy. My chest started to feel heavy and it was hard to take a full breath. The next thing I remember was waking up in the hospital and every inch of my body hurting."

Dawson squeezed my hand, drawing my gaze up to his. The sadness I saw was enough to cripple me, but I kept going, giving him as much of the truth as I could spare.

"My dad was there when I woke up. I'd never seen him scared before, but he looked so terrified then. He told me what had happened and how close I'd come to...well, you know. He'd had Narcan in this kit from work that he used and it saved my fucking life. Guess being a pharmaceutical company CFO has its perks," I joked weakly. The look Dawson gave me showed that my lame attempt to lighten the moment was not in any way appreciated.

"That still doesn't explain why you disappeared on me the way you did," he remarked without reproach.

This was the point where the truth fractured into pieces I had to sort through before sharing. He wouldn't get why I was so adamant that he stay ignorant about what I really went through. I didn't want him to know what I had learned about myself a few weeks before that had spiraled me out so badly I bought oxycodone off a shithead dealer at school just to cope. And that was only the first of many spirals I'd gone down in the years after.

"I slept for a few more hours and Mom was there the next time I woke up. She and Dad told me that I was being admitted to a rehab facility close to where she and Doug lived and after I was released, I'd be staying with her from then on. They said that I needed a "reset" to help me get better."

Anger and despair spiked through my blood thinking about how I'd broken down when they'd told me the news. I'd begged, cried, screamed at them that I couldn't leave Dawson. I even threatened things that didn't help my case and cemented their decision to send me away for treatment. It was as though my whole world had been ripped away from me in a heartbeat and I had been powerless to stop it.

Dawson yanked his hand from mine and stumbled out of his chair. "So...you almost *died* and then told your Dad to keep me in the dark while you got shipped off to rehab hours away from here? Why the hell didn't you trust me?"

"It wasn't about not trusting you..."

That was my first lie.

"That's exactly what it was about," Dawson barked. "Tell me why you didn't trust me with the truth."

"I didn't want to hurt you more when there was nothing I could do to change it. I was leaving either way," I replied weakly.

Dawson scoffed coldly, marching up to me and coming within inches of my face. "You have always been a terrible liar, Theo. One more chance. Why did you not trust me?"

With him this close to me, stealing my breath and sanity, I panicked. We were tap dancing perilously close to the secret I'd held for years now. I had tried so hard to keep it from him, to not taint what we once had, but I cracked under the pressure of his glare.

"I didn't trust that you'd still see me the same if you found out," I whispered hoarsely. "I didn't want you to know I was broken. I couldn't stand to see you stop loving me."

Dawson's face crumpled, tears flooding his lash line in a wave of pain. I wondered how much I would inflict before he turned his back on me forever. It would only be what I deserved.

"You—" He broke off, his breath stuttering. He took a large step back and cold swept over my body at the loss of his warmth.

"You didn't trust me to keep loving you? So when I gave you my class ring and I promised you my heart, my future...you thought I was what? Lying? Did it even mean anything to you?"

A sobbed broke through my chest, forcing its way out. He didn't understand. His promise was the one thing that kept me alive every time the darkness came for me.

Every time my thoughts screamed at me to end it, to quit trying, to just stop feeling, I held his ring to my heart and remembered that Dawson had promised me forever...and I couldn't take that away from him by giving up. His ring was all I had of him, the physical proof that I'd once owned his heart. I had promised him that I would always keep it close to me so I'd never forget that he was mine.

But fear can kill even the strongest of resolves, break the most powerful of promises. And it had broken mine.

"You're wrong," I choked out as my own tears broke free. "I didn't think you were lying. What you said, it meant everything to me. *You* meant everything to me. I was just scared and I...I really thought it was better that way. I was losing you anyway, but at least you still loved me. If you knew the truth, I risked losing that too..."

I watched helplessly as he cried, wet trails running down his beautiful face as he turned away from me. His hands laced together on top of his head and he stared up aimlessly at the sky.

In all the years we'd been apart, we'd never felt as broken as we did in that moment. I had broken us over and over with my secrets and lies, and now finally, with the truth. What did we even have left to help us to repair the damage? I wasn't sure it was even possible.

The worst fucking part was that I was still holding back the rest of the secret, the core of my distrust. He assumed the overdose was the source of my shame, and I was too much of a coward to let him think otherwise.

After an interminable silence, he turned around with a defeated slump in his shoulders. Dread slid down my spine at the cold, empty look in his eyes. I'd read once that the most beautiful, colorful cornflowers were meant to be worn by men in love to reflect the love given to them in return. But if the flower's color faded before its time, it meant their sweetheart's love for them had faded as well.

Dawson's cornflower blue eyes were dull and muted as though the color had drained away. I fought to breathe, trying to stifle the alarming hysteria building inside me. I had been terrified of losing Dawson's love, of seeing the shift in the way he looked at me. Seeing him now was every nightmare come true, every fear come to fruition. He looked right through me and I wanted to die.

"Thank you for being honest with me," he intoned. "I don't want us to fight anymore, and to be honest, I don't have the strength to keep being angry with you. I'll agree to no longer bring up the past and wipe the slate clean if you will."

"What does that mean? Does...does that mean you forgive me?" I asked, failing to keep the hopefulness from my voice.

"It means I don't want to keep living in the past. It's exhausting. I might one day be able to forgive you, but I'm not there yet."

I nodded dumbly. "So we agree to just be...friends?"

His gaze darted away from mine and my stomach sank. I was so fucking stupid to hope.

"I'm not there yet either," he admitted quietly. I caved in on myself, my lungs deflating.

"What even are we then? I mean, we can't just be acquaintances, Dawson," I argued. "I've known you since you were nine years old. We grew up together. We fell in love. Jesus, we were best fucking friends and got matching tattoos to prove it."

I lifted my hand in evidence, a slanted beamed eighth note inked on the back between my thumb and pointer finger. Dawson stared at it and I knew he was remembering that day the same as me.

On my seventeenth birthday, we'd bribed a friend's older brother to sneak us into the tattoo shop he worked at after closing, paying him way more than the stupid things were worth. It had taken so much convincing to get Dawson to agree, so I let him pick the design. When I'd seen the music note he'd chosen and he told me it symbolized our unbreakable connection, I'd fallen for him even more.

He clenched his jaw the longer he stared at my tattoo until finally dragging his gaze up to mine.

"I covered it," he confessed almost inaudibly.

My hand dropped to my side as all the air left me in a painful rush. He shifted on his feet, waves of anxiety pouring from him as I stared at him. All the betrayal and anger I had felt evaporated in a second. The only thing I felt now was cold.

"You'd do anything to erase me from your life, wouldn't you?"

I wasn't sure he'd heard me, but his noticeable flinch said otherwise. I let out a deep sigh, fatigue setting in and clouding my mind. There was nothing else for us to discuss. Our slate was wiped clean, after all.

"I get it, Mercury," I replied calmly, walking past him toward the house. "I'd erase me too."

CHAPTER TEN

It's quiet here. Neverland never used to be quiet. It was always filled with our laughter and Dawson's music. I miss it. I miss him.

It hurts to be here without him, but it's the only place I can pretend. Pretend he's still mine. Pretend I'm still the man he loves.

This is too hard.

It's all too much.

I'm always too much.

And yet never enough.

I remember the day I told Dawson I loved him for the first time. It was right here in the hayloft, in this very spot. If I close my eyes, I can almost feel him next to me. I can almost hear his song.

Does he remember that day?

Does he remember he said it back?

Or would he erase that too if he could?

CHAPTER TWELVE

I keep thinking it will hurt less, but it doesn't. I still come back here every day though. This is where I want to stay forever, here in Neverland.

So I can always be connected to him.

And when the day comes where I can't fight it anymore, this is where I'll do it.

I'll lie down on this very spot where I gave him my heart and let it stop beating.

Not now.

But someday.

CHAPTER THIRTEEN

I cursed as I hit another sour chord on my keyboard. I had been going at it for almost two hours and it sounded progressively like I was having a stroke. Even when I was keyed up about something it was unusual for me to mess up like this. A soft whine drew my attention to the bed where Penny was curled up next to my pillow.

"Yeah yeah, I know. I suck," I grumbled. She merely yawned and dropped her head back down lazily in response.

I dialed it back and began Für Elise instead, a return to form. I mastered it when I was five. No one would believe me of course because once again, I fumbled my fingers so much that I slammed my hands down on the keys repeatedly like a toddler throwing a tantrum. Penny jumped up at the noise and darted out the door.

Everyone's a critic...

"Woah. Who pissed in your cornflakes, Beethoven?" Dani leaned against my doorframe, slurping down a bowl of cereal at three in the afternoon.

"Gross," I griped. "And no one. I'm just having an off day."

That was an understatement. I almost regretted my decision to stay the remaining two weeks before returning to school for football practice. Mom and Dad had been so excited for some "family time" before Dani and I went back to school that I hadn't had the heart to turn them down.

Hah! Yeah fucking right, Hayes. Whatever you need to tell yourself.

"Hmm, right. And this would have nothing at all to do with the hunky boy next door who has been moping on down to the barn for three days now?"

Flutters of guilt set off in my gut thinking about Theo. His last words to me had ruined my sleep since that day, playing on a horrible loop in my head.

I'd erase me too...

Christ, what had he even meant by that? And it was all my fault. I don't know what possessed me to lie to him about the tattoo, but for some selfish, stupid reason I hadn't wanted him to know that I still had it. That not only had I taken to running my fingers over it every night where it lay inked on my hip, but that I had added to it last year. Expanded it. Marked it with even more meaning to memorialize what we once had.

What. A. Dumbass.

He'd looked so crushed when I said I'd had it covered. I was a piece of shit for saying it. I knew that. I was a hypocrite too, accusing him of purposely hurting me to push me away, yet that's exactly what I had done.

"Why would I care about that?" I groused, keeping my back to her.

"Oh hell no, we're not doing that," she exclaimed. A surprisingly strong hand landed on my shoulder, whipping me around to face her. "Do not lie to me and try to play that nonchalant, unaffected bullshit when we both know that you're still head over heels for him. You forget that I was there from the beginning and I saw your browser history."

I blinked at the bizarre comment. "Am I supposed to know what that means? What does that have to do with anything?"

Dani let out a frustrated grunt, rolling her eyes at me as she yanked her phone out of her back pocket. She scrolled through her photos for several seconds, her finger swiping furiously. When she found the one she wanted, she thrust it under my nose with a little huff of satisfaction.

Blood crawled up my face and set my cheeks on fire when I saw the photo she had snapped of my computer, the engagement ring website clear as day on the screen. I forgot that I had started looking those up back around the time of Homecoming.

Well, tried to forget.

Failed to forget.

Shit.

"Why the hell were you snooping on my computer, creep?" I tried to sound indignant, but it mostly came out strangled.

She smirked down at me. "Because I'm your younger sister and I'd never pass up an opportunity for blackmail. But also because my friend Sarah bet me that you two would break up before graduation and I wanted to rub it in her face how wrong she was."

Her eyes flared in remorse as she realized what she'd said. "Oh damn it, I'm so sorry! I wasn't thinking! I didn't mean...*shit*."

"It's okay," I reassured her, my voice dull. "I mean, she was right in the end, wasn't she?"

Dani's eyes flashed with regret, but she let it go. I turned off my keyboard and trudged over to my bed, flopping down onto my back. Dani's small form plopped down next to me, both of us staring up at the ceiling in contemplative silence.

"Why did he leave us like that?" she eventually asked in a tiny voice.

Her question squeezed my heart. In all my years of fuming and hurting over Theo's abrupt departure, I never thought about how Dani was affected by it.

I should have, but I was so far up my own ass that I hadn't thought about the fact he was, for all intents and purposes, another brother to her. They'd loved each other. When I'd lost him, so had she.

"I'm not sure it's my place to tell you," I started off carefully.

"Well, he sure as hell isn't telling me anything! He hasn't even tried to talk to me once this summer. I keep missing him when he's over here, but I shouldn't have to be the one to reach out first anyway," she pouted. My heart ached for her because I knew exactly how it felt to be ignored and avoided by him.

"I'm sorry, Dani. I'm not sure why he hasn't come to see you, but I know he's not meaning to hurt you. He's just...got a lot going on. And every time he and I have talked, it's been pretty rough so I imagine it's not easy for him to think of coming to you, Mom, or Dad yet."

Dani nodded slowly, blowing out a heavy breath. "Yeah, I understand that...but it still sucks. You really can't tell me anything? What happened for him to push us away?"

"He left for some...health reasons and made a bad call to cut ties to try to make it easier."

"Ugh, easier for who?" she grumbled sadly.

"For himself. He was really scared and he didn't want it to hurt worse than it already did."

I stopped, my own words echoing back to me in a clarity that stole my breath. I'd been so caught up in feeling betrayed, abandoned, and disposed of that I had lost sight of how much pain Theo must have been in to do what he did.

I knew Theo. Down to his very soul, I knew him better than anyone. He was romantic, goofy and loyal. He loved hard and deep and had never once made me doubt his feelings when we were dating. He never would have left like that without feeling like he had no other choice... like his world was ending and it's all he could do.

God fucking damn it, he also *had* a choice. He could have fucking talked to me, not blocked me and shut me out when we needed each other the most. But I couldn't honestly say I know what I'd do if the situation were reversed.

It's easy to judge when the choice isn't yours to make.

This merry-go-round of past mistakes couldn't keep spinning like this. I had told Theo that I wasn't ready to forgive him or be his friend, but that was the problem. The forgiveness wouldn't be for him. It would be for me, to release me from this purgatory of anger and pain.

Yes, Theo had fucked up royally and hurt me in many ways, but deep down I know he hadn't truly meant to. I can't remember a time growing up that he had ever caused me pain, so why was I clinging to this resentment so damn tight? For all he was and used to be to me, I could forgive him his mistakes. I could let go of what we were and start fresh as friends.

Regardless of the years of distance and heartache, Theo was still my soulmate. Maybe it was only meant to be platonically. Maybe that was our real destiny despite the hopes we once held for our future. Either way, I could no sooner erase Theo from my heart than I could physically tear it from my chest.

I launched off the bed and Dani squawked in complaint as I jostled her. I grabbed my guitar off the wall and slung it over my shoulder.

"What the heck are you doing, weirdo?"

"I have something I need to do," I said hurriedly, looking around for my phone and catching a glimpse of something odd out the window. "Uh, by the way, Stella is swimming in the pool and gnawing on your inflatable dolphin."

“What?!” Dani screeched, hopping off my bed and rushing out my door at record speed. “How did she get out again? *Goats don’t even like the water!*” I heard her screaming as she rushed down the stairs.

I laughed for the first time in days, a renewed sense of determination fueling me. I quickly made my way out to our golf cart and zoomed across the expansive lawn toward the back of the property. If what Dani said was true about his habits the last few days, I hoped I’d find him there.

The golf cart crawled to a stop far enough away from the barn that he wouldn’t hear me coming. I didn’t want to give him time to ask questions or talk first. My words had gotten us into enough mess and I was never good at them anyway.

Music had always been the easiest way to communicate for me. I thought in quarter notes and responded in eighth notes. My pulse beat in 4/4 time and lyrics filled my head, giving me the words that didn’t come easily. This was the best way I knew how to get through to Theo.

I slowly slipped up the side of the barn, listening for any sound that could tell me he was there. After a few seconds, I heard sniffling and a long, drawn out exhale. He sounded so profoundly sad that it made my heart clench. I shook it off and readied my guitar, my lucky Queen pick in hand.

Gentle, warm chords echoed in the quiet summer air, the song coming to me easily despite my nerves. The lyrics hit me in a wave of nostalgia, remembering how often I would play this for him...for us.

I had played for Theo countless times, serenaded him for every special occasion and random romantic moment in between, but this was different. It was an apology. My act of contrition.

I sang to him as a plea to let me in, to not let this be the end of everything. I couldn’t think of any song more fitting for this place, our Neverland. Somewhere only we knew.

The last chord faded into the rustling of trees and birds warbling. I walked around to the front of the barn and set my guitar down gently behind me. I couldn’t see Theo lying down on the loft above, but I could hear the slight crinkle of hay from his movement. I fidgeted with the pick, twirling it in my fingers as I waited on bated breath for his response, any response.

“You know, I haven’t been able to listen to that song since the last time you played it for me.”

Warmth spread through me at the sound of his familiar rasp. It was ridiculous how desperately happy I was to hear his voice now that I'd let the veil of anger fall away. But his admission cramped my insides.

Theo rolled to the edge of the loft, propping up on one elbow to stare down at me. The dark circles under his eyes and stringy, unwashed hair worried me, but they did nothing to detract from how truly beautiful he was.

"It hurt too much to listen to," he said flatly. "Still does."

"Oh...I'm sorry. It was meant to make you...happy, I guess," I finished lamely.

"Hmm."

"Yeah..."

"Okay."

Jesus. What an epic start to the U.S. leg of your Apology Tour, Hayes. You're getting booed off stage.

"Do you mind coming down here? I...there's things I want to say to you."

Of course, the song was supposed to speak for me, but apparently it was as effective as speaking Farsi. Perfect.

Theo cocked his head slightly, appraising me with bleak, lifeless eyes, rimmed in red. Unease rippled through me the longer he stared at me with that hollow expression, but eventually he rolled onto his feet and climbed down the ladder.

He sauntered over to me, his movements heavy and slow. His clothes were wrinkled and even from where I stood I could tell he didn't smell the best. Guilt curdled in my gut knowing I was the cause. The last time we spoke, I had gone with the intention to smooth things over and instead made everything worse.

"Why are you here?" His voice was uncharacteristically quiet and monotone.

"I, um...so the thing is..."

Good Lord, why was this so hard? I had found the words to tear him down easily enough, so why couldn't I find the ones to fix this? Theo only continued to stare, not even a flicker of emotion crossing his face. I blew out a flustered breath and tried again.

"I thought about it and uh...would you—I mean, is it possible for us to be...friends? Like actual friends who talk and hang out and stuff. Not "stuff" like dirty stuff, but just...you know what I mean."

Wow. This. This is why I can't be trusted to talk.

Theo didn't react to my bumbling ineptitude. In fact, he didn't react at all. The only indication that he'd heard anything was the tiniest furrow in his brow. Heat flooded my face at the uncomfortable silence that settled over us.

I could feel him slipping away from me with each second. I could see the fractional slump in his shoulders, the slightest droop in his mouth, his chest deflating with a long, slow breath. Panic surged and I scrambled for how to fix it before he walked away from me.

Again.

"Wait, I know you may not trust me because of what I said about not being ready for that, but I want to try. I really do! The truth is that I wanted to keep punishing you for how things ended with us, but I understand that it wasn't entirely your fault and the parts that were were only done because you were scared and hurting too. I get it now. I didn't want to before, but I do now! I know you were scared and all I did was blame you and hate you for it. And I know we can't get back what we had, but I hate this, Theo. I really fucking hate this. I miss you and I *hate* hating you!"

My confession ended in a breathless tumble, desperation pouring from every syllable. I was flayed open, things coming out I hadn't quite intended but I couldn't hold them in. I only hoped it was enough.

Theo's eyes flared the slightest bit and he swallowed hard. My breathing was labored, my breaths coming in quick pants in time with my racing heart. I fought the instinct to go to him as much as I did the urge to run away. Time felt stretched out like taffy, slowed down as if to drag the moment out.

Finally, when I was sure I'd pass out from lack of proper oxygen, Theo took a step closer. And another one. And another until he was standing so close to me I could see the striations of silver in his clear blue eyes. Eyes that were coated in misery, but sparked with the tiniest flicker of hope.

"Mercury?"

I broke. My lips crashed into his, inhaling him like a sweet drug. His lips were dry and chapped, but somehow so perfect moving against my own. I licked the seam of his lips and when his tongue lashed mine, I moaned into his mouth. I felt his hand settle tentatively on my waist and I slipped my arm around him, pulling him closer. It felt right in a way I'd long forgotten existed.

"Theo," I grated, my voice raw. A low whimper escaped him and he reclaimed my mouth, kissing me with an intensity that radiated down to my marrow. I walked him backwards until his back met the ladder, pressing against every inch of his tight body. Hands raked through my hair, tugging and scraping my scalp in a delicious pain that tore a groan from my throat.

This wasn't what I intended to happen. There was too much damage between us, too much that had to heal for us to even consider this, but in that moment I couldn't have cared less. I needed him, needed his taste and his heat. His moans and his gasps.

"Fuck, Dawson," he breathed against my lips. "Please don't leave me."

My chest squeezed painfully at his whispered plea. It hurt to hear the fear in his voice, but it also cleared away the lust long enough to get my bearings. I pulled back just enough to look him in the eye. He tensed as I put a little more space between us, but I cupped his cheek to calm him.

"I'm not going anywhere this time, I promise. But we need to take a beat before we get too carried away. Okay?"

Theo sighed in relief, but I noticed the wariness in his gaze. I understood he didn't fully trust my sincerity in starting over, but I was committed to this. It wasn't like all the pain had disappeared and I was over everything. I had a lot of open wounds still where Theo was concerned, but I was done letting rage and bitterness consume me. I wanted us to have a second chance at being in each other's lives, whatever that looked like.

And I couldn't jeopardize that by mauling him and diving into the desire that had always stirred between us. We needed to take this slower. Much slower.

I took his hand and led him over to my chair under the loft, gesturing for him to sit down as I pulled a stool over for myself. I shot him a bashful look, rubbing my hands together nervously.

"I'm sorry for jumping you like that. I got caught up in the moment," I explained. I tried my best to ignore the wince he failed to hide. "I meant everything I said though. I want us to be friends again.

More than anything, I miss my best friend. I'm hoping for a chance for us to get that back."

He absorbed what I said, gnawing on his bottom lip and hunched over, deep in thought. My knee bounced relentlessly while I waited for his answer.

"Friends, huh?"

I couldn't quite place his tone. I wasn't sure whether he was disappointed or relieved. His gaze slid up to mine, piercing through me. So many memories passed through my head and I wondered if he was remembering them too.

Days enjoying video games and inside jokes. Nights spent kissing and fucking under the stars. A future of happiness plotted out in eager anticipation. Everything we once meant to each other being boiled back down to innocent friendship seemed wrong, but necessary.

We were different men now. We couldn't go backwards.

"Yeah...friends."

"Who's giving whiplash now?" he teased lightly.

I dropped my chin to my chest, feeling like a huge hypocrite. I tried to regret kissing him, but I couldn't. It had been a hit of pure oxygen to my veins. When I looked back up and saw his lips kick up slightly and his face soften, I smiled gratefully in return.

"So what does this mean for you and that girl?"

I grimaced in confusion. "Who, Aly? Why would it mean anything for us?"

He looked at me with a bewildered expression. "You don't think your girlfriend will care that we're friends again and we just...made out?"

I choked on my spit. "She's not—I don't have a girlfriend. We're just friends, I swear!"

"Like I'm just your friend?" Theo smirked sadly. I ran my hand down my face, frustrated with myself and my stupidity.

"Not at all," I said firmly. "Aly's just a very good friend. She and I haven't even kissed before. I'm not seeing anyone right now."

"But...at the party, you said—"

"Something fucked up because I was pissed and hurt," I interjected.

There was no mistaking the relief on his features, but there was also regret too. The last thing I wanted to do was bring up anything from that shitty night, but there was something we needed to discuss before we left it behind for good.

"What about you and Corvin?" I questioned, acid bubbling in my stomach thinking about them together.

Theo broke our eye contact and I swallowed down the bile that threatened to come up. Whatever his answer was, I wasn't going anywhere. I would need to eventually accept Theo dating other people just like he'd need to do the same for me. Not that I had the desire to right now, but I also couldn't be alone forever.

"He asked me out and I turned him down," Theo replied, still avoiding my eyes. "But I gave him my number and said we could grab coffee sometime."

Somehow that hurt worse than I expected. Not that them hooking up didn't rip me apart, but Theo agreeing to grab coffee with Corvin, leaving that door open for more between them sent shocks of pain down my limbs.

"Oh. Okay," I responded lamely. What else could I even say?

"That doesn't change things for you, does it?" he asked worriedly.

"No, it doesn't. I mean, you're gonna have other...friends and I've gotta be cool with that. I'm still in this."

And I was. Even if I was seething at the thought of Theo being *friendly* with Corvin or anyone else.

"Good," he smiled weakly. "Me too."

I returned his smile as best I could. Emotionally, I was wrung out. All the anguish and struggle since the first day we ran into each other again caught up to me and I was close to crashing. I'd probably sleep for days if allowed to.

"I should get back. I promised Dad I'd go on a run with him before dinner."

We both stood and I went to grab my guitar from where I left it on the grass. I turned back toward the golf cart, but stopped when Theo bent over to grab something. Theo smiled to himself as he examined my guitar pick, caressing it gently. I hadn't realized I'd dropped it earlier when I'd kissed him.

"You kept it."

Maybe it shouldn't have, but it hurt a bit that he sounded surprised I had. I let out a hum of acknowledgment, crossing over to him when he held it out. My fingers brushed over his as I took it, that quick touch enough to ignite my blood and make my pulse stutter.

We stood there for seconds, minutes, who fucking knew? I wondered if he was as reluctant to leave as I was.

"So, I'll text you later?" It came out as a question rather than a statement, maybe to hear him tell me that's what he wanted or even that he still had my number.

"I'd really like that," he admitted softly, giving me a tiny version of his lopsided grin that stopped my heart every damn time. This one was no less powerful.

I laid my guitar on the backseat of the cart and climbed behind the wheel, déjà vu hitting me from the last time we were here. When I left the barn that day I first came home, I was miserable and convinced that Theo and I were doomed forever, but maybe now we could start to rewrite our ending.

"Why did you choose that song?" Theo called out. I lifted my head, catching and holding his gaze intently.

"Because it's still ours."

Dawson, Age 15

I WIPED my sweaty palms on my jeans for the umpteenth time. Theo would be here soon and I was trying not to freak out. I couldn't help it. I was filled with anxiety over what I was about to do.

I grabbed my guitar and tuned it one more time, just in case it had gone flat in the summer heat. Today was the first day of summer vacation and I couldn't wait any longer to tell him.

"Freebird!"

I rolled my eyes at his shouted request and played the opening lick, just to be a smartass.

"It's not as funny when you don't get all cranky about it," Theo pouted up at me.

"It stopped being funny thirty years ago."

Theo huffed in fake annoyance before climbing up to sit beside me on the edge of the hayloft. My heart beat faster the closer he got, stealing my breath and my focus in one go. That happened more and more lately when he was around.

He dropped on his butt next to me, tossing me his signature lopsided grin that did weird things to my stomach. I'd been living with that reaction for all of freshman year and if I didn't do something about it, I was going to snap.

But I couldn't just tell him. No way. I'd say something stupid and screw everything up and then what the heck would I do? I couldn't live without Theo. I just couldn't. I'd sooner stop playing music and that would be the same as bleeding my veins dry.

"You okay, Mercury?"

I glanced over at Theo's worried tone and I'm pretty sure my heart stopped. Full-on stopped beating for a whole ass second. He was so...beautiful. I'd watched him through every awkward stage of life so far, but somehow at only fifteen years old he was now unfairly pretty. Braces gone, clear skin, perfectly styled ashy blond hair, and eyes so blue they were almost translucent.

Yeah. My best friend was stunning. And I was in serious trouble.

"I'm good," I muttered. Theo smiled in relief and leaned back on his hands, looking out over the small clearing of land that bled into the treeline.

"Dude, can you believe it? First year of high school down, only three to go."

"Yeah. It's kind of crazy."

"For sure," he smirked, but it faded fast. "I saw McKenna give you her number before we left school yesterday. What did she want?"

"Oh, uh, just wanted me to text her to hang out this summer."

"Hmm. Cool," Theo said in a clipped tone. There was something off about the way he said it and it made me worried that I upset him.

"I don't want to though," I rushed to explain. "Hang out with her, I mean."

His lips twitched a bit, but his eyebrows were still scrunched together. "For real? You don't like her or something?"

I shook my head because I couldn't force myself to tell him why. Not yet. He seemed to relax then and I realized it was now or never.

"I-I learned something f-for you. To play. I-if that's okay," I stammered. Ugh, I was such an idiot.

"Why are you nervous, weirdo? You know I love anything you play for me," he beamed, his smile setting off flutters in my chest. I breathed out anxiously before settling my guitar on my lap. Here went nothing.

I started playing, ignoring how Theo's body stiffened in my periphery.

He'd listened to the Keane song so many times that I was scared he'd get sick of it before I could learn it for him. Last weekend, when we were sleeping out here in Neverland and it was playing softly on his camping speaker, he told me what this song meant to him and I knew. I knew it would be how I finally told him.

"I love this song so much. Whoever my Person is, this will be our song. I want it to belong to us."

My voice was soft, but steady as I lost myself in the melody. Every chord strummed was a confession about how I felt, about what he truly meant to me. Each note was a commitment to him. I was claiming this for us.

This was my love note.

I wasn't sure when I'd closed my eyes, but I slowly opened them as the last note faded. Theo was silent and still. I wasn't brave enough to look at him. All my courage was gone, poured into the music.

He grabbed my hand off my guitar, squeezing it and running his thumb over my skin until I finally turned to him. We stared at each other and I was scared to breathe.

I wasn't prepared for it when he grabbed my face and brought me close to him. Close enough to feel the warm puffs of his breath on my lips. I wanted him to kiss me so badly. I'd wanted it for over a year. I had avoided every girl who ever showed interest in me this year because I never wanted them. Only him. It's always been him.

"Dawson?"

"Yeah?"

"I love you."

Then his lips were on mine. Soft, but intense. Shy, but confident. It was everything and nothing like I imagined it would be. Theo was kissing me and my heart felt like it was going to explode right out of my chest. He pulled back and I couldn't hold it in anymore.

"I love you too."

And then he kissed me again.

CHAPTER FOURTEEN

I let out another frustrated growl as my phone vibrated for the twentieth time in the last minute, but I couldn't freaking find it. I was tossing pillows off the couch and shaking out blankets, trying to follow the incessant buzzing like a homing beacon.

"Hey buttface. Catch!"

I turned a second too late and my phone slammed right into my sternum. "What the hell, Dani?" I groused, rubbing at the area.

"Wow. You'll definitely be a first round pick with skills like that."

I flipped her off, but her sarcastic remark made me cringe internally. I'd been home for almost two weeks now and I had managed to chicken out of every single opportunity to tell Dad the truth. I must have done a piss poor job of keeping a straight face because Dani pounced.

"Wait, what was that look for? What's up with you? Holy crap, are you injured or something? Dad's gonna flip out if you're hurt before the season even starts!"

Her rapid fire comments were like needles poking at the flimsy bubble of silence I'd put around myself to keep it all in.

Poke. Poke. Poke.

"Have you talked to your coach yet? Oh snap, what if he benches you and you miss the first game? I mean, it'll definitely help my Baylor boys out if you aren't on the field, but I don't—"

POP.

"Oh my god, I am not injured," I spit out. "I'm quitting!"

Dani's jaw dropped so fast I half-worried that it would snap clean off. I sank back into the cushions of the sofa, releasing a huge sigh of relief. I hadn't said that out loud to anyone yet and it felt damn good. Dani gingerly sat down next to me, tense and quiet before patting my leg awkwardly.

"That makes a lot of sense actually."

"How do you figure?"

Dani cocked her head at me like the answer was obvious. "I mean, even with being King Quarterback all these years, you never really talked about football like it was your future. Like, I never saw you light up talking about it or get all wrapped up in it. Not like you do music. Your piano and your guitar are your escapes, not the sport."

I chewed on my bottom lip, thinking about her assessment. When I thought about what I wanted in my life, music was indispensable where football wasn't. If God forbid an injury did take me out this year, I'd be bummed but not devastated. Thinking of keeping up with football after college wasn't exhilarating, it was exhausting.

"You're not quitting this year, are you?" Dani asked nervously. "You know Dad would riot if that happened."

"No, I want to play my final season, but I'm withdrawing my eligibility for the NFL draft."

"Yikes...when do you plan to tell him?"

"Oh, about four months ago."

"Ahh, so right on track then."

"Exactly."

"What *are* you planning on telling Dad?"

"Just that football isn't what I want long term," I shrugged. "I don't care about playing professionally. I really want to get involved in the music scene in Austin. I don't know exactly what yet, but Mom's got all these contacts to get me started and I'd be willing to work my way up."

My love and talent for music had all come from my mother. She played dozens of instruments and had been a pianist for the Chicago Philharmonic when she met Dad. Of course, she gave it up to move to Dallas when he'd been traded to the Cowboys. She was now a professor of music at UT, but also heavily involved in the indie music industry in Austin and I wanted to follow in those footsteps.

"You sure you're good with giving up that pro-football money?" she teased.

"It's not about the money. Even if I didn't have my trust fund, I wouldn't change my mind. I'd rather be happy and living paycheck to paycheck than do something that I'll end up hating and stressing over."

"I'll remember you said that when you're eating your hundredth cup of ramen and drinking instant coffee."

I rolled my eyes and planted a hand on her face, shoving her away gently. She laughed and nudged me with her shoulder before pinning me with a serious look.

"You know Dad might be mad at first, but he wants you to be happy. As long as you don't plan to just play on a street corner with a hurdy-gurdy, he'll support whatever you decide to do. And so will I."

"Thanks, gremlin," I smiled. "But I guess now that you've shit on my first plan, I've got to move to plan B."

"Eh, hurdy-gurdying is a dying art anyway. You'll thank me later," she replied. "But for real, if you need help telling Dad, let me know. I've got your back, big brother."

I gave her a grateful smile and she hugged me before leaving the room. Would Dad actually be okay with me giving up a shot at the NFL for a different dream? I still didn't have a full plan for what I wanted to do after graduation, but I had time. Sort of.

My phone buzzed once more and I remembered I hadn't checked it yet. I had about a dozen missed texts on our crew's group chat, the latest ones directed at me.

KENJI

Anyone up for hitting the lake tomorrow on a party boat?

MICAH

Isn't that expensive?

KENJI

All taken care of courtesy of my uncle. We've got it 10-2, but it's BYOB

GRIFFIN

Fucking sold. I'm in.

MICAH

Count me and Bash in too. Thanks Kenji!

ALY

Why not? I could use a tan.

FIN

Ugh, I hate you. My skin never tans…but sure, sounds fun!

GRIFFIN

Are you sure you can risk it, Snow White?

FIN

Mirror mirror on the wall, who's the biggest dick of all?

GRIFFIN

I definitely have the biggest dick of all. But you don't need a magic mirror to confirm that, cutie ;)

FIN

I would slap you, but I'm against animal abuse.

RHYS

I joined this conversation at the way wrong time…

CAL

Come on, Sweetness. You and I know better than anyone fighting is the best foreplay. Looks like you're gonna lose our bet.

GRIFFIN

Woah, what bet??

FIN

EW. I'd rather deep throat a cactus, thank you. Also hi, yeah, I'm taken, remember?

GRIFFIN

Riiiight. How could we possibly forget about Dan, the human participation award…

FIN

NATE

Dude, this is better than my Hulu subscription. I'll be there! Dawson, you coming?

NATE

D-man, you there??

NATE

Don't make me spam your phone, bro!

I snickered at the ridiculous text thread. I couldn't remember the last time I'd gone out to Lake Travis. I had free range to use Dad's boat if I wanted to, but the last time I'd taken it out had been...well, my last summer with Theo. I couldn't bear to look at it after that. An idea sparked and I texted back before I could overthink it.

ME

Kenji—is it cool if I bring someone?

KENJI

No prob

I wasn't sure if I should invite Theo or not, but I wanted him there. It was the perfect activity for friends to do. And that's what we were. Friends.

What a stupid fucking word.

My thoughts were interrupted by an incoming call and I swiped to answer.

"What's up?"

"Duuuude, you excited for the lake?" Nate squawked, his infectious energy pouring through the line.

"Sure. It'll be great."

Nate made an obnoxious buzzer sound that crackled loudly in my ear. "I'm sorry, but that level of excitement isn't going to cut it, mi amigo. I need you pumped! This is the last summer before we graduate college and become boring-ass adults. These are the days you'll tell your kids about. How you used to be fun and hot and did crazy shit just because you could! Well...not you, you don't do crazy anything, but you know what I mean."

I blew out an amused breath as he rambled on about his hopes for a water slide and hot girls on the boat tomorrow, exclusively in that order.

"So..." Nate started, dragging out the word like it had fifteen letters. "You asked Kenji if you could bring someone. Anyone I know?"

My annoyance piqued at his smug tone. "Shut up. You know I meant Theo."

"Hah! Knew it, love it, here for it. I call best man at your wedding! Is that a thing? Can you call shot gun on a best man spot?"

"Oh my god, I'm inviting him to the lake. Not proposing," I muttered, but Nate barreled on.

"You know, I actually thought you might be ace—that's the right term, right?—because you weren't into hooking up or anything. And I would know because your wall is next to mine and you are *not* quiet when you're 'strumming your guitar', if you know what I mean..."

I pinched my brows, trying to ward off the headache that threatened. I was not prepared for this conversation, but what else was new?

"I mean when you jerk off—"

"Yeah, I got that," I cut him off. "And no, I'm not asexual. I like sex and stuff, it's just only been with Theo. He's the only one I've ever wanted like that."

"Huh...so have you tried to want it with someone else? Like put yourself out there and see who wants to take a ride on the D-train?"

"Jesus Christ," I muttered, silently praying for strength. "Look, I don't know how to explain it, man. It's like...okay, I got it. I hate Pecan pie."

"...is that supposed to be code for something?"

"Just shut up and listen. I hate all Pecan pie unless it's my mom's homemade pie. It's the only one I love and will eat, and no other Pecan pie has ever tasted good to me."

"Wait, say that again."

"Which part?"

"The pie part."

"It's the only pie I love?"

Nate let out an exasperated sigh. "No, say the name of it."

"Pecan pie?" I repeated slowly.

"That! Dude, why did you say it that way?"

"What way? The right way?"

"No, the dumb as fuck way."

"What do you mean 'the dumb as fuck' way? That's how you pronounce Pecan pie."

"Hell no, it's *Pee-can* pie!" Nate protested indignantly.

"Why would you say it like that?" *And why the fuck am I entertaining this crazy-ass conversation?*

"It's the right way, numb nuts!"

"No one in Texas says it like that! You are literally the only one who I've heard say it that way."

"I call bullshit. I can't be the only one who says it right...and the right fucking way is Pee-can pie!"

"Oh for the love of God, Theo is just *it* for me, alright? No one else. Just him. He's the only one I have ever wanted."

"Okayyy...so you've never been interested in another pie—I mean, guy?"

"I haven't really been interested in any *person* besides him. I find other people objectively attractive, but not enough to want anything with them. Others hold no interest for me, sexually or otherwise."

I sighed tiredly, the weight of a confession I didn't want to admit sitting heavy on my tongue.

"And almost four years later, after all he's put me through, I've still never felt for any person what I feel for Theo. He was my first and he's been my only. I'm beginning to think he'll always be my only."

"Damn. He's your pie," Nate said softly, like it was the most romantic shit he's ever heard.

"Stupidest fucking analogy I could've thought of..."

Nate chuckled before falling quiet, his tone growing serious. "All I want is for you to be happy, D. You're the best fucking friend in the world and you deserve it. So invite Theo and get your man back."

I couldn't go into why that was impossible where Theo and I were concerned, not right then.

"Thanks, Nate. You're the best fucking friend too."

"Aw, don't make me blush, Dawby-Bear," he joked, laughing as I growled at the sickening nickname. "Alright, I'm out. I've got people to do and things to see."

"Pretty sure you have that backwards."

"I said what I said. See you tomorrow!"

He hung up and I breathed a laugh at the chaos of the last few minutes. I tried to start a message to Theo, but my fingers just hovered over the screen. It was stupid, but I felt nervous about texting him. It'd been a couple of days since we'd struck up our truce at the barn and I still hadn't gotten up the nerve to talk to him again. Fuck, I was being a pansy about this. I wanted to be his friend again and friends texted each other. Nothing weird about it.

Yet I typed, deleted and retyped more than a dozen times before finally shooting off something simple.

ME

Hey, how are you?

I cringed at the lame attempt, but whatever. It was out there. My phone buzzed in response thirty seconds later.

THEO

Okay, I guess

Be honest. How long did you overthink that text before you sent it?

Damn it, he knew me too well.

ME

Don't know what you're talking about

THEO

That long, huh?

ME

Shut up...

Do you have any plans tomorrow?

THEO

Nothing right now, but you know I charge for appearances. What did you have in mind?

ME

My friends and I are taking a boat out on the lake for a few hours. Interested?

Text bubbles kept popping up and disappearing, but no response came. I wondered if he was nervous about seeing my friends again after we'd made epic asses of ourselves at my party. I didn't really blame him. I was even a bit anxious to reintroduce Theo to them, but I didn't want to hide him away. I wanted him to know my friends and be included in my life.

THEO

Are you sure they're cool with me coming?

ME

For sure. It won't be a big deal, trust me

THEO

What about my appearance fee?

ME

You aren't generous enough to just grace me with your presence?

THEO

My dad taught me that if I'm good at something, never do it for free.

ME

Jesus, I'll throw in a case of Corona. Deal?

THEO

...agreed. But you better have lime wedges for those or the deal's off

ME

So demanding

Meet me at my truck at 9am

THEO

Can't even pick me up properly like a real gentleman. I thought your mama taught you better than that

ME

Nvm, the invitation is rescinded

THEO

That was deeply uncalled for... 😒

See you at 9, Mercury

I sent a thumbs up in response with a stupid grin on my face. It was weird slipping back into our normal banter, but it also felt good.

Natural. It made me wonder if there was more of my old Theo buried in there than he let on.

All I had to do was focus on treating him like any other friend and not kissing him within an inch of his life like I'd been dying to do since the barn. My resolve would definitely be tested, especially when Theo was all wet and shirtless and sun-kissed and...

Shit...I might have made a mistake.

CHAPTER FIFTEEN

I was glad my instincts hadn't been rusty when I'd told Theo to meet me a half hour before we actually needed to leave. In typical fashion, Theo stepped out of his house at 9:28, his button down linen shirt flapping open as he ran over to my truck. My eyes followed the lines of his abs and the light trail of hair that ran from his navel down to his swim trunks. Flashes of tattoos peaked at me from behind the fabric and I wanted to trace them all with my tongue. He flashed me a megawatt smile that did dangerous things to my stomach.

My mouth went dry and I felt uncomfortable pressure behind my own shorts, so I adjusted myself covertly and hopped behind the wheel. Within seconds of us setting off, Theo propped his legs up on the dashboard and started flipping through radio channels. Flashbacks of autumn drives and heated nights in the backseat ran through my head. I needed to get it together or I was going to crash the damn truck.

"So who all will be there?" Theo asked, disrupting my train of thought. *Thank fuck.*

"Pretty much everyone you met at my party," I said dismissively. "Maybe a few others, but I don't really know. This is Kenji's deal. We were all just invited along for the ride."

Theo nodded, but his knee bounced rapidly and his hands tapped out an erratic rhythm on the side of his thigh.

"You don't have to be nervous. My friends are chill and they'll like you once they get to know you," I tried to reassure him. Theo's eyes looked aimlessly out the window and I saw the slight tick in his jaw before he shot me a cocky grin.

"What's there not to like?"

He cranked up the music a bit more, drowning out my chance to respond, but I had nothing to say. The words were said confidently, but sounded hollow. I let the silence between us linger until we parked at the lake and got out to walk down to the boat slip. I turned to check in with him before we boarded, but was pounced on from behind, nearly losing my footing on the dock.

"What's up, brother! You ready to get your lake on?" Nate's energetic shout rang in my ears as he clung to my back like a chimpanzee. I dropped him unceremoniously, but he just landed gracefully on his feet. Asshole.

"Hitting the sauce already, Nate?" I ribbed.

"I'll have you know I'm as sober as a judge, Sir Rudeness. This is all God-given enthusiasm right here," he grinned. "Hey, look at you bringing a date! Theo, right?"

I almost choked on my spit and saw Theo visibly blanch. His posture was rigid and he was regarding Nate with a mix of wariness and anger. I couldn't understand where the latter was coming from. Nate definitely gave off unhinged squirrel energy, but he was harmless. But seeing it from Theo's perspective, Nate was the best friend who had replaced him. My stomach curdled at the idea that Theo imagined he could ever be replaced.

Nate gave Theo a wide, genuine smile and held out his hand patiently. Theo finally shook it and gave a tight smile in return. "Nice to see you again."

I nudged Nate to help me with the large cooler I'd brought, Theo tagging along behind us. The party boat was huge, a double decker monstrosity with a water slide attached at one end and a long floating mat at the other. It was already filled with at least twenty five people, half of whom I'd never seen before.

Kenji made his way to us and showed us where to drop our stuff. "Glad you guys could make it. Great timing too, we're about to head out."

We followed him onto the boat, and I quickly spotted Micah, Rhys, Fin, and Aly situated on one of the bench seats at the far end.

They stood to hug me and Nate before turning their attention to Theo.

"Guys, you remember my friend Theo?" My emphasis on the word *friend* was a signal that this was a fresh start for us all, and I saw their faces light with understanding.

"So glad you could make it!" Aly beamed, wrapping him in a huge hug while the others smiled and welcomed him. To my relief, Theo seemed to visibly relax at their warm greeting.

"Where are your men at by the way? Tossed them overboard already?" I teased once we'd sat down and the boat started to move.

"Captain Cal-drenaline decided to rent two jet skis to take out because the boat wasn't enough," Rhys explained with a dramatic eye roll. "So he and Bash took off a couple minutes ago to 'test them out', as they put it."

Like clockwork, a buzz of engines and joyous shrieks zoomed by us, waves rippling in their wake. I could just make out Bash and Cal's manic laughter as they raced away from us. By the time we reached the middle of the lake, they slowly maneuvered the jet skis to the edge of the boat and Kenji threw them each a tow rope.

"Fuck man, that's the way to spend a day on the water!" Bash said happily as he climbed aboard.

"I wouldn't know because my boyfriend ditched me before we even left the dock," Micah jokingly griped. Bash snatched him around the waist and hauled him in for an obnoxiously sweet kiss that Micah melted under.

"Aw, don't worry, baby. I'll take you for a ride later."

"We don't need to hear the details of your bedroom exploits, Dupont. There's not enough booze for that," Cal smirked as he wrapped an arm around Rhys. He shook out his drenched curls like a dog drying off, all of us protesting as we got hit with the spray.

"You jealous, handsome?" Bash winked.

Their playful bickering continued as we were immersed in Kenji's guests. I recognized a bunch of them from school, but most were from the lacrosse team. Of course, a good half of the crowd were girls in bikinis, so Nate was in heaven. I was amused watching Micah cling to Bash and shoot the evil eye at a couple of girls who attempted to flirt with him, but Nate was quick to swoop in for their attention.

"Your friends seem pretty awesome."

I startled at Theo's voice right behind me. He held out a beer bottle to me as he took a slow pull from the other one in his hand. There was a wistful look in his eyes that made me curious what he was thinking.

"Yeah, they're the best. Do you have any friends back in Huntsville that you still talk to?"

"Not really."

His tone said that was all to the conversation he was going to share. I couldn't help wondering what had happened over there. We never really got into the reason he came home, but I could guess it wasn't his idea. The thought made me inexplicably sad.

"Well, now that I've brought you around, these guys will suction to you like a squid. There'll be no getting rid of them," I joked awkwardly. Theo whispered something under his breath that I couldn't quite make out, but he plastered on that fake, bright smile before I could ask about it.

"Thanks for bringing me out by the way. Jet skis, drinks, and new squid-friends all in one day. Hell of a first date, Hayes," he grinned cheekily, but his words threw me off kilter.

"Oh—well, you know, this isn't..." I stammered, feeling my cheeks heat. Theo's gaze dimmed and his smile slipped the slightest bit.

"Yeah, I know. Just friends," he said dully. He drained his drink and pursed his lips. "I think I'm gonna go...mingle or whatever. Who knows? Maybe I'll get lucky and find myself an actual date."

My stomach sloshed as I watched him walk away. Then it threatened to revolt as I watched him easily jump into conversation with a couple of the guys I recognized from the lacrosse team. I needed to get my shit together if this was going to work. I wasn't going to lie to myself anymore and say that I didn't still want Theo, but that ship hadn't just sailed, it had crashed into an iceberg.

Cancel the mayday. Call off the search. There are no survivors.

I shook off the shitty feelings and beelined for Aly and Fin on the other side of the deck. They were both whispering harshly back and forth, their voices growing as I got closer to them.

"—don't deserve that shit. And you keep going back to him for some godforsaken reason!"

"For fucks sake, I'm not just gonna throw away almost five years. We're working on it and he's promised me..."

"Oh my god, that piece of shit has already broken a hundred

promises to you, Fin. I don't know why you brought him with you when all he's done is—"

"Just stop! I don't want to talk about this anymore!"

"But he's—"

"Hey guys, everything okay?" I interjected quickly, noticing tears forming in Fin's angry teal eyes. Aly shot Fin a plaintive look as he stormed off, sidling up next to a tall guy who easily could have passed for a linebacker. He was chatting up a girl by the drinks cooler while Fin meekly tried to get his attention, and that alone had my guard up. I was pretty sure Fin ran on nothing but pure sass and confidence. I had never known him to be as submissive and subdued as he looked now.

"He never listens to anyone about that douchebag," Aly muttered softly.

"Is that the boyfriend Fin got back together with a couple months ago?"

"In the cheating, narcissistic flesh. Dan is the drug Fin can't ever seem to kick. I don't get why he keeps going back to him."

"Maybe he really loves him?"

"He only thinks he does. But it stopped being about that a long time ago. Fin just can't ever seem to say no to him." Aly's face pinched with concern and my thoughts darkened.

"He's never hurt Fin, has he?"

"Not physically that I know of...but you know there's more than one way to break a person."

I looked on worriedly as Dan finally allowed himself to be dragged away, snapping something at Fin as he did. The wince on Fin's face told me enough about what was probably said. "You'll let me know if I need to step in, yeah?"

"You'll have to beat Griffin to it. You see his face?"

I searched for Griff in the crowd and sure enough, his face was a mottled red and the grip on his beer bottle was noticeably tight. He was glowering at Fin and Dan who were now huddled in the corner with Fin smiling tightly and trying to not draw anyone's focus over to them even as he was being berated by that drunk asshole.

"I'll keep an eye on them today, but there's nothing we can really do until Fin is ready to listen," Aly said defeatedly. "Anyway, how is it going between you and Theo?"

"I don't know," I sighed. "It's like one step forward, two steps back with us. But we finally talked and agreed to leave the past in the past and move on as friends."

Aly pinned her bottom lip between her teeth, assessing me carefully. "And is that really what you want? To only be his friend?"

"That's all we can be."

"Why?"

"There's something so...different about him. It's like he's my old Theo one second and then this switch flips. I can't shake the feeling that he's hiding something from me. And until he tells me, I can't trust him enough to be anything else."

"I'm sorry, babe. I really am," she said, squeezing my arm sympathetically. "Do you still love him?"

My throat clenched around the words, forcing them down. I couldn't admit it. Not now, not here. Something told me she already knew the answer anyway. Aly hugged my arm and rested her head on my shoulder.

"Life is seriously twisted sometimes. Especially since the ones we love most have the power to hurt us the worst."

I grunted in agreement. I knew that better than most. It was a painful lesson I was reminded of when I glanced over at Theo, his perfect smile aimed at a guy I didn't recognize. He was gorgeous, with shoulder length dreads and dazzling white teeth. They looked really good together too with Theo's pale skin next to the guy's darker tone. A beautiful contrast that twisted my insides torturously.

The guy laughed at something Theo said, knocking his shoulder in a way that seemed flirty but maybe only appeared that way through my jealous eyes. I tried to look away, but it was like rubbernecking on the highway when passing a car crash.

Our gazes collided and it punched the air from my lungs. Theo's smile seemed stale as though he'd been holding it in place too long, his lips slowly sinking from the weight of it. His eyes glazed over the tiniest bit and I saw it.

Exhaustion.

Emptiness.

Hopelessness.

I craved to go to him, hug him to me and demand he tell me what put that look in his eyes. What was he hiding that he couldn't trust me with? As he emptied his drink and reached for another one from a cooler, the thought struck me. Was it that obvious and I just missed it?

The drinking, the drugs at my party, the overdose in high school that came out of nowhere?

His erratic behavior and mercurial mood made sense now. I could even trace moments back in high school, like pins on a timeline where Theo had started to change. Staying up later each night, not sleeping as much, his grades slipping from A's to C's, becoming more temperamental and irritable between weird bouts of happiness and energy. Everyone assumed it was his ADHD, but medication had never seemed to help and it just got worse the older he got.

Fucking fuck, how had I missed that? Was this all stemming from an addiction? How is it possible that I hadn't noticed how much he was struggling back then? He was my best friend, my boyfriend, my fucking *everything*. Why hadn't I seen?

The realization sank in like a weight on my lungs. The answer was simple. He hadn't wanted me to.

Or maybe it was because I hadn't wanted to see it.

Theo

CHAPTER SIXTEEN

My gaze was pinned on Dawson's. I thought I was crazy (*probably because I fucking was*), but I caught the shift in the way he looked at me. It was subtle, but it was like someone slotting a puzzle piece into place. That lightbulb moment when a solution finally hits you. I felt dizzy and panic sizzled in the back of my brain that he'd figured me out. That he knew I was nothing but a ticking time bomb.

Then the look slowly melted into one I recognized very well. Disappointment and pity. I couldn't stand seeing Dawson look at me like that.

Does he know? Does he really see now? How did he figure out that I'm...

I slammed the door on that train of thought before it sent me over the edge. It was impossible. There was no way he knew.

He can't...I'm not ready to lose him again.

I spent the next couple of hours like a social magician, conjuring up smiles and creating illusions of joy. Drink after drink gave me power, but it didn't stop my brain from firing off in a million directions.

"Hey man, you alright?"

I focused back on—*shit, what's his name?*—the lacrosse dude I'd been talking to earlier. I had tried to enjoy the conversation, but I was just so damn tired. It never ended.

"Yeah, sorry. Zoned out. I'm gonna grab something to eat real quick."

He waved me off with a smile and I stumbled quickly up the stairs to the deck where the food was. I wasn't really hungry, but I needed an excuse to get some space. I leaned up against the railing, looking out at the myriad of boats, paddlers, and kayaks dotted across the water. I used to love coming out to the lake, but I always had Dawson by my side then.

I let myself get lost in past summers spent out here when we were kids, eating way too much junk food and using way too little sunscreen. My thoughts drifted to later times, when we were much older and things had shifted between us. I had touched Dawson's dick for the first time out here. Under the water, I'd snuck my hand into his swim trunks and gave him the world's most inexperienced and shortest handjob before he blew his load.

And it had been fucking epic.

That was the summer I'd first kissed him, when he'd played my favorite song because for him, there was no better way to tell me how he felt. That was the summer that changed everything for us. We had always known we'd have a lifetime of friendship, but it was then that we promised each other so much more. There had been no doubt in my mind that Dawson was my forever.

And now my future was uncertain, unstable in a way that left me doubting whether I'd have one at all.

The dark cloud threatened to invade my head, but I refused to let it in. I spun around and ran smack into someone I actually recognized.

"Oh shit, I'm sorry! I swear I usually have better depth perception, but my brain's a little scrambled from the jetski," Dawson's friend apologized with an embarrassed smile.

"Ahh, not your bag?"

"Probably would have been if I hadn't been flung overboard when Bash took a corner too fast," he said with an exaggerated eye roll. "So I'm gonna blame any faux pas on the gallon of lake water I unfortunately ingested."

"Should also give you a nice parasite or two. I bet you could blame a few offenses on that."

"Like if I get the urge to tell someone to eat a shriveled up bag of dicks, I can blame it on parasitic Tourettes or something?"

"Something tells me you'd say it even without the excuse."

"That's an awfully rude and accurate assumption," he sniffed delicately and my mouth tugged into a reluctant smile.

"Well, I'm shit with names, but if Bash is your boyfriend-tossing jet skier, then that must make you...Micah?"

"Ten points to Theodore!" Micah exclaimed, giving me a golf clap.

I fake-gagged and shuddered. "Agh! Nope. I'm not Theodore. Just Theo."

"Got it," he snickered. "Are you having fun so far, not-Theodore?"

"Yeah, it's a blast," I lied. Micah's eyes narrowed at my obvious bullshit.

"Hmm. Is that why you raced up here like someone dropped a piranha down your shorts?"

"Oh, uh, I was...feeling a little queasy, that's all. I came up to get some air."

"Because the air five feet below us was so contaminated?"

"It was. With people," I muttered. Micah smirked and grabbed a popsicle out of a cooler nearby.

"It's cool that you came today."

"Oh yeah?" My head was beginning to swim slightly from the alcohol and heat, and focusing was becoming a chore.

"Yep. You know, I haven't known Dawson very long, but I like to think I can read people pretty well. He's different with you," he said without looking up at me, opening his treat.

"Different how?" I asked cautiously.

"In the several months that I've known him, I've only ever seen Dawson sweet, calm and perfectly put together. He's like the hot lovechild between a Ken doll and Prince Henry from *Red, White and Royal Blue*...only less British and plastic-y."

I snorted at the comparison, imagining how Dawson would react to hearing that. "What are you trying to say?"

He let out a deep sigh as though I was boring him or a moron...or both. "The point is that from the minute Dawson saw you in our apartment building that day, he's been a lovesick, tortured mess. He tries to hide it, but we all see it. Well...most of us. Nate and Griff are clueless idiots most days."

My heart gave a hopeless flutter hearing that Dawson was so affected by me before I remembered to squash that idea flat. He'd already erected the Great Wall of boundaries between us to keep us firmly in the friend zone, so there was no use going there.

"Maybe you're reading him wrong. I mean, you said it yourself, you don't know him that well."

"No, I said it hasn't been long. And I'm not wrong," Micah said simply. "I also know that you've done a bit of damage already since that day too."

His tone was gentle, but sweat still slithered down my back and my skin grew clammy. This was it. This was where he told me to leave, that I was a screwup, trash, a jackass not worthy of breathing Dawson's air.

You're all that and worse. Did you really think they wouldn't notice?

I stammered, but Micah gave me a patient smile and cut me off.

"Take a breath. I'm not here to judge or bitch at you. I only say that because it's relevant. Dawson once helped me when I was struggling with being hurt by someone I loved." Micah's voice grew soft, and an echo of pain crossed his features.

"How did he help?"

"He helped give me the courage to give Bash a second chance. He said that even though Bash hurt me deeply, he was the only one who could fix it. And that as long as I was missing a piece of myself—missing Bash—I'd never really heal. That we made each other whole. Knowing what I know now, I'm pretty sure he was talking from personal experience...and that you might be *his* missing piece."

Air burned in my lungs as the guilt stifled me. Had Dawson been thinking of me and what I'd done to him when he'd talked to Micah? Has he been as broken as I have been without him?

"Why tell me all this?" I croaked.

"Because it helps him. I figured I owed Dawson a solid," Micah shrugged. "And I'm hoping I'm not wrong, but I don't think you intended to hurt him. My advice is to start by fixing what you broke. No bullshit apologies, no excuses. If you screwed up, find a way to make amends. I hear groveling can do wonders."

He fluttered his eyes at me obnoxiously, my lips tugging up involuntarily. I wasn't sure how to even begin fixing things with Dawson. I was still terrified for him to know the whole truth, but one thing was damn clear to me.

I'd never be whole again without Dawson. He was my other half. He had loved me on my worst days and embraced every flaw and scar I had. No one but Dawson ever made me feel like I truly mattered.

And all I'd done since returning was hide from him like a coward and when that didn't work, I pushed him away. He deserved better than me. I was so far beneath him, Hades himself couldn't find me.

But I needed him. God, I needed Dawson like a vital organ. I was fucking lucky that I even got a second chance at his friendship, but I wanted more. I needed more. I didn't want Corvin or any other man.

Only him. It was always him.

"Thanks, Micah. Not only for this, but for looking out for him too."

"Eh, that's a member's perk for our group. It also goes for you too now," he told me with a pointed look. "I get you don't know me, but if you ever need to talk or get some more unsolicited, but well-meaning advice, I'm around."

I scanned his face for any sign that he was messing with me, but all I saw was sincerity. It was a bold move to make with someone he didn't know from Adam, but part of me longed to take him up on it, to unload all the shit I carried and have someone possibly understand. But I'd done that before and ended up losing everyone I thought was on my side.

"I appreciate that," I thanked him, even knowing I'd never use the invitation.

"Absolutely," he smiled warmly. "Also I think I saw Dawson waiting for his turn on the jetski if you wanted to maybe go find him. You know, for some reason or whatever."

I rolled my eyes at his super subtle hint, but set off down the steps to do just that. My gaze zeroed in on his windswept brown hair, his eyes crinkled in laughter at something Nate was saying. He wore a UT branded t-shirt that stretched across his chest and hugged his biceps just right. He was so beautiful my lungs seized looking at him. My pulse beat a dangerous tempo as I got closer, drawn to him, but I froze at the not-so-quiet whispers behind me.

"Holy shit, Dawson Hayes is *so* gorgeous. I'm lowkey obsessed with him, but there's no way he's single."

"I've never heard that he has a girlfriend. He's supposedly phenomenal in bed though. My friend Gillian told me she met him at a party, like, a year ago and he rocked her world. I mean, he had to be single, right? He doesn't strike me as a cheater."

"No way! I've talked to him once, you know? He's, like, super nice, but I bet he's a beast in the sheets. He's like the kind of guy who would carry your bags for you, but then fuck you so good he'd throw your back out."

"Mmm, I'd pay good money for that ride. I've got an awesome chiropractor, so I can take it."

The shrill female laughter grated on my nerves like a dentist's drill. My jaw popped under the strain of holding back a scathing retort at their lewd comments. I hated them for talking about Dawson that way. *My* Dawson. They didn't fucking know him.

My stomach roiled at the thought of him fucking someone else. It was hypocritical as fuck, but it didn't stem the nausea one bit.

One of the girls sashayed over to Dawson, interrupting his conversation with a hand on his elbow. He gave her a warm smile as she flashed a flirtatious grin and looked up at him through heavily lined eyes. Who the fuck wore makeup out on the lake anyway?

She laughed prettily at something he said, slapping him lightly on the arm before rubbing that same spot. I could practically feel my skin turning green as my face heated with jealousy. *Ugh, could she be more fucking obvious? Gross.*

She then gestured to one of the jet skis moored to the boat and Dawson helped her into a lifejacket, slipping one on after her. Dark thoughts overwhelmed me watching them, lacing my veins with fury, fear and helplessness.

"You really gonna race a girl, Daws? How ungentlemanly of you," I heard myself saying. I hadn't realized I'd walked over until I was standing next to them, and I hoped the slur in my voice wasn't noticeable. I gave him a grin to hide the emotion broiling under the surface and his mouth pinched in annoyance.

"Actually, Heather asked me to take her out for a ride since she didn't feel comfortable by herself," he corrected me. One look at the chick confirmed she knew exactly what she was doing. Her face lit up as Dawson settled on the watercraft and held a hand out to help her down.

The second their skin made contact, panic zapped me like a cattle prod. Disturbing images of them tangled together in bed struck me when her chest met his back, her arms wrapping around his waist tightly. An icy sensation blanketed me when I saw her hands splay across his abdomen and I wanted to vomit.

Please stay...don't leave me here. Don't ignore me...

I heard the jetski take off and in the next second, I was climbing onto the other one after haphazardly throwing on a lifejacket, not bothering to buckle it. Voices called out to me from the boat as I shot off, but they were quickly drowned out by the roar of the engine.

Heather's blonde hair waved behind her as Dawson drove at a leisurely pace, and her laughter carried as I caught up to them. Dawson threw a look over his shoulder, his brows crashing together in a double-take upon seeing me.

"What the hell are you doing?" he shouted over the whine of engines and crashing water.

"What's the matter, Mercury? Afraid you'll lose?" I taunted loudly, gunning my jetski.

The spray of the lake hit my face and in that split second, I felt free. Free of the voices, the gloom, the constant buzz under my skin. My vision wavered at the edges and my hand slipped on the throttle a bit, but I shook it off and kept pushing. Dawson drifted into my periphery and I caught the shake of his head and pursed lips before he sped off, the chick shrieking in laughter and tightening her grip on him. My heart squeezed painfully and a lump bobbed in my throat.

Don't leave—see me—stay with me—give me your eyes—give me you...

The voice screamed in my head, desperation clawing at me for his attention. Every inch of space he put between us was a stab between my ribs. All I saw was him running away from me, leaving me behind. I squeezed the throttle in a vice and the jetski lurched forward violently. A wave of dizziness washed over me and I could just make out Dawson's jetski ahead of me as I raced by them.

The craft pitched sharply to the left and I was suddenly airborne, flipping ass over head before crashing into the water. A pain shot through my shoulder as the lifejacket ripped off me as I broke the surface. White noise filled my ears while water filled my lungs.

I was so disoriented, I didn't know where the surface was. I wasn't sure if I was immobile or flailing. The only thing that registered to me was quiet.

Nothing but quiet and darkness.

It was peaceful.

I wanted to sink into it.

And never come up.

A crushing force anchored under my arms and around my chest, yanking me upwards and a small voice told me to fight it. To stay in the quiet.

Cool air rushed over my head as we cleared the surface and I instinctively dragged in oxygen to my depleted lungs. Hoarse coughs wracked me as water was forced from my body and my head pounded from the effort.

"It's okay, I've got you. Breathe, Theo, you're okay," Dawson gasped out. I choked out his name, the fear that was curiously absent before slamming into me all at once. That I had even been tempted to let go horrified me because in the quiet, there was no Dawson. He was music and song, and that didn't exist in the cold silence.

"Shh, it's okay, you're safe. Can you help me kick? There's a stretch of shore close by."

His voice was strained and rough from the struggle. I didn't know how far away he was when I went down or how deep I'd sunk before he grabbed me. He draped my arm around his shoulder and started swimming us toward the shoreline. His lifejacket was gone and even the thought that I could have endangered him had dread coursing through my system.

I tried my best to kick and paddle us closer, but my limbs were heavy and fatigue was setting in fast. It seemed an eternity before my feet hit the silt at the bottom and we were able to stagger out onto the muddy bank. Dawson kept a tight hold of me until we were far enough away from the water before releasing me, and I wanted to cry at the loss of his touch.

I fell to my back gracelessly, that old dizziness swirling as I stared up at the sky and tried to catch my breath. Dawson dropped to his knees beside me, his warm hands cupping my face and forcing me to look at his worried blue eyes.

"Christ, are you okay? Does anything hurt? Can you breathe alright?" I hated the fear that shook his voice, knowing I put it there. But I couldn't help the sense of victory that swept through me at having every ounce of his attention on me. Dawson was here with me...where he belonged.

"Heh...I win...got you..." I panted through a weak smile. Dawson's face scrunched in confusion as he peered down at me.

"What do you mean 'win'? What are you talking about?"

My eyes slid shut as I tried to will my thoughts back into order. "Y-your...eyes. On m-me...not her...I got you back."

Dawson scoffed loudly and my head lolled towards him. He stood and angrily brushed off his legs. I slowly sat up and willed my stomach to settle. Whether it was the beers on the boat, the crash, or the nerves of making Dawson angry, my gut gurgled uncomfortably. He finally spun toward me, his hands fisted at his sides and his chest heaving.

"You've got to be fucking kidding me," he growled at me. "You climbed on that freaking thing after God knows how many drinks and took off like a bat out of hell because you were *jealous*? Seriously?"

I wasn't entirely sure it wasn't a rhetorical question, so I stayed silent. I couldn't exactly defend myself. That was what I'd done after all.

Another fuck up for the books. If he only knew this was all I was destined for, he never would have pulled me out of the water.

"Theo, what the hell were you thinking?" he snapped, but there was no hiding the tremor in his voice. "You scared the ever-loving shit out of me back there! Do you have any idea what that was like? Seeing you go under like that and not come back up? Goddamnit, I just got you back!"

His face twisted in a grimace as his voice cracked. It was clear he hadn't intended for that last part to slip out, but that single sentence made my heart soar.

"I'm sorry I scared you..." I said shakily.

"Oh! You're sorry. I guess we're all good then," he sneered.

"I didn't mean—"

"You had no reason to be jealous. Nor did you have a right to be. She was harmless. It's not like I screwed her on your bed and then got her number afterwards," he finished bitterly.

His pointed reply spiked my temper. I didn't need the reminder of my massive screw up. I already hated myself enough for driving that wedge between us that I could never take back.

"That's not fair," I ground out, standing up on shaky legs. "I'm not exactly proud of it, but I was fucking rolling that night. I didn't plan for that to happen and we weren't together at the time."

"We aren't together *now*," he bit back. The comment drove straight through my sternum. I understood logically it was just the truth and not thrown out to hurt me, but it did. Fuck, did it hurt.

"Why not?"

The question rushed out on a rough whisper. Dawson's eyes flared in surprise before his face fell, regret lining his features. He abused his bottom lip while avoiding my gaze and my heart sank further than I had at the bottom of that lake.

"You know, there are times when I look at you and all I see is that loud, wild-haired boy who used to bribe me with sour skittles to play my guitar for him and sang along at the top of his lungs. The one who drew a Freddie Mercury mustache on me the night before my recital when I accidentally fell asleep beside him in the hayloft."

Pressure built behind my eyes and stung with tears. Vivid memories assaulted me and I mourned for the boys we were. They had been so happy, blissfully ignorant of just how much they stood to lose.

"But then there are times where...I don't even recognize you anymore," he confessed thickly. Those cornflower blue orbs rimmed with red and I ached to go to him. I wanted his arms around me again to hold me together before I fell apart.

I opened my mouth to respond, to promise him that I was still the same Theo he knew, the one he loved. But my throat locked up, sealing the words away as though my body protested the lie. I wasn't the same. I'd told him as much. I couldn't even be sure that version of me was the real one, or if this fragmented, labile mess was who I was always meant to be.

"I would have given anything to get you back after you left. I spent night after night in that barn waiting for you. I screamed at the stars to bring you back to me. I promised my voice, my instruments, my goddamn soul to whoever the fuck was up there in exchange for you... but you never came back."

The anguish in his words cut to the bone, tearing through nerves until I was shredded and ruined. His face was wet with tears that mirrored my own.

"The worst part was that when you finally came back, I realized it wasn't *to me.* You were back, but you weren't mine. And I made peace with that. You didn't leave me much of a choice, but I did it."

"I am yours," I grated out. I stepped towards him only for him to retreat even further away.

"But you're not," he smiled sadly. "You're holding something back from me. I don't know what or why, but I do know there's something."

"I'm not," I swore, yet it didn't even sound convincing to my own ears.

Dawson let out a long, exhausted sigh, his shoulders sagging under an invisible weight. A weight I placed there with my secrets. A dull buzz of an engine drew our gazes to the lake and we saw Bash and Nate making their way towards us on the jetskis we'd abandoned.

Dawson ran his fingers through his hair, looking more defeated than I'd previously seen him.

"And that lie right there should answer your question," he replied dully. He pinned me with glassy, miserable eyes. "What's even sadder about this whole thing is that it didn't have to be this way. You're your own worst enemy, Theo."

I was cemented in place by the raw truth in his words. Dawson couldn't even begin to understand how right he was. This hell was of my own making. There was no outside force, no man or woman that was as much a threat as the one that lurked inside me.

Everything I truly had to fear was in every fiber that made up my body. My own being worked against me, an enemy within my veins.

Sometimes there was no battle like the one fought within your own mind.

CHAPTER SEVENTEEN

The pill bottle seemed heavy in my hand as I twirled it around, working up the courage to open it. I had fought this for so long that willingly going back to it was fucking with my head a bit. There was always a rough adjustment period for me, but I'd been through this enough to know what the first wave would bring. Oddly enough, the nausea and dizziness were something I could deal with within reason. The diarrhea was...highly unfortunate, but the hand tremors tended to be the worst. It was like a physical reminder of how out of control I truly was. But I wasn't backing down.

Dawson's fear and anguish yesterday were bad enough, but it was his parting shot that had struck me like a blow to the chest. Things didn't have to turn out this way between us if I could just learn to get out of my own way. I wanted to fight for us, to silence the malicious voices in my head that said I wasn't good enough and win him back. And clearly I couldn't fucking do that with my brain left to its own devices, so it came down to this. The pharmaceutical leash meant to rein in the excesses of my nature.

I fucking hated it though. I felt like a wild animal thrown into a cage designed to keep me safe and contained, but without the freedom to breathe. The medication created as many problems as it solved. However, I was willing to do whatever it took to earn Dawson back. He deserved a stable, reliable partner, and I couldn't be that for him when my brain was a yo-yo of reckless impulses and sinister notions.

So stop being such a pussy about it and open the damn thing. It's not like it's fucking arsenic...

Dad's footsteps coming up the stairs made me jump and I quickly dropped the bottle into the drawer of my nightstand. I whirled around just as he appeared in the doorway.

"Hey, I was about to run some errands and figured I'd grab dinner on the way back. You good with pizza?"

"Yeah, sure. Hawaiian for me." I prayed that my voice sounded steadier to him than it did to my own ears.

Dad made a disgusted grunt. "Where did I go wrong in raising you?"

"Don't be a hater because I have a much more refined palate than you."

"Coming from the kid who actually tasted the mud pies he used to make in the backyard..."

"Now, those were a delicacy. My stuffed pig, Gordon Pigsmey, raved that they had a unique umami flavor and delicate earthy aftertaste," I said haughtily.

"I'm sure the Pepto Bismol aperitif you had to take afterwards really rounded out the experience."

"I will admit the stomach cramps did taint the enjoyment a little bit."

"Yet it still sounds better than pineapple on pizza," Dad snickered affectionately. "I'll be back in a couple hours. Text me if you need anything."

I gave him a lazy salute as he left. I sauntered over to my window seat and sank into the corner, knees curled up to my chest as I looked longingly towards Dawson's house. Only their backyard was visible from my window, but I still watched and waited, hoping for even a glimpse of him. The second we stepped foot back on the boat yesterday, he went out of his way to avoid me the rest of the time. He surprisingly hadn't left me to fend for myself to get back home, but the silence in the truck had been thick enough to choke on and Dawson had bolted inside his house faster than I could blink.

For the twentieth time today, I pulled out my phone to check for a response, but my texts had still gone unread.

ME

I'm so fucking sorry, but please let me explain??

I know I screwed up, but can we at least talk about it?

Okay, you need some space, I get that...I'm here when you're ready to talk

Can you just tell me how much space we're talking here? Like an hour or a day or...?

Please don't shut me out, Mercury. Give me a chance to fix this.

I blew out a deep, long breath that did little to release the tension in my body. I had fallen so far in Dawson's eyes with the shit I'd pulled that I had a long ass climb ahead of me to get back in his good graces. My head dropped back against the wall with a painful thud like it was weighed down with all the regret and frustration I felt.

A flash of black and white outside drew my gaze. Stella made a frenzied dash across the backyard, tossing her head wildly and I could just make out her distressed bleating through the window. Then Dani seemingly came out of nowhere, fruitlessly trying to catch up with the frantic animal. I cursed and shot out of my room, racing down the stairs and out my back door.

I vaulted over the fence and when I got closer, I saw the barbed wire wrapped around Stella's horns and heard Dani crying at her to stop, as pointless as it was. I clicked my tongue to get the goat's attention and I saw Dani's steps falter out of the corner of my eye, but I ignored her and focused on avoiding Stella's thrashing head.

"Hey sweet girl, it's alright. You remember me, don't you?" I spoke soothingly as I could, approaching cautiously. I always had much better luck with Stella than Dawson had, but it wasn't unheard of for her to charge me every once in a while if she was feeling testy. She could be a literal ballbuster.

"Theo, be careful," Dani warned tearfully. I nodded without taking my eyes off the animal.

Stella continued to bleat loudly, but calmed enough for me to get close and swing my leg over her to hold her steady between my thighs.

"Come hold her head while I get this shit off."

Dani rushed over and tried her best to hold her still, but Stella was jumpy as hell as I worked to free her horns. By the time she was loose, my fingers had been nicked several times and I was going to have more than one bruise on me. The instant I released her, the goat trotted away as if it hadn't happened. I breathed in relief that she didn't seem to be hurt, but then the breath was punched out of me as small arms banded around my stomach.

"I missed you," Dani said, her voice muffled against my chest.

I gingerly wrapped my arms around her, unsure of how to respond. I'd been dreading this inevitable confrontation for weeks. Dawson wasn't the only one I had worked to avoid after coming home. Half of me worried it was a trick to let my guard down so she could claw my eyes out for hurting her and her brother, but when I heard her sniffling my heart cracked and I hugged her back fiercely.

"I'm sorry," I grated out, squeezing her to me. "I'm so fucking sorry. I missed you too."

We stood like that until my back twinged from being slightly hunched over her smaller frame. I gently released her and forced myself to meet her gaze. Her eyes were glossy with tears and her cheeks reddened with embarrassment.

"Sorry. I just really needed that," she mumbled, wiping the wetness off her face.

"Please don't apologize. This is all my fault," I said gruffly. Dani crossed her arms, shoulders bunching up as she looked up at me sadly.

"Yeah, it is. I kept wondering when you'd get the balls to come see me this summer, but then you never did..."

I swallowed roughly, fighting to stay put and not rush back to the safety of my house. I hadn't been prepared for this.

"Look, I'm not mad at you anymore for ditching us back then because I know you had your reasons, but you didn't have to ignore me when you got back. And now even Dawson's seen you a bunch of times, but not me. That's not fair. I loved you too..."

Her accusation cut deep even though it was completely warranted. I had been so fixated on everything with Dawson that I got tunnel vision about everything else. I also hadn't had the guts to face the people who were my second family for eight years. Their rejection would have been the final nail in my coffin.

"I swear, I didn't mean to hurt you. I loved you too, Dani. I still do. I mean...*fuck*." I choked up, guilt suffocating everything I wanted to say to her. I pinched the bridge of my nose that was stinging with tears I refused to let free.

"Did you think I'd give you a hard time or something?"

"No, that wasn't it..."

"Then why didn't you come see me?"

"I guess I was scared."

"Of me?"

"Of you hating me too," I admitted quietly. "I know how badly I fucked up when I left and that Dawson wasn't the only one I hurt. I didn't want you guys to hate me as much as he did."

She scoffed softly and looked at me like I was an idiot. Which...was fair.

"Dawson never hated you, dingbat. He probably wished he could. He'll never admit this to anyone, but he never stopped believing you'd come back to him."

A burning pressure squeezed my throat and I worked to swallow past it. I kept shaking my head like refuting her words made them less real. It was too much to hope for that Dawson had held a flame for me all this time, a twin to my own. No matter what I did to douse it, it never went out.

"It doesn't matter. He won't want me back now. I keep screwing everything up."

"So stop screwing up," she said bluntly.

"Like it's that easy," I exhaled sharply, annoyance flaring.

"Uh, yeah, pretty much. You're the only one who controls your actions, so do better. Self-fulfilling prophecy, you know?"

"What do you mean?"

"If you keep saying you're a problem, then you'll *be* a problem. If you keep believing you won't get him back, then you never will. You have such a strong fear of what could happen that you end up acting in ways that bring about the outcome you're so afraid of."

I chewed on my lip, weighing her words. It wasn't that simple. It couldn't be...could it? Fuck, what if she was right?

I thought about all the anxiety and fear I had about Dawson dumping me and hating me when he discovered the real reason I moved away and cut off contact. Except Dawson wasn't the one who left, I was.

He didn't choose to shut me out and block me, I did. His anger and hate had been a consequence of my own making with my secrets and lies.

I scrubbed my hands over my face roughly, the realization hitting me upside the head. I had been the architect of my own pain and I had no one to blame but myself.

"He deserves so much better than me, Dani," I whispered defeatedly.

I cursed when a sharp smack landed on my arm. I gaped at Dani while she stared me down angrily, hands perched on her hips.

"Stop with the fucking pity party, Theo Bishop. Yes, you've messed up a shit ton, but you can work to deserve him. I've seen it before. Do you remember what I said when you guys were dating and really getting serious?"

I ran back through my memory, but came up short. I shook my head helplessly and it only seemed to frustrate her further.

"I told you to make sure you treat him like gold because there was a line of people who would gladly take your place if not, and you said—

"—that I would never let anyone treat him better than I could because he was always meant to be mine."

"Exactly," she smiled smugly. "I might have shipped you guys a little too hard back then, but I still stand by it."

"I've kept something from him though," I whispered hoarsely. "And I'm terrified that if...when he finds out, he'll see me differently. He won't see a future with me anymore."

Dani absorbed what I was saying, chewing on her bottom lip in thought. She then straightened with a determined look.

"Or maybe he'll see you clearer now and still love you like he always has. Different isn't always bad, Theo. And if you continue to lie to him, you definitely won't have a future with him, so really, what do you have to lose?"

"Dani, you out here?" Mr. Hayes called out from the back door. He scanned the backyard until his gaze landed on us, and the expression on his face was inscrutable. "Sorry to interrupt, but your mom is looking for you. Better go see what she wants."

Dani nodded, but held out a finger for him to wait. She looked back up at me, her eyes pleading.

"You and Dawson are meant to be together. I know it. You can work things out, but you have to stop running and talk to him," she implored. "Stop assuming you know how things will turn out. You've trusted Dawson your whole life, so trust him enough to love you through whatever you're scared of now."

She didn't let me respond. She only hugged me again tightly before jogging past Mr. Hayes and back inside. My mind couldn't even process what she'd said as Mr. Hayes closed the distance between us slowly. Nerves fizzled in my gut over what he was thinking and the urge to run was so goddamn strong.

I wasn't prepared when he pulled me into his arms, gripping me in a hug that rivaled his daughter's. I eagerly wrapped my arms around him, relief coursing through every limb of my body. There wasn't an ounce of hate in his embrace and it healed a tiny fraction of me. He held me for a few more moments before stepping back, hands planted on my shoulders.

"I think that was long overdue, don't you?" he smiled at me. "Emilia and I are glad you're home, son. And I know your dad is so happy to have you back."

I couldn't stop the scoff from escaping, but the thought of anyone being happy to see me was ridiculous. He frowned at my reaction, but he didn't understand the reasons behind my departure or even my return. If he truly knew, he'd be threatening me to stay away from his son and ordering Dawson to drop me like a bad habit.

"No offense, Mr. H, but that's a load of BS. Dad only took me back in because he had to. I haven't made him happy in a long-ass time."

"Interesting," he hummed, sticking his hands in his pockets. "That's not the impression I got when he called me in December, so excited about you finally coming home. He's been a miserable bastard since the day you moved out."

That news hit like a slap across the face. "That's not true."

"Theo, you going to live with your mom wasn't his idea. He told me he only agreed because she convinced him it was best. Your dad was so damn worried about you that he would have agreed to anything to make sure you were safe."

Tears blurred my vision and I fought to make sense of it all. Something about what he'd said curdled my stomach.

"Wait...do you know about why I left in the first place?"

Mr. Hayes gave me a sad smile and nodded slowly. I suppressed the urge to vomit or scream, hating that he might have known the entire time how damaged I really am.

"How much of it?" I asked tightly.

"If you're asking whether I know about your illness, I do," he replied gently. "Grady has kept me updated on you every year you've been gone. I think part of it was to process what he was feeling, but Emilia and I also wanted to know how you were doing."

"Seriously?"

"Of course. You're as much our child as Dawson and Dani. Why wouldn't we want to know?"

"But if you knew I've been back since December, why didn't you tell them?"

"I didn't think it was my place. You would have reached out to Dawson and Dani if you wanted to. But I'm...ashamed to admit that I also kept it to myself because I was nervous about what your coming back would do to Dawson."

His face flushed at the admission, and my heart sank. I wanted to curl up into myself. Of fucking course he still wouldn't want me around Dawson. He knew the truth about me, so there was no way he'd want that future for his son.

"Right. Makes sense," I muttered petulantly.

"Now wait, it's not for the reason you think. It's not because of the overdose or your illness. You had just transferred into UT and were trying to get healthy again. Dawson had a football season to finish, scouts coming around, and a 3.8 GPA to keep up. I knew that any reunion between you two would most likely be messy and complicated because of how it ended, and I didn't want either of you derailed by that. Neither did Grady. The codependent relationship you two had was manageable when you were younger, but you're not kids anymore. There are very real stakes this time and a lot more complications involved."

I knew I wasn't good enough for Dawson, but hearing that both of our dads thought as much made my chest tighten painfully. I hadn't noticed I was digging at the barbwire cuts on my fingers until I looked down and saw red. The pain grounded me and kept me from spiraling about how worthless and broken I was.

"I'm not saying that you and Dawson shouldn't be together. I know you love each other, but you two have a lot of healing to do first. Being heartbroken as a teenager is one thing, but at this age, it can change the trajectory of your futures. It might sound dramatic, but people have ruined their lives over a lot less. We only want what's best for both of you."

I was only half-listening, dark thoughts crashing in my head like storm clouds. I had made the decision to try harder for Dawson, to commit to whatever pills and coping mechanisms I could to be worthy of him again, but what was the point if our own parents thought I wasn't good for him?

"Gotta get home. Dinner time," I muttered, whipping around and speed walking towards my house. I ignored Mr. Hayes' calls for me to come back, his voice being drowned out by the negative screams in my head.

Every kind word I'd heard from Dawson's friends morphed into criticisms. Dani's encouragement twisted into sneers of derision. Mr. Hayes' assurances of love mutated into animosity.

Logic couldn't penetrate the toxic fog that was overwhelming me. I barreled into my room and yanked open the drawer I'd thrown my meds into. The rattle of the pills sounded deafening. Remembering all the side effects I'd suffered through each time I was forced back on the regimen made me want to toss them out the window. They had hardly seemed worth it when the meds didn't seem to make much of a difference. All it had accomplished was anchoring me to a neutral setting where everything felt slowed down and lifeless. Bleak.

And being stuck in that hole made living feel pointless.

The idea that had been swirling around those three days of hiding out at Neverland crooned to me, tempting me with the sweetest relief that only it could bring. That idea of *someday*...someday I would be free. For good.

Yet even as I thought it, I clutched Dawson's ring that was back around my neck where it belonged. I couldn't count the times I'd clung to it and the promise that Dawson had made me. That alone had the power to wipe out that malignant idea, to silence every doubt and worry in my mind, to evaporate any outside opinion that we shouldn't be together.

I wanted Dawson. I couldn't lose him again. I would push through any pain and darkness that came because nothing felt as good as being loved by Dawson Hayes.

I popped the lid on the bottle and shook out a pill, steeling myself before throwing it back and swallowing it dry. I jumped at the furious voice behind me and fumbled the bottle in my hand.

"What the fuck do you think you're doing?"

CHAPTER EIGHTEEN

My whole body shook and my ribcage felt like it would crack under the building pressure as I tried to tamp down my rage. My focus was zeroed in on the orange bottle in Theo's hand and ice slid down my spine.

I'd almost talked myself out of coming over here after I spotted Dad talking to Theo outside. The miserable defeat that shadowed his features before he took off compelled me to follow him. Dad had tried to tell me to give him space when I'd rushed past him, but I wasn't having it. As pissed as I was at Theo for his stunt on the lake, I couldn't bear to see him upset. I'd seen that look enough recently to last a lifetime and then some.

But watching him toss back whatever the fuck pill that was made me want to wring his neck. Any doubt I had of Theo's addiction vanished and I surged forward, snatching the bottle out of his grip.

"No, don't!" Theo protested with wide, panicked eyes, but I held it out of his reach.

"I can't fucking believe you. Why do you keep doing this shit to yourself?" I snapped.

"Wait, what? What do you mean?"

"Don't play dumb. You know exactly what I mean. Did you get this crap from Corvin?"

"What? It's not—just stop freaking out and let me explain!"

"No, I'm done with your excuses. Since you won't do anything to help yourself, I'll do it for you."

I made a mad dash for the hallway bathroom with Theo close behind, yelling frantically. He caught up and he began wrenching, yanking, pulling at anything to stop me. It was a cacophony of curses and shouts, grunts and shoves until I made it through the doorway and came to an abrupt stop in front of the toilet, holding the bottle above it threateningly.

"Stop! Fuck, please! I need those," Theo gripped at his hair wildly, looking close to tears. I had a moment of pity that the drugs had such a hold on him and it broke my fucking heart. How could he have gotten this bad?

The sheer desperation on his face gave me pause and I suddenly felt exhausted. I wondered if I'd even be able to save him if he didn't want to be saved. If the pills and alcohol were most important to him now, where did that leave me?

My eyes burned and I grimaced at the spike of pain behind my ribs.

"Why? Why did you do this to yourself?" I choked out.

He tilted his head, shooting me a bewildered look. "What do you mean? I have no other choice. I was doing it for *you*."

I reared back, my brain going a hundred miles an hour to try to make sense of what he was saying.

"You did...what? Theo, there is always a choice! How could poisoning yourself with drugs and getting high be for me? I can help you, but you can't keep turning to this shit!"

I could practically hear his gears turning and saw when it clicked for him. He let out a sharp breath and grimaced, gesturing at the bottle.

"It's really not what you think. Read the label."

I was weirdly nervous to look away from him, but did as he said. The first thing I noticed was Theo's name printed neatly on the sticker, which made me feel like a huge tool. It was *his* prescription, not some party drug he scored. But printed under that, in bold, was Lithium Carbonate.

"What is this?"

Theo's gaze met mine, fearful and resigned. "It's used for bipolar disorder."

Hundreds of pieces snapped together in quick succession. Everything I thought I understood about Theo and his issues dissolved and I was left floundering. Weird, stuttering sounds came out of my mouth as I struggled to process four simple words.

"So...that means you're...bipolar?"

"Yeah."

"Is that the reason—"

"Uh huh."

I was reeling from this new revelation. A dozen emotions spun in my head interspersed with several questions I needed answers to. I set the bottle down on the counter with all the care of handling a live bomb, and scrubbed a hand over my jaw.

"Okay. This is a lot. First, let's get out of this bathroom so we can talk."

"You're not leaving?"

My forehead creased at the surprise in his voice. "No, of course not. Why would I?"

He lifted a shoulder in a half-hearted shrug before dropping his gaze to the bottle on the counter. Tension radiated from Theo's slouched frame and it hurt to see him so unsure of himself, so afraid of how I'd react. I'd jumped to so many conclusions that I'd only managed to drive him further into that protective shell he'd been hiding inside.

I gingerly reached out to grab his hand, relieved when he didn't pull away from me. He didn't look at me and his palm felt clammy against my own. I slid by him and led us to his room, gently steering him to sit down on the edge of the mattress before I wheeled his desk chair over for myself.

"I'm not even sure where to start." I leaned forward on my knees and tried to gather my thoughts. "When did you find out you were... um..."

"It's not a bad word, Dawson. You can say it," Theo said icily.

I winced, but nodded in agreement. "You're right. I'm sorry. When did you get diagnosed as bipolar, I mean?"

"A couple weeks before Homecoming," he murmured.

"You've known that long?"

"Yeah. Remember when you started to notice I'd been acting weird senior year?"

His brows furrowed for a bit before they softened in realization. "I do. I couldn't figure out what was going on with you..."

"You weren't the only one. Dad had been worried when my grades started slipping, my sleep turned to shit, and my moods had been up and down every few months. He took me to see a psychologist because he didn't think my ADHD was fully to blame for my issues, and he was right. When I found out what was actually wrong with me, I just couldn't deal. I freaked out and ended up buying that Oxy on a whim."

"Does that mean you don't have ADHD then?"

"No, I do. I just have both. It's actually common to have bipolar disorder and ADHD together. At least that's what the psychologist said."

"I'm guessing this is part of the reason you went to live with your mom out of nowhere?"

Theo's chin dipped in confirmation. "Mom hadn't known about the diagnosis before I ended up in the hospital. Once Dad told her, she found some bougie mental health facility close to her place, paid out the nose to secure me a spot, and it was a done deal before I even woke up. She'd even decided I'd go to college close to her so she could keep an eye on me."

He picked at his nails, staring absently at my knees as he spoke. His voice was detached, emotionless. Worry clawed at me that this was too much for him right now, but I also didn't want to give him the chance to escape the long overdue conversation.

"Did rehab help at least?" I asked cautiously.

"It did...until it didn't," he answered cryptically.

"What do you mean?"

"That first time, I was there for four weeks. They were able to stabilize me, start me on meds, and got me into therapy. I did okay for a couple months after that, even got my grades back up while I did homeschooling. But I hated the medicine they gave me. The side effects were trash and they made me feel off."

"Off how?"

Theo's brows furrowed and he nibbled his lip in thought. "It's hard to explain. It's like experiencing the world through a pane of glass. Everything is muted and just...distant. Emotions, creativity, all of it. My brain was like a rapidly depleting battery and I was always tired. Schoolwork that I used to do in thirty minutes took me hours. I didn't find anything interesting or funny anymore. It was fucking miserable, so I stopped taking them."

I had trouble imagining Theo like that, limited and restrained. As long as I'd known him, he'd been spirited, magnetic and impossible to ignore.

"What happened then?"

"I felt amazing. I had this uncontainable energy. Everything was funny, everything held appeal. Books, music, people, ideas. Nothing could bring me down or scare me. I could function on just a couple hours of sleep and still take on anything. I felt like the best version of myself."

A knot formed in my stomach at his wistful tone. It sounded like an exhausting state to be in, but Theo spoke as though he longed to have that feeling back.

"But the problem was that others didn't agree," he chuckled mirthlessly. "Mom and Doug would say I was talking too fast, that I didn't make sense, I was too temperamental, I didn't get enough sleep, and I was 'too much' to handle. Where I thought I was creative, they saw me as chaotic. I felt strong, they saw reckless. I felt invincible, they saw delusional."

"They sent you back to rehab?" I hazarded a guess.

"Right after I stayed up all night painting a giant mural on their dining room wall. I didn't have paint in the house, so I had to improvise with permanent markers, different sauces from the kitchen, and Mom's very expensive makeup."

A startled laugh escaped me and I clapped a hand over my mouth. "Wait, seriously?"

Theo gave a quiet snort of amusement. "Yeah, she didn't exactly appreciate that. But they said it was obvious I was manic and off my meds, so they carted me off again. That time was different though."

Something haunted flashed in his eyes and he fidgeted with his hands. I glanced down and noticed blood where he was picking at little scabs scattered across his hands. Instinctively, I grasped both his hands in mine to stop him hurting himself.

Theo's gaze darted to mine, scared and glassy. My thumbs started rubbing soothing patterns into the back of his hands and I felt the tension leach from his body.

"Tell me how it was different," I urged him softly.

"They immediately upped my dose when I was admitted. I leveled out after a couple of days, but the side effects were worse and instead of only feeling dimmed, I felt hopeless. Helpless. Like I'd never be happy again. Like I was in a hole I had no hope of climbing out of."

"Oh, Theo..."

"That was the first time I thought about it," he whispered. A shiver raced down my limbs, dreading what he meant by that.

"Thought about what?" My voice was raw, shredded with emotion.

"About how nice it would be for it all to end...to just go to sleep and not wake up the next day. And I wanted it."

I folded in on myself, a strangled noise caught in my chest. The implication stabbed at my chest, straight through bone and into my lungs to collapse them. I was sick to my stomach that Theo, my sweet, sunny Theo, ever considered leaving this world. Leaving me.

Theo's hand cupped my cheek and tilted my face up, my vision blurry as I peered at him. I hated his concerned look, that he was even worrying about me when he was the one who had suffered.

"Did you ever..."

My throat pinched close and I couldn't get the question out. It might break me to hear, but I needed to know how bad it had gotten for him. Theo's eyes darted away, breaking our connection and I suppressed the surge of bile that rose.

"I had it planned. For those weeks, it was all I could focus on. I said all the right things in group therapy. I took my meds daily. I smiled and laughed and felt so at peace with my decision that I convinced myself it was the right call. Finally, they released me and I was free to follow through."

"What stopped you?" Fuck, it hurt to speak past the ball of grief lodged in my throat.

Unflinching, Theo looked me dead on and gifted me with the smallest, beautiful smile.

"You."

"What?"

"You're the reason I didn't go through with it." He pulled his necklace out of his shirt, fingering my class ring. "You were wrong when you said that your promise meant nothing to me. Dawson, you have no idea how deeply your promise is lodged in my heart, in my fucking soul. The night I...was going to, I took your ring out and put it on. If I was going to go, I wanted you close to me."

I squeezed my eyes closed against the onslaught of tears that flooded me hearing that. I felt wet trails down my cheek that Theo gently wiped away, but that only made them come faster.

"The ring was supposed to bring me comfort, but instead brought me clarity. I remembered what you told me the day you gave it to me. You promised to love me forever and that you were going to spend your life with me, and I...couldn't do it. I couldn't end my life when it was supposed to belong to you. I didn't know if I'd ever be brave enough to see you again or tell you the truth if I did, but it felt so wrong to take away my future when you promised me yours. And every time those thoughts invaded, I held your ring and kept myself alive for you."

"*Fuck*, Theo."

My lips crashed into his, my hands cradling his face to keep him close. I felt his shock before he molded his mouth to mine, his tongue sweeping in to taste my sorrow, my regret, my fear that I had come so close to losing him permanently.

"I'm sorry," I whispered the words against his lips. "I'm sorry you were ever in that much pain. I'm sorry I didn't make you feel safe enough to tell me."

A warm tear slid down his cheek and it felt like acid when it hit my hand. I fucking hated that I was the cause of it. I kissed him again, infusing it with every drop of remorse and sincerity I had. When we pulled back, we were both breathing hard and gripping at each other with quiet desperation.

"Come here," I ordered softly, pulling him to stand with me. I crawled up to recline on his bed, holding out my arm for him to do the same. He hesitated slightly, but the second he laid down I tugged him to me, wrapping him in my arms and guiding his head to my chest. I inhaled his fresh, clean scent, and a rightness settled in my bones having him next to me again.

I didn't let myself think of what we'd do about this tomorrow or where we'd go from here. I only cared about the beautiful, broken man in my arms and giving him what he needed most right then.

"Why were you so scared to tell me about your illness, Theo? How could you think I would have ever stopped loving you because of it?"

He squirmed in my hold, so I raked my fingers along his scalp to soothe him, pulling a breathy sigh from his lips.

"Did I ever tell you about my aunt Shannon?"

"Um, no? I don't think so. Why?"

"She was my mom's sister. Mom told me she was a total nerd and really smart, but was also always bubbly and cracking jokes. I only got to meet her a couple of times growing up, but when I'd ask about her at family gatherings, everyone was really sketchy about her. They would give vague reasons she couldn't be there and would change the subject whenever she'd come up. Mom and Dad didn't tell me the truth about her until I was sixteen."

"She had bipolar disorder, didn't she?"

"Yeah. She had been diagnosed in college. They told me she'd have periods where she was able to manage and do really great, but something would inevitably happen that would spin her out of control. She'd lose her job and disappear for months at a time before calling Mom up and letting her know she was settled again and feeling healthy. It was a seemingly endless pattern with her until..."

His body tightened against mine and I ran my hand up and down his back. "Until what?"

"Something changed apparently. Shannon had been holding a steady job for a couple of years, even got married and was thinking about children. Mom was thrilled for her. Then her husband called one day and told her that Shannon was dead. They'd found her in a hotel an hour away."

"Jesus Christ," I breathed, hugging Theo to me a bit tighter. "What happened?"

"The husband told mom that Shannon had been cheating on him for a few months, had quit her job, been partying and taking drugs. She'd moved out of their house and was hotel hopping, and I guess it got to be too much for her. She left a note, saying that she was tired of fighting and just wanted to have some peace."

Theo's voice broke and it ripped into me. I pressed a kiss to his temple and wished like hell I knew what to do to make it better for him. It was becoming clearer where the root of Theo's fear came from.

"What your aunt went through was unimaginable," I started to say, continuing to rub his back in soothing circles. "I hate that she felt so lost that she thought that was the best way out, but Theo...you are not her. Her story isn't yours."

"But don't you fucking see it could be?" he barked, ripping out of my hold and leaping off the bed. "Mom could barely look at me once she found out my diagnosis. She was so paranoid that I'd turn out like

Shannon that she shoved me into rehab three times, forced me to take meds that I despised, and regulated every minute of my life until she felt satisfied I was "normal" again. And honestly, I don't blame her. Sometimes I hate her for it, but I get it. What makes me any different from Shannon?"

I jumped up and rounded the bed, trying not to let it show how much it hurt when he stepped back from me.

"I'll be the first to admit I don't know much about mental illness, but I *do* know that not everyone experiences it the same way. Do you even know why her cycles were that bad? What triggered them? Was she on and off meds, or did she take them at all? There could be a hundred reasons her story turned out that way, and you could do the exact same things and still have yours turn out differently."

"It's more than that. This is a lifelong disease, Dawson. There is no cure. There is no break from it. I have to live with it every day, never knowing when the switch will flip. When I found out, all I could think was how it would affect us. I was scared that when you looked at me, you'd only see the 'bipolar boy' like everyone else would. Or worse, maybe you'd stand by me anyway and I'd do something unforgivable when I was fucking manic and drive you away like Shannon had done to her husband."

"And you decided to take the easy way out and push me away on your own terms?"

"Yes, because at least you would have been happy! There was nothing I could do but accept it, but you had a chance at something better."

"So what? You just gave up?"

Theo's expression sobered, snagging my ring around his neck and fiddling with it. Knowing now what it truly meant to him, what it had done for him, clenched at my heart.

"You don't know what it's like to have your brain turn against you, to be terrified that one day you'll hear that voice telling you to end it all and you won't be able to fight it. You don't know how fucked up it is that I crave the highs that get me into so much trouble because the lows just hurt too damn much. I'm left waiting from one day to the next for my control to be taken from me and turn me into someone I don't recognize..."

He stepped closer and my pulse kicked up.

"Someone who would rather be coked out of his mind than deal with reality, or who would go out on a jetski after drinking because of a jealous fit—"

He was close enough now that his body heat seeped into my skin. My eyes fluttered close when his finger traced over the light freckles that dusted my cheeks.

"Or who would make the worst decision of his life and walk away from the man he's loved since he was fifteen because he was too scared of his own mind."

My breath hitched when his lips ghosted over mine. My heart was pounding a frantic rhythm that I was sure he could hear. I didn't stop him when Theo captured my mouth in a tentative kiss, licking over the seam of my lips and coaxing me to open for him.

Tingles spread over me and my head swam. He didn't linger long and I was grateful. I wasn't confident in my ability to say no to him right now. If he asked, I would drop to my knees and rip out my bleeding heart for him.

He put some much needed space between us, allowing me to think somewhat clearly again. I rubbed at my scratchy, swollen eyes and then glanced up at Theo, sadness clouding his features.

"What is it?"

"Have I lost you for good?"

"I told you I'm not going anywhere and that hasn't changed," I explained gently.

"That's not what I meant. Will you ever be able to love me again, Mercury?"

My heart wrenched at the yearning in his voice, his nickname for me sounding like the sweetest torture. I wasn't sure how to respond because it wasn't a simple answer. Theo's chin quivered and he gave me a shaky smile, a bone deep ache blooming behind my ribs at the sight.

"I never stopped," I told him honestly. The relief and hope that spread across his face almost made my knees buckle. "But..."

His face fell and his skin paled, but he didn't say anything.

"I'm not ready for us to be together again. Not yet."

Theo's eyes snapped to mine. "Yet?"

I reached for his hand, lacing our fingers together. His chest wasn't moving as he held his breath, waiting for me to put him out of his misery.

"I want to trust you again. More than anything. I'm just not there yet. Please give me some time?"

"I'll give you all the time in the world, Dawson. I'm not going anywhere either. And I'm willing to take the pills and do whatever else is needed to be as healthy as I can for you."

"But you hate taking them. You were...suicidal before," I forced out. "Why on earth would you put yourself through that again? I don't want that for you. There's got to be some other way..."

Theo pressed a finger to my lips, halting my rambling. "I've told myself for months that I didn't need the pills, that I was fine and in control of myself. But it was a lie and deep down I knew that. My head is clear enough right now to see that without them, I have no control. I do horrible things like get bombed out of my mind and give myself to others when all I want is you."

I reflexively tried to pull away at the painful reminder of seeing Theo with those other guys, especially Corvin, but he only grasped my hand tighter.

"I fucking hate myself for what I've put you through, and I don't care about some crappy side effects and feeling "off" as much as I care about you. I'll do anything to prove that your heart is safe with me. Nothing could be worse than hurting you, so bring it on."

"And what if the medication brings back...those thoughts again? That's not worth it to me."

Theo raised our joined hands and sweetly kissed my knuckles, making butterflies swoop in my gut.

"It's impossible for me to feel hopeless if I have you by my side, Mercury. Your ring was my anchor, but you're the reason my heart beats. You're my reason for wanting to be strong, for wanting to fight for every breath. I have faith in that and it's worth the risk. *We're* worth it."

I smiled at the conviction in his voice, choosing to trust that he knew what he wanted. I squeezed his hand before releasing him. There was so much I still wanted to know and ask, but he'd given me enough for tonight.

He walked me downstairs and all the way out to his back patio, but once I crossed the threshold, I wasn't able to leave. We stood there with our gazes locked, that ever-present electricity sparking between us.

"Thank you for everything you shared with me. I know that wasn't easy for you."

“I should have told you a long time ago,” he said regretfully. “I don’t think I ever gave you a real apology for how I left you and for...really any of the shitty things I did that hurt you.”

“No, you didn’t,” I reluctantly admitted. Those crystal orbs pierced right into me, misty with remorse.

“I am truly sorry for everything, Dawson. I never wanted to cause you pain and I will do whatever it takes to make it up to you. Even if you’ll only have me as your best friend, I won’t ever quit trying to make you happy. I hope you can forgive me one day.”

I leaned forward and brushed my lips across his cheek in a soft kiss. His sharp intake of breath made my lips quirk up.

“I already have.”

I turned and headed back home, a lightness in my step. Learning the biggest piece of the puzzle released a huge weight off my shoulders. That tiny spark of hope flared bright and hot, disintegrating any trace of doubt that we’d find a way through this.

I only wondered if I could be brave enough to let him love me again.

MERCURY

Were you planning on coming over anytime soon or are you just leaving us in suspense?

ME

Aww, missing me already, Mercury?

MERCURY

I'm only missing those sour Skittles you promised to bring.

ME

Ouch! Is that all I'm good for?

MERCURY

Well, it certainly isn't punctuality.

ME

Gasp When did you turn so cold, Hayes?...

DANI

Stop flirting and get over here. Let's get this marathon on the road!

I smirked down at the group text we had resurrected several days ago. Just like old times, we were having a *Fast and Furious* marathon tonight since Dawson had to return to UT in two days for practice. Dani and I still had a few weeks before we had to go back, but the thought of being here without Dawson depressed me.

The last two weeks had been better than anything I could have wished for since coming home. I'd spent every day with Dawson playing video games, swimming, watching movies, and doing pretty much anything we could think of. It was the first taste of the old Theo I'd had in years and I was starved for more.

The only thing we hadn't done again was set foot in Neverland. I'd hinted at taking our sleeping bags and spending a night out there like we had done a hundred times before, but Dawson was hesitant. I had a feeling he wouldn't return there until he could trust me again.

I could wait. I had nothing but time and love to give him, so I'd wait as long as he needed.

Stuffing the two packs of sour Skittles in my pockets and grabbing my phone, I traipsed down the stairs with an eager buzz thrumming in my veins. I logically knew my medication hadn't had time to kick in yet, but it already felt like I had turned a corner. My thoughts weren't racing, I wasn't constantly on edge, and I felt grounded in a way I hadn't for months. It was as though all I had needed was a new focus, a new purpose.

Or rather a return to what my purpose was supposed to be all along: loving Dawson.

The sound of arguing reached me as I neared the open back patio door. They were so wrapped up in their squabbling, I slipped into the kitchen unnoticed.

"Holy crap, Dani. You drowned the whole tub of popcorn in butter!"

"Uh, yeah? I'm doing us a favor. Without butter, we might as well be eating cardboard."

"Well, *you* might as well inject the fat straight into our asses. I swear to God, your eating habits are worse than a toddler's."

"Not true! I had a salad just yesterday."

"That you doused in dressing and croutons!"

"Yeah, because I don't hate myself. And don't go throwing stones when you regularly eat your weight in sour skittles."

"That's totally different...it's self-care. Plus, I'm an athlete so I can work it all off. You won't be young forever and that crap will catch up with you."

"Go preach to someone else, Dr. Oz. And I get plenty of exercise, thank you."

"You do know running your mouth doesn't count, right?"

"Oh, I do cardio alright, just with a workout buddy. Horizontally. In bed."

I joined in Dani's cackling as Dawson's face contorted in disgust and horror. "You walked right into that one, Mercury."

I made my way over to lean back on the counter, my legs crossing at the ankles. Dawson swept his gaze over my sweatpants and white tank, and the look he leveled at me heated my blood. I'd done my best to be a complete gentleman while hanging out, but I was only human. I'd caught those gorgeous eyes of his trailing over my body more than once the last few days, stripping me of my restraint layer by layer.

Luckily, their parents sauntered into the kitchen with the dog trotting behind them, killing my urge to leap over the island and suck Dawson's perfect, pouty lips off.

"Uh oh. That's Dani's evil laugh. What did she do now?" Mr. Hayes asked sardonically.

Dani scoffed indignantly. "Why do you always assume I did something?"

"Years of experience has taught us that you're usually the culprit, honey," Mrs. Hayes teased.

"Only because Captain America here is a rule-following kiss-ass."

"Don't pout because I'm the favorite," Dawson snickered. Dani lobbed a handful of popcorn at him, laughing when one piece pegged him in the eye.

"I doubt he'd be the favorite if your parents knew where that scratch on their new Mercedes came from when we were—"

I was cut off by a volley of popcorn pelting me in the face.

"You Judas!" Dawson shouted, grabbing another fistful and throwing it my direction. I howled with laughter at his panicked outrage, catching some of the over-buttered projectiles in my mouth.

"Hey! Not in my clean kitchen, you heathens!"

"Relax, Emilia. That's what the canine vacuum is for," Mr. Hayes soothed his wife, gesturing towards Penny who was happily scooping up the shrapnel of our mini-food fight.

Being around Dawson's parents after everything was strange, but also comfortingly familiar. His mom welcomed me back with open arms and a ton of food. Making me fat was her love language. What worried me was how silent our fathers had been about Dawson and I spending time together. No warnings, no words of advice. Nothing. Somehow that put me on edge more than anything. I was stuck waiting for the proverbial shoe to drop.

It'll probably be a fucking steel-toed boot drop, knowing my luck.

"Don't worry. I'll try my best to keep them in line tonight, Mama Em." I shot her my most charming smile while Dawson and Dani booed in the background.

"And that's why you're my favorite," she said, smooshing my cheeks together.

"Don't you two have a date night to get to?"

"Yes and our show starts at five so we need to get going. Don't forget to lock up after you let Penny out tonight," Mr. Hayes reminded us as he herded his wife towards the door. "And double-check Stella's pen too. I swear, that damn goat could escape from Alcatraz."

"Remember to call us if you need anything! Our hotel is downtown so we're not far!" They disappeared through the door, only for their dad to pop his head back in quickly.

"But only call in an emergency or you're all disowned."

"Alright, I'm gonna go set up the movie in the theater room," Dani said. "You guys know we're never gonna get through all of them at this rate, right?"

"It's cool. We always skip two and three anyway," I explained to her.

"Why would you do that?"

"Well, two is boring and doesn't have Vin Diesel, and we all pretend three doesn't exist. If we make it through number eight, I call that a win."

"I second that," Dawson agreed. "Why don't you grab the popcorn and the chips. We'll bring the drinks."

Dani's eyes bounced between us and rolled her lips. "Okay. Just don't take too long. Or at least keep it down..."

"Oh fuck off and go start the movie." Dawson flushed and I laughed at his obvious discomfort. Once her footsteps receded, I sauntered over to him, loving the way his pupils dilated and his breathing quickened the closer I got.

"She's not wrong. You were always pretty loud during...you know."

Dawson gulped audibly, tensing slightly as I leaned into him. I reached into my pocket for the Skittles, dangling the bags in front of his face enticingly. His lips twitched as I rattled them obnoxiously, finally swiping them out of my hand.

"You know, those used to be worth a song or two."

Dawson's brow quirked up. "Maybe my prices have gone up."

"Maybe I'm willing to negotiate," I rumbled.

His lips parted on a shallow breath and my gaze darted to his tempting mouth. When his tongue swiped out, my dick jerked in response. I sensed his nerves though and reminded myself he asked for time, so I pulled back.

I went to the fridge, grabbing several cans of soda and turning just in time to catch Dawson's gaze dart away from my ass. My smirk told him he'd been caught and he quickly snatched a couple of the cans from my arms, heading downstairs. I took a steadying breath, willing my erection to go down before I followed him.

And if I snuck a peek or two at Dawson's ass as I did, that was nobody's business but mine.

"Oh come on, why did you hit mute?" I griped. I was sprawled out on one end of the large U-shaped couch with Dani curled up in one of the corners and Dawson in between us.

"Because this scene always makes me cry and I can't listen to that song anymore," Dani whined.

"Why not?"

"Dawson was obsessed with it when this movie came out and played it on his piano for *months*. Even Charlie Puth himself would be sick of it after that."

"Christ, you're so dramatic. I didn't play it that much and it's been years. Get over it already."

"Yeah, you did and I still have the migraine to prove it. Also don't forget all the weeks your mopey butt spent playing it after Theo moved."

Dawson went rigid next to me, but I caught the nervous sidelong glance he shot me in the glow of the giant screen. A weird rush of emotion hit me. I thought about the lyrics and what Dawson would have been trying to say through the music. Was it meant to mourn me and my absence, or had he believed and perhaps even hoped that he'd see me again?

"Do you have any filter for that mouth?" Dawson grumbled, sinking lower in the cushions.

"Oh, was it supposed to be a secret that you missed your boyfriend? Because spoiler alert, it wasn't much of a secret," Dani whispered sarcastically.

"Neither was the time you snuck the captain of the basketball team in your room when you were sixteen, but maybe I should finally let your mom in on that secret too," I stage-whispered back.

"What the fuck? You knew about that?" she squeaked loudly. Dawson barked out a laugh and I winked at him playfully, enjoying the spread of pink on his cheeks that told me he'd caught it.

"Whatever. It's like two thirty in the morning. I'm out. You guys have fun," Dani yawned, dragging herself off the sofa. We said our goodnights and Dawson spooled up *Fate of the Furious*.

My attention was spotty at best after that. Being alone with him was a test of my willpower. His laughter, his smell, and even the way his throat bobbed while he drank hypnotized me. I loved that he was still the same Dawson, but also subtly different. His scent was more masculine, his jaw shadowed with faint stubble, and his body was carved with new muscles. I studied each little change in him I could find, seeing fragments of the boy I once knew in the man he was now.

"You're staring."

Dawson's soft words snapped me out of my daze. I probably should have been embarrassed, but I had no shame when it came to appreciating him. I rested my elbow on the back of the couch, angling myself towards him.

"I was thinking about the day this movie released in theaters. You remember?"

Dawson's face split into a grin and my heart seized in my chest. After hearing that the theater was doing an all day screening for the movie series, we'd convinced a bunch of our friends to skip with us to go see it. We'd of course gotten caught and grounded for two weeks, but it had been totally worth it.

"Oh my god, I forgot about that. And we tried to shove like, fourteen people in two cars because only two of our friends were old enough to drive."

"Right," I chuckled. "And then I sat on your lap and you complained the whole way there."

"Because your bony ass was digging into my thighs."

I smacked Dawson square in the face with one of the throw pillows. I cracked up at the shock on his face, but gave him a clear opening to nail me right on the nose in payback. We grappled for the pillow, yanking it back and forth, but I only ended up pulling Dawson closer.

His eyes were bright with laughter and the air crackled between us. I relinquished my hold on the pillow and we slouched back, still huffing out breathless laughs. I felt the brush of Dawson's pinky against my own.

"You know what I remember most about that day?" I murmured.

Instead of answering, Dawson stretched out a finger, drawing slow circles on the back of my hand. My skin tingled from the contact and I soaked in the tiny, intimate gesture. He used to do it all the time when we were younger to ground me when I was anxious or upset. The fact he remembered made my throat tighten.

"I remember being so jealous I could barely breathe. McKenna had been flirting with you for weeks and when she sat next to you, I was so pissed. I watched you all day for any sign that you liked her back, terrified that you'd hold her hand or put your arm around her when the lights went out. Especially when I would have given anything for you to hold my hand in that theater instead."

"You never told me that," Dawson whispered roughly. I smiled weakly, stroking my little finger against his lightly.

"I'd been hiding how I felt about you for almost two years at that point. If I had let on that I was jealous, you would've figured it out. But then a couple months later we got together and it didn't matter anymore."

"I never liked her like that. I never liked anyone else before you."

His voice was low and smooth, like honey poured in my ears. His eyes were molten, heating me from the inside out. My heartbeat thudded a heavy, uneven rhythm I could feel everywhere. Dawson's pinky ensnared mine and I almost fell to pieces at his feet.

"It's always been you."

He'd barely gotten the words out before my lips were on him, devouring him in a slow, desperate kiss. His tongue tentatively slid against mine and a low growl vibrated in my chest. I cupped his jaw, deepening the kiss, chasing his sweet taste that I'd craved for years.

I worried he'd push me away, but Dawson's fingers tangled in my shirt and he pulled me closer. The kiss grew hungry, leaving me lightheaded as all my blood rushed south to my cock. Dawson leaned back and tugged me down to cover him. Our dicks rubbed together through our sweatpants and I groaned as pleasure shot down my spine. Dawson moaned into my mouth and I swallowed it down greedily, wanting to coax every delicious sound from him I could.

"Fuck Mercury, I missed this...missed you," I panted, our steady rocking driving me closer to the edge. He let out a pained whimper, rutting against me frantically. He clawed at my back as we chased our releases, trading gasping breaths between us.

"Oh god, Theo," Dawson cried, his voice wrecked with lust. His head dropped back, eyes clenched shut as I quickened my thrusts.

"That's it, baby...shit, I'm close."

Dawson's body tightened and his eyes shot open. Panic replaced pleasure as he scrambled to push me off him.

"No no, wait. Stop," he begged.

Immediately I pulled back, even though my dick throbbed with my impending orgasm. My stomach cramped painfully at being denied release, but I ignored it, focusing on the shaken look on Dawson's face.

"What's wrong? Did I hurt you?" I asked in a rush.

Dawson scooted back into the corner, putting as much distance between us as he could manage. It hurt like hell after what we'd just done and I cursed myself for pushing him too far, too fast. He shook his head as he caught his breath, pushing his sweaty hair back with shaking hands.

"You didn't hurt me," he replied unsteadily. "I, um, I'm just not ready."

"I'm so sorry, I thought you wanted it..."

"I did—do want it. What you said...nevermind."

"No, wait. What did I say?"

Dawson looked uncomfortable, avoiding my gaze. He chewed the inside of his cheek as though debating whether to tell me or not.

"The last thing you said...it was the same thing I overheard the night I found you and Corvin together."

Guilt rushed to the surface and a chill swept through me. A queasy feeling settled low in my gut, but I knew it wasn't a fraction as bad as Dawson must have felt. Even thinking of anyone else touching him made me physically ill, and he'd witnessed my shameful moment firsthand.

"I know nothing I say will make it any better or make you hurt less, but I can't even begin to explain how fucking sorry I am for that night," I rasped. "God, how can you not hate me for everything I did?"

"Would you hate me if the roles were reversed? If I'd been the one to sleep with someone else in those circumstances?"

"Never," I answered instantly. I didn't even have to think about it. It was an innate truth, as real as the blood in my veins.

"Then you understand how I feel. I don't hate you, regardless of what I said when I was angry."

"Do you want me to go?"

"No, no I don't want that. I'm just struggling with the memories of it and...what it means for us, I guess."

My stomach knotted harshly. "What do you want to know? I'll tell you whatever you need."

"I want to know why." His voice cracked, cutting me with the broken sound.

"I get this might sound like an excuse, but you have to understand something. When I'm manic, I become...self-destructive, I guess. I get these impulses that are hard to ignore. And with the drugs I took, I was a walking disaster."

"So you're saying you just couldn't help yourself? You got the impulse to screw someone and you couldn't stop no matter what?"

I exhaled heavily, fighting not to let that sinister voice back in that whispered I would ruin everything. Dawson was giving me a chance to earn his trust back. I'd be damned if I messed that up.

"No, not exactly. When I have a manic episode and things get really bad, sometimes I feel...well, horny, but it's more than that. It can be intense and I don't always think through the consequences of things like I normally would. I don't necessarily lose all control, but my inhibitions are way down, kind of like being drunk. It doesn't happen often and what you saw that night was a...milder version of that. I had some awareness, but with the drugs..."

"Then did you realize what you were doing or not? I'm not even sure what's worse. That you had no control over your actions and it could happen again in the future, or you could have stopped it but you didn't."

Through his frustration, I could hear the fear about what this said about me. What he was worried I was capable of if we were together. I knew in my bones I would never cheat on Dawson, never even consider it, but I couldn't lie to him about this. Not even to assuage his fear.

"The only times I couldn't curb the impulse was when I was high or wasted," I said warily. "But at your party, I had started to come down a bit by that point. I honestly wasn't aware of it at first, but...eventually I realized what was happening and I chose to let it. All because I thought you were with Aly, and I was jealous and miserable."

Dawson drew in a shuttering breath, wrapping his arms around himself. He was quiet for so long that I wondered if I had finally managed to push him away, if he'd decided I wasn't worth the risk. I picked at my nails anxiously, weighing the pros and cons of getting on my knees and begging him not to give up on me yet.

"Were you unmedicated at my party?" He peered at me and I nodded solemnly. "What about the other times you couldn't control it?"

"I hadn't been taking my pills during any of those times. As much as I hate taking them, the meds definitely suppress any manic symptoms like that."

Dawson's head bobbed slowly, but he was still curled into himself and unwilling to look me in the eye. I carefully slid a few inches closer, giving him time to stop me if he wanted.

"Mercury, look at me," I ordered gently. Glossy, sad eyes met mine, tearing my heart out. "I know you're scared to trust me and that you think I won't be able to control myself, but I promise you that I will never hurt you like that again. I would never cheat on you."

"You can't promise that," he whispered brokenly.

"Yes I can. I don't want Corvin, at all. And I have no desire to get high or drunk, not when I have you. I will take every medication, go to every therapy session, do anything I need to stay strong for us. And if I ever feel like I'm slipping, I will tell you and you can help me stay grounded. We can do this together."

"Do you really believe that?"

I reached for his hand, bringing it up to rest above my heart.

"There's not much I trust about my mind, but I trust this. I've known you were meant to be mine since we were fifteen. I know I got lost along the way, but I found my way back to you. I am completely devoted to you, Dawson. This heart only beats for you."

His hand curled into my shirt, dragging me towards him. Our lips met in a soft embrace, a quiet promise that we would find a way through this. Dawson was my anchor, my safe place, and I knew in the deepest parts of me that I could weather any storm with him at my side.

He restarted the movie and we settled into the cushions next to each other. I hated the few inches he left between us, but I wanted to give him what he needed. Space, time, patience, my whole goddamn heart carved from my chest. Anything he wanted of me, it was his.

Dawson reached for my hand, his fingers sliding between mine like a key finding its lock. Eventually, I fell asleep with a smile on my face and Dawson's hand in mine in a dark theater.

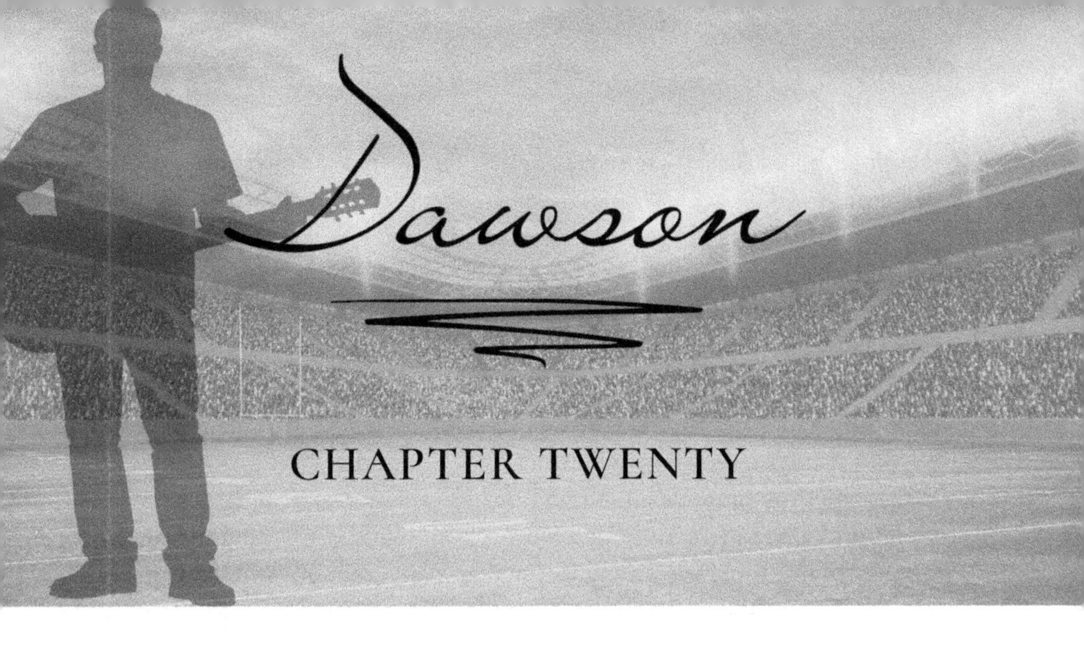

CHAPTER TWENTY

My head throbbed in the harsh, afternoon sun and sweat slid down my temples as I called out the play. The feel of the ball hitting my hands usually snapped me into action, but my focus was all over the place. I moved around the pocket, trying to find the right opening before the bubble of safety around me collapsed. A shoulder caught me in the side and I went down, hard.

I rolled onto my back, wishing like hell I could just lie there and bake into the ground. Coach's whistle blew and he shouted at a few of the offensive players before barking at me.

"Hayes! Get your ass up and run it again!"

I groaned and attempted to roll to my feet, but a hand reached into my field of vision. I grabbed it, allowing whoever it was to yank me up even though my ribs protested the movement.

"Hey man, you alright?" Corvin asked. All week I had managed to ignore him during practices. It had been awkward as hell to see him again, especially with visions of him and Theo together screwing with my sanity.

"Yeah, just got the wind knocked out of me," I rasped, coughing from the effort. My side was on fire and I could almost feel the bruise developing.

And yet that will still hurt less than being this close to the guy who had his mouth around Theo's—ugh, fuck. Now I'm gonna be sick too. Fucking delightful.

Corvin's brows zipped together and when he opened his mouth to say something, I rushed to cut him off.

"We better get back to it before Coach flips out. Thanks for the hand up."

I hobbled over to the line and got back in position. My head was already a chaotic jumble without hearing what he had to say and I needed to get my ass in gear before Coach reamed me out.

By the time practice ended an hour later, I was soaked through with sweat and a headache pounded in my skull. I kept my head down in the locker room, avoiding any attempts at conversation and taking the world's fastest shower, more than ready to head home and pass out for an hour or ten.

Of course, the universe chose that moment to give me an enthusiastic middle finger as I was leaving the practice facility.

"QB, wait up!"

I contemplated acting like I didn't hear Corvin, but my less dickish side prevailed when he caught up to me.

"What's up?" I asked as casually as I could.

"I've actually been meaning to talk to you for days, but kept chickening out. I owe you an apology for what went down at your house." He fiddled with the strap of his gym bag, shoulders hunching up around his ears. I forced myself not to bolt even though there was no topic on earth I'd rather discuss less than this.

"Don't worry about it, man."

"No, seriously," he pressed. "I'm a huge jackass. I know shit happens at parties and whatever, but I wouldn't want anyone boning in my room either. That wasn't right of me to disrespect your space like that. We've always gelled well on the team and I don't want to screw that up. I'm really sorry, Hayes."

I blinked at him, my brain shorting out. He thought I was upset that I'd caught him in my room? I mean, it wasn't *not* an issue, but that was microscopic next to the fact that I'd caught him with Theo. My fucking Theo.

Not your Theo. Not then and still not now. How's that for a nice slice of reality with a scoop of "fuck you" on top?

"Thanks, Corvin. I appreciate that. We're all good," I forced out through a tight smile.

The tension left his shoulders and his features relaxed into an easy grin. "That's good to hear. You got any plans this weekend?"

"Other than a lot of sleep and a slightly torturous ice bath, not much. You?"

"I think me and some friends are gonna hit up a few bars on Sixth Street. It's always a pretty good time. Why don't you come with us?"

As nice as his extended olive branch was meant to be, I had no desire to be in his presence longer than required. I forgave him because I didn't need the drama, but I was only human. There was still a part of me that wanted to go all *Misery* on his ankles for touching Theo.

"Thanks man, but I'm exhausted. Maybe next time?"

"For sure. Hey, this is probably weird, but do you know if Theo is back on campus yet?"

The question was a blitz attack, hitting me so abruptly I nearly tripped over my own feet. "Uh no, not yet. Why?"

"I thought I'd text him and see if he wanted to come out with us, but it's cool. I'll text him later. See you at practice tomorrow, yeah?"

I nodded in a daze as he took off in the opposite direction. Knowing Corvin had a line to Theo was a sour reminder I didn't need. I wondered if Theo would take him up on his offer. Corvin had already triggered his manic urges once before. What if it happened again? I was the one who'd said he needed time, but did that mean Theo would wait for me or would he want to explore his options? What if I was only the comfortable option? The safe choice?

My mood plummeted and my brain kicked up a maelstrom of anxiety. Nate was with his family and for some reason I didn't really want to be alone like this. I tugged my phone aggressively out of my pocket and shot off a text.

ME

Mind if I come hang out for a bit?

Within seconds, I received a reply.

BASH

Anytime, D. Micah said lunch is almost ready and get your ass over here lol.

I ordered a rideshare to their off campus apartment, making it in record time. I hurried across the foyer, but intrusive images of the last time I was there shoved in. The time we'd all stumbled across Theo walking his...overnight guest out.

Ugh, why the fuck do you do this to me, brain? Haven't I been good to you, fed you well, treated you to top-tier porn on occasion? Is this payback for that concussion?

I reached their floor and came up on their unit, but froze when grunts and gasps reached me from inside. Bash's dirty words filtered through the door and it was all I could do not to gag.

I pounded my fist on the door loudly and took great pleasure in their startled voices and frantic footsteps. Several moments passed before the door opened on Bash's flushed features and painted-on smile.

"Hey dude! We, uh, didn't think you'd get here that fast."

"Clearly," I smirked as I spotted Micah wiping off his mouth in the kitchen before coming over to greet me with a hug. I pointed to the corner of my mouth, unable to resist fucking with him. "You missed a spot...just there."

Micah's eyes sprang wide and he swiped at his lips before realizing my joke.

"You dick," he chastised without any heat. "Come on, I made pasta. It should be ready by now."

We dug into lunch, talking about upcoming classes, football, and other mindless stuff. I had hoped coming here would distract me, but my focus was split, registering only a fraction of what they were saying.

"You doing okay, D?" Bash asked, drawing my attention back.

"Sure, just tired. Six days of practice have kinda kicked my ass," I said, picking at the food on my plate.

"Sooo, how has it been going with Theo?" Micah asked tentatively. Bash muttered something under his breath to him. "What? I'm curious! I figured that might be why he's all mopey."

"I'm not mopey," I rolled my eyes. "And he's fine. We're fine."

"That gives me literally nothing," Micah complained. "Are you guys dating again yet or are you still deluding yourselves into thinking you can be 'just friends'?"

"Dupont, control your man."

"No way. He's your problem right now," Bash snickered, rubbing the back of Micah's neck and I half expected him to purr. *Yuck.*

"We just want you to be happy, Dawson."

"I am happy."

"If that's your happy face, then that's just appalling," Micah complained. "For real, what's going on?"

I blew out a heavy breath, nearly second-guessing my decision to come over. But then I remembered why I had thought to come here of all places to deal with my hang-ups about Theo.

"Uhh Bash, would you mind if I talked with Micah about something...privately?"

Bash's brows shot up and his gaze bounced between us. "Sure, no problem. I promised Mom I'd call her soon anyway, so I think I'll go do that."

He placed a kiss on Micah's forehead before closing himself up in their bedroom. Micah gave me a quizzical look, sipping at his wine as he waited for me to speak.

"You're a psych major, right?"

"Yep, clinical psychology. Why? Thinking about changing majors?"

"W-what do you know about...bipolar disorder?"

His features quickly lit with recognition, empathy and understanding bleeding through.

"I know more than the average person. It was actually part of a major project I did last year."

"Yeah, I thought I remembered Bash saying something about that. Hypothetically, what would the risks be in dating someone who is bipolar?"

Micah pursed his lips in a tiny frown. "Well, for one, it's best to say that they *have* bipolar disorder, to show that's not all they are and it doesn't define them."

I winced lightly and my stomach clenched with embarrassment, but he gave me a gentle smile.

"Honestly, the risks really wouldn't be that different in dating someone who didn't have a mental illness. It definitely has its challenges, but there's no reason you can't be a healthy, functioning couple. What risks are you worried about exactly?"

I couldn't really answer that without betraying Theo's confidence, but I also trusted Micah's discretion.

"You promise this stays between us?" I asked and Micah nodded in agreement. "I want to be with Theo. More than fucking anything. But something happened between Theo and Corvin at my party, and it really fucked with me. Now I can't shake this overwhelming fear that one day he'll get these urges again and...cheat on me."

He pinned me with a sympathetic look. "That's a completely normal and valid fear to have. I won't lie and say that it can't cause problems, but it doesn't have to. If your partner is stable, either with medication, therapy or both, then the chances of them cheating aren't any higher than for anyone else in a relationship."

Frustration lanced through me and I raked a hand through my hair.

"So what? Are you saying having a serious mental illness would have absolutely no effect on our relationship and we'd be just like everyone else?" I asked, bitter and sardonic.

"No, I'm saying that if someone were getting treatment and living a relatively healthy life *despite* their mental illness, they'd have just as good a chance as anyone else at a happy ending with the person they love."

"What if I open myself back up to him and this disease breaks him... breaks us? I can't go through this if I'm going to lose him again."

I hated this so much, hated feeling so damn conflicted and terrified. Micah's forehead creased and he drummed his fingers on the barter.

"Okay, I feel like I missed some chapters in this story. Start from the top and give it to me unplugged."

I dropped my head back with an exhausted groan, but I was too mentally drained to put up any kind of fight. I unloaded everything that happened between me and Theo from the night of my party up until I spoke with Corvin today after practice.

"Well, shit," Micah blurted once I finished talking. "I will say you're a much better person than I am because if I'd caught Bash with someone else, that room would look like a scene from *Saw*."

"Except I don't really have a right to be angry at him for it. We weren't together and he wasn't exactly in his right mind that night..."

"Let me ask you something. Did Theo reassure you that it meant nothing and that he only wants you?"

"I mean, yeah..."

"Did he ever cheat when you guys first dated or give you any reason to worry?"

"No, never."

"And he agreed to do whatever it takes to treat his disorder so this doesn't happen again?"

"He did..."

Micah rolled his lips and eyed me warily. "So correct me if I'm wrong, but it seems like that's not the crux of the problem then. What is it that's really bothering you?"

The question was a kick to the gut, forcing answers to the surface that I didn't want to face. I wasn't able to meet Micah's eyes, but I could feel him watching me. My shirt collar felt tighter and my body grew warm under his scrutiny.

"Theo is the only one I've ever felt anything for. He's been my only crush, only kiss, only...everything since we were kids. But I'm not *his* only anymore. I know that's unrealistic as fuck to think that when he moved away, he'd never be with anyone else, but he has and it hurts way fucking more than it has a right to. And no matter what I do, I can't stop this relentless voice that says I'm not enough for him anymore."

Micah's face crumpled in sympathy. I felt raw and blistered, my stupid confession burning right through me.

"I understand. Really, I do. And I can't tell you whether you're enough for Theo because only he can do that and prove it to you. It won't be easy, but no relationship is. It will take a lot of communication and trust, just like every other couple. Also everyone experiences this disorder differently, so you can't assume anything about how it will exactly affect him or your relationship."

"That doesn't make sense. Aren't the symptoms the same for everyone?"

"This isn't a cookie cutter disease. Every person has different triggers, severity levels, cycles—yada yada. The point is, don't base your decisions and fears off of a checklist of symptoms or other people's horror stories. Base them off of *Theo*. His actions, his effort, his love for you. That should be the deciding factor."

"I don't know," I sighed, exhaustion creeping up on me fast.

"If you want my advice—"

"It's cute you say that like I have a choice," I smirked weakly.

"You don't, so shut up and listen," Micah said teasingly. "If you really want to make it work with Theo, do your own research. Learn about his condition, explore ways to help him cope, try to understand him better so you can work together to help him fight this."

"That's actually solid advice..."

"You came to the right genius. I'll send you my bill."

I huffed a laugh and knocked him in the arm. Micah grabbed my hand gently, dragging my eyes back to him.

"Don't let him go again, Dawson. You and Theo have a chance at something most people would kill for. You just have to take a leap of faith. That's all any of us can do."

"Alright, I hope you guys are done because the season finale of *House of the Dragon* is tonight and I'm impatient as fuck for it." Bash proclaimed, waltzing out of his room. I thanked them both and made my excuses to leave.

Once I was home, I crashed on my bed and stared aimlessly at the ceiling. My fears hadn't magically disappeared, but they no longer felt insurmountable. Something had changed in me, shifted into place.

As Micah had said, there were always risks when it came to trusting someone with your heart. There were no guarantees in life. Theo's demons could be terrifying and unpredictable, yes, but he deserved someone who would stand by him, who would fight them at his side. Someone unafraid. Unflinching. Unbreakable.

What was I willing to risk to have him be mine again? What was Theo worth to me?

As sleep took me, Theo's bright smile filled my head, giving me the only answer I needed.

Everything.

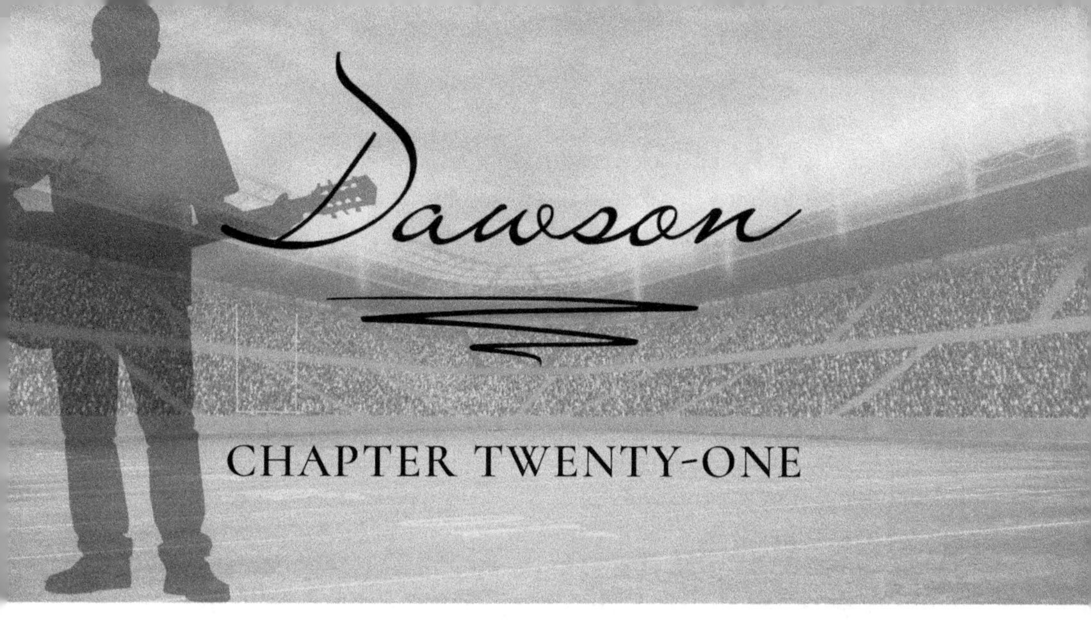

CHAPTER TWENTY-ONE

My feet tore up the ground as I sprinted down the field, blood pumping as I crossed into the end zone. I dropped the ball and leaned on my knees, breathing heavily from the exertion of the play and the heat of the afternoon sun.

Coach Walker clapped his hands, voice booming from the sidelines. "Excellent! That's how you do it! Great work, gentlemen. Hit the showers and get out of here. Have a good first day of classes tomorrow, but do not be late to practice. Be on the field at six sharp, ready to go."

I jogged over to the benches for my water bottle, chugging half of it in one go. A heavy hand clapped me on the shoulder, nearly knocking me over.

"Whoo! That was a fucking good scrimmage, yeah?" DeJuan, one of our wide receivers, beamed at me. "Fuck, if we keep playing like that, we're going all the way this year, baby!"

"You fucking know it," I laughed, his exuberance contagious. He congratulated me again as he made his way indoors, and I couldn't help but feel like a fraud. The game meant everything to some of these guys, and here I was, ready and willing to throw in the towel. Yeah, the championship would be awesome, but part of me didn't even give a shit and would quit right now if I could.

The team would probably be pissed if they knew. Who wanted to follow a captain that wouldn't even care if the ship went down? I ambled towards the locker room, lost in thought, when a loud voice pierced through my distracted haze.

"Looking good, Mercury!"

I whipped around and saw Theo leaning against the outer wall of the practice facility, a playful smirk aimed my way. My heart sped up at the sight of him with the sleeves rolled up on his t-shirt and faded jeans hugging his thighs. He tossed back his floppy blond locks and the world tilted slightly under my feet.

"What are you doing here?" I asked breathlessly, my feet carrying me over to him instinctively.

He shrugged, lips sliding into an easy grin. "I know we planned to meet up tomorrow after classes, but I got in early and thought I'd catch you after practice, see if you wanted to grab lunch."

I slammed into him, wrapping myself around him tightly. He tensed in surprise before his arms banded around my waist, squeezing me to him. I buried my nose in his neck and inhaled his cedar and citrus scent that did dangerous things to my cock.

"Well damn, what did I do to deserve this?" Theo chuckled softly.

I pulled back, slightly embarrassed that I'd thrown myself at him. Only a few weeks without him had left me unsettled and antsy, like I was terrified he'd disappear again. We texted every day, but it wasn't the same as inhabiting the same space, breathing the same air.

"Just missed you, I guess. Sorry, I probably smell disgusting," I grimaced, suddenly hyper aware of my shirt sticking to my sweaty, cooling skin.

"Nah. I always found it sexy, remember?"

My face heated at the burning gaze he swept over my body. A shiver rippled through me and the pressure in my athletic cup was hella uncomfortable now.

"R-right," I swallowed roughly. "Well, I'm gonna go shower real fast. Are you good to wait for me?"

"As long as it takes," he rumbled, an intense gleam in his eye. His double meaning wasn't lost on me and I fought against the grin trying to overtake my face as I darted inside.

I rushed through my shower comically fast. I couldn't seem to wipe the smile off my face knowing Theo was outside waiting for me, that he'd come to surprise me. It brought back memories of happier times, of him waiting outside my classes or by my truck after practices in high school. Maybe we could be happy like that again.

I gathered my things and got dressed, mostly tuning out the dying buzz of the locker room as the guys started filtering out. I wanted to race out the door, but was thwarted as I crossed in front of Coach's open office.

"Hayes, come here for a second."

I bit back the annoyed grunt as I stepped into the room, and Coach motioned me forward. His dark eyes settled on me and I struggled not to squirm under his appraising look.

"How are you feeling about this season?"

"Good, sir."

Coach let out a low, vibrating laugh. "A man of few words, just like your grandpa. You remind me of him. Quiet, determined, a strong leader. I learned a hell of a lot playing under him back in the day. It makes me proud to watch you follow in his and your dad's footsteps."

There was a sharp pang in my chest at his comparison. Growing up, those words would have meant the world to me, but now? They were a cruel taunt that I was only going to let them down, disappoint them and the legacy they left for me.

"You've been looking good out there, Hayes. It's exactly what I want to see from you this year. You keep this up and you'll have NFL scouts from here to Washington after you. I guaran-damn-tee it."

Something sour coiled in my gut at his praise, but I forced a smile. "Thank you, Coach."

I bolted out of his office. I wanted to tell him that I had no plans to enter the draft, that hanging any NFL hopes on me was pointless. I didn't think I could put it off for the rest of the season, but here we were, three weeks into practice and I'd pussied out every time.

All I wanted was to get to Theo. Since talking with Micah, it was like my need for Theo had been unleashed. I craved his scent, itched to feel his skin on mine, wanted to wrap myself in his warmth like I used to after a bad day.

I lengthened my strides and barreled out the doors, Theo's head swinging my direction. He broke out in a wide grin and my heart punched out a faulty rhythm at the sight.

"About damn time. I was beginning to think you'd stood me up. So am I worthy enough to score a lunch date with the hot quarterback?"

His teasing smirk set off a cascade of sparks throughout my body. An ache settled low in my stomach, a deep hunger that had nothing to do with food.

"Depends. Can we hang out at your place and order in?"

He waggled his eyebrows ridiculously and a smile stretched my lips. "That's why God invented DoorDash. Your wish is my command."

I WASN'T CLAUSTROPHOBIC by any means, but I had never struggled with enclosed spaces more in my life than I had in the last fifteen minutes. The car ride to Theo's apartment was torturous with his tempting smell permeating every molecule of air around us until I was damn near dizzy with it. I had to twist my fingers together at one point just so I wouldn't lunge at him across the console.

Then the elevator. Holy Dante's inferno, the elevator. Theo was so close, his body heat stoked a flame in my lower belly that was getting impossible to ignore and his scent was amplified in the tiny box. The surrounding mirrors made it almost impossible to hide my roving gaze, but Theo seemed blissfully unaware of my suffering. Unaware and unaffected. With his hands in his pockets and head nodding along to the elevator music, he was the picture of serenity.

I was clinging to my sanity by the time Theo opened his door and led us inside. I trailed him to the kitchen as I took in the space. It was a mirror image of Bash and Micah's unit, but without their lived-in feel. The apartment looked like a model, clean and cold. Nothing like I imagined Theo's place to be. I hated it immediately. It wasn't lost on me that my reaction had more to do with how I used to picture any place of Theo's actually being *ours*.

"Alright, so what do you want to eat? There's this great burger place down the street, or—oh! We could do pizza, if you're digging that. I also wouldn't say no to sushi, but you might not want raw fish after practicing in a hundred degree weather. Feels like a misstep," Theo snickered, tossing a glance over his shoulder. "Hey, you okay?"

"Yep, I'm good," I choked out. "Uh, how 'bout burgers?"

Theo cast me a suspicious glance, but thankfully dropped it long enough to order. We settled on the couch while we waited for the food, talking about the last few weeks we'd spent apart.

“How are you doing with the medication?” I asked warily. Theo’s brows pinched slightly and he pursed his lips in thought.

“It’s weird, but...okay, I think? It was hell on my body for the first couple of weeks, but I’ve actually smoothed out faster than the other times, which is good.”

I hesitated, not wanting to wreck a good evening so far, but I had to know. “And you haven’t had...umm, any *bad* thoughts, have you?”

“No, I haven’t,” he smiled softly. “I know it probably won’t always be like this, but I feel good right now. Really good. I don’t feel like I’m fighting through quicksand like before. I feel like myself again.”

“Really? You’re not just saying that?”

Theo gripped my hand resting between us, electric pulses zipping up my arm at the contact.

“I promise that if or when things change and I start feeling off again, I will tell you. I won’t hide that side of me from you ever again.”

His intense stare pierced through me, making my brain glitch as I got lost in his liquid blues. I was faintly aware that Theo was still holding my hand, his thumb smoothing over my pulse point that was beating erratically from his proximity.

Theo’s phone chimed with an alert, breaking whatever spell I was caught in. He stood and went to grab the food that’d been delivered. All I could do was sit there and convert oxygen into carbon dioxide, fighting to find even two functioning brain cells that would keep me from jumping his bones.

We queued up some action movie as we ate that I could barely focus on. Just like the weekend of our movie marathon, my attention caught on every tiny movement and sound that Theo made, but without the cover of a darkened room.

His damned scent wafted over to me every few seconds and I got the urge to rub against him until I was marked with his smell. He seemed infuriatingly unaffected by me again, just watching the movie, chill as could be. I let out a slow, deep breath, trying to get control of myself before I did something immensely stupid.

Like beg him to fuck me over the back of the couch. Or on the floor. Or on the kitchen counter. You know, for old times sake.

“You’re staring,” he murmured, mimicking my words from that night.

“Sorry,” I rushed out as heat flooded my face.

One of his brows quirked up and he smirked at me, siphoning the air from my lungs. Fuck, he was gorgeous. He had only seemed to grow more attractive in the years he'd been gone, more devastating to my senses. I idly wondered what he'd look like in twenty years, or thirty. Would I even be around to find out?

Theo's phone vibrated with a text on the table in front of us. His brows furrowed as he unlocked it, his fingers flying across the screen to type out a response.

"What's that about?" My mouth formed the words before my brain caught up and I winced internally. "Wait, never mind. That's not my business. I'm sorry."

"Dawson, it's okay. I don't mind telling you."

"No, it's not. That's...I have no right being nosy like that."

"I don't see it like that and I'm not going to keep secrets anymore," he said firmly. "It was Corvin."

Icy dread slid down my spine and I did my best to smooth out my features. "Oh? What did he want?"

"He asked me to go out with him and some friends tonight."

I wonder how much it would cost Dad to bail me out after I break Corvin's spine during practice tomorrow?

The burger I ate suddenly felt heavy and sour in my stomach. I couldn't place Theo's tone and how he felt about Corvin's invitation. My chest thudded uncomfortably and I dug my nails into my palms, the small bite of pain doing nothing to ground me.

"Gotcha. Well, that's, um...that's cool. He's, you know, a good guy and you'll have fun together."

"Do you really mean that?"

"Sure. Why not?"

Theo didn't answer and a cold sweat broke out on the back of my neck. My gaze was riveted to the TV, praying I looked calm on the outside while a fucking hurricane tore through my chest. Theo leaned back and draped an arm on the couch behind my shoulders. I barely held back from launching myself to the other side of the room, so I didn't sink into him and let him hold me while I fell to pieces inside.

"Hmm...it's a shame you mean that because I told him no."

I whipped my head toward him so fast my neck popped painfully. "You what?"

"I told him no."

"Why?"

Theo glanced at me, every line of his faces calm and sincere.

"He's not you."

"But you gave him your number. You hooked up with him, so you clearly liked him, and—"

"Dawson, I told you. None of that meant anything to me. I have no interest in him like that. And I only gave him my number because he asked if we could be friends and get coffee sometime. He's a nice guy. I don't...have a lot of friends anymore. Well, none really except for you and Dani."

His careful admission made my heart hurt for him. I didn't want to comfort him with platitudes and say it wasn't true when he clearly felt otherwise.

"Why do you say that?"

Theo fell silent, picking at the remains of his food while a dozen emotions ran across his face. I itched to reach out and comfort him, so I smoothed my hand over his thigh, squeezing it gently. His chin dropped as he looked at my hand, timidly grasping it and lacing our fingers together.

"I had some pretty good friends at Sam Houston State while I was there. But there were periods where I was on and off my pills, so I was in and out of cycles for a couple years. They knew something was up, just didn't know what. I finally got the guts to tell them I was bipolar when I got sick of them saying I was acting *crazy* all the time."

His disgust at the word was easy to hear. His reaction to me calling him crazy that night in my bedroom made perfect sense now, and I felt like shit for it.

"You're not crazy," I told him firmly.

"They seemed to think so. Everything changed once I told them."

"How so?"

"I became the disease," he croaked. "It was like Theo disappeared and all they saw was my disorder. They blamed it for anything I did. If I laughed too much, I had to be manic. If I was quieter than usual, I was depressed. They became scared of me, of what I'd do if they said the wrong thing or if I had a bad day. To them, I was a tornado without a warning siren. Eventually, they decided I wasn't worth the trouble and ghosted me. The irony of it all was that I didn't become truly unstable until I didn't have them around anymore. I started spiraling out of control and it got me sent back here."

My body moved without conscious thought, straddling him in one smooth movement. Theo's eyes bugged out even as his hands gripped at my hips. I cupped one cheek, tracing his jaw gently with my thumb. Theo's eyes slid closed and he leaned into my palm, flooding my chest with warmth.

"They didn't deserve you, Theo. You are one of the kindest, funniest, most captivating people I've ever met. You have a way of making everyone feel important, like they matter. Life is just better with you around and if they couldn't see that, then they didn't fucking deserve you."

Tears rimmed his lashes and he blinked them away, huffing a dismissive laugh. "Nah, I'm nothing special. I'm a fuck-up, Dawson. I'm good for a few laughs maybe, but I'm still just a fuck-up."

The self-effacing comment cut through me like a blade, completely unlike the Theo I had known for half my life.

"You are *not* a fuck-up," I ground out. "This isn't you. The boy I fell for was so confident and full of life that he fucking glowed with it. Don't let this disease or those assholes dim any part of you."

His expression shuttered, defeat washing over his features.

"I'm not the boy you fell in love with, Dawson. I'm damaged. A ticking time bomb. I'm not the same person I was back then..."

My heart beat a loud confession in my chest, echoing out so strong I was sure he could hear it.

"It doesn't matter who you came back as. I only needed you to come back to me. I will love each and every version of you I can get, for as many lifetimes as I can get."

He inhaled sharply, searching my face for any hint of uncertainty. He wouldn't find any. I knew what I wanted, fears be damned.

"I need you back, Theo," I whispered, hovering right above his parted lips. "I'm willing to try, no matter what."

"What changed your mind?"

"Some good advice," I murmured. "We've both been cowards and it's already cost us so much time. I don't want to let fear take anything else away from us."

"Are you sure?"

I nodded slowly, skimming my nose lightly over his and his lids fluttered shut at the touch. His fingertips dug into my hips, shaking hard enough to vibrate into my skin. The air shifted, charged particles sparking and zapping between us, drawing us together.

"Please…"

His tremulous plea wrapped around me, my restraint hanging by a thread. "Please what?"

Theo whined low in his throat, chasing my mouth as I continued to tease my lips against his, never quite touching.

"Kiss me. Remind me who I belong to."

My lips slammed down on his, devouring his needy groan that shot straight to my dick. I swept my tongue inside and the first taste of him made me ravenous for more. I rose up on my knees, tilting his head back and taking complete control. This hadn't been our usual dynamic. I loved being at his mercy, but now he was at mine, mewling and clawing at my back as we ravaged each other.

"You belong to me, baby," I growled into the kiss, grinding down on his erection. He moaned long and rough, thrusting up against my ass, desperate for friction. "Say it. Say you're mine."

"I'm yours. *Ffuck,* only yours…"

I tugged his hair hard enough to tilt his head back, staring into his eyes, his pupils nearly eclipsing the blue. I was shaking with a need that only he could satisfy. I needed something more. I needed to hear him say it.

"Tell me I'm beautiful…"

His eyes widened a fraction, something fierce and reverent in his gaze. Something I had missed beyond all measure.

"You are so goddamn beautiful, Dawson. I can barely fucking breathe around you…"

I shivered at his hoarse, sweet voice, molten honey pouring in my ears. His praise lit me up inside like liquid fire running through my veins. I moved a little faster, heat blazing a trail up my spine as I rode him. We moved together seamlessly, a rhythm we knew by heart.

"I'm so close," I gasped, rocking faster, harder, driving us past the point of no return.

"You gonna come for me, Mercury? Come on, baby. Show me how badly you want it and soak yourself with your cum like the perfect boy you are."

The rough command pushed me over the edge, my release

exploding out of me. Hot spurts flooded my boxers and I bit down on Theo's shoulder to muffle my shout. He groaned loudly as he tensed underneath me.

"Oh, *fuck fuck fuck*...I'm coming."

Theo tossed his head back, his body convulsing from the strength of his orgasm. I drank in the sight, memories swirling. Theo was breathtaking when he came apart for me.

He panted heavily, holding me close as we came down from our mutual highs. His lips brushed my sweaty temple in a sweet kiss and the gesture crumbled the last brick of the wall between us.

"Don't hurt me, Theo," I begged in a wrecked whisper. "Don't break me again."

"Never," he swore fervently. "I swear to you, I will never break us again. I'm all in. This time, we'll be stronger together, Mercury. We'll be fucking bulletproof."

CHAPTER TWENTY-TWO

I reread the paragraph for the sixth time, no closer to understanding it than I had been ten minutes ago.

Fuck my sadistic Sociology professor for giving homework the first week of classes. I hope his coffee is never the right temperature and his khakis fucking wrinkle.

I slammed the book closed with a huff, trudging into my kitchen. I opened the fridge and stared at the contents longingly. I was starving after waiting the last two hours for Dawson's Friday evening practice to end so we could eat together.

Since last weekend when he'd come over and agreed to give me another chance, we'd been inseparable outside of classes and his practices. We reconnected effortlessly as though no time had passed, two halves becoming whole again. We fell into an easy routine of texting all day, having dinner at my place, watching TV, and just enjoying each other's presence.

We also made out like a couple of horny teenagers every day, but we hadn't made each other come since the last time on the couch. It was like we had a tacit agreement not to rush things, to wait until it felt right again. It was strange since we knew each other's bodies better than our own, but four years was a long time. In a lot of ways we were relearning one another, discovering new things that had grown in the other's absence.

But each day we were growing more impatient, more eager, that unquenchable desire that had always been there bubbling just below the surface. Dawson's need radiated from him and I wanted nothing more than to spend hours worshipping his body like it was our first time. All he had to do was say the word.

I would be as patient as I needed for him to be ready though. I considered myself on probationary status with him, so his comfort was all that mattered. All might have been forgiven, but it wasn't forgotten and I had to prove to Dawson that his heart was safe with me this time around.

I wanted to sweep him off his feet again, to show him that my world started and ended with him. I used to love doing the most romantic shit I could come up with when Dawson and I were dating in high school. I took great pride in the deep blush that would steal over his skin, darkening those beautiful, pale freckles that I'd catalogued with my tongue over and over.

A loud knock startled me out of the memories and I almost tripped over my feet racing to the door. I threw it open to Dawson's bright, wide smile and my pulse sped up dangerously. I fisted his shirt, hauling him inside and shutting the door before pinning him against it.

I grabbed his face and kissed him fiercely, his lips parting on a gasp and giving me easy access to his addictive mouth. Dawson sucked on my tongue like a fiend, tearing a deep groan from my throat as he feverishly kissed me back. Goddamn, I missed him so much. How the hell did I function without him for so long?

I snuck my fingers under the hem of his shirt to rip it off, needing to feel his skin on mine, but he swatted me away.

"Is this you playing hard to get or something?" I pouted as he pulled away, chuckling at my pitiful expression.

"No, we just don't have time for that. We've got somewhere to be."

"I hope you mean my bedroom..."

"More like game night with my friends at Bash and Micah's place," he explained, sidling around me to drop his gym bag by the couch.

"That'sss...one option, sure. Or we could tell them I had a medical emergency and just stay here. Naked. In my bed."

"And what emergency would that be?"

"Acute ejaculatory deprivation."

Dawson barked out a laugh. "Is that medical lingo for orgasm denial?"

"Who the fuck knows? I made it up," I muttered, snatching him around the waist on his way to the door. I licked a path up his neck, my breath ghosting over his ear and eliciting a violent tremble from his muscled frame. "I missed you. You have no idea how much I thought about you today."

"Oh y-yeah?" he breathed shakily. "What did you think about?"

"I thought about tearing off your clothes and spending an hour mapping your body with my tongue. About making you come apart and marking every inch of your skin with my fingerprints. About drinking you down and seeing if you're just as sweet as I remember."

"Oh, fuck," he gasped as I nipped his earlobe, sucking on it hard enough to pull a helpless whimper from him. He melted into me, his hips thrusting into me lightly. I went in for the kill.

"Doesn't my beautiful boy want to shoot down my throat? You're so fucking pretty when you come for me, Mercury."

A ragged moan vibrated from Dawson's chest. He attacked my lips, frenzied and greedy, his fingers tangling in my hair to pull me closer. His back hit the wall and I pressed against him, my erection dragging along his slowly, both of us groaning at the feeling.

"What do you need? Tell me and it's yours," I said between swipes of our tongues.

"Suck me," he pleaded roughly. "I need your mouth, Theo."

My fucking pleasure.

My knees hit the ground so fast, the impact rattled my bones. I jerked his joggers and boxer briefs down in one swoop, freeing his rigid length quickly.

Fuck me, Dawson had a gorgeous cock. He was just above average length, but thick and smooth, with a dark blue vein running underneath that made him leak like a faucet with the right stimulation. His swollen pink head peeked out from his foreskin and saliva flooded my mouth as memories of how it felt on my tongue made my own dick harden to the point of pain.

"Sweet hell, you have such a perfect dick, baby," I purred, lapping up a pearly drop of precum. His taste exploded on my tastebuds and I growled appreciatively. "God, you taste even better than I remember."

I ran my hand slowly up his shaft, coaxing out another pump of his flavor. I slipped my tongue into his foreskin, circling the velvet head and Dawson hissed in pleasure, pulling on my hair hard enough to unhinge me. Fuck it, I couldn't wait any longer. I swallowed him down, taking him to the back of my throat until I gagged.

"*Holyfuckingshit,*" Dawson cursed, curling over my shoulders as his legs quaked.

I slurped up and down his cock noisily, relishing in the helpless grunts and whimpers he couldn't contain. I only made a few passes before he let out a sharp cry as his balls drew up close to his body and his grip on my hair tightened.

"Shit shit shit...I c-can't—baby, I can't stop it. Oh my fuck, I'm gonna come. I'm...oh god!"

Hot, thick ropes spurted down my throat, and I swallowed it down like a man dying of thirst. I milked him for every drop, his hoarse cries driving me out of my mind. His head thudded back against the wall as his soft cock slipped from my mouth. I sat back on my heels, looking up at his gorgeous, sated face, but he refused to make eye contact.

"Dawson, what's wrong? Are you alright?"

His face was red with more than just a post-orgasm flush, and my stomach fluttered anxiously, my own release forgotten. I stood up fast and cupped his cheek, forcing him to turn back to me.

"Was it not good? Did I push you too fast?"

"No! No, it was amazing and I wanted it, I promise," he rushed out, but he looked anxious, a vulnerability in his eyes that I wanted to soothe away. "It's just...I know it was really fast, and I..."

"That's okay, it happens to everyone. You don't ever have to be embarrassed about that, babe." I stroked my thumb against his warm cheek, loving how he leaned into my touch.

"I know. It's just been a long time," he mumbled, a weird inflection in his tone that gave me pause.

"How long has it been exactly?"

He blew out a sharp breath. "Since our last time together..."

"Well duh, but I meant before we dry humped each other's brains out last weekend," I chuckled, but Dawson wasn't laughing.

"No. I mean our *last* time together."

The words clanked around my head, refusing to make sense. There was no way I was understanding him right, but dear God, I wanted it to be true.

"You really haven't been with anyone else since I left?"

Dawson shook his head stiffly, but his eyes stayed pinned to mine, embarrassment giving way to something softer.

"I don't feel things like that for other people," he explained, his brows furrowing. "Not before you and definitely not after. I tried to look at others and feel...something, but it never happened."

I drew his face to mine, my lips ghosting over his and inhaling his shaky breath like a drug. "Never? You haven't let anyone else touch what belongs to me?"

His Adam's apple bobbed and shook his head, trapping his bottom lip between his teeth. I tugged it free, running my thumb over it lightly.

"No one has kissed these plush, soft lips?" I rumbled in a husky whisper. Another shake of his head. I ran my hands slowly down his torso.

"No one has held this strong, gorgeous body in their arms?"

Another shake. I snuck a hand back to his still naked ass, feathering over his crack.

"And no one has taken this sweet hole and filled it like you need?"

He keened softly, thrusting his ass back against my questing finger. "No. Only you."

I grasped his jaw to push him back just enough to look into his eyes.

"Are you truly only mine, Dawson?"

"You own every piece of me, Theo. No one else ever stood a chance after you. There was never a time that I wasn't yours."

He leaned forward and kissed me gently, tenderly, infused with so much meaning it made my eyes sting. I poured all my love and devotion into the kiss, wanting it to soak into his skin and stain his soul so that he never doubted that I was his. Wholly. Irrevocably.

We finally came up for air, breathless and clinging to each other like we could stay frozen in that moment while time moved past us. Dawson eventually pulled back, a shy smile on his face that unleashed a swarm of butterflies in my gut.

He opened his mouth to say something, but he was interrupted by someone pounding on the door next to us, making us both jump an inch in the air. A loud, muffled voice came from the other side.

"Stop sucking face or whatever body parts you've chosen to defile and get your asses upstairs! Micah won't let any of us eat the pizza until you're both there and I'm so hangry, I'd murder someone for their crust!"

"Give us five minutes, Fin!" Dawson called out.

"You've got two or I'm pulling the fire alarm and blaming you!"

Dawson cursed under his breath and started yanking up his pants. He stood and coasted his gaze over my body longingly, my cock twitching in response.

"You didn't get to come," he said apologetically. I reached out and cupped his jaw, his barely there stubble scratching my palm.

"You gave me something so much better, beautiful," I promised, stealing a quick kiss from his frowning mouth.

He graced me with a smile that was pure sunshine, chasing away all the shadows that lingered in my soul. It filled me with light until I overflowed with it. My hand found its way into his and I brushed a kiss over his knuckles, never looking away from those soulful blues.

"Let's go before our escort out there gets trigger happy with the fire alarm."

Dawson led us out of the apartment to where Fin was waiting impatiently in the hallway. He griped to Dawson about how hungry he was as we made our way to the elevator, but I barely heard their conversation.

My mind was still spinning with the knowledge that Dawson hadn't been with anyone else since me. I wished more than anything I could say the same, but I couldn't change the past.

Loneliness and heartbreak were a potent cocktail that my disease fed on, fueling poor decisions that I'd regretted as soon as I could remember what I'd done. I didn't have a lot of other partners, but even one was too many. They may have had my body, but only Dawson had my heart.

Theo

CHAPTER TWENTY-THREE

"An exploding crayon? A laser pointer? Oh! A butt plug!"

"Why the fuck would 'butt plug' be an option in Pictionary?"

"Excuse me, Bob Ross, but you're the one whose happy little drawing over there looks like a butt plug. Hawkins, back me up on this."

"Again, this a game for *normal* people, not a Rorschach test for the Sexually Frustrated, Griffin. Feeling a little pent up, are we, neighbor?"

"Hey, I haven't exactly heard you and Dan rattling the walls lately either, cutie. Trouble in paradise already?"

Fin's and Griffin's arguing had been going for several minutes and neither of them even heard the timer when their turn was over. It was infinitely more amusing than the actual game. Everyone had given up trying to stop them during Scattergories earlier, and I was living for the free entertainment.

"You know, we can stop now and just hang out," Aly suggested loudly over their verbal barbs.

Fin capped the marker with a huff, shooting Griffin a glare sharp enough to cut glass. "Fine. It was a space shuttle launch by the way, you big boob."

Griffin's face twisted in bewilderment and he waved wildly at the easel. "How the hell was I supposed to guess that? Whoever chose to draw random names for teams, you can fuck all the way off. I got cheated."

His comment drew Fin into another round of bickering and the knowing looks that were tossed around the room suggested everyone but those two morons saw what was going on between them. Oh well. They'd figure that shit out eventually.

We all settled in the living room afterwards, drinking and laughing about shit that wasn't half as funny without alcohol. With every sip, my anxiety about feeling like an outsider drained away.

I was a bundle of nerves and tension when we'd walked in, wondering if I was going to be ignored or looked at like I was "crazy" again. I'd suffered through awkward silences and judgmental glances from my so-called friends before, and I'd do it again. For Dawson. To carve out a place for me in his world.

I also didn't want to admit that a part of me was afraid that Dawson would hide what we were, playing the part of long lost friend rather than reunited lover. I'd embarrassed myself twice already in front of his friends, proving repeatedly that I wasn't good enough for Dawson. Why would he want to claim a disaster like me anyway?

I had steeled myself for his dismissal. Instead, he'd squeezed my hand and pecked me on the mouth in view of all his gawking friends before going to grab food. And when Fin, Aly, and Micah had pounced on me with a dozen excited, but intrusive questions, Dawson had chastised them all for overwhelming his boyfriend.

Boyfriend.

A title I hadn't held in years. One I never expected I'd be lucky enough to earn back. It was a shot of adrenaline straight to my veins, and I was still flying high on it hours later.

I was stretched out on the floor, reclining against the couch with Dawson pressed up next to me. He threw a leg over mine and fiddled with my left hand absently, laughing at something I'd missed because I'd been caught up staring at him. I had four years to make up for, after all.

Dawson elbowed me in the side, jolting me out of my daze. I glanced around to eyes staring at me expectantly.

"Sorry, what did I miss?"

Nate chuckled, tipping his beer bottle towards Dawson. "We asked if you were coming to the game next Saturday. It's a big one too since it's the season opener and the Hayes family showdown. It's a can't-miss event!"

"Hayes family showdown?" I asked Dawson.

"We're playing Baylor. It's been a whole thing since my freshman year here. Dani rooted for them even before she got into the damn school, so the first time we played against them, there were some... heated exchanges in our house. Ever since, it's been me and Dad versus Dani and Mom. They even decorate our family suite at the stadium in both school colors, really driving home the whole 'house divided' shtick, but I always invite some friends to come too."

There was a sharp pinch behind my ribs that felt a lot like grief. A feeling of loss for the years and family traditions I was always meant to be part of. Inside jokes and memories I'd never get to experience. That darkness that lurked in the corners flooded in, the specter that the pills could barely keep away. It poisoned my thoughts, tainting them.

Did you think you'd be missed? They got along fine without you. What makes you think you're good enough to be part of his family, his life? You're a childhood memory that was better off locked away...

"Will you come next weekend?" Dawson asked, his voice instantly calming me, an antidote to the darkness.

"A chance to see your sexy butt in action? I wouldn't miss it for the world." Dawson kissed the smirk off my face and the last of my tension bled away.

"Oh my god, you two are so adorable. I can't even..." Aly simpered, watching us with dreamy eyes.

Dawson's cheeks stained pink from the attention that swung our way. She was right about that. He was so damn cute. And so damn mine.

"Yeah yeah, whatever," he grumbled. "What about you guys? You all able to come?"

There were nods and excited agreements from everyone with plans being made about where and what time to meet.

"Hey Theo," Bash called. "Why don't you come up to our place and hang out with us since Dawson will be with the team? We can ride over together."

I agreed and thanked him and Micah around an unexpected lump in my throat. It was a simple question. Nothing special, yet knowing that I was welcome here, even in Dawson's absence, settled something inside me.

Once he and I made it back downstairs to my apartment, I was deep in my thoughts, filtering through every interaction that night. I didn't feel a sense of obligation from any of them, like they had to accept me for Dawson's sake. Every smile, laugh, or question directed my way tonight radiated sincerity. Maybe like Dawson, they'd actually stay when they learned the truth about me.

Strong arms slipped around my waist from behind. "Did you have fun tonight, baby?"

"I love hearing you call me that," I breathed, sinking into his incredible warmth. Dawson rested his head on my shoulder, his breath coasting across my cheek, smelling like the fruity drink Micah had made him.

"I thought it would be harder," he mused softly, almost to himself. "Harder to go back to how we used to be. Kissing you, calling you baby, wanting to be with you all the time...it hasn't been hard at all. It's been as easy as breathing. Nothing feels different, but everything is."

I turned and slid my hands down to his wrists, bringing his arms up to drape around my neck. I wrapped mine around his waist, trailing my hands up and down his back.

"Not everything. The important things are still the same. How you like your burgers plain and your coffee iced. How the sun shows the strands of gold in your hair and how you close your eyes when playing a song makes you emotional. How you kiss me and I forget how to breathe, and how you crave being adored and praised during sex because it makes you feel confident and sexy."

I framed his face, using my thumb to smooth away a tear that silently fell. Dawson stared at me unblinking, his eyes wet and a tremulous smile pulling at his lips.

"And what hasn't changed is how deeply and endlessly I love you. There is no corner of my soul that you don't fill. I ran away because I forgot how to trust, but I could never forget how to love you. Even when I was gone, I carried you like a brand on my fucking soul. We could rewrite our story a million times and that will never change."

Dawson leaned into me and his lips met mine in a sweet kiss. He kissed me languidly, stealing my breath with every move of his lips. No tongue, no lust, just a promise made in a language only we knew.

"I love you so much, Theo," he whispered into the kiss.

My heart pounded and I worried it would tear through my chest and right into his hands. Where it belonged.

"Go on a date with me."

"For real?" he grinned widely.

"Yep. I have four years to make up for," I winked. "How about after your game Saturday night?"

"That should work. It's an afternoon game, so I should be out by six. What did you have in mind?"

I mimed zipping my mouth shut.

"Fine. Keep your secrets," Dawson scoffed, but he couldn't hide the excitement I saw in his eyes. It quickly dimmed when he checked the time on his phone. "It's later than I thought. I should probably get home. I've got practice tomorrow afternoon."

"Stay," I blurted, hoping like hell that this wasn't a push too far. "Stay with me tonight. I'll wake you up with plenty of time before you have to leave."

Dawson ducked his head and my chest constricted. Fuck, he wasn't ready. I'd gone a step too far and now he would—

"I'd love to," he replied evenly, head tilting up with a small smile.

My breath left me in a rush as relief flooded in. I grabbed his jaw and took his mouth in a hard kiss. He let out a soft groan that I swallowed down. I kissed him deeper, pouring my gratitude for his answer into the embrace.

We separated slowly and I took in Dawson's dazed, glassy expression. He looked undone and needy, and I soaked it in. I'd never get enough of him.

"Let's go to bed," I purred. "No sex, just...let me hold you."

Dawson bit his lip and bobbed his head, taking my hand and leading me to the bedroom. We slowly stripped, peeling away the layers as though it would strip us of the past. Strip away the pain until only love remained. We climbed into bed and Dawson gravitated into my arms, his back pressing to my front, our briefs the only barrier between us.

Nothing in the last few years ever felt as right as this. Nothing made me feel as strong as having this man love me. I silently vowed that I'd never do anything to lose this. I'd lock myself away before I let my illness consume me and cause him pain again.

"Do you think your friends would still like me if they knew?" I whispered under my breath. My scalp prickled with embarrassment at how pathetic I sounded, like a boy wanting kids on the playground to play with him.

Dawson wove his fingers through mine and coasted them up to rest over his sternum. He didn't answer right away and in the space of those few seconds, a dozen intrusive images swamped me, overriding any kindness or act of acceptance I'd been shown tonight.

"My friends are no strangers to pain like yours," he replied softly. "Most are fighting their own silent battles. Bash and Cal have been more open than others in the group, but we all support them however we're able. The biggest is by being there and holding space for them on the hard days. Never turning away. That's what you will get from them, Theo. They won't turn away."

I swallowed roughly, squeezing my eyes against the sting brought on by his promise. I couldn't speak past the tightness in my throat, so I buried my face in his neck, the scent of his skin a heady mix of his earthy body wash and something uniquely Dawson. He smelled of summers in the woods and nights under the stars. Of memories and innocence and home.

Dawson's breathing evened out, the rise and fall of his chest slowing down. The thump of his heartbeat under my hand played like my favorite lullaby and I clung to him as though he'd fade away with my dreams.

When morning came, I woke to him curled around my body, but it still felt like the best kind of dream.

CHAPTER TWENTY-FOUR

The commotion of the pre-game festivities could be heard before the stadium was even in sight. Parking in the city was a nightmare on a good day, so it was a hike to get there and sweat was cooling on my skin by the time we reached our destination.

Food trucks, parade floats, and people littered Bevo Boulevard, affectionately named for the one-ton steer that was the Longhorn's mascot. That cow was practically Texas royalty and treated like it too. Tailgaters were scattered around the outskirts, with girls dancing on truck beds, guys chugging beer, and the smell of BBQ wafting from every grill in the Texasest of Texas traditions. Yee. Freakin. Haw.

Even with the high energy surrounding us, enjoyment eluded me. I floated in that foggy space between feeling indifferent and melancholy. It'd been a month and a half since I'd been back on the meds and though it wasn't nearly as bad as the other times, I was starting to slip back into old patterns.

I'd been here before, where the anchor of my medication kept me from soaring too high, but sometimes weighed me down too heavily, sinking me into that oppressive abyss. But I was determined not to give in, kicking to the surface to keep afloat. I'd be damned if I let my twisted brain ruin this for me.

It was a fight to push through the crowds to find the rest of the group, but we finally caught Aly and Fin flagging us down. Cal, Rhys, Kenji, and Nate were standing around in the little shade they could find.

"Heyyy, you made it!" Nate cheered around a mouthful of hot dog.

"Good grief...cover your mouth, barbarian," Rhys chided. Nate just laughed it off with a wink, even as Rhys tried to cover his mouth with a napkin. If it weren't for the fact that he'd replaced me as Dawson's best friend and I was territorial as fuck, I'd probably really like the guy. As it was, I found him...tolerable.

"It took for-freaking-ever to park and walk over here. It's insanity! I mean, we almost got trampled by some wasted guys from Delta Kappa Himbo or whatever pulling an actual rickshaw of girls behind them. Like what even is that? Plus my dumbass had to forget my Fitbit, so my steps don't even count," Micah ranted.

Bash wound an arm around Micah's neck, yanking him close and planting a kiss on his temple. "Ignore him. He's just hangry."

"At least he isn't threatening violence or to pull a fire alarm illegally," I snorted. Fin blew me a kiss and waggled his brows mischievously.

"Uh oh, I know that face. What did Tiny Terror do now?" Griffin drawled as he strolled up with a pretty brunette tucked under his arm. Fin tensed up noticeably and he narrowed his eyes at the pair.

"Oh, Griffin. How not nice of you to join us," Fin snarked. "And who is this lovely victim of yours?"

Aly sputtered and choked on the water she was sipping, failing to hide the laugh that bubbled up. Micah rolled his lips as his eyes bugged out, looking between the men with rapt attention. Griffin scowled at Fin and his jaw clicked repeatedly as the girl with him flushed pink and huddled closer to him.

"She didn't do anything to you, so why don't you keep your comments aimed at me? Or better yet, keep them to yourself," Griff sneered. Fin blanched, sadness clouding his features while he watched Griff pull his date over to a food truck without another glance his way.

For some reason, I was compelled to comfort him. Rude as he had been, I recognized his behavior for what it was. A mask, a shield for his silent battle. The group started towards the stadium, and I sidled up next to Fin who was dejectedly bringing up the rear.

I bent down to murmur in his ear. "We all screw up from time to time. He'll forgive you."

I saw Fin peer at Griffin up ahead as he whispered something in the girl's ear that made her laugh out loud, and Fin seemed to fold in on himself even more.

"Maybe he shouldn't. Some of us don't deserve it," Fin muttered, almost inaudible with the noise around us. The self-loathing in his tone hit me low in the gut, a familiar ache that I'd felt for the last four years. "I don't know why I care. I have a boyfriend, for Cher's sake."

"Where is he by the way?"

He mumbled something about him being busy and wrapped his arms around his middle. It didn't sit right with me to see him so upset. I shoved him hard enough to knock him off balance, drawing a small giggle as he righted himself and pushed me back. We caught up with the crew as we drew close to the stadium entrance, but my attention snagged on the massive orange and white horned beast ten feet away.

"Holy shit, that's Bevo," I blurted. The bovine's horns seemed much more intimidating in person than in the photos I'd seen, stretching longer than my arm span. He was chewing away on something as people came up to pet him like he was a dog rather than a 2,000 pound bulldozer.

"Oh yeah. I was wondering where he was," Bash mused. "They bring him out for all the home games. It's crazy how chill he is around all this. Did you know in the fifties, Bevo actually escaped and charged through the Baylor band?"

"You're shitting me," I laughed at the visual in my head.

"I swear! He's also taken out a car, a cheerleader, and at one point, he stampeded his way through campus."

"I wonder if this Bevo will be just as bloodthirsty. Maybe if we're lucky, he'll break free and charge the Baylor quarterback this time," Nate interjected gleefully.

"And if he charges Dawson instead?"

"Then Bevo will be sacrificed for the greater good and we'll all be having steaks!"

We made our way into the stadium and up to the floor that housed the suites. The Hayes suite was centered almost at the fifty yard line. Inside it looked like a luxury hotel room without a bed. It held a kitchenette, a leather couch, a wet bar, and a built-in shelf that was laden with food. Straight ahead were steps down into the four short rows of theater-style seats that overlooked the field and a TV hanging in the corner to broadcast close-ups of the game.

Dawson's parents were sitting on the couch, chatting with a few people I assumed were their guests. Emilia's head turned towards us and she jumped up excitedly. She greeted everyone, but her eyes softened when she got to me, folding me into a big hug.

"I'm so glad you came, sweetheart. We missed you," she said warmly. I hugged her tighter, telling her without words how much I'd missed them too.

She released me and squeezed my cheeks together like she used to do when I was a kid. I brushed her off with a laugh and sauntered down the steps to the bottom row of seats, sliding in next to Dani who was scrolling on her phone.

"What's up, gremlin? You ready to lose?"

She slowly tilted her head my way and pursed her lips. "You've been a Longhorn for all of two minutes, so don't even with me. But it's good you're here. Dawson's going to need you when we send him home crying."

"Don't you worry about your brother, traitor. I'll be taking *very* good care of him tonight, especially when we're celebrating his win," I taunted with a wink.

"Nope. Ew. Stop it...I don't need to hear about any of your celebrations," she gagged, covering my face with her hand. I licked her palm and she shrieked in disgust, wiping it on my shoulder. The glare she aimed at me quickly dissolved into a smile that reminded me of happier times.

"Does this mean you guys are back together?" she asked hopefully. A grin spread across my face instinctively and she clapped her hands in delight. "Ohmigod, finally! I've been waiting for this! Tell me everything. Wait...not everything. Fast forward through the spicy bits."

I filled her in on the relevant stuff, couching the salacious details and my more embarrassing moments. Soon, the UT band blared the fight song as the players burst from the tunnel, spilling onto the field.

Even from up high, I recognized Dawson instantly. Seeing his lean form jogging across the turf, commanding and fierce, took me back to Friday nights spent in the stands watching him dominate the field. Even in high school, Dawson was a force to be reckoned with, and I was the lucky asshole who got to call him mine.

And yet you threw it all away like the coward you are...how long will it take you to lose him this time? Maybe he'll be the one to run away when you become too much...

I slammed my eyes shut against the toxic invasive thoughts. They'd been a little harder to ignore this week when Dawson wasn't around, but I worked to shut them down each time. I pulled Dawson's ring out from beneath my shirt, the cool metal bringing me a measure of relief.

The first half of the game was explosive. Our offense was on fire, but Baylor matched them play for play. Every time our team pulled off a touchdown, the Bears would come back with one of their own.

Watching Dawson was a religious experience. The way he moved was breathtaking, a holy union of strength and grace, agility and power. I couldn't take my eyes off him.

Each time the TV flashed his gorgeous face, my stomach somersaulted and flames of lust licked my skin. Images flickered through my mind of him writhing under me, moaning my name, begging for something only I could give him. When my dick twitched in my jeans, I quickly redirected my wayward thoughts.

Thirteen seconds left in the second quarter and we were tied with Baylor. Dawson caught the snap, searching for an opening before sprinting left and down the field. All of us jumped up, the suite thick with tension and anticipation as we watched him eat up the yards with one of the Baylor players closing in behind him.

He rushed twenty yards, then thirty.

Forty...fifty...fifty-five yards...

Dawson was slammed into from behind, hitting the ground as two defensemen tackled him hard right across the goal line. The referee's arms shot up vertically and the cheers of the crowd pierced through the viewing glass as we all shouted along in the suite. Dawson sprang to his feet and was swarmed by his teammates, knocking into his helmet and jostling him enthusiastically.

The camera panned to Dawson jogging to the sidelines while he removed his helmet and shook out his sweaty hair, but when the blinding, perfect smile slipped, his eyes were blank. Joyless. Empty. It was hardly noticeable, easily missed by the crowd. But not by me.

"He looks incredible out there, doesn't he?"

I turned towards Mr. Hayes as he sank into the seat next to me, watching Dawson on the screen with a mix of pride and awe.

"He always does, sir."

Even as I said it, I wondered whether anyone else saw what I did. I took in Dawson's flawless features as the camera followed him and the team to the tunnel for halftime. Outwardly, he seemed confident and at ease, but to me he appeared disconnected, drained of the life that used to shine out of him when he played.

Mr. Hayes loves his son, but he has always pushed Dawson a bit too hard when it came to football, constantly instilling that "commitment to the Hayes legacy" as Dawson put it. I knew how important it was to him to make his dad proud, enough to bury his own needs and problems under his dad's and everyone else's expectations.

"I can't believe that he's graduating this year. That you both are," Mr. Hayes continued. "It's like no time has passed since you were a couple of kids joined at the hip, hauling ass down to that barn of yours and camping out every night. Emilia was convinced you'd both start sneaking stuff out of your rooms to live down there permanently."

The nostalgia in his voice made warmth bloom behind my ribs. The years we'd spent as a couple were the best of my life, but the years before that were pretty perfect too. Just two best friends against the world.

"Believe me, we definitely considered it," I confessed with an impish grin. "We even hid some blankets and a stash of snacks out there once. A couple days later, the blankets had been shredded and pissed on by an animal and the box of snacks was covered in ants. Thus ended all our attempts at relocation."

Mr. Hayes let out a low chuckle, his eyes still fixed on the TV but he seemed to be lost in thought. He finally looked over, pinning me with a pensive stare that unnerved me a bit.

"I'm glad you and Dawson seem to have worked through some stuff. I'm assuming that's the case since you're here. I really hope you're both in a better place and you're happy."

"Why do I sense a 'but' coming, Mr. H?"

His faint smile did nothing to calm the anxiety that was quickly rising. "It's not a 'but' so much as a...loving warning. Every source I have says Dawson's on the fast track to the NFL. He's been working towards it his whole life and it's finally within his reach."

"You think I would somehow mess that up," I replied woodenly.

"Not at all," he clarified. "Believe it or not, I would love to see you two work out and be able to call you my son-in-law one day. I just want you to be prepared for what that might look like."

"What do you mean?"

"As you can imagine, being a professional athlete comes with a lot of sacrifice. He'll travel frequently for games, have a grueling schedule during the season and for off-season training, and he'll be heavily in the public eye. There will be media obligations and events to attend. It's a high-pressure and intense life, but it's also everything Dawson has worked for and deserves. That will have ramifications on your relationship."

"Such as?"

"For one, it's likely that your condition will be discovered and become public knowledge, especially since you are a queer couple. That draws attention. And probably most importantly, his job will demand most of his time and energy, which means he won't always be able to support you like you need with your illness. There is no shame in it at all, but you two can't ignore that it matters and it will have a big impact on you both."

Ice slid down my spine and the anchor grew heavier, dragging me down a little further as I struggled against it. I tried to remind myself that he wasn't against us, that it was out of genuine love and concern, but my brain kept latching onto the negative space, the things he wasn't saying.

"We aren't ignoring it, sir," I ground out as evenly as I could manage. "We've talked about my illness and have a plan. We've been honest with each other and I...I'm stronger with him. I don't care about anyone finding out about me. They don't matter, only Dawson does. He promised to stand by me, and I'll do the same for him. I'm willing to do whatever it takes to be someone he can rely on."

His lips curved up at the sides, his eyes gleaming with the same pride he held for Dawson.

"I believe you. And I'm rooting for you both, honestly. Emilia and I will do whatever we can to help, but at the end of the day, you both have to put in the work and take on the risks. I don't want either your health or Dawson's path to the NFL to suffer because you two didn't go into this with your eyes wide open."

My chin dipped down and I toyed with the ring around my neck. When it was clear I wouldn't respond, Mr. Hayes gripped my shoulder affectionately before he walked away. I wasn't sure how to process the last several minutes. I felt ambushed, a microscope aimed at all the cracks and fissures that still ran through my relationship with Dawson.

I was barely aware of the second half of the game starting up. My eyes drifted back up to the screen in the corner, catching a glimpse of Dawson as he got into position behind the line of scrimmage.

I couldn't shake the sense that something was off with him, and for once, I wasn't worried it had to do with us. All week, Dawson had been glued to my side every chance we got. He'd stayed a few more nights at my place and though we still hadn't crossed that final barrier when it came to sex, it was more than I'd allowed myself to hope for.

We were happy. I trusted us. Trusted what we were rebuilding. I wouldn't let outside doubts blind me to what was real, and Dawson's love for me *was* real. He had proven it everyday since he took me back and that's what mattered. Everything else was white noise.

My attention was drawn back to the field. Dawson pivoted smoothly in the pocket, waiting for his moment, and then lobbed the ball fifty yards downfield for a passing touchdown. Another wave of thunderous applause rippled around the stadium. Whether he was truly happy with it or not, Dawson was in his element out there and it was the biggest fucking turn-on.

I crossed my legs to hide the growing erection in my jeans, but it was useless. The TV flashed a shot of Dawson whipping off his helmet to run a hand through his damp locks and his biceps flexed temptingly. His football pants clung to his form, highlighting his firm, toned ass, and once again my dick took notice.

I'd wanted something to distract me from the shit of the day and by God, if it wasn't delivered on a silver platter in the form of a two hundred and nineteen pound walking wet dream in cleats.

Suddenly, all I could think about was our date tonight and how much I wanted to tear down every remaining barrier between us. I wanted to rediscover what made him gasp, and moan, and cry out in pleasure. I wanted to lay claim to his body again. With my fingers, my lips, my tongue, and finally, my cock.

I only hoped he was as ready as I was.

CHAPTER TWENTY-FIVE

Adrenaline surged. Blood roared in my ears. My eyes sharpened. My focus whittled down to nothing but the turf under my feet, the sun on my back, and the unwavering need to win.

Not for myself, but for them. For my coach, my teammates, my dad.

For Theo.

I could feel him watching me and I wanted to pull off this win for him. He had been my biggest cheerleader back in high school, always front and center in the stands and chanting my name into the wind. Then chanting it again when he would bury himself inside me hours later.

Here's to hoping history repeats itself.

We lined up and I could feel the energy pouring from my teammates. They were hungry for it, the taste of victory tantalizingly close. All we had was this one chance, this final play.

I caught the snap and through a frenzy of players, I saw Corvin open on the left and sent the ball flying into his arms and he ran straight into the end zone.

The stands erupted with noise, a sea of burnt orange and white rippling with deafening cheers that shook the earth. For the first time that day, I felt elation sweep through me as I was surrounded by my team. I tilted my head up and kissed two of my fingers before pointing them at our suite...at Theo. He would know it was for him.

It was always for him.

The next two hours were a blur of interviews, photos, and back slaps. The high of the win faded quickly as reporter after reporter asked me about Dad and Grandpa like I hadn't been asked the same questions a million times since I was sixteen. How did it feel to follow in their steps? How did it feel to be part of a football dynasty like the Matthews or the Mannings? How did it feel to be the "prince" of college football?

How does it fucking feel? Like a goddamn noose around my neck, strangling me with a life I don't want.

I ignored the bitterness that coated my stomach and instead thought of Theo and our date. Excitement buzzed under my skin as I wondered what he had planned for us. He'd be the first to admit that when it came to date nights or surprises, he could be cheesy as fuck.

I secretly loved it. Theo used to make me feel treasured, adored, loved in a way no man had a right to be. There was a sliver of apprehension that maybe that part of him was no longer there, but I wouldn't dwell on it. Having him back was more than enough and if the sacrifice was some cheesy, romantic gestures, then so be it. I just needed him.

I waited a little longer than I wanted to steal the only private shower stall so I could be a bit more...thorough in my cleaning. I'd thought about it for weeks now and I wanted him inside me again. Craved it like nothing else. I was ready. I had no clue if Theo was up for it, but I wanted to be prepared because I was ready to beg for it if necessary.

The energy in the locker room hadn't dwindled by the time I was done showering. Guys were yelling across the room, taking friendly digs at bad plays and tossing around plans for partying after. I opened my locker to grab my clothes and checked my phone for any messages, finding one Theo sent twenty minutes ago.

THEO

I'm parked by the doors to the locker room.
Don't keep me waiting, Mercury 😉

"Hayes! You're coming out with us to celebrate, right?" someone called out.

"Sorry man, not tonight. I've got plans."

"Ah damn! You got a hot date?" one of our tight ends asked. "I bet it's that hottie with the pink hair you're always hanging out with, am I right?"

"Actually, it's with my boyfriend. But I'll send Aly your compliments."

A shiver of trepidation went through me at my casual mention of a boyfriend, knowing how locker rooms were sometimes a breeding ground for toxic masculinity bullshit, and I braced myself.

"Right on, right on. Well, go get your freak on with the boyfriend, but we're dragging your ass out after next week's game! Capeesh?"

"Yeah yeah, I hear you," I chuckled. I sat on the bench to pull on my shoes and clocked Corvin plopping down beside me to do the same.

"Awesome fucking game, Hayes. That was a sweet play there at the end. I almost shit myself when I thought I might fumble it."

I breathed a laugh through my nose. "Nah, you were solid. You did great out there."

"Thanks, dude," he shot me a crooked grin, then stood to grab his things. "Anyway, I'll catch you later. And have fun with Theo tonight. I'm happy for you guys."

My head shot up in surprise and I returned his smile, tipping my chin at him. A sigh of relief left me as I grabbed my bag and headed out, feeling like we'd somehow turned a corner. The air was muggy and warm outside as I reached the parking lot, swiveling around until I spotted Theo leaning against his car under a street light close by. I made my way over, scanning the length of him hungrily.

His dark wash jeans molded to his long legs that were paired with wine red Vans. His white t-shirt clung to his torso with a black button-down hanging open and the sleeves rolled up, showcasing his veiny, inked forearms. My mouth watered at the sight and arousal heated my blood. A cocky smile graced his face when he caught me checking him out.

"That was quite a win, Mercury. Congratulations. Also you brought Dani to angry tears, so double win."

"Yeah, I'm truly blessed," I said dryly. "What are you hiding behind your back there?"

With a flourish, he presented me with a bouquet of white flowers wrapped in shimmery black paper, though I noticed something...odd about them.

"Are those roses...made out of sheet music?" I asked baffled.

Theo's grin widened and he swaggered over, holding them out for me to take. My breath caught as I examined the petals, taking in the complex notes and time signatures as though I could somehow read the music enfolded there.

"You're not going to feed me some horrible line like 'I'll love you until the last flower dies', are you?" I snickered, trying to hide the emotion clogging my throat.

"Oh please, I'd never say something so corny."

"I'm sorry, have you met you?"

"So damn cheeky tonight," Theo smirked, reaching out to tuck a strand of hair behind my ear, my pulse faltering at the contact. "Do you like them?"

The vulnerability in his voice squeezed my heart and I cupped his neck, pulling his mouth to mine. His lips parted under my prodding tongue and I swept inside to taste him. He let out a guttural moan that I inhaled greedily. The kiss was slow and deep, both surrender and control. I reluctantly pulled back and my gaze roved over Theo's spit-slicked lips and blown-out pupils.

"Clearly you're disappointed. Noted," he panted.

I huffed a soft laugh, trailing my nose slowly up his cheek.

"Thank you," I whispered, unable to resist stealing another kiss. "They're perfect."

I could feel Theo's smile against my mouth, but he stepped back and snatched the gym bag from my shoulder. He tossed it in the backseat of his car, then moved to hold the passenger door open for me. My teeth clamped down on my bottom lip to stifle the smile that threatened to overtake my face as I buckled myself in.

"So what are we doing tonight?" I asked once he'd climbed in behind the wheel.

"I'm sorry, that's classified."

"Are you for real?"

"Yep. Unless you know the codeword."

"Please?"

"That's not it."

"You fucker..."

"That's *really* not it."

"You honestly won't tell me anything?"

"Nope. That actually reminds me..."

He leaned over me to pop open the glove box and pulled out a dark swath of fabric. He dangled it between us and I gaped at him.

"A blindfold? Seriously? I thought this was a date, not an episode of *I Survived*."

"It's the only way to preserve the surprise factor," he explained patiently.

"Or I could just, you know, *close* my eyes. But what do I know?"

"Dawson...do you trust me?" The soft plea in his voice drew me in and he held my gaze. "I won't make you wear it if you really don't want to, but I'm asking you to just go with it. For me?"

I knew before he finished that I'd cave for him, like the complete love-struck idiot I was.

"Fine...fork it over," I muttered begrudgingly, but the way his face brightened made it impossible to regret as I slid the blindfold in place. "You're excessively high maintenance, you know that?"

"You love me anyway," he sang. He reached over and squeezed my upper thigh, rubbing his thumb in circles that sent tingles down my leg.

He started the car and we pulled out of the parking lot, and for a little while I was able to keep a general sense of direction, but by the third turn, I was lost. Theo rustled around for a few seconds until "Dangerous Night" crackled out of the speakers.

"Thirty Seconds To Mars. Nice choice," I said while tapping out the beat on my knees.

Theo's quiet laugh barely reached me over the music and I wondered if I'd said anything unintentionally dumb or funny. Maybe it was how fucking ridiculous I looked in the stupid blindfold. I decided to ignore it and relax for the drive. When Sum 41's "With Me" and Quietdrive's cover of "Time After Time" followed, something scratched at my memory.

"Wait...this isn't our old date night playlist, is it?"

Silence stretched and told me I was right on the money. Theo clasped my hand and brought it to his mouth, placing a firm, warm kiss to the back of it. My eyes stung under the black silk and I clamped them shut to keep the tears at bay. Jesus, why was I getting so damn emotional?

The playlist ran through all the songs we'd added over the course of months and months of dates, songs that held special meaning for us or that were just constantly stuck in our heads at the time.

The car slowed to a stop right as the closing licks of "Don't Fear The

Reaper" faded away, and I suddenly became aware that we'd been driving for a long time.

"You know, I wouldn't have agreed to the blindfold if I'd known I'd be wearing it for over an hour," I grouched.

"It was only thirty-five minutes, drama queen. I need to grab something real quick. Hang tight and don't even think about taking that thing off."

I heard the driver's door close behind him before I could protest. My head slumped back on the headrest, my ears straining for any sound that might tip me off to where we were or what Theo was doing. Faster than I expected, the door next to me opened and Theo guided me out of the car, instructing me to step up and sit on some kind of vinyl seat. It kind of felt like—

"A golf cart? What the...are we at *my house*?"

"Two minutes and you'll see."

The golf cart lurched forward, bumping along uneven ground while crickets chirped loudly around us. The musky scent of the Cedar Elm trees hit me the closer we got and my heart started to thump out an unsteady rhythm.

We slowed to a stop and Theo carefully pulled the blindfold off. I blinked hard to clear my vision, but I didn't need to see it to know where he brought me. After all, it was our place, our hideaway. And the location of our very first date six years ago.

But my mouth fell open at the view that greeted me.

Lights were strung across the top of the barn like spider webs and battery-powered lanterns were placed strategically on the ground. A blanket was spread out in the center with a fancy-looking picnic basket sitting next to a small cooler.

I gawked at the space with stilted noises coming from my slack mouth as I tried to process what I was seeing. My chest ached from the overwhelming sensations running through me, and I rubbed at my sternum absently.

"How?" I gasped out. I refused to look back at Theo because I was ninety-nine percent certain I'd crack right down the middle if I did.

"Dad," he answered simply. "A couple weeks ago, he and I had a long chat about....pretty much everything I'd kept him in the dark about. It wasn't pretty. Lots of truth, *lots* of yelling, some tears, but we ended in a good spot. I called him last week and asked for his help setting this up. He said it was his gift to us...for all we'd been through."

My head shook frantically and I couldn't stop it, like my brain was rejecting the enormity of what he and his dad had done.

"You didn't have to do all this for me. This is..."

Theo came up behind me, heat emanating from him and warming me all over. His hand grazed my arm in a featherlight touch, finally sliding down to weave our fingers together.

"There's nothing I wouldn't do for you, Dawson. I'd give you the breath from my lungs if that's what you needed. All of this? It's a fraction of what I want to give you. I wanted to go back to the beginning, do it right this time. Our story started here and so should our new chapter."

CHAPTER TWENTY-SIX

My eyes blurred and I sucked in a harsh breath. I spun around and gave Theo a bruising kiss. I pressed along the length of him, clawing to get close enough that not even a whisper could fit between us.

Theo's hands dove into my hair, scratching at my scalp in a way that almost made me purr for him. He sucked on my tongue and my dick pushed angrily at my zipper, begging to be freed. All too soon though, he pushed me back and I blinked lazily at him.

"Later, baby," he promised huskily. "We don't want the food getting cold."

I let him lead me over to the set-up where we dropped down, leaning against each other as though any space between us was intolerable. Remarkably, the food was still fairly hot inside the insulated basket. Whatever the pasta dish was smelled amazing and when I snuck a bite of a breadstick, I was happy to note they were garlic-free. That wouldn't have stopped me from sucking the lips off him later, but it was a perk. There was even a bottle of wine that he uncorked expertly and poured for us in glasses out of the basket.

"What, no dessert?"

"Oh, I brought that with me," he said throatily, running his heated gaze down my body slowly. My cock thickened at the promise in his voice. I was so wound up from the last few weeks, I almost begged him to skip the dinner and devour me instead.

We started in on the food, falling into easy conversation like normal. It still amazed me that we never grew tired of talking with each other, moving seamlessly from one topic to the next.

"Do you remember the week during junior year you had the flu, but you didn't want to miss the big rivalry game against the Timberwolves?"

I tipped my head back, releasing a loud groan. "Holy shit, I had blocked that out. I snuck out, drove to the game and somehow convinced Coach Eames that I was fit to play."

"And were you?" he asked rhetorically.

"Nope."

"Nope indeed! You were sick as a dog, yet you still suited up and went out there. I was honestly impressed you made it to the second quarter, but then..."

"Not the 'then'..."

"*But then* you lined up for the snap, bent over, and...what happened again?" He leaned over, cupping a hand behind his ear and waiting for my reply. Instead, I stuck a finger in my mouth and shoved the wet digit in his ear, causing him to yelp and knock over his half-empty glass. I cracked up at his appalled expression.

He gave an exaggerated shudder. "That was uncalled for...and unsanitary."

"Kind of like after I bent over and proceeded to projectile vomit on the field right as the ball was passed to me?" I asked wryly, a shiver of revulsion sliding down me at the mortifying memory as he laughed.

"So much for blocking it out," Theo chortled. He glanced at me as his laughter died down, his gaze turning wary. "Speaking of football, I wanted to ask you about something I noticed at the game today."

"What was that?"

"A couple times when the cameras caught you, you looked...well, hot as fuck, just to put that out there, but also kind of...empty. Like you wanted to be anywhere but there."

His words struck me like a blow to the solar plexus, knocking the wind out of me. I had tried to smile big every time I knew the cameras would likely be pointed at me, hiding the soul-deep exhaustion I felt while playing. It evidently still hadn't been enough.

"I'm almost positive no one else saw it, babe. I swear."

"You did though," I pointed out. Theo shrugged.

"I've always seen the real you."

That had been true from the beginning. Theo had looked past what others had dismissed as weird or aloof, taking the time to peel away the layers and find the real me, even when I made it damn difficult sometimes.

"I don't want to play professional football," I began slowly. "I love the sport and all, it's just not what I want to do with my life. But every time I play, I think about how I'm letting down my coach and disappointing Dad and Grandpa, and it's starting to get to me."

Theo scooted closer until we were connected from shoulder to ankle, side by side, leaning his forehead against mine.

"What do you want to do instead, Mercury? What do you see when you think about the rest of your life?"

I thought about all the plans I had for the music industry and building something so others could connect with music the way I had growing up. However, there was only one answer that came to mind.

"You. You're what I see, Theo."

He moved back just enough to pierce me with those brilliant pools of blue.

"You have me. Whatever you want out of life, wherever that takes you, I will be there. I'd follow you across time itself. There's no version of me that doesn't include you."

I didn't know who moved first, but suddenly all I could feel, taste, and smell was Theo. His wine-laced lips attacking my mouth, his strong hands gripping my hips to haul me onto his lap, his citrus-cedar scent that infiltrated my senses like a seductive drug.

I ran my hands down his defined chest, smoothing my hands around his shoulders to push off his button-down. When I gripped the hem of his undershirt, he took hold of my wrists to halt me.

"How far do you want to take it tonight? I need the words."

"As far as we can go," I rasped. "Fuck me, Theo."

His eyes flared with desire and he gave me a quick, hard kiss. "Up the ladder, baby."

I climbed off his lap and went for the loft ladder. I was only halfway up when Theo reached from behind me, undoing my jeans and yanking them and my briefs down my legs.

“Woah, what the fuck?” I blurted, clinging to the rungs and shooting Theo a bewildered look. My ass was now level with his face, and he was grinning wickedly up at me.

“Sorry, babe. I just wanted dessert first.”

He nipped me with his teeth and I let out a curse that morphed into a deep groan as he sucked a mark into my flesh. He carefully parted my cheeks and heat flooded me when I felt him drag his nose along my crease.

“Fuck me, you smell so damn good,” he sighed, his warm breath coasting across my skin. “Can I taste you, get you ready for me?”

I nodded even as I shook slightly, suspended there for his pleasure. Of course he noticed and he swept his hand up my back tenderly.

“Hey, what’s wrong?”

“Nothing. A little nervous, I guess...”

“It’s just me,” he whispered, kissing the dimples in my lower back that he used to spend hours tracing with his fingers and tongue. It didn’t make a lick of sense that I was nervous. This man had taken me apart time and again, memorizing every inch of my body, yet this time it seemed bigger, greater, as though I wasn’t hanging from a ladder, but the edge of a cliff.

“We can stop if you want—”

“No, please don’t,” I rushed out. “I want this. I want all of it.”

He rubbed soothing circles up and down my thighs, planting soft kisses anywhere he could reach, leaching the tension from my bones so I was putty in his hands.

He bared me to his gaze again then licked a long, wet stripe over my hole. I cried out at the feel of it, clutching at the rungs to hold me up. With a desperate growl, he dove in and ate me hungrily, licking and sucking until I loosened under his carnal assault. His tongue probed my entrance, tearing a ragged moan from my throat.

“God, I fucking missed this ass. Your hole is so greedy for it, isn’t it?”

All I could do was whimper as he plunged back in, making me dizzy with need as the wet, sloppy sounds of him feasting on me echoed in the barn.

“Theo, please—oh shit...I need you,” I whined, low and rough.

Finally, he released me and I sagged, panting against the ladder. He righted my clothes as best he could and swatted my ass lightly to get me moving. We climbed up to the loft and my lips quirked up at the thick pallet of blankets and pillows laid out with candles flickering around it.

"Wow, nothing says romance like a fire hazard," I sassed. "Wait, your dad didn't set this up too, did he?"

"As hot as that would be—literally—they're not real. Also no, I came down and did it early this morning before the game. Our date wasn't the only thing I wanted to go back and improve on."

"But our first time wasn't up here."

"Yeah, well...I have a lot to make up for and giving you a perfect second-first time is part of that," he murmured and I understood what he meant. Unwelcome images of Theo and Corvin on my bed mingled with the memories of Theo taking my virginity there, but I shoved them down before they could ruin the moment.

I turned and drew him to me, kissing up the column of his neck. "So take me. Make me yours again."

Theo claimed my mouth in a searing kiss, walking me backwards and guiding me to lie down on the bedding. He started a slow grind with his hips, rocking against my hardening cock in a steady motion that drove me crazy.

We shed our clothes between drugging, unhurried kisses while the air around us thickened and crackled. Theo trailed his lips down my throat to my chest, circling my nipple with his tongue before biting it gently. I hissed and dug my nails into his shoulders while he sucked the tiny bud into his mouth, working it over torturously before moving to the other side, giving it the same attention.

Theo continued his sensual exploration until he was right above my swollen, leaking dick. He blew on it, chuckling soundlessly when it jerked and strained towards him. With no warning, he swallowed my length and I arched off the mat, moaning helplessly as he took me deep. I peered down to see his plush lips stretching around me in the sexiest fucking way and I nearly came at the sight.

He sucked me down over and over, messy and loud, his spit running down into my crease. I felt his fingers tap my hole, swirling the wetness there and teasing me with the slightest pressure. I keened, my hips thrusting up involuntarily to get him closer.

He slurped off my cock, flushed and teary-eyed. "Are you ready for my fingers, beautiful? "

My head lolled in some semblance of a nod and he sat back on his heels, widening my legs before his movements froze. I glanced up to see him focused on my hipbone, and I swallowed roughly when I realized why.

"You didn't cover it..." he said barely above a whisper.

He traced over my tattoo reverently, the ink different than the last time he saw it. The music note was identical to the one on his hand, except for the opaque blue watercoloring now splashed behind it that matched the shade of his irises, curling around a quote in small script underneath.

When words fail, music speaks.

"I couldn't do it...even if it hurt to keep it, I never wanted to forget."

My whispered admission made his mouth curve up, his features flooding with relief. He leaned down, pressing a warm kiss there and making goosebumps erupt over my sensitized skin.

Theo had lube stashed in the corner and he slicked his fingers, bringing them to my puckered flesh. His eyes never left mine as he sank in, pumping in and out of me slowly. One finger became two, then three, stretching and opening me for his cock. Anticipation thrummed through my veins, overcome with my need for him.

"I'm ready. I want you inside me," I pleaded hoarsely.

"Just a little more. It's been a long time for you and I refuse to hurt you," he crooned. I whined impatiently as he scissored and prepped me longer. After what seemed like an eternity, he slipped free of my body.

I yanked him down for a heated kiss, the intoxicating smell of his sweat and skin enveloping me. I felt him stretch an arm out and fumble for something. I stopped kissing him long enough to see the condom he held up and nausea churned in my gut. As much as I tried not to think about Theo's exploits in the intervening years, the condom was a cold reminder that there *had* been others after me. We'd never needed protection before, but that was no longer the case and I felt sick.

"Dawson, please listen to me." I reluctantly tipped my head up to meet his steady gaze. "I got tested the day I surprised you after practice. That's why I was back in town early. I wanted to be ready if I ever got the chance to be with you again, but I also didn't want to assume, hence the condoms. It's entirely up to you if we use them. I'm okay either way."

Something cold slid down the side of my temple and Theo swiped his thumb to catch the tears that escaped. Unbearable pressure built up in my ribcage, threatening to explode out of me with everything I felt for this man.

"I love you," I said thickly.

"God, I love you so fucking much, Mercury." He kissed me slowly, passionately, our chests heaving for air.

"No condoms. Only you. I just want you."

A rush of air left him, resting his forehead on mine and swallowing audibly. He grasped my wrist, squeezed some lube in my hand, then brought it to his half-hard length. I stroked him firmly, twisting over his head and relishing in his tremors as I got him hard for me.

Theo notched himself at my opening, waiting for my eyes to meet his before pushing into me. I breathed and bore down to allow his head to breach the first ring of muscle. As he tunneled his way in, the burn intensified to stifling levels, but I gave into it. My body lit on fire, burning away all the years of anger and pain we'd been through without each other. When he was fully buried, he stilled inside me, our chests heaving as the ashes settled around us.

What was left was only us. No past, no pain, no fear.

It was right in a way nothing else had felt before, taking me over, remaking me into who I was meant to be. Completely and forever his.

"God, I can't believe I have you back," he murmured, voice wrecked and thick with emotion. Words wouldn't come, buried under the intensity of the moment. I drew his lips to mine, hoping he could taste how much I loved him.

"Tell me when to move," he ground out, muscles shaking from holding back.

"Now, baby...I'm good."

He slid out an inch then pushed back in, starting a steady roll of his hips that made me see stars. I wrapped my legs around him and dug my heels into his ass, encouraging him to go harder, deeper. Soon he was pounding into me, his cock thick and impossibly hard inside me.

"Fuck, babe, you're so tight. You were always so fucking tight for me. This hole remembers who it belongs to, doesn't it?"

I mewled at his filthy words, rocking up to meet his thrusts. Our sweat-slicked bodies slammed together as I answered him grunt for grunt, moan for moan as we escalated into a chorus of shouts that drove my need to incinerating levels.

"You're so fucking sexy, Dawson. I love watching you fall apart on my cock."

Pleasure spiked my blood at his praise, sending me higher. He rose up on his knees and threw my legs over his shoulder, dropping his face to mine for a kiss, bending me in half and driving himself even deeper.

"Harder," I begged. Theo angled his hips up and nudged my prostate. I keened at the electricity that coursed up my spine.

"Goddamn, I'm not gonna last," he growled, his warm breath puffing against my lips. "Get there for me, baby. I want to see you shoot everywhere like my perfect little slut so I can fill you up like you need."

I had forgotten how dirty his mouth could be and a shudder ripped through me at how much I loved it. His hand closed around my shaft and I whimpered at his touch as he stroked me in time with his thrusts.

A low string of curses rushed out as prickles of heat spread through my groin. Theo drove into me faster, hitting that perfect spot and I exploded with a cry as the orgasm he demanded split me in two. My back bowed off the mat, cum erupting from my tip and covering my stomach and torso.

"That's it, Mercury. Fucking come for me, beautiful. You want my load?"

"Please please please," I chanted deliriously, every pump of his hips drawing out my orgasm.

Theo's pace grew urgent as he moved in and out of me. My name tore from him on a shout, his hot cum spilling inside me. He kept going, pushing his release as deep as it would go, marking me like I craved.

My heavy arms went around his back, clutching him to me as he buried his face in my neck, aftershocks still rocking both our bodies. Eventually, he carefully pulled out of me and I winced at the sting, feeling the loss immediately. He rolled onto his back next to me, playing with my fingers beside him. I squirmed uncomfortably as his cum slowly trickled out of my used hole.

"What is it?"

"Uh, I just need a towel or something. I kind of forgot what *that* feels like down there."

"Oh, shit..."

"What?"

"I don't have anything to clean up with."

A sharp noise burst out of me and Theo whipped his head toward me. Another sound bubbled up and then I was laughing uncontrollably, my abs clenching painfully as I wheezed.

"What the—what's so funny?"

"Just...you thought of every fucking thing...except that," I choked out, fighting for air.

Theo snorted, his laughter joining mine as we struggled to calm down, and I was pretty sure we were just delirious from our euphoric orgasms. He crawled over to grab his undershirt and gently wiped me clean, my heart stuttering at the intimacy of the gesture.

When he was finished, he slid back onto the pallet with me. We turned on our sides towards one another and I knew his smile mirrored my own. My cheeks ached from it, muscles stretching that hadn't felt this used in years.

A peaceful silence blanketed us as we basked in the afterglow, hands roving slowly over each other, not to arouse, but to cherish, recommitting every detail to memory. We drifted closer without conscious thought, ending up tangled together and exchanging lazy, sated kisses.

I didn't want to overwrite a second of our shared history, only create new ones to add to our story. Theo said nothing had changed between us, but he was wrong. As much as we loved each other before, we were still teenagers, naive and innocent of what it meant to truly love someone. We grew up, experienced pain, and struggled without each other. Now we knew what was at stake. What we had to lose.

We might not have made it without enduring what we had, both the highs and lows, all the lessons learned. Our love grew up just like we did and it just might have saved us.

CHAPTER TWENTY-SEVEN

Forty two.

That's how many gouges were in the wood table top in front of me. I counted them five times to be sure. My head was offline, buzzing with static and disconnected from everything around me. For a moment, I even forgot what I was doing there or who I was with. It was difficult to concentrate on anything other than dragging in oxygen. And counting gouges.

"Theo, do you want a refill?"

Someone nudged my shoulder and my head rebooted enough to catch that Aly had asked me a question, pointing at my empty soda. I shook my head, awareness surfacing once again. Aly and Nate had dragged me to lunch between classes.

Without Dawson.

Who wasn't here.

Fucking away games...

Six weeks into the semester and I was already battling the gray void left in the wake of the Lithium that suffused my system. That vacant place where every emotion and thought had the edges shaved off, dulled just enough to leave me "functioning" and floating in that safe space between the highs and lows.

I had good days and bad days, but the only real exception was any time spent with Dawson. He injected life into my world and reminded me what it felt like to be happy when everything inside me started to flatline. But he couldn't be around all the time and those quiet moments were always where I was weakest.

Things were...manageable when he wasn't around, but his away games were rough. Those forty-eight or so hours shouldn't have been a big deal, but with Dawson far away and no classes to distract me, it was harder to keep from getting sucked into that lifeless vacuum. That first weekend he was gone, I'd spent two days in bed feeling like I'd fallen in the lake again.

Panicked, tired, then nothing. The nothingness was what truly scared me.

Thank fuck he'd only had two away games so far, including this weekend. With football in high gear, it was an act of the gods to get any quality time with Dawson. If it wasn't practice or conditioning that was stealing him away, it was exhaustion from the week and whatever energy he had left was devoted to his coursework.

Oh, and orgasms. Sometimes all we could manage were mutual blowjobs before he passed out, but the times we really needed to connect, I would sink into that sinful body of his, feeling like I could finally breathe. I either fucked him into the mattress and made him scream, or I made love to him until he was crying beautiful tears as he came for me.

We hadn't been able to go on another date since the Neverland do-over last month. I worried I was letting Dawson down, like I was a poor substitute for the boyfriend I'd been before. We couldn't find time for another real date and all the gifts I thought of weren't good enough. There was a low-hanging sense of dread that I was screwing up this relationship after we'd only just gotten off the ground.

There was a bustle of activity as everyone gathered their stuff, bringing an end to my morose thoughts. We stood and started a slow meander towards the Tower at the center of campus. I stared up at it, beautiful and imposing, and wondered what the view would be like from the top. In that quiet moment of curiosity, an old idea flickered. A wondering turned morbid. A spark in the deepest recesses of my brain that whispered words I didn't always try hard enough to ignore.

Let it stop—you'll be free—

Someday...

"How many more classes do you have today?" Aly asked, jarring me back to reality. Guilt rushed up from the void, turning my skin clammy and restricting my lungs as the realization of what I'd allowed into my head hit me.

"Uh...just one. Over in the, um...McCombs building," I stammered like an idiot.

"Oh sweet! That's where I'm headed," Nate chimed in. "You can walk with me."

"You boys have fun. I'm off to chem lab...oh, joy," she deadpanned, heading in the opposite direction.

I wanted to tell Nate I wasn't in the mood for company, that I needed to call Dawson immediately. I had to tell him what happened. I promised not to hide it so he could help me.

I need Dawson's light to chase away the darkness.

"Man, Dawson's got a fight on his hands this weekend. You know about the Red River Rivalry, right? Woah! Try saying that five times fast," he giggled. Actually giggled. Why the fuck was that endearing on him?

"Yeah dude, I grew up in Austin. I hate OU as much as the next guy," I snickered.

The Red River Rivalry game against Oklahoma University was a cutthroat tradition dating back to the 1900s. The fans on both sides could be vicious and winning the game was considered "a matter of honor", like we were the fucking Hatfields and McCoys. The reminder of how major the game was tomorrow pulled me up short. I couldn't tell Dawson what was happening with me, not now. He couldn't be distracted or worried about me when all his focus needed to be there. He might not want that for his future, but Dawson still cared about the game. Especially this one.

"Oh yeah, I forgot you were from here. Anyway, a few of us are watching the game at our apartment tomorrow if you wanna come. Come cheer on your man while he kicks some Sooner ass," he pressed, wagging his eyebrows and elbowing me playfully.

"Yeah, maybe. Sounds fun though."

My noncommittal answer wasn't doing it for him though. "Look T, I'm gonna level with you. Dawson asked me to keep an eye on you, make sure you were having fun this weekend and felt included."

I bristled with irritation that Dawson might have told Nate about my situation. I didn't need a fucking keeper. I just needed *him*.

"I think he's only worried that you're still adjusting to being new here and wants you to feel at home with his friends. I mean, we're a cluster of stone-cold weirdos—present company excluded of course—but we're family. That makes you family too. And even though you've totally stolen him away from me," he paused, flashing me a wink, "I'm really glad that he has you back. I always thought he was happy before, but seeing how he is with you now, I don't think that was happiness. I think it was survival."

I wasn't sure how to respond. It hit too close to home, thinking of how Dawson had been *my* survival the last few years. He'd been the beacon that saved me from the darkness, a tourniquet to stop the hope from bleeding out of me. I survived because of Dawson. I had him even when I didn't. But Dawson had needed someone too.

"I'm glad he met you, Nate. I hate to admit it, but I was jealous as hell that he had a new best friend. I'd been the only one he had for almost ten years, so it was a tough pill to swallow," I revealed sheepishly. "But I'm grateful you were there when I couldn't be. He's told me how much you mean to him. You've been a great fucking friend and I can't thank you enough for being there for him."

Nate gave me a pensive look that I'd never seen on his normally carefree face. Then his lips tugged up at the corners and his arms opened wide. "Aww, bring it in, brother. There's plenty of D-man for the both of us, but that means you've got me too!"

I coughed out a breath as he crushed me to him in a surprisingly strong hug. I awkwardly returned it, but a tiny smile cracked through at his claim.

"Hey, do you know what time it is?" Nate asked abruptly, shoving me back and holding me at arms length.

"Uhh, no?"

"It's two-fifteen...and OU still sucks!"

I couldn't help answering Nate's Cheshire Cat grin with my own. He seemed pleased with himself as we headed off towards our classes, and I decided having Nate as a friend didn't sound so bad. In fact, it sounded pretty good right now. Maybe Dawson wasn't my only source of light after all.

:♡:

It was pandemonium in Dawson's and Nate's apartment as the clock ran down the final seconds of the game. UT was trailing OU by three points and if they got this touchdown, they'd clinch the Red River showdown.

Dawson was locked in, hunting for his opening and feeling the pressure. I saw the offensive line caving and my heart plummeted, bracing myself to watch Dawson get sacked. The line broke and just as the defense rushed in, Dawson launched the ball with a force that made my own arm throb. It sailed cleanly into the hands of his wide receiver who shot off like a rocket.

"Holy shit! Let's goooo!"

"Run, motherfucker, RUN!"

"Come on, you've got this! Go go go!"

Loud shouts from Nate, Griffin, and Bash rang in my ears as they all leapt from their seats. When my throat started to hurt, I noted incredulously that I was yelling along with them. The bubble of anhedonia I'd been trapped in for weeks popped without me noticing, even if only temporarily.

Soon, everyone joined us, our shouts coalescing into a booming cheer as the receiver sprinted into the end zone, sealing the win. Limbs flailed around me in excitement, hugging and shaking me vigorously while we watched Dawson and his team celebrating their victory on the sidelines.

"Holy fucking Sooner-balls! Our boy kicked ass!" Nate cried, clapping his hands to my cheeks, which were sore from how wide I was grinning.

I turned my attention back to the TV, hoping to catch as many glimpses of Dawson as I could. The cameras slowly panned over the team, and when I saw Dawson's smile, there was no emptiness behind it. No exhaustion. Only pure, undiluted joy.

And it was so fucking beautiful.

He'd been different since getting his decision to quit off his chest, and I was glad our talk seemed to bring him some relief. My fingers itched to dig out my phone and call him, to hear the triumph and laughter in his voice. But I knew he wouldn't get it, not for a few more hours at least, especially with the celebration that would undoubtedly follow.

Instantly, that dark cloud rolled in and washed out any happiness I had. Irrational and toxic feelings of sadness, jealousy, and abandonment filtered in, the bubble around me trying to reform into something thicker and more potent.

I fucking hated this. I hated myself for being this way. It wasn't fair that I didn't get to hold onto my happiness, my peace. This illness was always there to taint it or steal it away. Even when I did what I was supposed to do—take my pills, be honest with Dawson, lean on my support system—it still wasn't enough.

Why am I never enough?

When do I get to be normal?

I was only half-aware as I snuck away from the group and slid into Dawson's empty bedroom. I closed and locked the door, his warm, woodsy scent wrapping around me like I wished he could right now. I crawled into his bed, burying my face in his pillow and clutching my phone to my chest, waiting for his call.

But it never came.

I WOKE up groggy and confused, sleep and reality weaving around one another in a disorienting haze. Keane was playing somewhere in the ether around me, bringing me sweet memories of Dawson singing for me. I finally shook off the fog of sleep, slowly piecing together that I was in Dawson's bed and my phone was ringing the muffled song under the covers.

I frantically dug around in the sheets until I found it and elation rushed through me seeing the FaceTime request. Dawson's face filled the small screen and the void fell away.

"Mornin' baby," Dawson rumbled happily, the softest smile on his pretty face. It was a hit of serotonin, infusing my system with a heady pleasure.

"It's not fair for you to look that sexy this early," I griped without heat. He really was so fucking hot. Dawson's bed-rumpled hair, sleep-swollen lips, and scratchy morning voice were doing it for me.

"Trust me, I'm not. I'm hungover as fuck," he grimaced. "I'm sorry I didn't get to call you last night. I got in later than planned."

"No need to apologize, babe. So what does a victor of the Red River Rivalry do to celebrate exactly?" I asked dramatically, ignoring the twinge of paranoia that seeped in.

"A bunch of my buddies dragged me out for drinks, but we had a curfew so we snuck some more drinks back in the hotel and got pretty wasted."

"What, no stripper cake for the champions?"

"I'm pretty sure that's for bachelor parties."

"Ugh, what kind of meathead jock are you? There's never a wrong time for a stripper cake, Dawson. Don't be a spoilsport."

Dawson huffed a laugh, looking up at me through his ridiculously long eyelashes that had the ability to melt my brain. Holy hell, I missed him.

"You know, I can't remember the last time I let loose like that, especially with football. It's like I've finally let myself enjoy playing again now that I've accepted these will be my last games. I think I also distanced myself from my teammates because of it, so hanging with them last night felt damn good."

While Dawson's smile was radiant and relaxed, mine felt wooden and difficult to hold in place. I was so proud of him for letting go and finding joy in the sport again, and of course he deserved to celebrate a major win. I couldn't ruin that by dumping my problems on him. I promised him I'd be honest when things became difficult for me, but there was no way I could be that selfish now.

He'd been through so much because of me and we were finally in a good place. A great fucking place actually. Burdening him with what amounted to a few emotional cuts and bruises would only jeopardize what we had now. It hadn't even been two months and this shit was happening to me. What would he think being with me months or years down the line would be like?

"Theo, what's up with you? I can see on your face that something is wrong."

I didn't know how far I let the mask slip, but I refreshed my smile and tried to brush it off.

"Nothing. I'm fine." I gave him the most convincing look I could muster, but my stomach roiled with guilt. How can the smallest words carry the biggest lies?

I pivoted quickly to attempt to salvage the conversation and throw him off the topic.

"I'm really fucking proud of you, Mercury. I can't wait to brag about my sexy, OU-crushing quarterback boyfriend," I winked, lowering my voice to that register that made him stupid for me. Dawson wasn't the only one with brain-melting powers.

Unfortunately, mine were apparently on the fritz because Dawson wasn't biting.

"Baby, please don't lie to me," he pleaded softly. "I know you, I can tell something is off. I trusted you to tell me if you were struggling, so please don't betray that."

His words gutted me, sucking the air from my lungs and replacing it with shame. My reasons for protecting Dawson from my issues dissipated instantly. I blew out a deep breath, trying to remind myself that Dawson was strong enough to handle my demons.

"You're right, I'm sorry. I didn't want to say anything because you're so damn happy and you had this incredible fucking achievement. I didn't want to ruin it with my bullshit problems."

I expected him to be fuming, to get pissed at me for almost breaking my promise to him, yet I didn't expect to see empathy lining his features or his sweet smile return.

"Theo, I need you to listen to me carefully. You are *not* a burden to me. Your problems are not bullshit and it would kill me to know you were suffering alone when I could have helped you. I know I can't fix it for you or make it better, but I want to walk with you through it anyway. That's what I mean when I say I love you. Your hell is my hell. Your pain is my pain. I'll carry you through it if I can't carry it for you."

My breathing stalled and my lash line flooded. My chest ached from the raw emotion that had been hiding behind the wall of drugs in my system, and it spilled over in warm tears down my cheeks that I rushed to wipe away.

"Did you just quote *Lord of the Rings* in your epic romantic speech?" I laughed wetly.

"It wasn't an exact quote," Dawson grumbled. "Blame Nate. He's the one who has those movies on a near constant loop at our place. I hear Gollum in my fucking sleep sometimes."

I chuckled, feeling some of my worry bleed away. I tried hard to keep my shit under wraps and get some control over how the pills made me feel, but with Dawson I felt safe to fall apart. It wasn't easy to blindly trust that I wouldn't scare him off or become too much for him. However, it was a mathematical certainty that I would lose him if I started hiding parts of myself away again.

"I was doing okay for a while, but lately it's been...hard."

"What's hard, baby?"

I chewed my bottom lip aggressively, trying to find the right words to make him understand. "Everything."

Dawson was patient as I filled him in on the blunted emotions, disrupted focus, and depression that I recognized was creeping in. It wasn't until I told him about the Tower and the dangerous direction my thoughts had turned that his calm exterior cracked.

"Fuck, Theo...I'm so sorry I wasn't there."

His distraught face broke my heart. "Dawson, even if you'd been here, it still probably would have happened. That's just...how this drug affects me. The mania gets contained, but it sort of leaves the door open for the darker shit..."

"Have you ever tried getting a different prescription?"

"I tried once when I was at SHSU after the third or fourth time of going off my meds. The doctor said pretty much the same thing as the psychiatrist at the rehab place. 'Lithium is the gold standard for bipolar disorder' and 'you'll adjust to it eventually', blah blah fucking blah."

Dawson seemed to process that, a wrinkle forming between his brows that I wanted so badly to kiss and smooth away.

"We'll figure out how to manage this, Theo. I promise you. Even if I have to hire a whole damn team of specialists to create a treatment specifically for you."

I smiled at the fierce determination in his voice. And even though it was an outlandish promise he could never keep, his conviction made me want to believe it was true.

"I love you so much, Mercury."

"I love you too," he whispered through that sweet, shy smile that was close to unmanning me. "What are you doing tonight?"

"Nothing really. Why?"

"How about going on a date with your—how did you put it? Your sexy, OU-crushing quarterback boyfriend?"

“Wait, seriously?” I beamed while a swarm of butterflies took off in my stomach.

“Absolutely. We get back around three-thirty, so how about I pick you up at five?”

“That works for me. Where are we going?”

Dawson’s lips kicked up into a devastating smirk and I forgot how to breathe.

“You’ll see.”

Theo

CHAPTER TWENTY-EIGHT

AGE 17

The ferris wheel loomed ahead and suddenly, I was thinking this wasn't my most brilliant idea. My dumb ass just had to let Dawson pick the date tonight. It wasn't going to be a very sexy look when I got to the top and puked from the height.

The things I did for this guy.

"Come on, it won't be that bad. You've ridden roller coasters with me before. How is this worse than those?"

"Because on those, I'm strapped in a harness and going two hundred miles an hour. The fear doesn't have time to sink in. Up there"—I gestured to the giant death wheel—"I'm wide open and exposed...the fear doesn't just sink in. It fucking marinates."

The tiny snort he tried to hide was so damn adorable that I couldn't even be annoyed with him. It was still kind of crazy to me to think that I stumbled across my soulmate at nine years old. In the woods of all damn places.

"Look, I won't make you if you really don't want to go. But I would love to do it together," he said, leaning close but not close enough to raise eyebrows. We always had to be careful outside of Neverland. A stupid side effect of the closet we kept ourselves in.

But Dawson was intensely private and worried for us, so I'd do anything to make him feel comfortable. Once we went to college together, we'd be free to be ourselves. We could hold hands and kiss in public. We could smile at each other without tempering it so others couldn't see the love behind it. I could be patient...ish.

"Alright, I'll go," I grouched. The smile that swept Dawson's face set off butterflies in my stomach. I still remember the day that first happened at his twelfth birthday party. He was opening presents and when he got to mine, he turned and gave me the brightest, most perfect smile. One he only gave to me.

And I was never the same. He had me.

I handed over our tickets to the operator who looked half-asleep, trying not to let my mind go all Final Destination *on me. I stopped cold when I saw the red, metal bucket that was supposed to hold us. It had high grated sides and a metal bar to cross our laps, but other than that it was completely open.*

"We're gonna die."

Dawson released an exasperated breath and pushed me onto the seat, sliding in after me and latching the safety bar in place. The second we lurched backwards, my lids slammed shut and my hand clamped down on the bar. My breathing was loud and unsteady, sharp pinpricks stabbing at my lungs as I worked for air.

"Baby, it's okay! You're safe, I promise. Just listen to my voice," Dawson soothed. "I brought you to the carnival because I've been worried about you lately. You've been really moody and temperamental, which isn't like you. Plus you haven't been sleeping much, so I'm sure that makes it worse. I know I've been crazy busy with football, but I thought doing something fun, just the two of us, would help you feel more like yourself. Maybe make you feel a little better."

I didn't even realize that I'd opened my eyes to look at him until we slowed to a stop at the peak of the wheel. I glanced out cautiously and my breathing quickened again, but Dawson's warm hand prying mine off the bar pulled my attention. He was holding my hand...in public.

Dawson's smile was small and unsure, but when I squeezed tightly, he let out a relieved sigh and his lips curved up higher.

"I also wanted to ask..." he paused, rolling his lips in, "if you would want to come out with me."

"I'm already out with you," I teased breathlessly, still fighting off that slight panic.

"No. I mean, out out. *Like I want to be honest about our relationship. Homecoming is in a couple of weeks and I want to take you as my date, not my best friend. I don't want to keep us a secret anymore."*

My heart beat wildly behind my ribs with enough force to crack them.

"Mercury...are you sure? You really want to stop hiding?"

"I do," he said firmly. "I'm tired of pretending. I just want to be with you and be happy without worrying what anyone else thinks. I want to win that Homecoming game for you and then walk into that dance with you on my arm."

Damn it, I wanted to kiss him so fucking bad. But I knew we weren't quite ready for that level of PDA yet. Baby steps.

"I say yes," I said excitedly. "Let's do it. I cannot fucking wait to show them all that you're mine. That I'm the luckiest asshole in the whole universe to get to love you. But let's meet at Neverland first and then after the dance, I want to take you back there, lay you down, and make love to you all night long."

Dawson huffed and flushed with embarrassment like he usually did when I got mushy as fuck, but there was no hiding the joy in his eyes. We'd looped the ferris wheel while we talked and I was surprised when we came to a halt back at the top.

"It feels like we're on top of the world," he murmured.

"I always feel that way when I'm with you," I confessed softly. This time around, I thought the view was a lot more beautiful than before.

When Dawson said he wanted to take me on a date, I should have seen this coming. That night at the carnival was a turning point for us, when we'd decided to be brave together and stop hiding. It was one of the happiest moments we'd shared as a couple. I only wish I'd known that would be the last date we'd have before it all disappeared.

The fairgrounds were buzzing with people, a cacophony of lights and sounds that were as exhilarating as they were overstimulating. Dawson bought our tickets and then took my hand, weaving us through the crowd like a man on a mission. I stumbled a bit as something dawned on me and Dawson glanced at me over his shoulder, frowning.

"You alright?"

"It just hit me that the last time we were here, we couldn't hold hands like this."

His face lit with understanding and he yanked me to him. My eyes widened when he slipped an arm around my waist, pulling me close.

"We can do a bit more than that," he purred before taking my lips in a soft, lingering kiss that I felt in my bones. When he released me, I felt dizzy and warm all over.

"Why Dawson Hayes, are you trying to seduce me?"

"Depends. Is it working?"

"I could show you just how much, but then I'd get arrested for public indecency," I muttered, subtly adjusting myself. Dawson's heated gaze flickered down to the slight bulge in my jeans, sending another rush of blood south.

"Maybe we'll save that for our next date. Come on, I know the first stop I want to make."

He led me towards the snack stands, and the smell of funnel cakes and turkey legs made my stomach grumble loudly. Dawson made me wait while he went through the line and when he came back, I barked out a laugh.

"I thought you said cotton candy was carcinogenic insulation on a stick?"

"Eh, YOLO," he shrugged, handing me one of the blue and pink swirled confections. "I figured I oughta see what the big deal is with this stuff since you're obsessed with it."

"That's a gross exaggeration," I scoffed. I grabbed a mouthful of the cotton candy and the second it melted on my tongue, I let out a moan that was downright indecent. Dawson glared at me, unamused.

"Would you two like to be alone?" He rolled his eyes and tentatively bit into his treat. His face contorted as if he'd tasted battery acid. "Nope. That was a mistake. Failed experiment."

"Amateur."

I swiped his candy and devoured it as we worked our way around the carnival games. Dawson wasn't nearly as hand-eye coordinated as I suspected he'd be, and I immensely enjoyed his growing pout each time I beat him. For the health of our relationship, I decided the rides were a safer alternative. And I couldn't complain when Dawson's hand never left mine during every twister, flipper, sizzler, or whatever ride we were on.

After the tenth ride, our bruises had bruises and we were aching in places no twenty-one-year-olds should be.

"Christ on a cracker, I don't remember those being so...violent when we were younger," I groaned, rubbing at my sore arm as we disembarked the bumper cars.

"If my coach knew I was this beat up by some fold-up carnival rides, he'd double my conditioning sessions every week. On the bright side, the ferris wheel shouldn't seem so bad anymore in comparison."

"I beg to differ. I'd argue the emotional trauma of that wheel far outweighs any physical damage I have now."

"Don't be such a baby, baby," he snickered, earning himself my middle finger.

I followed him towards the lit up ferris wheel that I noticed with a sinking feeling was bigger than the one we'd ridden years ago.

"Oh my god, you look like you're walking the Green Mile," Dawson laughed. He looped a hand behind my neck, bringing my lips to his for a quick kiss. "You don't have to do this, you know."

"I didn't back out last time and I won't today," I gulped, staring up at the monstrosity. "You jump, I jump, Jack."

"That would definitely put a damper on the evening."

I laughed sarcastically as he pulled me onto the ride behind him. Thank fuck it had enclosed gondolas this time instead of the death-buckets. My hand remained cradled between Dawson's as the wheel started circling around.

"I've been meaning to ask you something..." he began warily.

"Talk about déjà vu..."

"Zip it," he demanded affectionately. "I wanted to ask how you'd feel about starting therapy."

I tensed at the suggestion, not expecting it. "You think I should see a therapist?"

"Actually...I thought we should both see one. Separately, of course, but maybe sometimes together?"

"Why would you want to do that?"

"Because you're not the only one who has to put in the work with us. You know I've forgiven you, but there are still things I wrestle with from time to time. None of that is on you, it's all my own shit, but I refuse to let it become an issue for us." He put a finger to my mouth when I went to speak, cutting me off gently. "I also want to learn more about your illness and how I can be the best partner for you. I won't go into this uninformed and blind, letting you figure it all out on your own. I'm in this, whatever it takes."

My nose stung and I blinked rapidly to clear the stifling emotion that built up. There was no way I was deserving of this man. I wished more than anything that I was normal for him...that I could give him a happy, easy life rather than this never-ending battle.

"Dawson, I—" I cleared my throat, finding it hard to push the words out. "That means more to me than you fucking know, but you shouldn't have to change your life for me. If I wasn't so selfish and didn't love you so goddamn much, I'd let you go find someone better. Someone who doesn't come with so much baggage."

Dawson's face turned stormy and he gripped my chin to hold me in place.

"Don't you *ever* say that again," he growled, each word clipped and firm. "You have already changed my life for the better, in ways I could only dream of. I wouldn't trade you or change you for any fucking thing on this planet because then you wouldn't be my Theo. I love you just as you are. There is nothing I won't face for you. If you start to sink, I'll pull you back up. I'll save you, just like that day on the lake. I promise I won't let you drown."

"You can't save me, Mercury," I whispered, grated and broken. His eyes burned and pierced straight through all my armor to reach me in the void.

"Watch me."

Then right there, on top of the world, he kissed me. It was a promise and a challenge, a vow that he embedded into my soul. He was my lighthouse and my lifeboat, my guide and my rescue for when the storm inside became too strong.

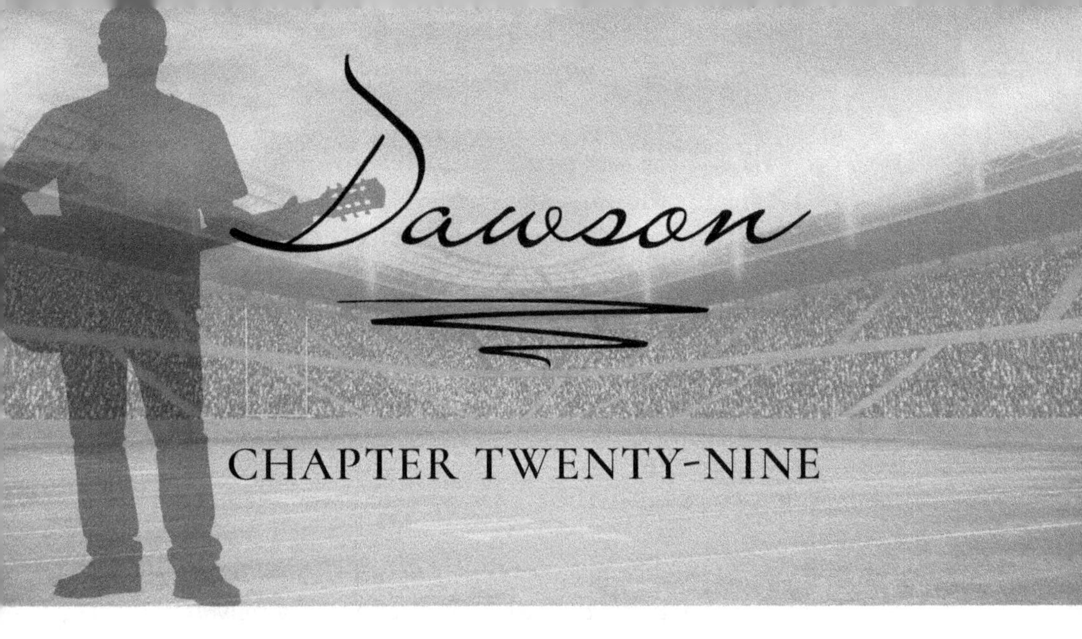

Dawson

CHAPTER TWENTY-NINE

"No. Absolutely not. Pick something else."

"Bro, it's my turn to pick. You don't get veto power."

"And I'm telling you I will *veto* the TV out the fucking window if you pick it."

"Uh, I'm like, eighty-five percent sure that's not how a veto works. Also fuck you, I'm picking it anyway."

Nate plucked the remote from my hand with a triumphant little sneer and I let out a small growl of annoyance.

"Fine...but only the first one or you don't get to pick the movies for the rest of the semester."

"What?!" Nate squawked loudly. "You can't stop at just one! What kind of emotional blackmail is this?"

"One or none, dude. And I'm like, one hundred percent sure that's not how blackmail works."

"And I'm one hundred percent sure I hate you," Nate grumbled, scrunching his face into an exaggerated pout.

I cracked a smile at the ridiculous expression and shouldered him until he caved and grinned back. That was one of the best things about Nate. He never stayed mad or upset long, always snapping back to his golden retriever setting pretty fast, pouring sunshine into everyone's lives. It was how he'd gotten through to me when I'd been an angry, heartbroken jackass rolling into freshmen orientation.

He'd dropped into the seat next to me, all floppy platinum hair and bright eyes, talking up a storm about how excited he was to be there. It was such a gut punch seeing him, bouncing in like we were going to be the best of friends, reminding me so much of another sweet, guileless boy who blew into my life much the same way. It had hurt to look at him. The scars from Theo's disappearance were still open and raw at that point, so I'd almost changed seats to escape the reminder.

But I couldn't. Something inside pulled me toward him, telling me I needed someone like him in my life. Nate helped me find joy again and for the first time since I met Theo, I had someone who I felt I could be myself around.

"Alright, I give," I sighed deeply. "*Lord of the Rings* marathon, it is."

Nate let out a whoop and tackled me to the couch happily. It wasn't exactly what I had planned for the day, but making him happy was worth it. Hell, I owed him a lot. Ten hours worth of movies was the least I could give him.

"Where's Theo, by the way? Did you invite him?"

"He went to see his dad for the weekend since I had an away game yesterday. I thought this was a good time for us to hang out, one-on-one. It's been a while."

"That happens when you get yourself a hot boyfriend who can sex you up all the time," Nate grinned wickedly.

"Yeah, but that's no excuse to not spend time with you, man. I missed you, weirdo," I teased.

"Aww I missed you too, Dawby-Bear!" Nate lunged, smacking a wet kiss on my cheek. I groaned and shoved him off, wiping at the gross feel on my face, but couldn't wipe my smile off with it.

By the end of the second film, my ass was numb and my eyeballs were dried out. I had tried not to text Theo during the day to let him enjoy time with his dad and focus my attention on Nate, but I was itching to hear from him. I eventually caved and pulled up our text thread.

ME

How's it going over there?

THEO

Pretty great. I think we're finally getting back to how close we used to be before everything.

ME

That's awesome, baby. It was good you went to see him.

THEO

It was.

But I still miss the fuck out of you. Are you spending the night with me tomorrow?

ME

Try and stop me

THEO

Not a chance in hell, beautiful

Your bye week is coming up soon, right?

Shit, I'd almost forgotten that was in a couple of weeks. It was the one week that we didn't have a game, a blissful reprieve from the stress of the season.

ME

Yeah, the weekend of the 19th. Have any ideas for us?

THEO

You + me = naked on the beach

ME

...is that it? Is that the whole plan?

THEO

What, you need more than that? I thought that was an A+ plan.

But if you're gonna be needy...

ME

THEO

Ok, ok. I saw your Mom today feeding Stella and I might have asked if we could use the beach house for the weekend...interested?

That...was actually a great idea. I hadn't been down to our Port Aransas vacation place in forever. I bit my lip thinking about having

Theo all to myself with no interruptions, no football, no classes. Nothing but us in our own little world.

Things with Theo had been a lot better since our night at the carnival. He and I had scheduled therapist appointments a couple of days later, and from what Theo had told me, he was feeling good about it. It'd been three weeks since he had another "dark episode" as he called it. He still felt like he was wading through molasses some days and his schooling was harder to keep up with, but he was dealing with it.

I'd just had my third session this week and I'd been able to unload some of the abandonment and jealousy issues that lingered. It wasn't that I didn't trust Theo, but when wounds ran deep enough, they didn't always heal as fast beneath the surface. The biggest issue I had yet to confront was that constant, nagging worry in my gut about Theo's depression.

All that played on a loop in the back of my mind was what he'd told me the day I found out about his diagnosis—the plan he'd once had. The medication that was supposed to help had pushed him to the edge, made him think there was only one way to end his pain.

Theo told me repeatedly that this time was better and that he had a lot going for him that he didn't have back then. He had his dad back, new friends who cared about and included him, and he had me. He said I couldn't save him, but that wasn't entirely true. I didn't have the power to cure him and in some ways, I was helpless when it came to easing his struggles.

But I could, in some way, save him. I could help keep his heart beating by giving him something to fight for, by showing him how beautiful and worthy his life truly was...by loving him. I had loved him through every season of his life so far and would love him until the world stopped turning.

And I had to trust that would be enough.

ME

Let's do it 🩶

CHAPTER THIRTY

"Damn, it looks bigger than I remember. Has it grown since the last time we were here?" Theo remarked as we pulled into the driveway of the two story, waterfront property.

"Yeah, I think my dad paid extra for that feature," I replied sardonically. Theo flipped me the bird as I climbed out to unload our bags from the trunk. He'd argued that I didn't need luggage because he planned to keep me naked all four days we were here. As enticing as that was, our stretch of beach wasn't private and we had one neighbor next door, so he'd begrudgingly agreed to clothes.

It had been a long two weeks waiting for my bye week to arrive. The season was ramping up big time and I'd been exhausted both mentally and physically, leaving no real time to spend with Theo. Of course, he'd been understanding each time I came over only for me to pass out within an hour, but I'd be lying if I said it wasn't starting to wear on me. I worried that it would eventually create a wedge between us, leaving Theo more vulnerable to the side effects of his medication.

But that's what this getaway was for. Ever since Theo and I had started dating again, we hadn't really had any time alone to reconnect, not without the stress of school or football or other people around. I wanted to explore every new facet there was to him, to fill in every gap that existed between us, to bare every fraction of our souls to one another. More than anything, I didn't want to take this second chance for granted.

Especially not *this* weekend.

I took our bags up to the master suite we'd be using while Theo put away the groceries we'd bought. Our housekeeper had set up the room so everything was ready for us. I headed back downstairs, but Theo wasn't in the kitchen or living room.

I was about to search the rest of the house when I noticed him outside on the deck. Theo was leaning against the wooden railing, gazing out at the gentle waves that were tugging at the shore. The late morning sun cast a halo around his honey blond strands and when he glanced over his shoulder, the bright smile he flashed me sucked the air from my lungs.

"You gonna stand there all day or come kiss me, Mercury?"

My feet moved of their own accord, drawn in by the magnetic gleam in his eyes. I was powerless against it, inevitable as the tide being pulled in by the moon. I crowded him against the decking with my chest pressed to his back, bracketing him with my arms. I brushed my lips over his pulse point, feeling it jump under my attention.

"Not exactly what I had in mind," he taunted breathlessly, yet he tilted his head to give me better access. I sucked a bruise into the skin and his throaty moan filled my dick so fast I grew lightheaded.

"God, I've missed you," I rumbled, nuzzling him behind his ear and drawing the scent of him into my lungs. "Fuck, you always smell so good."

"Huh. Guess that bathing thing really works."

I nipped at his jaw with a growl. "Smartass..."

"What was that about my ass?" He arched his back slightly, dragging his tight ass over my half-hard cock teasingly.

My breath hitched and I dug my fingers into his hips, desire ripping through me like a storm. I whirled him around, grabbing his face and crashing my lips into his. I shivered at the low whimper he let out, his hands diving into my hair and tugging me closer. I swept my hands down Theo's back and hooked them under his ass, hauling him up.

"Holy shit," he sputtered as he clung to my shoulders. I started walking him back inside, pulling back a fraction to take in his blown out pupils and bewildered expression. "Well...that was new. And hot. And unexpected. But also *really* hot..."

"You said that twice," I teased, biting his lower lip and pulling it out enough to make him chase my mouth. I pecked a quick kiss to his swollen lips before dropping him unceremoniously on his feet.

"What the hell?" he asked indignantly while I strolled towards the laundry room.

"I've gotta grab some towels. I want to head down to the shore and swim some before lunch." I threw a wink over my shoulder and grinned at the icy glare I got in return. I adjusted myself in my shorts, understanding his frustration but also wanting to build the anticipation. I had plans for him later that I didn't want rushed.

I hunted down the beach towels and sunscreen and made my way back to him, but froze when I caught Theo staring intently at the calendar mounted on the fridge. He didn't turn when I came up behind him, but subtly leaned back until my arms circled his waist.

"I hadn't realized what this weekend was until I saw this," he murmured. I rested my chin on his shoulder, my eyes pinned to the third weekend of October. It was the first time my bye week had fallen on this exact weekend, and it felt like some kind of sign.

"It was supposed to be such a big day for us," he continued, voice tinged with sadness. "You would have been getting ready to meet me at Neverland about this time. I hated that I never got to see you in your suit and give you that stupid little flower thing."

"A boutonniere?"

"Yeah, that's what I said."

I breathed out a small laugh, pressing my lips to his shoulder. I had tried to ignore this weekend for a long time, finding it too painful to think about. Four years almost to the day, I was left waiting for Theo to show up, not knowing that he was in the hospital or that I'd spend our Homecoming night crying alone at the barn after learning he was gone.

"I'm so sorry I ruined our day...our plans. If I hadn't—"

I shushed him softly, sliding one arm across his chest and crushing him to me.

"I don't want that to be what marks this day anymore," I told him. "As far as I'm concerned, this day still belongs to us. We're just a little late claiming it."

Theo ducked his head, likely still beating himself up for mistakes long forgiven. I slid my hand across his jaw and turned his head towards me, those mesmerizing blues ensnaring me as always.

"You came home to me, Theo. That's what I'm choosing to remember. I couldn't ask for a better Homecoming than that."

I captured his mouth in a soft kiss, soaking in how his lips moved against mine. His tongue teased at the seam of my lips and I parted for him, feeding him a groan while he took over the kiss. He twisted to loop his arms around my neck, raking his fingers through my hair before yanking the strands just enough to send zaps of painful pleasure down to my dick.

I released him before we could get carried away, and the wild look he gave me had me stifling a laugh.

"Are you *kidding* me? Again?"

"Don't want to waste the daylight," I tsked. I only made it a few steps outside before Theo barreled into me, pitching us both into the pool on our right. Theo's bright laugh hit me when I resurfaced and he splashed me with another wave of water.

"Seriously?" I sputtered and coughed, but Theo only laughed harder, hooking me around the waist and reeling me in.

"You know what they say, beautiful; play stupid games, win stupid prizes," he purred, biting my earlobe and sucking it between his soft lips.

The air was punched from my lungs and a growl escaped me. I stole his mouth in a scorching kiss as he wrapped his legs around me. I could feel his smile against my lips that I couldn't help but return. After several long minutes of lazy kisses broken up by helpless laughter, we raced each other down to the shore. The minute we hit the water, shoving and splashing each other with childish enthusiasm.

Seeing Theo so uninhibited and happy filled my chest with an incredible warmth. I wanted to drown out every malicious voice and thought, chase away every shadow that plagued him. It wouldn't work forever, but for now it was enough.

Between hours of swimming, talking, and laying out in the sun, I was pleasantly tired and happier than I'd been in weeks. Well, outside of time spent with Theo.

We'd finally called it a day and came in for dinner. I was no great cook, but I could whip up chicken and pasta easily enough, which was more than could be said for Theo whose skills stopped at pouring milk over cereal. However, I wasn't going to turn down his offer to clean the kitchen instead.

I sauntered into the living room, eyeing the baby grand piano in the corner. Music had been running through my head all day, my fingers thrumming with need. I had barely touched my guitar in the last two months and it'd been even longer since I'd played a piano, leaving me unsettled and pent up.

The piano's closed black lid was like liquid obsidian in the setting sun coming in through the floor-to-ceiling glass walls. Dad had gifted it to Mom for their tenth anniversary because, like me, she could rarely go without the feel of the keys beneath her fingers. I sat on the bench and my hands began moving across the keys fluidly as I lost myself in the music, the rich chords filling the room and my soul.

"That's one I haven't heard in forever. I always loved this slower version of yours," Theo mused behind me. I smiled, continuing with the 'Viva La Vida' cover and eventually picking up with the lyrics. Theo slid onto the bench as I sang, leaning on me and sending sparks down my arm.

"You know, the looks and the sports talent were bad enough, but that voice of yours is proof that God plays favorites," he quipped, kissing my shoulder.

I scoffed at his teasing and elbowed him. His laugh washed over me and even after hearing it all day, it made my heart thump erratically in my chest. I rested my forehead on his, breathing him in.

"I'm really glad we're getting to do this."

"Me too," he replied softly. "I've been going kind of crazy barely seeing you. I might be your trophy husband, but I require more attention than this."

"Hmm no, I'm sorry. You only get conditional affection when it suits my schedule."

"I want a divorce...and my alimony won't be cheap."

"Oh good, I've been looking to trade in for a newer model."

Theo hip-checked me hard enough to damn near catapult me off the bench. I laughed at his disgruntled expression, curving a hand around his neck and reeling him in for a possessive kiss. I slowly pulled back and his hooded eyes seared through me. The words got trapped in my throat while a melody echoed in my mind, giving me what my voice couldn't.

I repositioned myself behind the keys and let the music flow. Theo recognized it instantly of course. "Faithfully" was one of the first songs I learned just for him and the blinding smile that spread across his face could have torn the heart straight from my chest.

I barely finished the song before Theo pounced, straddling me and claiming my mouth. He kissed me greedily, robbing me of coherent thought as his tongue dove in to tangle with mine.

I sought out the hem of his shirt, our mouths only separating long enough for me to rip it over his head. He quickly did the same for me, his fingers caressing my abs. I groaned when he moved them to stroke over my straining dick.

I reached behind him to close the fallboard over the keys and stood with him in my arms, gently setting him on top of the piano. My hand went to his chest and I pushed him back, a low laugh escaping me as he tried to chase my lips.

"Lean back for me, baby. Let me make you feel good."

Theo's eyes widened at my uncharacteristic display of dominance, but he fell back on his elbows and widened his legs. I tugged his swim shorts off and stood back to admire his lean, toned body and the ink covering his skin.

"You're so fucking stunning, Theo," I rasped, raking my gaze over him. "I want to spend hours tracing every tattoo of yours with my tongue and then mark them with my cum."

"Fucking hell, Dawson. Where has this filthy mouth come from?" he panted, his body flushing pink with arousal. I shrugged, not really having an answer other than I've been fucking dying to explore more with him, break out of the comfort zone of sex we'd had as teens. His blown out pupils and heavy breathing told me that he didn't mind one bit.

"I want to see you," he pleaded, staring longingly at the erection straining my own shorts. I pushed them down and stepped out of them, feeling the heated gaze he trailed down my naked form like a physical caress.

I stepped between his legs and ran my fingers teasingly down the coarse hair under his belly button that ran down to a thatch of trimmed blond hair, but it was his long, swollen cock that had me salivating. He hissed when I traced my index finger around the leaking head, gathering the precum there. I sucked it into my mouth, moaning from the hint of his flavor and then I fisted his length, stroking him slowly. I swooped down to kiss him again, plundering his sweet mouth as he fed me breathy moans and gasps that shot straight to my balls.

"Please suck me...I need your mouth," he croaked, a strangled moan tearing out of him as I twisted over the tip.

Without any more preamble, I took his head into my mouth, my tongue digging into his slit to steal the precum beaded there before swallowing him down.

"Christ, yes," Theo cursed, gripping my hair roughly. "Take me all the way in...that's it."

I moaned around him, savoring his needy sounds. Theo's hips pumped in time with my mouth as I bobbed over him in a steady, slow rhythm. I rolled his balls in my palm and hollowed out my cheeks to suck him harder.

"Oh goddamn...just like that, beautiful. Oh my *god*. Shit, I'm already getting close..."

Well, that just won't do...

I sucked off of him with a pop and he whined in complaint, but I wanted something else. My eyes met his and my heart thundered in my chest.

"Lift your feet and put them on the edge of the lid. Legs wide."

His eyes flickered with curiosity, but he did as I asked. My breath caught at the sight of his pink, puckered hole, and I bit back a groan as it fluttered under my gaze.

"W-what are you doing?" he breathed, excitement and nerves coating his voice.

"Can I rim you, baby?"

My voice came out husky and thick with uncontrollable lust coursing through me. It was something I'd thought about in passing, but now I was aching to hold him open and eat him until he screamed for me. I saw the apprehension in his eyes, seeing as this was new territory for us. As teenagers, we had sort of fallen into a strict dynamic of top and bottom, too naive and inexperienced to discuss and try anything else. And it was fucking great back then and I still loved it, but now...

"Are you sure?" His teeth sank into his bottom lip while he scanned my face for any sign of hesitation. I nodded slowly, my eyes locked on his as I rubbed his calves soothingly. Theo stayed silent, but widened his legs more and grabbed himself under one leg to hold it off to the side, baring himself to me completely.

"Have you ever..." I let the question hang between us, dreading his answer. Theo shook his head slowly and air rushed back into my lungs.

I leaned in and ran my nose along his crease, my head swimming with the smell of sea salt and his own natural musk. I felt a tremor run through him and I wasted no time licking a bold stripe over his center, the taste of him exploding on my tongue. His hips bucked in response and I pinned his waist down before burying myself between his cheeks.

"Shit! Oh, *fuck* yes...Dawson..."

I became unhinged as I devoured him, licking, sucking, owning him with my mouth as his cries grew louder. I swirled and circled his hole, softening it enough to breach it with my tongue. Fuck, why hadn't we ever tried this before? I was addicted after one hit, the feel of his hole spasming around my tongue arousing as hell.

I fucked him with my tongue, plunging into him as deep as I could get, but when his rim clenched down on me and his thighs started to shake, I stopped my sensual assault.

"Oh fuck," Theo gasped out. "Why did you stop?"

My lips curved up, a wicked desire racing through my veins as I took in how debauched and desperate he looked.

"Because I want you to fuck my face while I finger this greedy hole. I sang for you, so now I'm going to make your body sing for me, Theo. You'll make the prettiest sounds when you flood my mouth."

His mouth dropped open and a shudder racked his frame at my crude words. I sucked two fingers in my mouth, getting them sloppy wet before bringing them back to his puffy rim. His muscles tensed as I prodded at his entrance and I shushed him gently.

"I'll be careful, baby. Just relax and let me in. I promise you'll fucking love this."

I sealed my lips around the glistening head of his cock, flicking my tongue back and forth over the sensitive skin underneath it, and Theo's head dropped back on a loud groan. The blowjob was messy as hell, the obscene slurping noises making me damn near delirious. Spit slid down his taint and I swirled it around his hole, slowly sliding one finger into him. The heat of his channel was scorching and my balls throbbed at the thought of sinking inside him.

I continued to torment him with hard, controlled suction as my finger pumped in and out. Theo's grip on my hair tightened painfully as I shoved another wet finger in and the sting on my scalp made my own hips thrust forward uncontrollably. My fingers curved up, searching out that spongy button that would shoot him sky high and the second I hit it, Theo let out a hoarse shout.

"*Oh my god*, don't stop..." he mewled. "That's it. Right there. You look so fucking perfect around my cock. Fuck babe, I'm so damn close..."

I doubled down and sucked him to the back of my throat, gagging slightly as I swallowed around his iron length while my digits worked that magic spot of his. Theo's cries and groans filled the room as he fucked up into my mouth, chasing his pleasure. My own dick was throbbing as I humped the air, so fucking close to blowing my load just from the carnal sounds alone.

My jaw ached and tears blurred my eyes as I worked him over faster, craving his cum more than anything else.

"Gonna come," Theo grunted. "Holy shit, I'm gonna come...Dawson, *fuck!*"

I sucked him harder and pegged his prostate just right. His hot, salty seed filled my mouth as his length pulsed and his ass clamped down on my fingers. My balls drew up tight as my own cock jerked, spurting my release all over the floor as I moaned and tried to swallow everything he gave me. He tasted like sin and pleasure, a dirty treat that I wanted to earn every single day.

Theo finally collapsed back on the piano, untangling his hand from my hair and quaking with the aftershocks of his orgasm. I flopped down over his stomach, my shaky legs barely holding me up as I came down from the euphoric high.

"Give me a minute and I'll take care of you," Theo gasped between heaving breaths.

"No need. S'all good," I slurred, all cum-drunk and hazy.

He stroked my hair and peered down at me in wonder. "Damn, Mercury...did you come just from blowing me, pretty boy?"

Well shit, that was a new one...and I didn't hate it because truth be told, Theo made me feel pretty. And treasured. And perfect. I wanted to always be his pretty boy, his beautiful Mercury. It was a need in me as powerful and necessary as oxygen.

"Maybe...what's it to you?"

Theo's laugh was a sexy rasp that liquified my insides. He gingerly slid off the piano lid, grimacing at the cum painting his abs. I fell to my knees and started licking him clean, a sharp gasp falling from his mouth. Once I'd cleaned him of every stray drop, he pulled me to my feet and took my mouth in a devastating kiss. I melted for him, parting my lips and letting him claim me, do anything he fucking wanted to me.

"You're gonna be the death of me," he rumbled, his sweaty brow pressed to mine and my face cradled in his strong hands.

"Uh uh, you're not getting off that easy. I have plans for us," I chuckled tiredly.

"What kind of plans are we talking about?"

I ran my thumb reverently over his bottom lip, grinning when he nipped at it with his teeth.

"Enough to last a lifetime."

CHAPTER THIRTY-ONE

I woke the next morning with my arm draped over Dawson from behind, his naked, sculpted form curved into mine and my dick nestled temptingly between his cheeks. I nuzzled into his warm neck, inhaling his intoxicating scent that turned my morning wood diamond hard.

I slowly started rutting into his crease, my teeth sinking into my lower lip to muffle the groan trying to break free. We'd fucked twice more last night before my dick gave out on me, and I'd refused to let Dawson wash away the cum I'd left stuffed in his tight hole. I felt fucking insatiable for him, which was a goddamn blessing considering the meds had a history of killing my libido more often than not.

Dawson stirred slightly, a soft grumble morphing into a moan when I teased his nipple with my thumb. Shit, all I wanted was to bury myself inside him, but we hadn't ever talked about being woken with sex. It was another new territory for us, so I needed the words from him first.

I started stroking over his smooth skin, gently coaxing him out of his sleepy state and peppering his neck and shoulder with kisses and gentle bites. He let out a small whimper and began moving with my hips, pushing back on my rigid shaft.

"Can I fuck you, beautiful?"

He nodded his head vigorously with a quiet whine, reaching back and clawing at my hip to urge me closer to him. I rolled him onto his stomach and used my knee to push his legs apart. Dawson's hands dug into the sheets as I breached his entrance in one, slow shove, the cum from last night allowing me to tunnel inside easily.

"God fucking damn," I choked out, pausing to get a hold of myself so I didn't bust in two seconds. "Shit, Mercury...you're sucking me in so deep. Nothing feels more perfect than your sweet hole strangling my cock."

My name fell from his lips in a plaintive moan and he tilted his ass up to let me slide in even further. Our groans mingled together as I started thrusting, hard and fast, plowing him into the mattress as I came undone. The slapping of skin and squelching of my cum as I drove into him was overwhelming, spreading fire through every vein and artery.

"You're so good for me, baby. My pretty little thing...you fucking love when I split you open with my cock, don't you? You want me to fill this sloppy hole of yours again?"

Dawson's ass spasmed around my shaft as he cursed, his muscles tensing all over as I spewed dirty promises in his ear.

"Please Theo...oh god, please..."

His begging almost had me hurtling over the edge, but I needed him to get there first. There was no way I was coming until I fucked the cum from his body. I angled my pelvis up and he cried out when I hit his prostate. I pummeled it over and over, my orgasm rushing to the surface. I snuck my hand under him to stroke his swollen length.

"Fuck babe, I need you to come. I'm too close. Fucking bust for me so I can flood your tight little pussy just like you want."

"Theo!" Dawson shouted as he quaked beneath me, his release soaking my hand and the bed spread.

"That's it...*oh fuck*, that's hot. I'm right there..."

I slammed into him relentlessly until my cock pulsed, shooting off as his ass milked me for all I had. My orgasm washed over me so intensely I was sure I'd black out, grinding into him over and over as I filled him to the brim, my seed spilling out where we were joined.

Both of us were panting for air and tremors ran down Dawson's sated body. I carefully pulled out of him and seeing my cum leak out of his hole made my spent cock give a pathetic little twitch.

"Damn, that's a sexy sight..." I muttered, swiping my finger over his red, swollen rim and pushing my release back into him.

Dawson let out a low groan and shivered at the intrusion. "That's a hell of a wakeup call."

"I couldn't help it. I'd live inside your ass if I could."

His chuckle sounded like rolling thunder and it made my stomach swoop fiercely. The bed dipped beside me as he stood up and stretched, then checked the time on his phone.

"Hey now...where do you think you're going?"

"We're gonna take a shower and then I have a surprise for you."

"If that surprise doesn't involve you and me naked in bed for the next...eighteen hours, then I'm not interested."

"Eighteen hours?"

"Give or take," I shrugged. "I'm open to arguments for twenty."

"Theo..."

"Okay okay! Nineteen," I rolled my eyes.

The damn sacrifices I make around here, I swear...

He snorted and ripped the covers off me, tossing them to the floor. "Come on, get up. I promise you'll love the surprise. And I'll even throw in some naked time later to sweeten the deal."

I narrowed my gaze at him, contemplating whether or not to seduce him back to bed until he forgot about this little side quest of his, but I decided to be generous and let him have this one.

"Fine," I sighed. "You drive a hard bargain, but I accept your terms."

I followed a grinning Dawson into the shower where we spent longer than necessary soaping each other up. I was lighter and more refreshed than I'd been in weeks. Every moment spent here with Dawson so far was a shot of dopamine to my brain, neurons sizzling with pleasure and energy that I was desperate for more of. It was as though the Lithium didn't stand a chance against the full force of happiness that Dawson was capable of giving me.

My therapist Maggie warned me that I would likely experience a bit of a crash when I returned from our trip. It made sense since things couldn't always be like they were now with my unfettered access to Dawson and the reprieve we were both getting from our daily lives. Soon, we'd go back to school and away games and carving out time for each other when we could. That cloud of depression would sweep back in because not even the sun could last forever.

I tried not to get caught up worrying about those things while we drove to wherever Dawson was taking me. It was much more pleasant to occupy myself with staring at Dawson in his sexy as fuck sunglasses with a satisfied smirk kicking up his full lips.

Fifteen minutes later, he pulled up behind a beachfront stilt house and my curiosity piqued. The bold turquoise paint job was intensely bright in the midday sun, burning my retinas and making it hard to open my eyes. Somewhere above us, I heard a gruff voice call out to Dawson over the sound of the crashing waves and circling seagulls.

"Well, if that isn't my favorite nephew! 'Bout damn time you two showed up. The day's half over, boy." The man's deep twang tugged at my memory and when my eyes finally managed to adjust, I barked out a disbelieving laugh when I saw him. His skin was weathered from the sun and his taupe hair was woven with silver now, but there was no mistaking the hulking man.

"Holy shit! Uncle Don?"

Don squinted down at me from his deck before breaking into a massive smile.

"Look at what the cat coughed up," he said in a throaty chuckle as he made his way down the porch steps. "Bishop, you get uglier e'ry time I see you. I thought puberty was supposed to help you out with that."

"I think your eyesight's going, old man. I'm hot as shit now," I beamed. I crossed over to him and body slammed him in a giant hug, the familiar smell of his pipe tobacco comforting me.

It had been years since I'd seen Mr. Hayes' older brother, but he'd been a staple in my life as much as Dawson's parents had been. He used to sneak us both money whenever he visited and he was the first one we came out to the summer we started dating. Of course, that was because he'd busted us making out in the den, but beyond giving us shit for it, he had been incredibly supportive.

He placed his hands on my shoulders and pushed me back, assessing me from head to toe with a wry smirk.

"Eh, I guess you'll do...how long has it been? Six years since I seen you?"

"Sounds about right, sir."

"Ah, to hell with that nonsense." He swatted his hand as if to wave away my words. "I ain't no 'sir'. I'll leave that to my father."

"I didn't know you moved your decrepit ass down here," I snickered, dodging a backhand to the gut when he swiped at me.

"You keep laughing and I'll make sure you don't make it back home, you little shit," he chortled. "I wanted to spend my retired years by the beach but still close to family, so here I am. Dawson, you quit skulkin' over there and give me a hug."

"Now you notice me? I thought I was your favorite nephew?" Dawson teased, but allowed Don to sweep him up in a bone-crushing hug.

"That was when I thought you'd get here earlier."

"We were embracing the island time mentality. I thought punctuality wasn't a thing down here," he argued as Don led us around his property to a large shed.

"Maybe for them locals, but I still enjoy my schedule. Three years here and it hasn't got any easier, I tell you." He swung open the shed door and rummaged around, hauling out two thin boards with foot straps attached that he thrust at Dawson. He then handed my confused ass two large folded swaths of neon green nylon and two black harnesses.

"Anyone want to fill me in?" I asked as I followed the two of them down to the shoreline. Dawson stuck the boards in the sand and turned to me sheepishly.

"You said you always wanted to try kiteboarding, so I asked Uncle Don to teach us. Is that okay? Should I have asked first?"

I dropped my bundle of gear and seized his face, crushing my mouth to his. I swallowed his gasp of surprise and my tongue lashed at his, drinking in the way he melted under my touch. I pulled back just enough to take in his breathless and dazed expression.

"You were right."

"I usually am, but what about this time?" he asked, voice thick with both lust and amusement.

"I do love the surprise. And I definitely owe you some naked time for this one."

Dawson's lips curved into a coy smile and I dove back in for another kiss, unable to resist another taste.

"If you two take much longer, your mouths are gonna fuse together like that. Get your asses over here and let's get on the water already!"

I reluctantly released his lips. "You know, that wouldn't be the worst fate."

"Says you..." Dawson quipped, stealing a quick kiss before darting towards the water with a laugh. I raced after him, joy surging in my chest as I followed him into the waves.

I STARED into the flames of the small bonfire, my toes digging into the cool sand as the dreamy sounds of Dawson's guitar floated around me.

Yesterday had been a fucking dream. The adrenaline rush from kiteboarding was addictive as hell and I'd gotten the hang of it quicker than I thought. Afterwards, we'd spent a few hours swimming and fishing with Uncle Don, having an early dinner with him before heading back to our place for a lowkey night curled up on the couch.

This morning, I woke up early to Dawson's lips wrapped around my cock and I came so hard I almost broke the headboard as I held onto it for dear life. Once I'd dropped to my knees for him in the shower, we explored the island a bit, went out for lunch in town, and spent a few hours on the beach again before hopping on a private sunset dolphin cruise that Dawson had set up for us. We'd managed to spot a few as they jumped and splashed around our boat for a bit, not the slightest bit shy, and seeing Dawson's face light up at their antics had made my heart swell.

I turned my head to the side, watching Dawson's nimble fingers on the guitar and taking in the soft shadows cast on his face from the fire. I was secretly thrilled he had brought it along on our trip. Not only was listening to him play one of my favorite things, but it was also a turn-on like no other. His skill after all these years was unreal and it never failed to stir my cock watching his talented fingers pick across the strings. Add in the way he looked in his black-rimmed glasses and I was barely restraining myself from humping his leg like a dog in heat.

I vaguely recognized the next tune he began to play, the evocative melody stirring emotions in my chest I couldn't quite name.

"What song is that?"

"I can't believe you don't recognize 'Iris'," he smirked without even missing a note.

"Well excuse me, but you weren't singing and it sounds different, all slow and acoustic-y..."

His teeth flashed in the flickering light and he raised a brow at me. "You want to try to learn it?"

I looked at him like he was crazy, but he only beckoned me over with a crooked finger. He stared at me impatiently until I crawled over into the space he left me between his legs, scooting back into his chest. He settled the instrument in my lap, his arms coming around me to position my hands just right on the strings. I shivered when he placed a warm kiss to the back of my neck while he adjusted my fingers on the neck of the guitar.

"How is this supposed to work exactly?"

"Just give me a second," he grumbled while awkwardly trying to work through the first few chords with his hand moving mine. After a few beats, I stuck to strumming the strings as he did all the work on the frets or whatever he called them.

"Hey, look at me. I'm a natural," I grinned over my shoulder. Dawson chuckled as he continued to guide me sluggishly through the song, but the smile he aimed at me made my lungs seize. He then took control of the song and my hands fell to his legs on either side of me, sinking into his warmth as he serenaded me.

His soulful tenor drifted across me like velvet. Dawson was mesmerizing, losing himself in the soft power of the lyrics. I felt each one of the lines as if he'd plucked them from my heart and threaded them into his own. Every emotion was etched into his features and I was drawn to him like a moth to a flame. I couldn't tear my eyes away, desire thickening my blood as my gaze fell to his distracting as fuck mouth.

Dawson's voice trailed off and his gaze slid to mine, noticing the shift in my mood. His breathing sped up and when his lips parted, I leaned in and licked across the soft flesh. I heard the breath catch in his throat before he slanted his mouth over mine. His tongue darted out to tease mine and an embarrassing whimper escaped me.

Dawson set his guitar aside while he claimed my mouth, one of his hands weaving in my hair and tilting my head to deepen the kiss. I was falling apart, my mind gloriously clear of everything except Dawson and how he was owning my body.

"Fuck me," I breathed over his lips. My pulse raced as he looked me in the eye with a mixture of awe and wariness. "I want you to fuck me, Mercury. I want you inside me."

It was something I'd been wanting for so long, but it was a uniquely vulnerable position to be in. Not that I had any problem being with Dawson in that way, but I had been scared to ask for it. It would have been yet another layer of myself peeled away, exposed like a raw nerve that I hadn't been ready to face. Now, I wanted to obliterate every layer and let Dawson in on a cellular level, an immutable fusion of our souls.

"You really want that?"

"More than anything," I promised. I surged forward to capture his lips again and twisted around to straddle him, all the while ravishing his mouth with uncontrollable need.

"Baby...not here," he panted between my relentless kisses.

"Yes, here. I can't wait. I want to ride you right here at the edge of the fucking ocean and scream your name under the stars."

"You really know how to motivate a guy, you know?" he laughed breathlessly. I kissed the grin from his face, rolling my erection over his and devouring his pleasured groans.

"Please, beautiful...I feel so empty. I need you to wreck my hole with that gorgeous cock and make me yours in every fucking way possible."

Dawson growled and flipped us with impressive speed so my back landed on the large beach towel underneath us. It was past midnight and our portion of the beach was deserted, and lucky for us, Dawson's only neighbors were away on a cruise. There was nothing stopping us from giving in and I wanted this too damn bad to wait any longer.

We frantically stripped our clothes and soon Dawson's strong body was holding me down, his erection grinding against mine. He kissed his way down my torso and took my aching cock in his mouth, swirling that devilish tongue around my tip and lapping up my precum like he was starved for it. My balls tightened within a minute and I yanked at his hair to pull him off me.

"S-stop...I'm gonna blow if you keep going. Please Dawson, I need you," I begged. He let out a sexy chuckle as he licked up my length one more time before planting another drugging kiss to my lips.

"Wait, we don't have any lube..."

I could only wave in the direction of the bag I brought with us and Dawson huffed a laugh through his nose at my preparedness. He leaned over and dug through the hotdog and s'more supplies to find the small bottle of lube I'd stashed. He reached up to remove his glasses, but I grabbed his wrist to stop him.

"No, leave them on."

He smiled softly at my demand and doused his fingers quickly, bringing them to my quivering hole.

"If it hurts or you want to stop at any time, tell me."

I nodded and dragged him back down to my mouth as he circled my rim before entering me gently. I hissed at the slight burn, but Dawson moved to suck on my earlobe and my bones turned molten. My muscles loosened enough for him to fully breach me, carefully pumping deeper into my body. I let out a sharp cry when he swiped a spot that radiated electricity through me.

"Oh sweet Jesus, do that again," I gasped, rocking back on Dawson's finger involuntarily.

"Topping from the bottom a bit, aren't you?" he grinned down at me, but he aimed for that spot again and I convulsed under him, his name tearing from me in an agonized plea.

He didn't waste anymore time opening me up, scissoring and stretching me until I was practically sobbing for his cock. Dawson trickled some more lube on his length and smeared the excess on my puckered skin before sitting up and pulling me with him.

I straddled him once more and he lined himself up with my hole. Our eyes connected and my heart stopped, waves of all-consuming emotion washing over me and drowning me in the intensity.

I hovered above him, waiting for permission. He dipped his chin and I lowered myself onto him until he popped through the outer muscle, lighting me up like a fuse lit too close to the end. I bore down and he thrust in deeper, a strangled moan ripping from me while he sank in more. When his pelvis met my ass, I paused, shaking from the overwhelming sensation of finally having him this way.

I'd never felt so full, so fucking complete as I did with Dawson buried inside my body. The way he felt was beyond perfection, beyond nirvana. It was as if heaven was just a rest stop on the road leading to this moment with him.

I lifted up and dropped back down, riding him at a languid pace, each drag of his steely length against my inner walls making me tremble. I wrapped my arms around his shoulders, leaning my forehead on his as we moved together effortlessly. We vibrated on the same frequency, our bodies matching a rhythm that we started long ago.

"Dawson..." My voice caught as he swiped my prostate and a flare of heat shot through my groin.

"Am I making you feel good, baby? Is this okay?" he whispered roughly, his strong hands gripping my hips to help guide me.

"It's perfect...*you're* perfect. Oh fuck, give me more."

He sped up his thrusts, driving up into me with abandon, and I cried out at the building pressure. I was on sensory overload, my thighs burning as I rode him hard, the salty air mixing with his delicious, woodsy scent, and his slick muscles contracting under me as he fucked me within an inch of my life. I was high on the pleasure, my head swimming as bliss consumed me.

"I love you so much," I gasped out. "Oh god...you're fucking me so good. Shit, I'm gonna come..."

"Yeah, you are," he ground out, intensifying his strokes. "Do you love my cock, baby? Is this what you wanted? Do you need me to paint your insides with my load?"

"Jesus Christ, that mouth...give it to me. Shoot every drop in my ass and mark me as yours, beautiful."

He flipped us again and came down on top of me, fucking into me harder and deeper as my orgasm raced down my spine. Obscenely filthy sounds poured from me as Dawson pummeled my hole, his cock flexing inside me and I felt the telltale heat bloom in my groin.

"Come for me, Theo," he purred in my ear, hitting that sweet spot inside over and over.

Dawson's name tore from my throat as my release slammed into me, hot liquid coating our stomachs as Dawson continued to rut into me wildly. I was engulfed in flames, consuming me from head to toe like a wildfire of pleasure that ignited my entire body. My channel spasmed around Dawson's shaft and he cried out as he drenched my hole with his seed, still driving into me until he was completely drained.

It was everything I needed, filling in a hole I hadn't known was there. My eyes stung as the adrenaline slowly fizzled out and my heart pounded behind my ribs. Dawson dropped soft kisses across my collarbone and up my neck, his cock softening inside me.

I reached up and dragged my fingertips across his stubbled jaw, our heavy breaths mingling between us. His lids fluttered at the contact and my heart stumbled over itself seeing how my touch affected him.

"I love you with all that I am, Theo. No matter what we face, I am yours."

He took my lips in a long, deep kiss that rooted itself in my bones. We stayed outside longer than we should have, tangled together in a cum-soaked, sweaty mess that neither of us was in a hurry to leave.

I wasn't sure what would happen once we left this place, and a faint, ominous voice inside told me that something dark was coming. But I refused to let it steal the joy that was thrumming in my veins as Dawson held me in his arms, reminding me that the love of this man was enough to withstand any storm.

CHAPTER THIRTY-TWO

"So how have things been recently? I was sorry to hear you cancelled your appointment last week. The last time we saw each other, you were about to go on a trip with your boyfriend, correct?"

Maggie's calm tone and warm smile should have been comforting, but it only made my annoyance flare. I hadn't been prepared for how quickly my mood would nosedive after Port Aransas, and I wasn't handling it as well as I should have, hence the cancellation last Wednesday. Dawson hadn't been happy about that one, but oh well.

"Yeah," I muttered. "Almost three weeks ago."

"You sound a bit agitated. Did the trip not go as you had hoped?"

"No, it was incredible. It was better than I had imagined it would be. I wish we had never left," I mumbled.

Maggie hummed sympathetically, jotting down a quick note before regarding me with a knowing gaze. "I take it some problems arose once you came home then."

"You could say that," I scoffed, remembering how things had started to slide downhill within a few days of us returning. When I didn't elaborate, Maggie stayed silent and watched me with that open, nonjudgmental expression that always had me spilling my guts.

"I just...I know you warned me that I might crash out some when I got back, but I didn't think I'd get so fucked up in the head," I confessed quietly.

"How so?"

"The first few days back weren't so bad. It sucked going back to being buried in homework and having to play second fiddle to Dawson's football stuff. I mean, I don't blame him at all because that's his life right now and after this season, he'll be done. But it was really hard to go from having him all to myself for this one, perfect weekend to barely seeing him again. It's somehow even harder now than it was before."

"That's understandable. Why do you feel it's harder this time?"

I didn't want to admit to her what I was feeling. While I liked Maggie and felt comfortable enough talking with her, there was still that inherent distrust in telling her too much about what went on in my head. That constant fear that if I said the wrong thing, she'd shove me in a mental hospital and I'd lose everything I'd worked so hard to get back.

"I'm not sure," I lied, hoping she didn't press the issue. I squirmed under her scrutinizing glare.

"How would you describe your overall mood the last couple of weeks?"

Fucking abysmal.

"Not great, but not too bad."

"Mmm...and have you had any suicidal thoughts since the last time we met?"

Yes, and they're growing loud enough to fucking terrify me...

"Not really."

She squinted at me as though trying to see through the curtain of lies I was hiding behind. It took everything in me to hold her gaze and will her not to see the truth. I'd give it to Dawson...he's who I promised it to anyway.

"Theo, remember when I told you that therapy only works if you *want* it to work and you're willing to be open and honest with yourself?"

The words were spoken softly and without accusation, but I could hear the underlying warning in her tone.

"Yeah, why?"

She shrugged daintily, her lips quirking up in a sweet smile. "I just thought you could use the reminder. Have you thought more about seeing the psychiatrist I recommended?"

I bit back the angry reply that wanted to come out. We'd been having this particular discussion for the last three sessions after I'd detailed my horrible experiences with rehab and my medication.

"Still not sure about that," I said.

Maggie let out a deep sigh and her brows wrinkled. For the first time, she seemed frustrated with me. She was always so even-keeled when we talked, but I could tell my stubbornness was getting to her.

"I can't tell you what to do, but I honestly think you should get reevaluated for new medication. You told me you've been very inconsistent with taking the Lithium the last few years and its efficacy declines each time you go off of it. When you're not stable in taking it, it doesn't work as well as it should. Seeing a psychiatrist—a new one that *you* have chosen and trust, *not* your mother—could give you some answers and better options than you were given in the past."

I weighed her suggestion and I understood why she thought it might help, but I didn't want to go through that again. It got me nowhere last time and I was so fucking sick of taking meds just to fucking get by. This was why I felt so goddamn hopeless. I would never be able to have a normal life. I'd be constantly on guard, constantly medicated, constantly worrying that I'd finally be pulled so far down into that abyss that there would be no saving me.

I didn't want to fucking be like this anymore.

"I'll think about it," I told her. *Another lie.*

She didn't seem to believe me, but thankfully she moved onto other topics and we wrapped up the session forty minutes later. I got in my car to head back to my apartment and saw a text from Dawson waiting for me. I was relieved when my heart gave a little flutter at seeing his name.

At least I haven't gone completely numb yet...

MERCURY

Hey baby, are you out of therapy yet?

ME

Just got out. You coming over?

MERCURY

Yeah, I've got a couple hours before practice.
Want me to bring tacos?

ME

I drove home with a million razor-edged thoughts flying through my brain, each one more cutting than the last. I'd been honest with Dawson about feeling more down lately, and even though I knew he was trying not to, he worried more each time we saw each other. I fucking despised myself for feeling irritated with him when he asked questions or tried to cheer me up, mostly because I knew it wouldn't work.

It was like the last bits of happiness I had in my soul were wrung out on that beach and all that was left were the dregs of my own humanity. I didn't feel like myself anymore. I felt angry and hopeless, if I even felt anything at all. And that was the real truth I couldn't share with Maggie. It was harder to be without Dawson now because I was so fucking scared that not even he had the power to pull me out of this, that there was no way for him to help me keep my head above the water this time.

I walked in my door and threw my keys on the coffee table. I barely had time to change into comfy clothes before I heard the front lock disengage and came out of my room to see Dawson waltz in, a brown paper bag tucked in the crook of his arm. He gave me that dazzling smile of his and I wanted to cry at the lack of reaction my body had. His smile had never failed to unleash butterflies in my stomach, but it was yet another thing this goddamn disease had stolen from me.

His face fell when I could barely muster a smile in return and fuck, I hated myself so damn much in that moment. I hated disappointing him, but that's all I was good for. All I'd ever be.

"Hey baby, how did it go with Maggie?" he asked cheerily, attempting to brush off the hurt that I saw in his eyes.

"It was good. Same old, same old."

"Oh. Good then," he replied, avoiding my gaze while he laid out the food for us. We started to dig in, but the food was bland and went down like mush. Considering it was one of our favorite places for Tex-Mex, it meant that *I* was the problem. Yet another source of pleasure robbed by this fucking disease.

"How have your classes been lately?" Dawson asked between bites.

"They're alright."

"I mean, are you able to keep up with the coursework? Are your grades still okay? You know if you need any help, I can tutor you or see if any of our friends have old class notes they could share."

I understood logically that he was trying to help during an obvious rough patch. Unfortunately, my irritation still simmered and I barely bit back my retort. I sucked in a calming breath and reminded myself that he loved me and didn't deserve my shit.

"I appreciate it, babe, but I've got it. All under control. Promise."

Eh, mostly...mostly still counts.

In truth, I was struggling to maintain focus in my classes and my grades were gradually slipping. I was lucky that academics had never been overly difficult for me, so I was faring better than I likely had a right to, but it only made the slow decline that much harder to stomach.

Dawson seemed mollified by my answer and moved onto other mind-numbing topics until he came back full circle.

"By the way, did you ask Maggie about doing a virtual session the week of Thanksgiving? I don't want you to have to miss another one while we're back home."

"Uh, no. I forgot," I muttered. I could sense his frustration rising with mine, but I had just gotten out of therapy. I didn't want to keep talking about it.

"Just...try to remember to ask her next week, okay? It's coming up fast," he sighed.

"Sure, Dad." The sardonic reply was nothing more than a whisper, but I knew he heard it when he tensed beside me. "It's not like we'll even have much time together, so what else is there for me to do?"

"What's that supposed to mean?"

"It means you'll be too busy with your family since they'll want all your time. And it's also just more nights I'll have to spend alone..."

Dawson's brow furrowed and he huffed out a loud breath, dropping his taco on his plate. "Where the hell did that come from? Mom has already asked me if you're going to be staying with us since your dad will be out of town, so we'll be together almost the entire week. The only time we won't have is on Friday because of my game, but I'll be back later that night."

I grumbled under my breath, focusing on my food rather than admit he was right. He softened and leaned into my space, his lips brushing my ear as he spoke.

"And I don't know what crazy ideas you've got in that gorgeous head of yours, but there is no way I'd let you sleep alone that week, even if your dad *was* home. I'd just climb in through your window like old times and crawl into your bed every single night so you could fuck me hard and fill me with that hot cum of yours just like I need."

He sucked at the diamond stud on my earlobe seductively and his hand coasted into my lap, fondling my limp cock through my sweats. I closed my eyes and tried to surrender to the sensation, willing my body to respond to him like it always had...but it was useless. It didn't matter that I loved him and wanted him more than the air in my lungs. My mind was frighteningly numb and my body followed suit.

Dawson's hand faltered when he noticed I wasn't getting hard, and he leaned back to look at me. The rejection that streaked across his face cracked my heart down the middle and I caressed his cheek before pressing my lips to his. I kissed him with every ounce of love and devotion I had for him, but even I could tell it was different.

"Tell me what's wrong, baby," he pleaded.

"Nothing is—" I stopped before the lie could slip out. "It's just been hard to...get in the mood lately. I told you things have been off with me."

"Is it me? Did I do something—"

"It's not you, Dawson. It's me and my fucked up brain, ok?" I snapped and instantly wished I could tear my own tongue out. Dawson paled and put some distance between us.

"I'm sorry, that was a stupid question to ask. I didn't mean...I'm not trying to make it about me, I swear. I only meant..."

Hearing him stammer and fidget with nerves made me want to rip my hair out and beg God to fix me already so I would stop hurting this perfect, sweet man who didn't deserve any of my shit. But that didn't stop the deluge of frustration and anger at myself from coming out and finding the next easiest target.

"What do you want me to say?" I gritted out. "I'm doing everything I'm supposed to and I'm still a shitty, broken mess. It's not anything you did or haven't done, it's just me. Fuck, I haven't even wanted to masturbate in three weeks because the only thing I seem to feel anymore is exhaustion. I'm too tired to do anything but wake up each morning and try to function like a regular person, but I'm *not*."

"Theo, if that's true, then why haven't you talked to the psychiatrist that Maggie recommended? Maybe she can help—"

"Help do what, Dawson?" I practically shouted. "Nothing really helps! I've been lucky to get these small breaks of actual happiness with you between all the shit, but it never lasts. Lithium is supposed to be the big, shiny gold standard in treating bipolarism or whatever the fuck, so what could she give me that would work better? And what if it only makes things worse? I don't want to take that chance...not when it can cost me you."

Dawson reeled back as if I'd struck him, but I couldn't force my body to go to him. An aching sadness simmered in my chest, yet no tears came. It was like there was a barrier keeping me from feeling everything I was supposed to feel.

Dawson cautiously came around to me, leaving only inches between us that I desperately wanted to erase, but I didn't deserve it. I didn't deserve to seek comfort in his embrace or have him soothe my frazzled nerves. But when his strong hands gently framed my face, I leaned into his touch. His love was my gravity, his touch all that kept me grounded to the earth.

"Is that what you really think? That there is any chance in Hell that you could lose me?"

His broken whisper cut into my skin and I bled guilt and regret onto the floor between us.

"You shouldn't have to put up with all this just to love me," I choked out. "It's too much. *I'm* too much..."

"It's not a chore to love you, Theo," he said adamantly. "I know you think your illness will change how I feel about you, but I swear that will never happen. I will find every way there is to love you for every good and bad day, every high and every low. I will be with you through it all unconditionally, loving you as I always have. You are never too much for me because I can never get enough of you."

I crashed into him, taking his lips with a fervor that pulled a needy moan from his throat. I inhaled it like it was the antidote to all the poison within me, wishing it could cure me. But luck had never been on my side in this battle.

Dawson pulled away and gave me a hopeful smile at the same time all the hope I carried died away. Despite every promise I made him, I couldn't protect Dawson from being the collateral damage of my own demons. If I didn't do something soon, it wouldn't matter how much he loved me. I would sink too far under the surface where even he couldn't follow.

CHAPTER THIRTY-THREE

The bus ride back to Austin seemed to last forever even though it was only three hours from Fort Worth back to the city. We'd won the game against TCU and I should have been as psyched as my teammates were that we were one step closer to the championship, but all I could think of was getting back to Theo. However, I was still wrestling with the nerves of how he'd be when I got home.

It had been so hard to convince my brain that Theo still desired me under the haze of the drugs when we'd gone without sex since coming back from our trip. I understood logically that Theo would have ups and downs even with his meds, but it was fucking hard to go from one of the best weekends of my life filled with life-changing sex to having my boyfriend unable to stomach touching me.

Okay, that was a bit dramatic, but it hadn't made the rejection sting any less. After my therapist assured me that troubles with sex drive were common with Lithium use, I calmed a bit, but I still wasn't able to shake the sense that I was losing Theo.

He'd been acting strange since our argument a week ago and I didn't know whether to be concerned or if it was just normal weirdness from the pills. He was still Theo but...more. Like the dial was now cranked up too far on everything that made him *him.* His virtues and his faults, all magnified to an overwhelming degree. It was a bit jarring after the last two weeks of his moodiness and disinterest.

I was still in my head when we stepped off the bus at the practice facility, but the buzzing in my pocket brought me out of it. I swiped to answer the phone call, bracing myself for what I knew was coming and I was honestly shocked it hadn't come sooner.

"Hey Grandpa, now's not a good time. We just got back to campus."

"Well, that's too bad because we need to talk about what happened today after the game," he scolded. "Why on earth did you blow off Mike Hancock? Your father asked him to make time specifically to meet you while you were up there and he told me you spoke with Mike barely five minutes before dashing off."

I drew a calming breath into my lungs, trying not to snap that I had no damn interest in talking to the sports agent he and Dad had corralled into meeting with me without my knowledge or permission. He'd been waiting for me outside the visiting locker room, all smarmy smiles and hard handshakes like I was selling my soul to him already. I feigned nausea from the exertion of the game and ducked out of the conversation, knowing it would get back to both Dad and Grandpa fairly quickly.

"I didn't feel well. I wasn't really up to talking with anyone," I said, holding back my surly attitude.

"This is your future we're talking about. Sometimes we have to do things we don't necessarily want to do, but that are—"

"Gramps, I can't even sign with any agents before the season is over. I didn't see any reason to waste his time and I didn't want to violate any NCAA rules," I said, but my flimsy excuse didn't work.

"You know there is no violation if he's there simply to meet you and give you information, and in any case, you still should comport yourself like the professional athlete you'll soon be. If you're seen as difficult or flighty, that can count against you when agents are signing with players ahead of the draft."

A headache started to form behind my eyes from the pressure of holding in this secret for months on end. It shouldn't have been so damn hard to talk to them about it, but that didn't matter when the fear took you. Irrational or not, it had a way of digging in and poisoning the blood, whispering the worst case scenarios in your ear like a foregone conclusion.

"Yes sir," I ground out, only wanting to be done with this pointless talk and get back to my guy.

"Good. I'm sending you his number so you can call to apologize and maybe fix up another get together with him one weekend coming up. I'll see you next week for Thanksgiving and you can fill me in. You played very well today, Dawson. I'm so proud of you."

I hated how much the little bit of praise warmed me inside. I couldn't even fucking say why it mattered so much to me, especially knowing football wasn't in the cards after this season. We ended the call and now I needed Theo more than ever, no matter what mood he happened to be in.

"Baby, I'm home!" I called out as I let myself into Theo's apartment. I heard the sound of his shower running and decided it couldn't hurt to join him. The stupid, insecure part of me just hoped he wouldn't shoot down the idea. I was aching to be with him intimately again, but I was a little gun-shy after weeks of distance between us.

As I made my way towards his bedroom, my gaze snagged on his pill organizer in the middle of the island. A small niggle in my brain said something was off, and when I drew closer, I recognized why.

I knew Theo refilled his organizer every Sunday and seeing as it was Saturday night, one pill was all that should have been left. But the wells for the last four days were still full, the pills sitting there like little drops of betrayal. I tried not to assume anything, but anger and disappointment ripped through me. I was stuck in a trance, so I didn't notice Theo waltzing into the room with only a towel around his trim waist.

"Hey beautiful, I didn't know you were back yet! Why didn't you text me?" His cheery voice penetrated the fog I was in and I twisted to see a bright grin on his face. It was such a far cry from the Theo I'd experienced the last few weeks that my nose stung and my eyes blurred the slightest bit. This Theo was all I had wanted to see for nearly a month, but now I worried what the cost had been to get him back.

"Are you skipping your pills?" I croaked out, the question bursting forth before I could stop it. Theo's face fell and a gamut of emotion ran across his features. Guilt, anger, embarrassment, sadness, and finally resignation.

"Yes, but it's not what you think."

My stomach plummeted and my lids slammed shut against the stab of pain from his admittance.

"You promised me," I whispered roughly.

"I didn't break it! Not like you're thinking," he rushed out. "I haven't stopped taking them, I've just started...staggering them."

"Staggering them? Theo, you can't screw around with your medication like that!"

Theo let out a frustrated grunt. "I had to do something. I was fucking drowning again! Do you think it's easy for me to be this dead inside? To not feel things like a normal person? I've seen how much I've hurt you the last few weeks. And it fucking hurts me too!"

He closed the distance and gripped my face, his sad eyes flaying me alive with their intensity.

"I didn't want to slip further away from you. I wanted to *feel* something again." He leaned forward, growling the next words over my parted lips. "I needed to get back that uncontrollable desire that makes me want to tear off your clothes and bury myself in your tight heat until the world around us no longer exists. But I couldn't do that while I kept taking that fucking poison everyday."

My hands were wrapped around his wrists so hard I worried I'd leave bruises, but it was all that was tethering me to the earth right now. I felt so damn helpless. I wanted all the things back that we'd lost the last month, but there was a pit in my gut that didn't feel right about this.

"You told me you didn't want to try new meds because you were scared it could make things worse. What do you think this will do? You're not supposed to just...pick and choose when you take hardcore pills like this. What if—"

My voice failed as a dozen horrible possibilities buzzed in my head.

What if you become manic? What if your sex drive becomes too much to control? What if you become suicidal? What if you get into trouble?

What if I lose you again?...

"Mercury, listen to me. In the past, I've always been 'all or nothing' when it comes to the Lithium, but that's not what I'm doing this time. I know I need them and I'll never cut them out fully, so I skip some pills every few days and it's crazy how much better I feel already. I'm finally starting to feel like myself again!"

"And you really think there will be no repercussions to this?"

"I know my own body, Dawson," he said firmly, releasing my cheeks.

“Why hide it from me? You promised you wouldn’t lie to me about your health again, that you’d keep me in the loop.”

“I didn’t mean to hide it. I swear I was going to tell you once I knew if this staggering thing would level me out or not. I actually planned to tell you on the way out to your parents’ place on Monday.”

I wanted to believe that he was right. It seemed like he’d put actual thought into it and it wasn’t just a rash decision. And he was still taking the pills, which had to be better than nothing. I willed the anxiety brewing in my chest to go down.

“And you really think this is helping?” I asked cautiously.

Theo came towards me again and sank to his knees, staring up at me with a hunger that I had secretly worried I’d never see again. He brushed the backs of his fingers over my jean-clad cock and it twitched violently at the gentle contact.

“Let me prove it to you,” he purred, holding my gaze as he freed my length and began to stroke it slowly. “You don’t know how much it killed me to turn you down, to not be able to give you this. I would have given anything to bring back that fire you set off under my skin, the one that burns me up inside and makes me want to ravage your entire body until you’re completely drained.”

“Oh fuck, Theo,” I gasped as he brought me to full hardness, my tip pearling with pre-cum. His tongue darted out to lap at my slit and I cursed, grasping his shoulders tightly to keep from crumbling to the floor.

“Jesus, I missed how good you taste,” he crooned, running the flat of his tongue up the underside of my cock. “Tell me this is okay, baby. Tell me you want this as badly as I do.”

All I could manage was a frantic nod before he took me to the back of his throat, drawing a loud cry from my lips. Theo worked me over zealously, worshipping my cock with an enthusiasm that brought me to the brink too quickly. My body tightened and shook with my impending orgasm, but Theo pulled off and yanked me to the carpet, pinning me beneath his weight.

He tore his towel away and shoved my shirt up to my armpits. The image of his naked body against my mostly clothed one was strangely erotic, and when he began to grind his velvet length against mine, the stimulation was almost too much to handle.

“I need us to come together,” Theo grunted.

He leaned down and let a string of spit fall on my dark red head, then took both our cocks together in his fist. A gravelly moan poured from my throat as he started jacking us off in a frenzied tempo, my hips thrusting into his grip uncontrollably. His groans were buried in my neck and his filthy words seeped into my skin. I wanted him imprinted on my flesh, on my bones, on my fucking soul that was branded with his name.

I clawed at his back desperately, canting my pelvis up to meet his as he drove us closer to the edge. Theo latched onto my neck and sucked a bruise into the tender flesh, setting off my release. I came on a guttural shout, jets of cum shooting across my abdomen and even hitting me under my chin. Pure pleasure infused my veins, an elysian bliss that whited out my vision and devastated my senses.

Theo cried out my name as his orgasm overtook him and I felt the warm splash of his cum joining mine. He kept milking our cocks together and the stimulation bordered on pain, but I never wanted it to end. I didn't realize how badly I'd needed this connection to him until hot tears slid down the side of my temple.

When Theo raised his head, he kissed the tears away and his soft lips skimmed my face in sweet caresses. He kissed apologies on my eyelids and declarations of love on my cheeks. We just laid there on the floor, our bodies fused with the drying cum and cooling sweat, but neither of us moved. I didn't care if the world burned around us. I was exactly where I wanted to be.

But as my high faded, the worry swept back in. As much as I wanted to trust that Theo had a handle on his disorder, my gut fizzled with nerves and an undeniable sense of dread. The danger was in waiting to see what would happen as we stood on shifting sands.

CHAPTER THIRTY-FOUR

The world rocked beneath me and I was engulfed in the most incredible heat, ecstasy sweeping through me from head to toe. I was floating in that fuzzy place just before sleep faded away and I fought against it, not ready to give up the dizzying pleasure it brought me. My chest vibrated with a deep groan as the delicious sensations spiked in my groin.

"Shh, baby...let me use your body to get us both off. Good boy...just take it."

Awareness crept back in as I registered the sultry voice and the heavy weight on my thighs. I peered through blurry slits, a puzzle of light and shapes coming together in the sexiest sight imaginable.

I was incapable of speech as I watched Theo ride me, his hips rolling in a seductive rhythm that made my mouth water. I clung to his waist and tried to urge him to move faster, but he snatched my hands and pinned them above my head, content to keep torturing me with the slow, sensuous tempo.

"You have no idea how tempting you are...how much I want you. Mmm, *fuck*...I love how thick you are inside me."

His channel squeezed my dick from the inside and a desperate moan slipped out as electricity zapped through me. Theo's raspy chuckle made me shudder all over as he did it again, pulling another helpless noise from my lips.

"Oh, you like that, huh? Do you like being my beautiful little fuck-toy? This perfect cock was made for me, wasn't it? All that hot cum in there is only for me...you don't shoot that anywhere except deep in my ass or all over my body."

His dirty talk was my undoing and I used every bit of my strength to shove up and flip him underneath me. He let out a sharp cry as I drove into him, my arms bracketing his head as I set a steady pace. His pupils swallowed the blue irises as I held his gaze, thrusting slow and deep into his tight body.

Making love to Theo was a musical experience, every stroke inside him like a perfectly strummed chord. I licked and nipped and kissed at his skin, finding the right notes to play that would bend the pitch of his moans or increase the volume of his cries. The sound of our bodies coming together was a beautifully filthy melody that echoed through my soul, a flawless harmony that was beyond reckoning.

Theo was nothing but a chorus of needy sounds and grasping fingers as his body tightened around me. I closed my fist around his dripping length and pumped him in time with my thrusts.

"You're getting close...I can feel it," I rumbled in his ear. "Come on, baby. Let go and come for me..."

As soon the words left me, Theo shouted his orgasm as he poured over my hand, covering me in ropes of hot cum that set off my own release. I roared as a cascade of pleasure slammed into me with Theo's hole strangling my cock and milking me dry. Stars exploded behind my lids as I lost sense of time and the force of the sensations consumed me.

When I came to, I was lying on top of Theo as he sifted his fingers through the sweaty strands of my hair. I peeked up to find him watching me, an amused smirk on his flushed, sated face.

"Sorry I ruined your plan," I mumbled into his collarbone.

"You can ruin my plans any fucking time you want if that's the outcome, babe," he snickered.

We finally pried ourselves off each other and showered together, which was a feat since Theo couldn't seem to keep his hands to himself. Yesterday he'd been insatiable as though he was making up for the month we went without sex by cramming as many orgasms as he could in the twenty-four-hour period before we went home for the break.

Theo was restless all morning on the drive home, like he had a low hum of energy just below his skin. He changed the music in the car every other minute and fidgeted with his hands and feet to the point that it was making *me* feel restless. I tried to shove down the worry that bled through because he had been in such a good mood since Saturday. He did seem like my Theo again, that light inside him that never failed to brighten my world finally flickering back to life.

We turned onto the long driveway and noticed the chaos unfolding in the front yard as I slowed the car to a halt. Dani raced after Stella who was on the warpath towards Uncle Don, her head continually butting at his groin each time she got close. He made the mistake of turning his back on the goat and she charged, her horn catching him in the seat of his pants and we heard his howl of outrage even through the car windows.

As we climbed out of the vehicle, Uncle Don let out a slew of loud curses as Stella bleated at him, unrelenting in her quest to nail him in the goods.

"My nards are not a fucking piñata! I will roast you over a fire for dinner, you demon spawn!" Don yelled. Dani was becoming increasingly useless as her laughter turned into silent wheezing and she bent over, attempting to catch her breath.

Theo's own cackling subsided long enough for him to whistle at Stella who miraculously stopped attacking and trotted in our direction. I instinctively stepped back, my hands cupping my junk protectively. One time was more than enough to learn my lesson.

"What did that mean old Uncle Don do to my sweet girl?" Theo cooed at the evil creature, petting her while she cozied up to his side.

"I fed her," he gritted out. "Apparently she ain't ever heard you shouldn't bite the junk that feeds ya."

"Good advice for goats and blowjobs."

"Ugh, barf! Why the fuck would you say that around me? You are corrupting my innocent ears," Dani complained dramatically.

"Hell, *I* don't want to hear that shit and my ears are anything but innocent," Don chimed in.

"Sweet Jesus, can we just put the ball-chomper in her pen already and change the subject?" I begged. Dani helped Theo lead Stella to her enclosure, leaving me and Don to head inside.

"Have you talked to your Dad yet?"

I should have seen that one coming after I told Uncle Don about my plans to quit football and pursue music, as well as the struggle I had coming clean about it.

"I haven't found the right time."

"Kid, that's an excuse. There ain't no such thing as 'the right time'. You just come out with it and hope for the best," he chided. "Pops and my baby brother are hard asses when they want to be, but they love you and once they get over the shock of it, I know they'd be supportive as hell. But dragging your feet ain't helping matters."

I groaned internally, knowing he was right and hating that fact immensely. I was still pussy-footing around it and I was running out of time to tell them without the whole thing blowing up in my face.

"I'll tell them this week, but after Friday's game."

His brow hiked up in disbelief, but he merely grunted and gave me a hard slap on the back before trudging off to the kitchen. I went up to my bedroom and dropped onto my bed, blowing out a heavy sigh. I didn't realize I'd drifted off until I was gently stirred awake by featherlight kisses against my neck.

I moaned and tilted my head with Theo taking full advantage of the open, submissive gesture and sucking a deep bruise into the juncture of my neck and shoulder. I hissed at the exquisite pain, but managed to push him back far enough to take in his hooded eyes and mischievous smile.

"Be. Good," I growled, pecking a quick kiss to his lips. The pout that graced his mouth was so damn adorable I almost said "fuck it" and let him take me right there with the door wide open. "Later, baby."

"Ughhh, you're no fun..."

"Yeah, I know. I suck," I teased.

"But you're not sucking anything right now and that's the problem."

I barked out a laugh at his petulant tone and rolled off the bed, tugging my arm free of the half-hearted grip he had on my elbow. After a little coaxing and a promise to suck him dry later, we made our way downstairs for lunch.

"There are my boys! Late to the party, as usual." Mom set down the dish in her hand to hug us both. Dad, Dani, and Uncle Don were already seated and piling food onto their plates when Theo and I joined them. Grandpa wasn't coming down until Thursday and as excited as I was to see him, it also stirred up a hornet's nest in my stomach.

"Theo, we're glad you could join us," Dad said warmly. I was confused by the stiffness in Theo's frame and the tight smile he gave in return. "Grady is visiting your grandparents this week, right?"

"Yes sir. They couldn't make the trip out here this year, but he'll be back on Friday."

I was selfishly thankful that Theo declined to go with him since it meant we didn't lose any time together this week, especially after my back to back away games. Dad continued to try to make conversation, but Theo remained tense and awkward the entire time. I shot Dani a pointed look, silently pleading with her to interject and draw Dad's attention.

Her brow crumpled as she looked between Theo and Dad, clearly noticing the same weirdness that I had, but she quickly cut in with a story about a house party she went to last weekend. Predictably, it horrified Dad and set off his inquisition, so I knew I would owe her big time.

We finished lunch in record time and even though we typically stayed to help Mom clear the table, she waved us off. I grabbed Theo's hand and dragged him outside with me, leading him to the golf cart. He was quiet while I drove us down to the barn and he hopped out the second I hit the brakes, stomping off towards the structure. I was so thrown off by the abrupt change in Theo's mood that it took me a few seconds to snap out of it and follow him.

"What was that with you and Dad just now?" I called out as I jogged to keep up with him.

"Nothing."

"That's bull and you know it. Did something happen that I don't know about?"

"It's not a big deal. It was just a stupid talk we had last time I saw him. Forget it."

"What kind of talk? When was that?" I asked bewildered, both by the statement and his irritation. Theo rolled his eyes and shrugged, but the warning in my gaze urged him on.

"It was at your first game. Your dad sat by me and started talking about how important your NFL career was and how my bipolar disorder can screw everything up for you and I should think about that if we're going to try to be together."

"What? He actually said that to you?" I asked angrily.

"I mean, not those exact words, but I knew what he meant."

I shook my head in confusion. "Wait...what exactly did he say?"

"He just..." Theo broke off with a frustrated grunt. "He said something like your job would keep you crazy busy and you wouldn't always be there to help me with this shit, so we needed to make sure we knew what we were getting into because he didn't want it to mess with your career or my health. But it was clear he didn't think we should be together..."

"Did he ever *say* we shouldn't be together?"

"Well no, but why would he say any of that if not to scare me off?"

"Theo, it doesn't sound like he was trying to scare you off. That's not like Dad, he's always been supportive of us! And it's only because he thinks I'm going to the NFL and wanted us to be careful, but it doesn't matter since I'm not going. Why are you freaking out about this?"

"Because it's obvious he doesn't think I'm good enough!" Theo cried. "He clearly thinks that I'm going to mess up your life with this fucking illness..."

I widened my eyes at how far off the tracks this conversation seemed to be getting and I worked to make sense of it.

"Baby, what are you talking about? That's not what he meant, I can guarantee it. Both my parents love you and know you're more than good enough. Why are you being so...paranoid?"

Theo froze at the quiet question and I wanted to take it back. "Paranoid" was probably no better than "crazy" in his book, but there was no other word to describe it. He was starting to spiral for some reason and I didn't understand why. I saw a range of emotions dance across his face before he strode over to me, taking my lips in a heated kiss.

I clung to his waist as he forced us backwards until I hit the wall, attacking my mouth with a fervor that made my head swim. His tongue lashed out and sparred with mine while he ran his hands frantically over every muscle he could reach. It was an attack on my senses that left me reeling and in any other context, I'd be raring to go. But something felt off about it that made my stomach clench nervously.

"Theo, slow down," I gasped out as he nipped and sucked at my neck down to my collarbone, purpling my flesh.

"Let me show you...I'll show you I'm good enough. Let me make you feel good, baby," he pleaded, voice gravelly with lust and desperation.

His hands landed on the front of my jeans and he quickly undid my belt and fly, freeing my aching length from its confines. He spit in his hand and started a furious pace of pumping me in his tight fist, the sensation both divine and overpowering.

"*Ngh*...b-baby, wait. This is...hold on, p-please stop."

Theo stopped the frenzied rhythm without removing his hand from my cock. His eyes were wild and hazy as he stared at me in confusion.

"Why do you want to stop? Am I doing something wrong?"

I struggled to find the right words. "No, it's just—you don't seem like yourself."

"What's that supposed to mean?"

"I don't know. It's like...you're not really here or something. Your touch feels different somehow..."

Theo released me with a scoff, spreading his arms wide. "What do you want from me? You were hurt when I had no sex drive, but now it's finally back and you're still not happy? I'm either too much or not enough again, huh? This is as good as it gets right now, so please tell me what you want from me!"

I gaped at yet another rapid turn in his mood, but what shook me the most was the distress in his voice. My gut sank and I felt as though I was watching him come apart at the seams, helpless to stop it. I couldn't form words as too many things hit me all at once. Fear, worry, sadness, and confusion all grappled in my chest and stalled every response I could think of in my throat.

Theo watched me expectantly, chest heaving and his fingers twitching at his sides. When all I could do was stammer quietly, irritation and disappointment lined his features.

"Forget it," he muttered. He brushed by me and my heart splintered the tiniest bit. I knew he wasn't walking away for good, but that fear of being abandoned welled up from the pits of my mind where I'd worked hard to bury it. But I didn't stop him. I just stood there, caught between wanting to go to him and knowing it wouldn't even make a difference if I did.

I STAYED at Neverland until the sun sank behind the trees and the air turned chilly. I drove back slowly, lost in thoughts of Theo and the conflicting signs I'd seen the last few days. I was rudderless and baffled without a single clue what to do to help him or even knowing if that was possible anymore.

I slipped in through the back door and snuck past the living room where I could hear the family watching some loud action film. As I reached the first step, I startled at Mom's soft voice behind me.

"How is he doing?"

I blew out a sharp exhale through my nostrils, my eyes squeezing shut against the small headache forming.

"I honestly don't know. Every time I think he's getting somewhere with his treatment and doing well, something happens that drags him right back down. And now, he's acting weird again and I can't shake the feeling that something is really wrong."

She reached out and ran a soothing hand up and down my arm, coaxing my gaze to hers. Once I did, the dam inside broke and cold tears slid down my cheeks.

"I don't know what to do. I'm scared, Mom..."

Her arms came around my shoulders and I gave into the comfort her embrace brought me. It was a tiny reprieve to set down the weight that I was buckling under. I wondered if I was ever able to bring that sense of relief to Theo when he was this close to crumbling.

"I know you are, honey. But I have faith in you two. What defines a relationship is how well you both deal with the trouble that comes your way because it will always come. You and Theo love each other so much and you have what it takes to get through this."

"What if that's not enough?" I whispered despondently. She pulled back to cup my cheeks and keep my eyes on her.

"Love alone may not be enough, but it's what gives you the strength and determination to get through the hardest times. The deeper the love, the more willing you are to fight through anything and everything to make it work. So how much do you love Theo?"

Sweeping music rushed through my head as I thought about Theo and how completely he possessed my heart. Every emotion within me transposed into a melody that flooded my soul, a refrain of devotion that echoed in my chest. It was an anthem of a love without end, without borders. Ceaseless and all-consuming.

Mom smiled and pressed a kiss to my cheek. "You don't even have to say it. As long as you feel it, that's what matters."

She headed back to the living room and I trudged slowly upstairs. I was barely aware as I showered and got ready for bed. I slid under the covers, an ache expanding in my chest as I wished I had Theo by my side. I fired off a quick text to him since I knew I wouldn't sleep otherwise.

ME

I love you

We'd already lost four years of "I love you's" and I'd be damned if I wasted one more day without saying those three words. Theo's bipolar disorder tricked him enough, so I wouldn't give it any reason to make him doubt my love for him.

I wasn't sure how long I'd been out when I was jostled awake by the bed dipping behind me. Panic spiked for only a second before I breathed in the alluring scent of citrus and cedar. My heart hammered away for a whole new reason when Theo's arm wound around me, pulling my back into his sculpted chest.

Tears pricked at my lash line as he started trailing warm kisses across my bare shoulder and I sank into his touch. I reached for the hand he rested on my pec, linking our fingers and pressing them firmly above my thudding heart. I could feel the puffs of air on my skin as he whispered something repeatedly between kisses.

I'm sorry...I love you...I'm sorry...

The words severed the last, fraying thread holding me back and I flipped around to face him, my lips finding his in the dark. Theo explored my mouth with a slow, deep passion that bordered on worship. He stripped us both unhurriedly, cherishing my body with his hands and mouth until I begged him to take me.

And when he finally slid inside my body, I let the tears flow freely as he made love to me, creating the most beautiful music two bodies could make.

CHAPTER THIRTY-FIVE

My body was sore in the best way when I woke up, a testament to how well Theo had fucked me through the night. He'd taken me three more times before we both passed out from exhaustion and I fucking loved every second because he had been *my* Theo through all of it. There had been no trace of the wild, harried touches from the barn and my relief had been palpable.

My arm met cold, empty sheets as I stretched and felt around for Theo. I sat up and listened for him in the bathroom, but it was silent. As the fog of sleep cleared away, my brain caught onto something strange in my room and it took a solid minute before I figured out what was missing. I scooted to the edge of the bed and reached for my glasses, finding a note folded under them.

> You looked too cute to wake up, so I let you sleep in. Meet me at Neverland when you're up. I love you ♡
>
> P.S. I was bored and stole your guitar to practice.

A quiet snort escaped me, easily imagining Theo sitting up bored in bed while I snoozed away and looking around my room for something to get into. After a speedy shower, I rushed to dry off and get dressed, then hurried downstairs. Dani sat at the kitchen bar top, slurping down a cup of coffee.

"Do you know where Theo is?"

"I'll give you three guesses, but you'll only need one," she droned, eyes glued to her phone as she scrolled on Instagram. I took advantage of her distraction to snatch a piece of toast off the plate in front of her, ignoring the colorful curse she yelled on my way out the door.

Theo hadn't taken the golf cart, so I drove down to the barn where the stilted twang of guitar strings rang out through the trees. The sound was coming from above and I scaled the ladder, halting mid-climb when I realized the song was actually recognizable. I was stunned when I hauled myself up onto the loft and saw Theo peering down at the phone balanced precariously on his knee. His brows were wrinkled in concentration and his bottom lip was trapped by his teeth as he glanced back and forth from the screen to the guitar, his uncertain fingers forming chords on the neck.

He snapped his head up when he finally heard me, his features lighting up. "Babe! Wait til you hear this!"

My cheeks ached from the grin that stretched across my face when Theo started to play and hummed the melody of "Chasing Cars" as he moved through the song. He was slow and had a couple of minor stumbles, but the more he played, the more sure he became.

When he got to the end of the chorus, he flipped his blond locks out of his eyes and beamed my direction. My heart nearly beat out of my chest at how truly gorgeous he was, pride and excitement evident on his face.

"Pretty cool, huh? You impressed, Mercury?" he asked, wiggling his eyebrows.

"Beyond. If I had ten bucks, I'd stick it in your jockstrap," I teased with a wink.

"Hell, I'm worth at least a twenty, cheapskate," he scoffed.

"How long have you been up?" I asked, sitting down across from him.

"Eh, I couldn't really get back to sleep, so pretty early. Then I thought it'd be cool to try to learn a song for you before you woke up. I'm romantic as fuck like that," he joked. His eyes gleamed with mirth, but they softened a fraction as he gazed at me. “Come play it with me?”

As if I could ever deny this man anything...

I scooted until my back was against the barn wall for support and patted the spot between my legs. He carefully crawled over and assumed the same position he'd been in on the beach weeks ago when I tried to teach him to play.

“Put your fingers over mine,” I instructed. As soon as he was set, I began to play it at the correct tempo with his hands moving in time on top of mine. It wasn't a song I'd played much, but it was easy enough to figure out by ear. Within a minute, I'd gotten the chord progression down and the music flowed.

I sang the song to him, smiling at the shiver that coasted down his body when I crooned a few of the more meaningful lyrics right against his ear. I eventually closed my eyes and let the song take me, soaking up the way his back curved into my chest and the way his lightly calloused fingers on mine sent tingles zipping up my arm.

I continued to sing to him as though it were an invitation, a tempting proposal to drag him back to my bed and lay there in my arms as we tried to forget the world. Tried to forget everything but us.

Tried to forget that nothing gold can ever stay.

“Do we really have to go down to dinner?” Theo asked for the third time in the last hour.

While we'd hung out with my family most of Tuesday, we'd spent all of yesterday together while everyone else chose to do their own thing, so I understood his reluctance to give up our alone time. However, our tiny bubble had to pop sometime since we'd come to my parents' house specifically to spend the holiday with them.

I arched a brow at him as I ripped off my shirt and hunted through my duffel for the nicer clothes I'd brought. Mom wasn't a fan of gray sweats and t-shirts at the Thanksgiving table.

“Unless you want to piss off Emilia Hayes, the answer continues to be yes. And I thought you said you were hungry.”

My hands stilled when inked arms slid around me from behind and trailed up my naked chest. Theo tweaked my nipples and I hissed as sparks of heat rushed through me. My breath hitched when he lowered one hand down to my sweatpants, palming my rapidly hardening cock through the material while still tormenting one nipple.

"I didn't say what I was hungry *for*," he said. My sweats and briefs were shoved down under my balls, my dick standing at full attention now. His appreciative rumble vibrated against my back and I dropped my head back on his shoulder, giving in to the sinful sensations as he twisted around the tip expertly.

"Holy shit..." I breathed, my knees trembling as Theo fondled my throbbing length, smearing the precum down my shaft and using it to jack me off. "Baby...*fuck*, we can't..."

"But we can," he purred, shuttling his hand faster and I started thrusting into it. "That's right, fuck my fist, beautiful. I'm going to lick every drop of cum from my hand so I taste your flavor on my tongue all night long."

My orgasm barreled into me in less than a minute and Theo clapped his free palm over my mouth to muffle my cries of pleasure as he continued to milk my cock for all it was worth. Once he'd drained me, he brought his cum-covered hand up to his lips, lapping up my release with a low moan. The erotic sight and sound of him sucking his fingers clean of my seed was almost enough to make me harden again.

When he was done, he grasped my jaw and brought his lips down on mine. The hint of my essence on his tongue made my chest flare with possession, loving that he tasted like me. Tasted like *mine*.

Just then, the door flew open as Penny bounded into my room, her nails skittering across the hardwood floor. Theo and I sprang apart and I scrambled to haul my pants up, but ended up tripping over my own feet and stumbling into my dresser.

"Hurry up and get down here so we can eat, losers! We're all starving!" Dani called from down the hall. She whistled for Penny who raced out of the room as fast as she'd blown in, leaving us shellshocked.

"You didn't close the door?" I whisper-shouted at Theo with wide eyes.

"Sorry if I was a bit preoccupied!" he retorted. "It's your fault for wearing those gray sweatpants. I am only a man, Dawson...a weak, weak man."

A sharp snort of laughter broke free at the grave look on his face that melted into an impish grin. I finished getting dressed while Theo washed his hands and we traipsed down the stairs to join the family.

Thanksgiving for the Hayes clan was always a big affair and Mom had gone all out with the food. Everyone was already seated, including my grandfather who was in deep discussion with Dad about the Dallas Cowboys' game earlier that day.

"I'm telling you, Lincoln, they haven't had a decent quarterback since you retired. They only won today because the Commanders' defense was a joke. If those Cowboys know what's good for them, they'll draft our boy Dawson here and then—"

"Pops, how about you stow the football talk at least until after dessert? We already got enough of that today," Uncle Don cut in. I threw him a grateful look and found my seat, my gut churning with anxiety.

"Yeah, for real. I love football as much as the next Hayes, but we all need a break. You don't want to harsh Dawson's juju before his game on Friday with all your armchair quarterback talk," Dani added.

"What in the blue blazes do you mean 'harsh his juju'? Is that some new hippie phrase your generation came up with?" Grandpa barked.

Dani and Gramps started bickering back and forth over her choice of words as I sighed in relief that the topic had veered away from anything football related. But my relief was short-lived as Theo joined their conversation and I could tell right away that something was off.

"—and I find it funny how older people hate that our generation makes up all these words when they did it themselves back in the day, like with 'groovy' and 'far out'. And what does 'back in the day' even mean anyway? Is it like a time period or a certain amount of time? You ever find it weird that we use all these phrases and sometimes never know what they really mean? Like that one about blood being thicker than water, but that's only half the saying! It doesn't mean what people think it means, it's actually the exact opposite and most peeps don't even realize that they are arguing against their point when they use it and—"

I placed a hand on Theo's thigh to drag his attention back to me, cutting off his long, disjointed rant as he became increasingly animated. He cut off mid-sentence and looked over at me questioningly, his bright irises darkening as his pupils dilated.

"Baby, are you feeling okay?" I asked quietly so only he could hear me.

"Yeah yeah, of course, why? What's up? Do I not seem okay?" he spit out rapidly. I shivered at the sudden chill that blanketed me, but I forced myself to stay calm, hoping to project some of it onto him.

"Yeah, I just wanted to make sure you weren't getting sucked into the conversation and forgetting to eat," I replied with a light smile, even as my stomach turned over uneasily.

Luckily, it distracted him enough that my family continued talking and Theo turned back to the meal. When I caught my mom's worried gaze, I knew I wasn't the only one who'd noticed Theo's off-putting behavior and that she was probably remembering our talk from last night. My eyes slid to Dani's and saw the same concern mirrored there as well.

"Dawson?" Grandpa called across the table.

"Yes sir?"

"Did you ever call Mike Hancock back like we talked about?"

My skin itched uncomfortably and I tried not to squirm in my chair. "Uh, no sir. I haven't really had time."

He shot me a disapproving look. "That's a poor excuse and you know it. I'm sure you found time to run around with your friends and boyfriend, so you had time to call him."

"Who's Mike Hancock?" Theo asked, and the underlying jealousy in his tone made me balk. *Where the fuck did that come from?*

"He's just an agent that came to my game last weekend," I hurried to tell him.

"An agent that I personally asked to go watch your game and speak with you as a favor to me," Dad interjected. "Champ, you can't be this cavalier with your responsibilities this close to the end of the season. And when I called Coach Walker the other day, he said that you hadn't even met with the two agents he brought in to speak with the seniors last month."

"This is no time to drop the ball and screw around. You need to start getting serious about your career because it will be here before you know it," Grandpa scolded me.

"This isn't the time to be discussing this and you two are hardly being fair," Mom tried to defend me, but Grandpa was on a tear.

"Well, life isn't fair. He needs to act like an adult rather than some careless teenager. Lincoln and I won't always be there to hold his hand,

and if he can't get his crap together now, then how will he be expected to handle the demands of a professional athlete?"

"He's not going to be a damn athlete!" Theo snapped. The room went silent and my eyes went wide in alarm.

"Theo, don't—"

"You two are so worried about signing him off to some agent or talking his ear off about the stupid draft, but you don't even notice that he doesn't want that life. Have you even stopped to ask Dawson what *he* wants?"

"Now son, this really isn't your business—"

"Dawson *is* my business," Theo interrupted Grandpa. "He's mine to take care of. Have you never really noticed how miserable he is out on that field?"

"Dawson is a top-tier athlete in a division one football program, what does he have to be miserable about? Your dramatics aside, we understand you care about him, but we are his family and know what's best for him."

"I don't just care about him, I love him. He's everything to me and I won't let you two steamroll him just because you can't accept he wants something different than you want for him!"

"Theo honey, calm down. It's okay," Mom tried to reason with him, and even Dani tried her to best to diffuse the situation.

"Maybe we should all take a minute to chill out before this gets any worse..."

"What is he talking about, Dawson?" Dad's gruff voice reached me through the blood rushing in my ears. I tried to explain and give him an answer, but no sound came out. Like usual, my words failed when I needed them most, but no fucking guitar song would get me out of this.

"I'm talking about all the pressure you've put on him since he was a kid. It's done nothing but stress him out and made him feel like he has to be perfect to earn your approval," Theo said angrily. "You both set this insane bar for him to reach before he was even born, deciding his future without thinking about what he wants and what makes him happiest."

"Hey kid, take a breath..." Don's attempts to get him to relax were useless as Theo seemed oblivious to anything else.

"Have you ever seen the way Dawson lights up when he plays his guitar? Or have you really listened to him when he sings and heard the fucking emotion he pours into it? Music is his life and what makes him who he is and you can't force him to—"

"Music is a hobby, not something you can build a life on. He is not throwing away all that natural talent and years of training to go play a piano for tips," Dad grumbled.

"Daddy, you're not getting Theo's bigger point," Dani argued. "You aren't trying to understand what Dawson wants his own future to look like. When he told me he wanted to quit football, I honestly wasn't surprised because, let's face it, he's never once said the NFL was his goal. You and Gramps always pushed it on him."

"Young lady, we don't need more fuel added to this fire," Gramps bit out. "This is between your father, brother, and me."

"Lincoln and Bill, please calm down," Mom begged. "We are all talking about Dawson as if he isn't sitting right here. And no matter what he decides, it's up to him and no one else."

"So you're okay with him giving up a successful, prestigious career for some childhood hobby?"

"If you really think that music is just some childhood hobby for Dawson, then you don't know him as well as you think you do!"

"I appreciate you standing up for my son, Theo, but I think it's time he and I discussed this in private," Dad said firmly, his eyes cutting into me with all the hurt and disappointment that I had dreaded from the very beginning. I hadn't even realized I'd stopped breathing until my lungs burned as I pulled in a breath, and I nodded to him.

"But you don't understand..."

"Stop, Theo. Just stop," I barked. "You've done enough."

The color drained from his face as he stared at me, shocked and gutted by my outburst. Dad carefully pushed his chair back and stood, a somber expression on his face as he stiffly walked out of the room.

"Dad, wait," I called, shoving out of my seat to follow him.

I ignored Theo's own voice calling out to me, but I only made it as far as the foyer when a hand clamped down on my elbow, tugging me to a stop.

"Baby, I'm sorry, but I was just trying to help," he explained frantically.

"Why couldn't you leave it alone?" I gritted out. "I told you that I would tell them after tomorrow's game, but you ran off at the mouth and messed everything up."

"You were letting them sit there and attack you! What was I supposed to do?"

"Oh for fuck's sake, they weren't attacking me. They were being annoying, sure, but they would have stopped eventually—"

"How do you know that? It seemed like they were just going to keep pressing and pressing until you probably agreed to sign in blood with Mike Cockbag or whatever just to make them happy!"

"Do you even hear yourself? You're jumping to these insane conclusions and not even listening to me. I know my family. I would have calmed them down and been able to tell them in my own way like I'd planned if you had stayed out of it. Now everyone is either upset or pissed, and it's your fault."

"How is it my fault?" Theo cried. "I was only telling them the truth because you refused to."

"It wasn't your truth to tell! How do you not get that?" I stormed. Theo shrank back, but I was too angry to care. "Do you really not see how you were tonight? You were talking so fast, it was like you were on speed and you completely ignored me and everyone else who tried to chill you out. Then you pulled that crap with Dad and Gramps and made things harder for me, not better. God, I knew—I fucking *knew* that this would happen when you started skipping pills."

"Knew what would happen?"

"That you'd go fucking crazy again!"

My heart lurched to a stop when the words clicked in my head and I saw Theo pale. His face went blank, all emotion wiped from his features as he retreated into himself.

"Wait, I didn't mean that..." I started, but Theo shook his head. Anguish tore through me as he stepped away from me.

"I'm sorry, Mercury," he mumbled, his gaze meeting mine for one heartbreaking moment before he walked away. I heard the front door close a few beats later and I steadied myself, unable to worry about fixing things with him right now. I needed to smooth things over with Dad first.

I made my way up the stairs towards his office and tried to ignore the twisting, queasy feeling in my gut that only grew with every step I took farther down the hall and away from Theo.

Theo

CHAPTER THIRTY-SIX

I knew it.

I knew I'd ruin everything.

I always do.

It's my fault...I shouldn't have done it. Shouldn't have stopped my pills. But I didn't stop. I didn't stop them completely but I still messed it up. I mess everything up.

I'm a mess. That's all I am. Dawson is better without me.

But he loves me. He loves me and I don't know why. Does he still love me? What if I ruined that too?

Maybe he'll love me again someday.

Someday he'll understand.

Someday he'll see that loving him means setting him free.

Set him free—be free—be brave—you aren't brave—you aren't anything—you're nothing—you're wrong...

Everything is wrong.

But soon it won't be. I'll make it right.

I'll make it right and he'll be free.

He'll forgive me.

He'll remember he loved me.

Someday.

CHAPTER THIRTY-SEVEN

I knocked on the door to Dad's office and steeled myself when he called out for me to enter. My eyes adjusted to the low lighting from his desk lamp before settling on his form by the window. I heard him pouring a drink from the small bar cart he had stashed away in the corner.

My worry turned into surprise when he walked over and handed me a lowball glass, clinking it with his. I wasn't sure exactly what the caramel-colored liquid was, but at that point I'd welcome anything to take the edge off. I tossed it back in one go and Dad snickered quietly before following suit, holding his hand out to refill my glass.

He gestured over to the sofa with the refreshed drinks in hand and we sank onto the leather seats side by side. The silence was thick and stifling, a palpable entity that I could sense hovering in the air. I chanced a look over at Dad who seemed to be staring at my football photo on his desk with a forlorn expression.

"I'm really sorry you found out that way," I murmured, running my finger around the rim of my glass slowly.

"Did I..."

"Did you what?"

"Did I push you too hard? Make you think that you had to be perfect or go along with what I wanted just to make me happy?" he asked in a pained whisper.

"I wanted to make you proud..." I confessed. "You always talked about football being one of the best experiences in your life and you were so excited for me to go pro like you and Gramps had."

"Why didn't you tell me that wasn't something you really wanted?"

"Well, I saw how hard it was for you to be forced to retire after your injury and I knew how important it was for you to see me continue the dream that you'd lost..."

Dad ran his hand over his close-cropped beard. "I won't lie and say I didn't look forward to seeing you play out on a professional field like I had. To think about one day sharing that experience with you and... yeah, maybe living a bit vicariously through you too was exciting. But you never had to make that your dream just because it was mine."

"I didn't want to let you down..."

"Did you really think I'd be any less proud of you if you chose not to go to the NFL?"

I shrugged sheepishly, keeping my gaze averted. "I mean, you didn't exactly seem supportive downstairs when you heard I wanted to pursue music instead."

"I was a little thrown off downstairs, but that's no excuse. I'm sorry for reacting the way I did. This is my fault," he grated. "I kept putting all this pressure on you because I really thought you wanted the same things I did. I assumed you were stressed about the season or just procrastinating like Pop said and you needed an extra push to remember the bigger goal. I never thought you wanted something else."

"You didn't ask," I mumbled.

"Now, that's not exactly fair. You never told me that you were thinking about quitting football and I still don't understand why you hid it for so long. Why not just come to me when you started considering another career path? Were you worried I'd be angry?"

"It wasn't that I thought you'd be upset or pissed. I was scared that..." I ducked my chin, not wanting to admit the truth out loud. "I got scared that if I didn't have football anymore, our relationship would change...that we wouldn't be close afterwards."

His eyes flashed with hurt. "What? That never would've happened."

"Think about it, Dad. Most of our relationship was about football, or revolved around it in some way. You were my junior league coach for years, you've been friends with all of my school coaches and trainers, and almost every conversation we have involves football. Shit, when I was a kid, the number one thing you liked to do with me was toss a football around outside and work on my passes. I knew that if I ever quit, we would have nothing in common anymore," I said gruffly. "I guess I kept putting it off because I wasn't ready to lose that connection with you..."

"Champ, I...*shit*." Dad covered his face with one hand, his breathing shaky as he tried to collect himself. My throat tightened and I worked to swallow the lump of emotion lodged there. He finally dropped his hand and looked at me with glassy eyes.

"I am so sorry, kid. If I was doing my job right as a parent, you never would have worried about that. That's all on me. Of course I loved sharing the game with you, but I loved spending time with you for so many more reasons than that. You've always impressed me with your humor, your intelligence, your kindness...I have loved getting to know the man you've grown into and none of that has to do a damn thing with football."

I blinked back the tears that blurred my vision. "But we don't really talk about anything else...what if you get bored with me?"

"Never," he said adamantly. "I could never, for one second, find you boring. And again, that's my fault for not talking to you about your life and other interests. I may not know anything about music like your mom does, but I'd love for you to tell me about it. And I want to hear about your friends and the crazy stuff you've all gotten yourselves into the last couple years. I want to know it all!"

"Really?..."

"Really, really. And if music is what you want to do after college, then I'll do whatever it takes to support you. I'll admit, I always figured if you didn't keep playing football, you'd at least look into coaching the sport and doing something with all your talent and years of experience."

"It's not that I don't love football, but it's not what I want to wake up and do every day. Music is something I can't live without."

"But have you actually thought about what that would look like as a career?"

"To be honest, I don't have a hard and fast plan yet. I've been thinking a lot about what I could do with my business degree and what's possible with the music industry in Austin, and I think I want to work as a creative producer or talent manager."

He gave me a puzzled look. "Hold on, I thought you wanted to be a musician or something?"

"I don't want playing music to become a job for me," I explained. "What I want is to bring music to other people. You know, help indie artists work on their first big album or scout local talent and work to promote them. I want to make the magic happen behind the scenes, not out on a stage."

He regarded me with a narrowed gaze as his fingers tapped on his glass absently, the light clink of his nails sounding like gunshots in the quiet stillness of the room. I was two seconds from screaming out the anxiety building in my chest when he finally nodded at me, his lips curving up in a soft smile.

"I can see it."

Something inside me cracked open at his simple acknowledgment and I threw my arms around his shoulders. He set his glass down and wrapped me in a tight hug, telling me he loved me and how proud he was. I hadn't realized just how badly I'd needed to hear those words from him until the ever-present knot in my chest loosened and fell away.

"What about Grandpa?" I asked when we pulled back.

"Leave him to me. He's an old grump, but he'll listen to reason and he does love you, Dawson. Your happiness matters to him. Almost as much as it matters to someone else down there..."

My stomach soured, thinking of how sideways dinner went and how horribly I'd handled things with Theo afterwards.

"I'm sorry about the way he reacted back there," I said awkwardly. "He's just really protective of me and can get a little...intense about it."

"I don't fault him for that. Even if the way he went about it was a little over the top, it's clear that he loves you deeply and has no problem standing up for you. A parent can't ask for more than that for their kid," he smirked, but it fell just as quickly. "But there was more going on there than just protective instincts, right?"

The knowing look he shot me said enough and I could only nod. I didn't want to voice the concerns that were blaring in my head, the ones I couldn't ignore after tonight.

"You know this is a big commitment you're taking on if you choose to stay together," he said, not unkindly. "Mental illness doesn't only affect the person, but their partners and families too. As much as you love each other, it won't be easy to navigate that sometimes. Are you prepared to take that on and go through all of that with him?"

"Absolutely," I said without hesitation. "A future that doesn't involve Theo isn't a future I have any interest in. When it comes down to it, I'll choose him above everything. I'll always choose him."

"I had a feeling you'd say that," he smiled. "I'm so damn proud of the man you've become, Dawson. Theo is a very lucky man and for what it's worth, I think you two will beat the odds."

Warmth spread over me at the confidence he had in us. "Thanks, Dad."

He slapped me on the back and stood up. "I'm going to go downstairs and have a talk with Pops. I also have a feeling I'll be doing some groveling with your mother for ruining her Thanksgiving dinner."

"Yeah, good luck with that one," I chuckled, trailing him to the door. He stopped me at the threshold with a hand on my shoulder, pulling me into another strong embrace.

"I'll always be here for you, champ. No matter what you need, I've got your back."

I soaked in the hug, relieved that things with Dad were on better terms than I could have hoped for. At last, we were on solid ground and I was actually looking forward to hitting reset on our relationship and showing him the side of me he hadn't seen before.

I strode to my room and immediately went for my nightstand to check my phone. Theo hadn't called or texted since he walked out, but what the fuck did I expect? I was such a dick to him, even knowing that he wasn't in full control of himself tonight. I tried calling him, but it went to voicemail after a few rings. I called three more times, hoping to wear him down enough to answer me, but he never did.

Fighting the urge to march over there and demand he talk to me, I sent him a text instead.

ME

Baby, please pick up? I'm so sorry for what I said, I didn't mean it. Please talk to me...

I waited for several minutes staring at the screen, anxiously hoping to see the message marked as "read". I fired off a few more texts, each one increasingly more desperate as I paced my room and warred with myself over what I should do. If he needed space, I wanted to respect that, but I was chomping at the bit to fix what I'd fucked up.

Eventually, I settled back on my bed and stared up at my ceiling, going over the events of the last hour in my head. How had everything gotten so screwed up so fast? How did we go from passionate nights and guitar dates to yelling matches and thoughtless words?

A sick, ominous feeling coiled in my stomach. Something wasn't right and the more I tried to brush it off as guilt over our argument, the worse it got. Chills coated my body and a cold sweat broke out on the back of my neck, and for a minute, I worried my dinner would come back up.

Fuck it, I couldn't wait anymore. I'd given him more than enough time and space since he left, but it had been over two hours now. If he didn't want me around, he could say it to my face. At least I'd see with my own eyes that he was okay.

I darted out of my room and barely managed to keep from sprinting out the door. None of the lights were on in his house that I could see as I hurried across the sprawling lawn, and I wondered if I was overreacting and he'd just fallen asleep.

Please God, just let him be asleep...

I felt like an idiot after pounding on the front door for a solid minute without an answer. I could have scaled the old oak tree up to his bedroom window, but the polite part of me thought it'd be better to give him a chance to answer the door first.

Then the asshole part of me quickly said *fuck this noise* and I started marching around the side of the house towards the backyard. I peered into the darkened living room through the glass doors like the creeper I was, but there was no sign of Theo. I skirted the pool, the inlaid LED lights giving off a dark blue hue that helped light the way.

The massive oak that stood sentry at the far corner of the house felt like an old friend I had lost touch with. How many nights had he watched me climb his knots and branches to reach Theo's window? Theo used to joke that the tree was on our side and liked being part of our story.

"It makes sense, doesn't it? You've never fallen off or broken anything while climbing him to get to me, so I think the old guy is rooting for us...get it? 'Rooting' for us?"

A breathy laugh escaped my nostrils as his teasing lilt echoed in my memory and a pang hit my heart. God, I needed to see him. I notched my foot in the familiar spot and grabbed onto the lowest branch, ready to haul myself up when a thud and bit-out curse reached my ears.

I looked around until movement above me snagged my attention and my heart dropped into my stomach. One of the windows led out onto the lower roof and ran the length of the backyard where Theo was shuffling around on the roof's incline.

"Holymotherfuck," I gasped, gripping my hair in panic. I stopped from shouting his name out, terrified of startling him and possibly causing him to lose his unsteady balance.

He looked around as though searching for something, letting out a triumphant noise when he noticed the brown bottle in his hand. He took a long pull of the drink, belching noisily before it slipped from his fingers and somehow caught on the gutter, unbroken. He giggled drunkenly and dread snaked down my back.

"Theo?"

His head swiveled around until he saw me and a bright, goofy grin split his cheeks.

"*Baabyyyy!*" he slurred happily. He took a step towards me instinctively and stumbled slightly. I sucked in a sharp breath, torn between dashing upstairs to pull him back inside and not wanting to take my eyes off him for a second.

"What are you doing up there?" I called out, my voice shaking as badly as the rest of me. He tilted his head back and pointed up at the sky lazily.

"I was looking at the stars and I wanted to see them up close. I can almost reach them from up here," he said in a tipsy voice.

My pulse was rioting and my breathing quickened with each movement he made, every one of my muscles tensing painfully in anticipation of the moment this all went tragically wrong. If the height wasn't enough to kill him, the fall to the concrete below would. A quick glance at the pool showed me it was too far for him to jump into, especially in his condition, so that wasn't an option.

"Baby, listen to me. I need you to go back inside for me. Can you do that?"

Theo's head dropped back down in my direction, his brows drawn together and his lip jutted out in a tiny pout.

"But why? It's sooooo pretty up here. You have to see it, Mercury. It's like—like on that wheel thing. I'm on top of the world!"

He flung his arms out wide and he turned in a slow, awkward circle on the tilted surface, ending up closer to the edge. Curses flew out under my breath as I tried to think of a way to get him down safely while keeping him in my sights. Theo began singing "A Sky Full of Stars" at the top of his lungs, oblivious to my turmoil as I tried not to lose my damn mind. Jesus, I fucking hated myself for not rushing over here the instant my gut said something was wrong.

Suddenly, a lightbulb went off in my head and I whipped out my phone to call Dani. I practically vibrated with impatience as it continued to ring.

"This better be good because I'm watching—"

"I need you to come to Theo's house right now," I rushed out.

"What? Why do you—"

"No questions, Dani, just do it. Please! I'm by the pool."

"Okay, okay. I'm coming now."

"Hurry!" I hung up and mumbled to myself that it was going to be okay. Everything was going to be okay. He would be fine. He *had* to be fucking fine.

Theo's singing cut off abruptly as he stared at the pool behind me.

"Babe, look..." he whispered loudly with an awed tone. "The stars... they fell in the water."

I glanced behind me for a split-second to see the lights had timed out in the pool, leaving the water dark and glossy with the calm surface reflecting the starry sky.

"Yeah, it-it's beautiful," I agreed placatingly. "Why don't you come down here and enjoy it with me?"

Theo didn't seem to hear me as he stared almost longingly down at the water. "Have you ever wanted to swim in the stars? Get lost in them? Do you think it's possible?"

The words took on a morose quality that stiffened my spine even more. My attention was riveted on him as I fought not to blink, even as stinging tears threatened.

"I don't know," I croaked.

"Come swim in the stars with me, Mercury," he softly pleaded. He teetered on the edge of the roof, raising his arms slightly for balance.

"No no no no! Don't move, baby!" I cried, holding out my hands uselessly as though I could push him back by sheer will. Dani's loud gasp cut across the yard and I frantically waved her over.

"Keep him talking and try to get him to back up. Whatever you do, do *not* take your eyes off him," I told her firmly before calling to him. "Theo, I'm coming up. Don't move an inch!"

She nodded her agreement and her teary gaze clawed at my chest. I heard her start talking to Theo, but couldn't make it out as I bolted for the door, thanking all the fucking heavens above that it was unlocked. I bounded up the stairs to the smaller third floor, my chest heaving as I pushed myself as fast as my legs could carry me. I made a beeline down the hall, finding the unlatched window that provided access to the roof.

Dragging myself through the narrow frame wasn't as easy as it was when I was a kid, but I managed to crawl out and steady myself on the sloped shingles. I heard Dani's watery voice as she begged Theo to be careful, and I turned my head in time to watch him sway too far forward.

I let out a strangled shout, fear paralyzing my limbs as Theo pinwheeled his arms to stay upright. His eyes met mine when he found his footing and my heart splintered at the misery that crossed his features.

"You're here," he breathed, barely audible across the space between us.

"Always," I forced out past my chattering teeth, trying to control the shivers that racked my body. "I'll always come for you."

Theo's shoulders fell and he seemed to sag with an invisible weight. His face was drawn with pain and my chest stuttered with shaky breaths as I inched closer to him.

His lips turned up in the saddest smile that trembled at the corners. "I'm so sorry you had to love me...I wish I had been better for you."

"W-what are you t-talking about?" My face grew warm and my throat constricted around a painful knot that refused to go down.

"You didn't deserve this. I just wanted to make you happy...so happy..."

"Don't you talk like that. You *do* make me happy!"

My lungs were on fire even as my blood ran cold. Terror blanketed me as I felt him slipping away with each word, each second that he wasn't safely in my arms. I was still several feet away, but it felt as though every step I took did nothing to close the distance separating us, and I realized he was slowly backing up as I crept forward.

"Why are you talking like this?" I choked out. "You c-can't...you just—"

I clamped my lids shut to stem the wave of tears that rushed to the surface and drowned my words. I blinked rapidly to clear my vision as Theo let his own tears fall.

"Will you sing for me, Mercury?"

The softly spoken question broke me and I clenched my jaw against the sob caught in my throat. I pulled in a gasping breath, denial blaring in my brain that he was talking like a man at the end of his rope, at the end of all options.

"Don't do this...please don't leave me again..."

The smile that had graced his sweet lips fell, his features clouding over as more tears slid down his pale cheeks.

"I don't want to be like this anymore, Dawson. I just want it to stop." The despair that laced his words almost brought me to my knees, my legs quaking from the effort to hold me up.

"No! No, you don't mean that," I argued desperately, hot tears streaking down my skin. "You p-promised me...don't break your promise, p-please. I didn't give up on you, so don't give up on us! Come back to me, baby...just come back to me."

Theo's face crumpled and he wrapped his arms around his middle as shudders rippled down his frame. "Why do you even want me? Why do you want someone like me? You could find someone so much better... someone who isn't a mistake."

"You could *never* be a mistake. You are my whole fucking world, and I can't lose you again! Don't take this away from us...stay with me and fight through this because *you* deserve it. Don't let this thing take everything away from you. We'll find a way together, just like I promised."

"Don't make a promise you can't keep..."

"I'm not. If you keep your promise, then I swear to you I'll keep mine," I said, holding his gaze intently. "I'll do whatever it takes to keep you fighting and give you a reason to stay."

"You..." he whispered brokenly. "You're my reason, Mercury. And I don't—I don't want to die. I just don't want to be broken anymore..."

I rushed forward as he collapsed in great, heaving sobs. I wrapped him in an iron grip and tugged him backwards so he was lying beside me, his face buried in my neck. Theo clung to my shirt as he cried and fell apart, and I rocked him gently in my arms. I couldn't stop my hands from running over his hair, his shoulders, his back, any part of him I could reach. I gripped his hand and pressed a soft kiss to our tattoo, the touch cementing the fact he was safe and that I would never let him go.

“I’m sorry, I’m so sorry…” he wailed as I tried to soothe him. I petted his hair and whispered calming words in his ear, telling him over and over how much I loved him.

His anguish shredded me down to my core, tearing at the threads holding me together until there was nothing but our broken pieces scattered across the roof. I didn’t know what to say to make any of it better. I wasn’t sure what he needed to hear to convince him that a life with me was worth every ounce of fight he had in his bones.

A hum started in my chest, growing stronger and morphing into an aria carved straight from my heart. I started to sing to him, low and shaky from my dwindling tears, but eventually Theo’s sobs quieted and his tremors slowed. His fingers dug into my side and he hugged me tighter as the song filtered in through his pain and recognition hit.

There was nothing I could say better than what the music conveyed for me. I crooned our song to him, our chosen melody, hoping beyond measure that he took it as my solemn vow, my unbreakable promise that I would stand by him.

That we would build a beautiful life from the heart-shaped wreckage surrounding us.

That there was no better choice than the one he made to survive.

CHAPTER THIRTY-NINE

The smell was what I noticed first. That odious, antiseptic hospital smell that never failed to infuse your clothes and skin like a noxious gas. After waking up in a room like this following my overdose, it was an experience I'd never wanted to repeat and I refused to open my eyes.

I sifted through the shards of memory that stuck out, trying to remember how I'd ended up here this time. It was a big, fuzzy picture that slowly became clearer, pixel by pixel, until it all crashed into me in a tidal wave of images.

The family dinner I'd ruined. The guilt and self-loathing. The drinking that had gone too far. The roof I'd haplessly climbed onto. The pool of stars. The worst decision born of a dark moment of hopelessness. And Dawson saving me...like he'd always saved me.

My Dawson...

"I'm right here, baby. You're okay," a smooth voice purred. It ran across my skin like silk, lighting up my nerve endings. I slowly peeled my gritty lids open to see Dawson slumped on the chair beside my hospital bed, my hand tucked between both of his.

His sandy brown hair was shaggy and unclean, overgrown stubble covered his jaw, and dark circles underlined his red-rimmed, swollen eyes. He was a wreck and the most goddamn beautiful sight in the world.

Fuck, I love him so much...

"I love you too. More than you know."

I narrowed my eyes at him as my sluggish brain started to catch up.

"Were my inside thoughts actually outside thoughts?" I croaked out, wincing at the pain in my raw throat. Dawson chuckled roughly as he grabbed the water cup on the table and brought it to my lips. Instant relief hit me as I greedily sucked down the cool liquid.

"Yeah, you've been talking in your sleep for most of the day."

"Well, shit...scale of one to ten, how embarrassed should I be?"

"A solid nine, for sure."

"Eh, could be worse."

The smile that tugged at his full lips distracted me and I ached to kiss him. But then the reality of where I was and what I'd done settled over me, and I realized I didn't deserve to kiss him. I wasn't even sure if he was still mine to kiss.

"What happened?" I whispered gruffly as shame filled me.

Dawson's chin dropped and he fidgeted with his hands. "How much do you remember?"

"Mostly everything, but the details are iffy. The last thing I remember was...you singing our song to me."

His features twisted with a crippling sadness that cut me to my core and I reached for him reflexively, but I hissed at the sharp pull in my left hand.

"Be careful of the IV," Dawson warned softly, covering my other hand with his. "They've been giving you fluids since you came in. I was able to help you climb back through the window, but you made it maybe halfway down the hall before you passed out, so Dani called 911."

"Well, that explains the hospital bed," I said dryly. "How long have I been out?"

"Close to eighteen hours now. Your dad went to get something to eat since he's been here most of the day. He came straight from the airport after he got my message."

Remorse coiled tightly in my chest at how fucking scared he must have been to get that call. The first time I'd landed in the hospital had devastated him and I vividly recalled how broken he'd looked and sounded when I had woken up. Christ, I'd really fucked up badly this time.

"Why did you do it? Why did you want to—"

Dawson's voice cracked, but I knew what he was asking. Fuck, I wanted to beg his forgiveness until my vocal cords shredded. I fought to speak past the painful lump in my throat and clamped my lids shut to keep the tears at bay.

"I didn't choose to die...at first. That's not why I went up there. I was just angry and hurt and hating myself so goddamn much, so I started drinking. And once I started, I couldn't stop."

I pulled in a shuttered breath and Dawson rubbed my hand comfortingly, encouraging me to continue.

"The booze hit me really fast and that was when I decided to climb on the roof. I remember feeling weightless and free up there, like as long as I was up there, I didn't have to face who I really was. My problems didn't matter. Then the idea came to me. If I wanted to stay as free as I felt up there, then there was only one way. It was like something clicked in my head and all I felt was peace the second I'd decided. But then you found me and...I didn't want to leave you. I was scared to let you go."

A pained whimper slipped free of Dawson's lips and he dropped his forehead to my hand, clutching it so hard that my fingertips went half numb.

"There was this voice that kept telling me to do it, that it would all just end and I'd never hurt again. Never hurt the ones I loved again. But then you were begging me to stay, to fight for us, and you started drowning out that damn voice until all I heard was you. Just you."

I sifted my fingers through his tangled hair, coaxing him to meet my gaze, and my heart skipped when I saw how blue his eyes were in that moment, as vibrant and bright as a bloom of cornflower.

"You didn't just save me, Mercury. You reminded me I was worth saving."

Dawson surged forward and stole my lips in a hard kiss, electric pulses shooting down my limbs. He breathed life back into my body and for the first time since waking up, I was so damn grateful to feel so fucking...alive.

It ended far too soon when the door opened and my dad walked in, looking like he'd aged ten years since I last saw him. The breath left him in a rush when he saw me and he closed the distance in a few strides, crushing me in his embrace.

Hot tears hit my shoulder and he quaked against me as I hugged him back fiercely. He kissed my temple, muttering thanks to God or whoever was up there that I was okay. I was a blubbering mess of apologies and regret, clinging to him hard enough to leave bruises.

He leaned back and gave me a watery smile, cupping the side of my neck. "I am so glad to see you, kiddo. How are you feeling?"

"Better than I have a right to be."

He opened his mouth to respond, but the door opened once again and four familiar faces shuffled into the small room.

"Oh thank God, you're okay! I mean, you're okay right? How do you feel? Your color is a little off, but that just might be this disastrous lighting. Ugh, fucking fluorescents," Micah exclaimed in one, long breath.

"Breathe, baby boy. Try not to overwhelm him. Remember how disoriented you felt waking up in the hospital last year?" Bash told him, rubbing his back calmly.

"Oooh, you're right. My bad, Theo. In my defense, I've had a *lot* of coffee today. I'm so wired, I can practically see sound and hear colors."

"You might want to get that checked out, my dude," Nate chimed in with wide eyes. "But for real, are you doing alright, T? You had us really worried there for a while. Your boy was a total stress-mess waiting for you to wake up, but no worries, we took care of him for you. Made him eat and all that good stuff."

A stab of guilt stuck me between the ribs and I reached for Dawson's hand again. He raised mine to press a warm kiss on my palm, the small, intimate gesture making goosebumps sweep down my arm.

"I'm as okay as I can be, I guess. And I really appreciate you guys coming down here. You didn't have to do that," I thanked them sheepishly.

Aly elbowed her way past Nate and came over to give me a careful hug, which I returned as much as I could with the IV line attached to my hand.

"We wanted to be here for you and make sure you were both okay. Rhys and the others couldn't make it, but they wanted me to tell you they're thinking about you and Dawson, and as soon as they can, they're throwing a party to celebrate you getting out of here!"

The genuine warmth in her words and smile made my chest clench. It struck me just how much this group of people actually cared about me and made an effort to include me. And the craziest part was I believed they'd show up for me regardless of Dawson.

"You read my mind, Alycat! A party is just what we need and you, my fine man, are gonna get the Nathaniel Christensen Recovery Special," Nate beamed at me.

"Bruh, if you make him one of your drinks, he's gonna *be* in recovery," Bash deadpanned.

I winced at the joke and of course Dawson noticed. He leaned down to whisper in my ear. "They don't know anything. I just told them you'd passed out and were brought here."

Relief flooded me that they didn't know all the details. That old fear of them finding out the truth and then ditching me because of it curdled in my gut. But I couldn't hide it forever and it was honestly exhausting to try. Dawson had assured me that they wouldn't turn away from me, that they'd hold space for my issues and support me, just like he did. Maybe that was enough.

"Actually," I began slowly, "I won't be drinking much in the future, or probably at all."

The four of them looked at me with a mix of curiosity and concern. I blew out a big breath before continuing, catching Dad's encouraging nod to me across the room.

"See, the thing is...I have bipolar disorder. I've been kind of having a hard time of it this year—the last few years, actually—and that's why I'm in here. I had a really bad episode last night and I, um...I'm finally able to admit I need some serious help to get better."

Somehow, it set me more at ease that none of them tried to immediately brush it off and act like it was no big deal, watching as they processed the news carefully before their faces softened with understanding.

Aly affectionately squeezed one of my ankles over the thin hospital blanket, smiling softly. "I'm really glad you trusted us enough to tell us. I know that couldn't have been easy."

"Funny enough, I actually feel a lot better now that you guys know. I've spent so long trying to keep it under wraps and make sure no one found out, I didn't realize how much it was draining me."

"Was there a reason you didn't feel comfortable telling us until now?" Bash gently asked. "We didn't do anything to make you feel unsafe or judged, did we?..."

"No, it wasn't anything you guys did or didn't do, I swear." I explained what had gone down at SHSU when I'd told my supposed "friends" about my disorder and how I'd handled the abandonment afterwards.

"What a bunch of cuntbags," Micah snarled. "Oof, sorry about the language, Mr. Bishop!"

"No need to apologize to me. I was just fantasizing about putting their balls in a wood chipper," Dad growled. Nate let out a short squeak and dropped his hands in front of his pants, his eyes bugging out.

"Well, I can guarantee that you are a lifetime member of the UT crew and that comes with an endless supply of love, support, and ass-whoopings for anyone who fucks with you."

"And we'll help however we can, whenever you need anything from us," Bash added to his boyfriend's reassurance.

My eyes burned at the unconditional acceptance they were all showing me and I choked out a thank you. My throat was going to permanently close with all these damn tears that kept coming up.

God, I hope this is just a side effect of my weakened state and I'm not gonna become one of those people that cries during Sarah McLachlan commercials or some shit...

I finally remembered my manners and introduced everyone to my dad, who seemed very pleased with the show of support he'd seen from my friends. Pretty soon the door opened again and a tall, middle-aged lady with platinum blond hair waltzed in.

"Ah, I was hoping you'd be awake! I'm the psychiatrist on-call, Doctor Johansson," she said in a light Scandinavian accent.

"The white coat kind of gave it away," I joked lamely. She chuckled and shook my hand.

"Aaand that's our cue," Micah piped up. "Autobots, roll out!"

The guys and Aly gave us quick hugs and made us promise to text them if either of us needed anything. I brought my attention back to the doctor, who was waiting patiently.

"I'm sorry to interrupt your visit with your friends, but I didn't want to keep you waiting any longer for news. Now, from what I was legally able to learn from your therapist and from the information your partner here gave me about the past few weeks up to last night, I believe you had what we call a mixed episode. It was likely brought on by the irregular use of your medication, and the alcohol you consumed worsened the effects. It's incredibly dangerous to mix your lithium carbonate and alcoholic beverages. To put it bluntly, you are very lucky that you didn't cause more damage to your body."

My stomach curdled as my mind worked to understand the influx of information. Dawson stepped closer and gripped my forearm, and I wondered if he needed the contact as badly as I did then.

"Umm, sorry, but what's a mixed episode?"

Her kind smile put me slightly at ease even as embarrassment heated my cheeks.

"A mixed episode is when someone with bipolar disorder experiences both manic and depressive symptoms simultaneously. They are fairly common, especially in those who have a co-occurring disorder, like with your ADHD, or those who abruptly discontinue their medication. They can be quite serious. The risk for suicide is significantly higher since the depression often leads to suicidal thoughts and the mania can feed the impulsivity and energy to follow through on those urges."

Nausea swelled in my gut thinking how close it had come to that last night. I glanced up at Dawson, the tension around his eyes and the way he was abusing his bottom lip with his teeth told me he was just as affected by her words as I was.

"So what happens now? What are his next steps?" Dad asked.

"My professional opinion is for you to enter a clinical treatment program to help you stabilize on new medication and learn to manage your symptoms long-term."

My muscles went rigid at the suggestion. I knew that would probably be her solution, but everything inside me rebelled at the idea. Dawson slipped an arm around my shoulder and pressed his lips to my temple, rubbing soothing patterns up and down my bicep.

"You really think that's the best option for me?"

I wanted to do what was right, what would help me genuinely heal and grow stronger so that this never happened to me again. If she felt this was the way to go, I'd push through whatever bullshit fears I had from before and commit to it. For Dawson *and* myself.

"I do. However, your partner did share that you've had some problematic experiences in the past with residential treatment, is that right?"

I gave a jerky nod and leaned into Dawson more, breathing in his woodsy scent to calm my thudding pulse.

"If I may, I have a personal suggestion that I think you will be much happier with." She paused and gave me an assessing look. "My wife is the staff psychiatrist for a treatment facility just west of the city, Harbor House. I worked there myself for some years and I can honestly say I've never seen another program equal to it. They have an impeccable therapeutic record for recovery with a low rate of relapse and the facility itself is top-tier."

Dad jumped in with several questions about the treatment and types of therapy they used, even down to the building itself and the amenities it included. I had to admit, it sounded like a dream. Dr. Johansson pulled up photos that she'd taken herself from her time there, showing us the immaculate grounds and the swanky, yet comfortable rooms. It even put the bougie facility my mom had forced me into to shame.

She left us to talk it out and research the place ourselves, letting us know they were keeping me for one more night of observation and fluids before releasing me so we had some time to decide. Eventually, Dad set down his phone after looking into everything he could find about the place, perching on the end of the bed with a hopeful, pleading expression.

"Well, everything I could find online so far points to it being a really great place. So what do you think, kiddo?"

Despite the glowing recommendation from the doc, my mind couldn't help but cling to the idea that it was nothing more than another gilded cage, a beautiful tomb to rot in as I lost even more of myself.

"Dad, can I have a few minutes to talk it over with Dawson?"

To his credit, he didn't bat an eye at my request. He pecked a kiss on my forehead and went on a hunt for coffee, leaving us alone. I levered myself over and patted the bed beside me. Dawson climbed on and wound his arms around me, tucking my head under his chin.

"What if it doesn't work?" I whispered, like saying it out loud would somehow jinx me.

"Can I say something without you getting upset or mad?"

I tensed in his hold, but dipped my head in agreement.

"I think a large reason you've had so much trouble is the mindset that really dug its claws in when you first got diagnosed. You've had so much shame and anger around having bipolar disorder, it's like you've been in survival mode. You fight it and hate it, but it's a part of you. You have to learn to live *with* it instead of *against* it. It's okay to give yourself some grace when you stumble, baby."

"I don't know how," I admitted wetly. "I want to—to stop hating myself and not look at myself as a mistake anymore. I want to change, for good this time. I just don't know where to even start..."

Dawson tilted my chin up, his gorgeous blues boring into mine like two waves crashing together. He stroked my cheek in a feather-soft caress and I sank into the touch.

"I think you start with accepting that you'll have bad days, but they'll come with a ton of good ones too. You start by celebrating the good days, but having compassion for yourself when you mess up because we all do from time to time. You start by telling yourself you are worthy of every bit of goodness that comes your way. You start by not being afraid to adjust the plan if something isn't working, and remind yourself that you do not have to go through a single minute of it alone. I will be there every step of the way, forever and always."

He rested his forehead on mine, both of us breathing each other in as his words settled between us. I was scared at the idea of starting all over again with my treatment, of going back to the beginning and relearning how to be *me*, mental illness and all. But sometimes you had to hit rock bottom to know which way was up.

"I'll do it."

Dawson leaned back to look me in the eye, his lips slowly curving up at the corners. "You mean it? Are you sure?"

"I do and I am. I'm still anxious about it, but I want to do this. Not just for you though. You're right about a lot of things, but the biggest is that I'm worth the effort to get better and to live my life with you. If I'm supposed to love myself, I think this is the first step in that direction; giving myself my best chance."

The blinding smile he flashed me flatlined my heart, and the way his eyes crinkled with joy sparked it back to life.

"I am so goddamn proud of you, Theo. And I love you more than words can say."

I grinned back at him, but as I stretched up to kiss him, an odd thought hit me out of the blue.

"Oh fuck! Isn't your game tonight?" I panicked. "Holy shit, you're supposed to be over there! You don't have to stay, I'm good—"

His lips covered mine, effectively cutting off my freakout and I went boneless under the lazy assault of his tongue diving into my mouth. He released me way too soon, my head hazy as I looked at him through hooded eyes.

"I already told Coach I won't be there. I don't care about missing the game. There is nowhere else on earth I need to be than right here. My place is and always has been right by your side."

Before I could respond, he reclaimed my mouth and I melted into him. His kiss was liquid gold poured into all the cracks, reforging me into something new. Still broken, yet healed. Still imperfect, yet somehow all the more beautiful for it.

And maybe someday I'd find a way to love those imperfections too.

Someday.

CHAPTER FORTY

We watched the rain roll in like a curtain being drawn over the woods, the water pinging on the roof of the barn. The weather was as gloomy as my mood as Dawson and I sat in the hay loft, our legs dangling over the side. Nostalgia crept in as I remembered all the days we spent just like this, sitting side by side in Neverland, watching the world turn and wishing it would pause for a little while.

"When do you have to leave again?" Dawson checked for the fourth time. At this point, I wondered if he ignored the previous times I'd said it just to live in denial a bit longer.

"At nine," I replied dully, playing with his fingers and watching two birds take cover from the rain in the barn's rafters.

Thirty minutes.

Just thirty minutes before I left him one more time, only if everything worked the way I prayed it would, it would be the last time I ever had to walk away from him. Then our next chapter could begin.

"I don't know why this feels so...heavy," I wondered aloud. "It's not like I'll be gone super long. Thirty or forty days is nothing in the grand scheme of things, right?"

Dawson nodded, lips twisting in a sad smirk.

"And I think we made a smart choice to not call each other. It'll guarantee that my focus is on therapy and recovery, and it'll make it that much better when we see each other again, you know?"

"You're rambling," he pointed out amusedly.

"Oh, is that what I'm doing? How annoying of you to notice," I grumbled, drawing a breathy laugh from him. "It's just a lot to process and this is my last big chance to get stable."

"It's not."

Confused, I turned my head in his direction. "What do you mean 'it's not'?"

"It's not your last chance," he refuted. "Don't put that pressure on yourself. If this doesn't work out, then we'll try another way. And if that one doesn't work, then we'll try a different one. We'll do whatever it takes to find the right path for you."

"That could take forever and by then, you'd be sick of waiting around for my ass." The joke fell flat under the hint of truth in my fear.

Dawson's features lined with frustration, but under that I noticed the challenge too. He didn't say a word as he dug in his pocket, pulling out his phone and unlocking it to send a text. I tried to ask him who he texted, but he silently held a finger up for me to wait.

He sat there, swinging his legs and staring at the rain as we waited for a call, text, or whatever he wanted to come through on his phone. A couple minutes later, his phone chimed with an incoming text and he smiled at the screen.

"Let me get this straight," he started. "You think that there is a possibility that I could one day get tired of waiting for you."

"I was just kidd—"

"No, you weren't, because there's at least some tiny part of you that believes there is a chance that could happen one day."

I swung my head back to look out at the water pelting the ground, unable to look him in the eye where he'd see the truth. I didn't want to be insecure at all about Dawson's love and commitment to me. One of the major things I wanted to work on at Harbor House was learning to distinguish anxiety from reality and combat the thoughts that liked to... well, rain on my parade.

"I asked Dani to send me this picture because I think you really need to see it. It might put some things in perspective for you."

He held my phone out for me. Sighing, I took it and looked at the photo he had pulled up, and my brows pinched together.

"I'm not sure what I am looking at. I mean, I know *what* I'm looking at obviously, but I don't understand what it means because it couldn't mean what I think it means...could it?"

I couldn't tear my eyes away from the screenshot of a jewelry website and the platinum men's ring that was front and center on the image. The platinum men's *engagement* ring, according to the description.

"It means exactly what you think it means," Dawson replied simply. "And so will this..."

He snuck his finger over and swiped to the next photo, this one of a different, but equally as beautiful engagement band. I scanned the entire screen, taking it all in until my gaze blurred. Dawson removed the phone from my trembling hand and grasped it instead, pulling my attention to him.

"Dani took that first photo when she was sneaking around my computer the week of Homecoming. And that second photo was one I took when I was looking at the website when you were in the hospital."

My pulse took off like fucking Secretariat as his gaze grew more intense, waiting for me to make the connection out loud. I couldn't. I didn't want to say it on the sliver of a chance I was wrong. I was too fragile, too weak to be wrong about this.

"Why were you looking at those rings, Dawson?" My voice was filled with gravel, shaking with all the terrifying hope that rushed through my blood.

"Because I intend to spoil the fuck out of you when I propose one day, so I need plenty of time to pick the right one."

All the air whooshed out of my lungs so fast I felt lightheaded. Small, aborted noises were all that came out as I tried to formulate a response, but what the fuck could I say?

How about "fuck yes"? Is that too soon? Is it allowed if he hasn't asked the question yet? Probably not, right?...

"I started looking for a ring four years ago because I was just as serious then as I am now that you are the love of my life and I want to spend every second of this life I have with you. So don't for one minute think that I will *ever* get sick of waiting for you, Theo Bishop. One year, ten years, fifty...it doesn't matter. I'll wait for you forever if I have to."

I gripped his face between my hands and seized his mouth in a fierce kiss. I licked the seam of his lips and he moaned as I dove in to taste him, so beautifully responsive for me. Our mouths moved together as we deepened the kiss, my tongue teasing his until I forgot my own name.

Oh well, fuck it...I want his name anyway.

My phone alarm pierced the air and we sprang apart, startled by the sound. I tried not to let my mood sink at the reminder that we only had ten minutes before I had to meet Dad up at the house for him to drive me to Harbor House for intake.

"I don't want to let you go," I confessed on a hoarse whisper, clutching at Dawson's hair to keep him close to me.

"Then don't." He stood and held out a hand to help me up, pulling me towards the center of the loft. "Dance with me?"

Those damn pesky tears lined my lashes, and I let him yank me into his chest, my left arm sliding around his shoulders as he held my right hand out.

"I need to grab my phone for the music." He tried to disentangle himself, but I held him tighter.

"You don't need it, Mercury. We'll make our own music. Sing to me."

Dawson grinned and brought his mouth to my ear, singing his favorite Jake Wesley Roger cover that sheeted my body in chills. I closed my eyes as the hypnotic sound soothed every nerve in my system, his voice warm and silky with a subtle rasp that scratched a part of my brain that made me come apart at the seams.

Just like always, he crooned the lyrics in a way that tore my heart out, emotional and passionate as if telling me a story. He twirled us around in the loft in a gentle sway, the world falling away and leaving us in this perfect moment with Dawson speaking to me in a language all his own.

All I need is you...only you.

We stood in the silence as his final words echoed in the quiet barn and the rain slowed to a stop. Dawson kissed me sweetly and then led me down the ladder. We stood there, staring unseeing towards the houses that were obscured by the thicket of trees.

"I have to go," I mumbled.

Dawson cradled my cheeks and tilted my head down, his warm lips brushing a firm kiss to my forehead. I clung to his waist, cementing this moment to memory.

"Please don't give up," he begged softly. "Remember what you have waiting for you here. You were supposed to be my forever. Don't you rob me of that. Don't you dare take that from me again."

The quiet words were spoken with such desperation that I had trouble breathing. I gripped his wrists and pulled back enough to lock eyes.

"Then what if we make a trade? Give me your forever and I'll give you mine in return."

A wet, soft laugh escaped him. "I'll give you anything you want as long as you come back to me."

I reached up to unhook the silver chain around my neck. Taking his hand, I held it up so his class ring slid off onto his open palm, curling his fingers around it.

"Keep it safe for me. I'll be back for that."

I brought his closed fist up and brushed a kiss over his knuckles, meeting his piercing gaze. "I will always come back. It doesn't matter how many turns I take, all my roads lead back to you. I'll always find my way back to you, Mercury."

I took his lips in a bruising kiss, hoping to leave a mark that he couldn't erase, couldn't hide. I kissed him until all the breath left my body and we were both panting as we held onto each other like it was the world's ending.

Theo

JOURNAL DAY 1

Mercury,

I miss you.

One day and I already hate being here. I mean, not really because I'm getting help, but I hate that I'm not with you.

Ugh, okay. I'll try to think more positively.

The group shrink told us we should keep a diary or journal during our time here to process everything and look back on it in "times of struggle". I thought that was stupid because I'm not an angsty teenage girl, so I decided to write to you instead. I'd rather talk to you anyway. I already miss your voice. I miss your laugh.

God, I just fucking miss you.

I know I let you down, but I will get better. I will get this under control. I will come back to you.

I love you.

Just please wait for me...

Mercury,

It's harder than I thought to be here. I don't regret it and I'm trying to stay positive, but I promised I'd always be honest with you.

The truth is I'm scared. I'm scared that this won't work, or that it will and everything will be different after.

I'm trying to trust in you and in us. Every morning I wake up, I remind myself that I need to do this to get better, to heal, to keep my promise to you that I will always come back.

I'm fighting, baby. I'm fighting with everything I have to do this for us and come home to you. Remember you own my heart, Dawson. I promise to keep it beating for you.

Don't forget our trade. You gave me your forever and you have mine in return.

I love you.

Please wait for me.

Theo

JOURNAL DAY 4

Mercury,

I met with Dr. Johansson's wife today, Dr. Kay. Honestly, I was nervous as fuck after what we learned at the hospital and it was a long visit, but she helped me understand a lot.

Apparently the doctors at my previous facility weren't doing their damn jobs right. She figured out I have rapid cycling, which basically means my inner yo-yo is fucked and goes up and down a lot faster than others. She said my ADHD was likely to blame, but normally one drug alone isn't enough to treat it effectively. That's why I kept getting so depressed even on the Lithium. Also did you know that shit can fuck up your kidneys?? Yeah, neither did I. Fuckers at the other place never told me that.

She put me on a couple new meds with names I'm not gonna even attempt to spell, but she also talked me through everything and what to expect. The drugs may need adjusting down the line and she wanted me to be able to advocate for myself.

Then I cried. Like, full-on breakdown. I was just so fucking angry. At those doctors, that place, my mom, and even myself. I felt so stupid for never asking questions and for trusting them to know exactly what to do. I kept thinking that was as good as it was going to get. I felt shitty, but not as shitty as it could be. I had accepted that I would probably always be a little bit broken.

I don't really think that anymore. It doesn't feel so hopeless now.

I think...I'm actually going to be okay.

I guess you were right again.

Theo

JOURNAL DAY 7

Mercury,

Did you know you have some fans here? My favorite tech, Meryl, was talking about your championship game tomorrow, and she lost her mind when I told her you were my boyfriend. She said she and her husband are UT season ticket holders and try never to miss a game. Beau (that's her hubby) swears you're one of the greatest college quarterbacks in the last two decades. I didn't have the heart to tell Meryl you aren't going pro...I'm worried it would give poor Beau a heart attack.

She did ask for an autograph though, so I said I'd hook 'em for her. Get it?..."hook 'em?"

Oh fuck off, I have limited entertainment here. Let me have that one.

I wish I could be there tomorrow to cheer you on. There's a lot of things I'm angry with myself about, but that's one of the biggest right now. If I wasn't like this, I would have been there. It makes me sick to think that if things had gone wrong that night, I wouldn't be here right now...and I'd miss everything.

I don't want to miss anything else with you. I don't want

to miss a single kiss, or hug, or morning waking up to you, or a night falling asleep in your arms.

I want to build a life with you. I want to be there for your final game, our graduation, your first job, our anniversary, our wedding. I want it all.

We still have so much life to live together, baby.

And I can't wait to start.

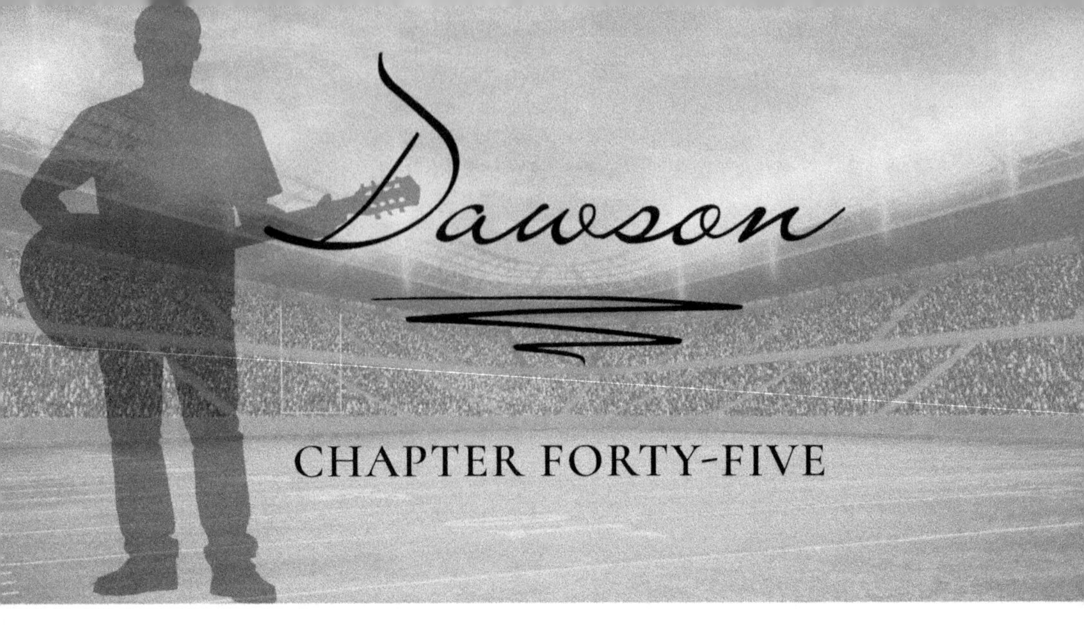

CHAPTER FORTY-FIVE

The air was thick with tension as my teammates and I rested on the benches during halftime, the sound of our heavy breathing and smell of our sweat permeating the locker room. Coach Walker came in and silently scanned the room with his hands on his hips, locking eyes with each of us as he went. I could almost feel the nervous energy coming off the guys around me as we waited for him to say something.

"This is it. This is the day you gentlemen have been working towards for months, some of you years. You have poured blood, sweat, and tears into preparing for this moment, pushed yourselves to the absolute limits, and proven your mettle against teams that have gone for your throats out on that field. We're down by sixteen, but I don't want to just make those points up. I want you to pull so far ahead of them that you can't see them in your goddamn rearview mirror. You can do this. You have earned this. This win is yours for the taking. Get out there and let's win us a fucking championship!"

Our roar reverberated around the room, vibrating our bones and firing us up. Coach called out our five minute warning as I opened my locker and checked my phone. I didn't know what I was expecting to find since my and Theo's no-phone agreement meant I hadn't heard anything from him in the week he'd been gone, and I wouldn't for another three weeks. Possibly more if things didn't go as planned with his treatment.

I locked it and went to put it back in my bag when the screen lit up with a missed call notification followed shortly by a voicemail alert. My heart flip-flopped seeing the unknown number because somehow I knew exactly who it would be.

I rushed to open the voicemail, plugging my other ear against the surrounding noise so I didn't miss a single syllable, and when I heard Theo's throaty timbre, my stomach somersaulted violently.

"Hey there, beautiful. Soooo I bribed my new bestie over here, Meryl, to let me borrow her phone so I could call you. We've been watching your game here and I couldn't help myself. Even just seeing you on TV makes it fucking hard to breathe...and I might have popped an inconvenient boner when you threw that eighty yard pass in the second quarter. Have I ever told you how sexy your arms look when you throw? And those pants should be illegal because your ass could start a prison riot, damn. Wait—fuck, I'm rambling. Not enough time for that. I wanted to tell you how sorry I am that I'm not there, but know that I'm watching and rooting for you, babe. Just imagine that I'm there, front and center, cheering you on. You've fucking got this. Don't let those assholes get to you out there. You are Dawson fucking Hayes, so go out like the champion you are. Bring home a win for me, baby. Fuck, I miss you so much, Mercury...and I hope you're waiting for me. Oh, shit, halftime is almost over...okay, go kick some ass! I love you! Bye!"

I choked out a watery laugh, my knees going weak hearing the longing in his voice. I sniffed and discreetly wiped at my eyes as I tried to pull myself together. A bittersweet ache bloomed behind my ribs, elation and heartsickness warring inside as I closed my eyes and tried to imagine him just as he said.

I pictured his flawless, white smile and the way one eyebrow always quirked up when he was feeling cheeky. I imagined him grasping my face and kissing me senseless before I ran out on the field, promising me a carnal reward if I won that would undoubtedly leave me hard and throbbing. And most importantly, I imagined his alluring rasp in my ear as he told me he loved me and he'd be waiting for me at the end.

Coach's whistle cut through the din of the locker room, signaling us to line up for the team entrance. The guys clapped my shoulder or knocked my helmet with theirs as I passed through to the front of the tunnel. I twisted around to face them all as it sank in that this could be the last game we played together, the last time we walked onto that field as a team.

"Listen up!" I shouted, all eyes swinging to me. "Playing beside you all has been one of the greatest privileges of my life, and I am damn proud of each and every one of you. But this is *our* field and *our* fucking championship. Let's show them that if they want to mess with Texas—"

"They'll get the Horns!"

Their collective chant thundered in my ears and made my chest swell with pride. I slid my helmet on and rolled my shoulders back before bursting from the tunnel, our fight song barely audible through the cheers of the crowd. I ran out with fire in my veins, my team at my back, and Theo's ring hanging right above my heart.

"Alright losers," Nate yelled over the noise in the bar. "Please raise your shot glasses to the real winner of the night, Captain QB himself! To Dawson!"

Whistles and whoops of celebration exploded from the crew before they knocked their glasses to the table and tossed the shots back. Rhys and Micah erupted in coughs while Nate, Griffin, Bash, and Cal howled like drunken wolves while some of the crowd around us joined in. Kenji and Aly gave each other matching looks of wry amusement at their reaction.

It'd taken some pushing and prodding from Aly to agree to come out with everyone tonight after our big win. It had been an intense game in the second half, but the guys back out with a vengeance. I played my heart out and we ended the game against Texas Tech thirty-six to twenty-two. And when I'd been lifted onto my teammates' shoulders, I'd looked right into the cameras to wink and blow a kiss, knowing without a doubt that he saw it as my silent message to him.

It wasn't that I didn't want to celebrate with my friends, but I was having second thoughts about the location. The karaoke bar was packed with the usual crowd, plus the fans who came to revel in the UT victory. My gaze trailed to the corner of the bar where I'd watched Theo that night last summer, nursing my broken heart as he'd flirted with his date. It seemed like a lifetime ago and the surreality of where we were now hit me.

Now, I was sitting there with my friends for yet another celebration, missing Theo just as much as I had back then, but with my heart finally healed over and stronger than before, waiting for him to come home and reclaim it.

"Earth to Dawson?"

I blinked out of my stupor and turned to see Aly smirking at me.

"Sorry, I kinda zoned out."

"Were you thinking about Theo?"

"When am I not?" I mumbled into my beer.

"Did you get to talk to him after your game? They allow phone calls there, right?" Rhys asked from where he was settled on his boyfriend's lap.

"They do, but we decided not to call each other and keep him 'unplugged', so to speak."

"But why? Oh no, you guys aren't on a break while he's away, are you?" Rhys gasped.

"I hope not, dude. That shit never works out...just ask Ross and Rachel," Cal chimed in. We all shot varying looks of surprise and amusement his way. "What? *Friends* is one of Rhys' comfort shows, I can't escape it at home."

"Yeah, but...you like, legit watched it, didn't you?" Griffin teased. Cal just looked him dead in the eye and double-bumped the sides of his fists together in true *Friends* fashion.

"No, we're *not* on a break. We both talked about it and we thought it would keep Theo focused on his treatment better," I explained. "But I think a large part of it is that he wants to prove to himself that he can do this alone, push through it without using me, or even his Dad, as a crutch. Even though he's doing this partly for us, this is about him."

It was weird to be able to talk freely about Theo's disorder and all the related issues with our friends, but I was also hella relieved to have them to lean on, to have people in my and Theo's corner that truly cared. None of this was easy no matter how strong we were trying to be about it. The episode, the rehab, missing him, and even what came next for us weighed on me more than I cared to admit, but they'd all been as supportive and compassionate as I always thought they'd be.

"That makes a lot of sense actually. The rough patch Micah and I went through last year was what pushed me to try therapy, but then it really became about me and my healing so I could be the best version of myself, regardless of whether Micah gave me a second chance or not," Bash added.

"Rough patch? Really? Is that how you'd describe how you were—"

Bash kissed Micah soundly on the mouth to cut off his snark, earning him a teasing glare from Micah when they pulled apart. "We don't need to get into that here. Different story for a different time, my love."

"That must be pretty hard though, going through all this without being able to check on him and know how he's doing?" Rhys flashed me a sympathetic look.

I was still getting used to opening up to my friends about how I was feeling, but it did make things easier to process and helped me not feel so alone in my own head.

"Harder than I thought it'd be, if I'm honest. I figured as long as he was there getting help and working through things, I would be fine with the radio silence, but all I feel is...useless. Helpless. I know this is something he needs to do by himself, but I wish there was something I could do to be there for him, or at least...ugh, I don't know."

I blew out a deep breath when I couldn't find the right words. All that played in my brain were memories of the romantic gestures Theo would always do for me back then. Surprise gifts, a playlist made of all the songs that reminded him of me, elaborate dates, random adventures to nearby cities. He had always used his actions to show me how much he cared, how much I meant to him.

All I had was music.

As if a beam of light landed on him by divine guidance, I spotted Cal's friend Mateo across the bar laughing with a group of friends. I didn't know him super well, but I remember that night last summer, he had gone up to sing right before me and he'd stunned the crowd with his natural talent. An idea was forming in my mind, small pieces snapping together as I thought of what I'd need to pull it off.

"Uhh, D? Whatcha doing?" Nate questioned. "You've got 'crazy eyes' going on over there, man."

"I need to go talk to Mateo real fast."

Nate blinked at me like a stupefied bird. "Okay. So. I have several questions, the first being why the *fuck* would you need to go talk to Colombian Hugh Hefner over there?"

I narrowed my gaze at him. "You know, we're eventually gonna have to talk about what happened between you two to make you hate him so much. The Cliffnotes version you gave me last year isn't cutting it."

"Yeah, I know," he sighed deeply. "How about I pencil us in for that talk on the twelfth of fucking never?"

I rolled my eyes and turned towards Mateo's table, but Nate snagged my arm before I could take a step. "No, seriously. What do you need to talk to him about? Also before you do, are you up to date on all your Hepatitis shots?"

"Jesus, I'm not going to proposition him, Nate."

"Bro, he doesn't even need the contact to pass on whatever he's got brewing in those overactive loins of his," Nate shuddered dramatically.

"Okay, first off, that's fucking gross. Second, what's with the slut shaming all of a sudden?"

Nate gasped loudly. "That's not what I'm doing! Is it? Ah fuck, maybe it is, but it's specifically against him! Let's just say he's not very... selective in who he screws around with. He can't be trusted."

I raised my brows at him, finally getting somewhere with his and Mateo's rocky history-mystery, but I couldn't dig into that right now.

"Look, that's his business and it's not really relevant to the favor I need from him. I'll be back."

"I'm coming with!" Nate followed me over to Mateo's table, and I caught him throwing a disdainful eye at him and the girl he had perched on his knee.

"What's up, Hayes? That was some fucking win, my friend. ¡Qué bacano!" Mateo flashed me a pearly white smile before his eyes slid to Nate beside me. "Well, Nathaniel, isn't this a surprise? I didn't think you could—how did you put it?—stomach being within a mile of my cocky, Playboy ass?"

"I took a Kaopectate," he said dryly, ice dripping from his gaze. It was the exact opposite of how Nate was with everyone that it had me a little worried.

"Uh, anyway, I actually wanted to talk to you and see if I could get your help with something?"

It took Mateo a few seconds to tear his eyes away from Nate and towards me. "Sounds mysterious. What did you have in mind?"

He patted the girl's hip and kissed her cheek to signal her to give us a minute, and I noticed Nate roll his eyes. I gave him the quick rundown of my idea and what part he would play in it.

"That's some romantic shit, Hayes. Count me in," he grinned widely. "¡A la orden, perrito!"

Mateo came back with us to the table so I could include everyone else in what I was planning.

"Hey Mateo, I didn't know you were here, man." Cal smiled at his friend, getting up to greet him with a complicated handshake they always did.

"Yeah, Hayes here looped me in on something he wants to do for his boyfriend that I can help with. Guess I'm an honorary member of the Scooby Gang now!"

"Ruh-roh, Shaggy...doesn't look like Nate's a fan of that idea," Micah whispered to Rhys, but it seemed like I was the only one who caught it.

"Aww, you're thinking of doing something for Theo? Can I help?" Aly asked.

"Actually, I kind of need all of y'all's help with what I have in mind. It's kind of a big thing..."

I spent the next twenty minutes going over the plan that I was now determined to put into motion. The crew's enthusiasm grew the more we got into the details of what we could pull off in the few weeks before Theo was due to come home.

"Dude, if we do that right, it's gonna be sick! He's gonna love it," Griffin exclaimed.

"I can hook you up with a pretty sweet sound system," Kenji offered.

"Micah, Rhys and I are on the decorations!"Aly clapped excitedly.

"Fin will definitely want to help too," Micah said. "Where the hell is he, anyway?"

"He was supposed to be here a while ago. Let me call him."

The rest of us continued talking about what we'd need and some obstacles to making it happen in such a short time. I cut off what I was saying when I saw Aly frowning down at her phone. She swiped to answer whatever call was coming in, walking away from the table with a grimace.

Griffin had also noticed and was watching Aly talk on the phone, presumably with Fin and it was clear it wasn't a happy conversation.

"Um, I'm sorry to drink and dash, but I need to go take care of something," Aly blurted as she made her way back to the table, grabbing her keys and leaving cash behind for the drinks.

"Wait, was that Fin? Is everything okay?" Griffin asked with concern.

Aly plastered on a smile that I instantly read as forced. "Yeah, he's good. I just need to go help him with something."

"Is it Dan? Did he do something?" Griffin's face darkened and venom had seeped into his tone. Aly paled slightly and her smile wavered the tiniest bit.

"No, not at all. It's nothing to worry about, I've got it handled. Dawson, call me later and let me know what I need to do first. Catch you guys later."

She darted off before any more questions could be lobbed at her, and my gut curdled slightly at how frazzled she'd seemed. I made eye contact with Griffin, worry and frustration etched into his features.

The rest of the table had been too deep in conversation to notice Aly's abrupt departure, so Griffin and I turned our attention back to them.

"Alright team, we've got this one," Nate said, slapping the table. "The Thawson Initiative is officially a go!"

"We're not calling it that," I griped.

"Oops! Too late, it's already been dubbed," Micah piped up. "This calls for more shots!"

"Way ahead of you." Cal glided over smoothly with a small tray of varied shots.

Bash cleared his throat loudly and raised his shot glass. "To Thawson and us not fucking up this epic, romantic gesture!"

"To Thawson!" They all cheered as one before throwing back their shots.

I laughed and took my own shot, the whiskey burning as it traveled down my throat. I wasn't sure if I'd be able to accomplish what I had in mind, but Theo was worth it. I wanted to sweep him off his feet like he had done with me a hundred times before. All I could see in my mind's eye was the surprise and joy on his face, and I'd do whatever it took to make it a reality.

When my baby came home to me, I'd make it a day he'd never forget.

JOURNAL DAY 10

Mercury,

We had music therapy today and it made me think of you. We had to choose two songs that we connected to. One that represents who we were before rehab and one that represents who we want to be after.

I'll tell you, it was a lot fucking harder than it sounded. And without my phone to browse through Spotify? Impossible.

But then I thought about you and all the songs you've played for me over the years. I thought about how you mostly choose to play piano when you're feeling some type of way and you need to process your emotions. But you play your guitar when you really want to pour your heart out and send a message, those times when the only words worth saying are better sung. You play the piano with your head, but the guitar with your soul.

So I thought of my own piano and guitar songs. My "head and soul music", as ridiculous as that sounds. Want to hear what they are?

I'm gonna tell you anyway.

But if you laugh, no blowjobs for a month.

My head song was Avril's "Head Above Water". Yeah, I know, it was a little on the nose. Stop laughing.

All I was doing was barely treading water, trying to survive before I came back to you. I never told you this, but there were a few seconds when I went under at the lake that I didn't want to come back up. And I'm not sure I would have. But then you saved me and a switch flipped inside. Suddenly all I wanted to do was fight to keep you. I wanted to keep resurfacing no matter how many times I went under because I couldn't be without you.

You saved me in more ways than you can comprehend, baby.

I think I'll save my soul song for when I see you again. It's better if I tell you in person.

Just wait for me.

JOURNAL DAY 14

Mercury,

Two weeks down.

All in all, this place has been pretty nice. Swanky. Definitely better than the rehab Mom and Doug shoved me into, even though it probably cost the same.

The pool time I get is great, group therapy isn't as bad as I thought it'd be, and the art and music therapy has been interesting.

But fuck yoga therapy. The only thing about me that's flexible are my morals. Also, child's pose put me to sleep and they frown upon that apparently.

I'm getting through it though. I haven't really noticed a difference with the new meds yet, but Dr. Kay said it'll take a couple more weeks to tell. I definitely feel more stable than when I came in, even though the depression is still there, but it doesn't feel so...big anymore. Like it's no longer controlling me.

It feels like forever since I've seen you, but also like it was just yesterday. Time moves weird in this place. It's disorienting to be cut off from the outside world like this. No TV, no phone, no social media. It's as if my life has paused while I try to get my shit together, but the world is racing ahead without me...like I'll have to run and catch the train back to my old life and there's a chance I won't make it.

But don't worry, baby. I'll always come back to you if you'll wait for me.

Theo

JOURNAL DAY 19

Mercury,

I had a dream last night.

I saw two little boys running through the woods, happy and laughing. Eventually I realized it was because I was chasing them. They seemed familiar the closer I got, but I couldn't see their faces.

Then I heard your voice. You called out to me. The boys turned around and I thought they were us, but they weren't. They were different, but I knew them.

They were ours. The best parts of us.

I think I know why I dreamed of them. Yesterday was rough...the hardest day I've had since coming here. I'm not sure why, but I was hit with so much doubt, wondering if all this was actually worth it, if it was worth putting you through this just for the chance to be with me. Wondering if I'd only let you down again.

Then I saw them and I remembered what I'm fighting for. Not just a life together, but a life with them...the family we could have. I never saw myself having kids before. It wasn't even something I thought I wanted, but I think I do. I want it all with you, Dawson.

Everything we could possibly have in this life, I want to give you. A home. A family. A love that never ends.

A life worth living for.

Theo

JOURNAL DAY 28

Mercury,

Well, this is it. My last day. It feels like I've spent a lifetime here.

Dr. Kay thinks I've made enough progress to move to outpatient status a couple of days early. I personally think a little Christmas spirit went into that decision, but who am I to argue?

Is it crazy that I'm actually fucking terrified?

I tried so hard not to think of this day when I first got here because it seemed so far off, but the last few days it was all I could think of. I've had so many questions on my mind that I gave myself a headache.

Would I feel different when I left? Would everything around me feel different? Would everyone treat me weird or walk on eggshells around me? Would I lose all my progress once I wasn't here? Would you be proud of me?

Would you still want me?

Will you still be there when I come home to you?

God, I hope so. I miss you so fucking much it's hard to

breathe. But if for any reason you haven't waited...if things have changed for you, I need you to know that you are the best thing that has ever happened to me. You are the other half of my soul. You loved me unconditionally and I will love you endlessly. Infinitely. Even when the blood dries in my veins, I will still be loving you.

But I also need you to know that I'll be okay. You gave me strength until I found my own and showed me that I'm so much more than this illness. It's not all that I am and I won't let it have power over me again. Even if I sometimes need help, I will still be okay because of you and what you've done for me.

Thank you for saving me, for loving me, for being my lifeline and my home. I love you, Dawson.

And if you're there waiting for me, I'm never letting you go again.

CHAPTER FIFTY

Stepping outside Harbor House was like taking that final step off the high diving board and free-falling through the air with excitement and fear swirling in your gut. I had been looking forward to this day for weeks, but now that it was here, I was inexplicably nervous.

My journal was clutched in my hand and I wondered how Dawson would take reading the contents. For as much as I fought the idea that first day in group, I ended up writing in it daily, sometimes two or three times depending on what was going on in my head. I was surprised by how much it had actually helped, so it was something I'd carry over into life outside the center. My group therapist had given me a smug, affectionate look when I'd come clean about that in our last session.

Meryl had gifted me a fancy leather-bound journal for a combo Christmas/Discharge Day present. She had become my surrogate mom during my stay, talking me through some of my hardest days here and even switching a shift around to be here on my last day. It was something I didn't know I was missing. My own mother hadn't reached out or said a word to me since shipping me back to Austin, but I couldn't even be mad at her. I just didn't care enough and in the end, that decision was the best one of my fucking life: it brought me back to Dawson.

Being two days away from Christmas felt a bit strange. I hadn't been out in the world in a month, so I hadn't been immersed in the typical holiday shopping music and over-the-top decorations that were everywhere. It felt like I had skipped over the last couple chapters in my book and I was trying to catch up to the storyline, not exactly sure what I had missed.

My veins thrummed with need as I impatiently waited for Dawson to arrive. Dad told me after our family therapy session yesterday that Dawson would be picking me up after discharge and I had lit up like the Christmas tree in Rockefeller Center.

I checked my phone for the time and saw he was almost fifteen minutes late. I mean...it wasn't a lot in the grand scheme of things, but this was important, damn it! I needed to feel his lips on mine and his arms around me more than I needed oxygen.

A grunt of frustration left me when I called and only got his voicemail, but just then, I saw Dawson's black truck turning onto the entrance road down the hill. I was damn near levitating by the time he pulled around the circular driveway and I raced around the back of the truck before he'd even stopped. I was about to fling myself into his arms when the door opened, but it wasn't Dawson who stepped out of the driver's seat.

"What the fuck?" I blurted as I stumbled back.

"You know, I take offense to that," Nate said, crossing his arms. "Is Dawson the only one allowed to get a hug? I mean, I drove all this way to pick you up and deliver you to your man and I don't even get a thank you or bro hug. I get a horrified curse. Nice."

"Hold up, I thought Dawson was picking me up? What do you mean you're 'delivering' me to him?"

"It means I'm cheaper than UPS. Where's your stuff? You've got stuff, right?" Nate walked around the truck before I could answer and picked up my small suitcase to toss in the back seat.

Disappointment swamped me as I realized something must have come up to prevent Dawson from being there. Why hadn't he at least called and let me know so I could have tempered my excitement and maybe *not* almost attacked his friend's face with my tongue?

I climbed into the front seat and buckled up as Nate did the same, shooting me a happy grin. "Alright, let's boogie!"

He started down the drive, but slammed on the brakes not even two seconds later, pitching us forward.

"What the hell, man? What's up?" I grumbled, rubbing my sternum where the seatbelt dug in from the force.

"I almost forgot!" he cried, leaning over to open the glovebox and grab something. He gave me a small square of black silk that unfurled in my hand.

"A blindfold?!"

Nate grinned wickedly. "Yep. Dawson says it's payback time."

I probably owed Dawson an apology. After wearing the offending blindfold the entire way back to the house, I was highly annoyed and a little bit queasy. At least he'd had a delightful date night playlist to listen to.

I had Nate.

Finally, I felt the car slow to a stop. I reached up to free my eyes, but was thwacked on the hand.

"Ouch! For why?"

"Hands off! The blindfold has to stay on until we get to our destination."

I groaned like a toddler having to wait for dessert as Nate came around and helped me out of the truck. He led me by my elbow several feet before coming to an abrupt halt.

"Woah, why did we stop?"

"Uhh, well...shit. I don't think they thought this through."

"Thought what through?"

"You see, part of the surprise is here, but Dawson said you had to keep your blindfold on a little longer."

"Can I take the blindfold off real fast to see this part and then put it back on?"

Nate seemed to think that over for a second. "Yeah, okay, that works. But it goes right back on afterwards or Dawson will sic Stella on my nuts."

With a sigh of relief, I peeled off the silk and blinked rapidly, trying to make sense of what I was seeing.

Large, car-shaped cardboard pieces were affixed to either side of the golf cart, painted to look like a black limousine. My brain worked overtime to figure out exactly how this worked into any surprise Dawson had planned, but at least I had the location pegged.

"Okay, all aboard! Or whatever the fuck they say when you climb into a limo."

"I think 'get in' pretty much covers it."

Nate shoved me and instructed me to slide my blindfold back in place once I'd carefully maneuvered through the door cutout to sit down. We took off towards the woods, but soon I caught the sound of cardboard ripping away and felt the jarring bumps as we drove over it.

"Fuck...my bad. I'll get that later. Umm, maybe don't mention that when we get there?" Nate rambled.

Within a minute, we came to a stop and Nate held my arm to keep me in place. I heard him typing something on his phone real quick and then he was hopping out and coming to help me as well. I gingerly stepped off the cart and my ears perked up at music filtering through the air.

Something was different though. This wasn't just Dawson strumming on his guitar for me. Other instruments joined him, creating an upbeat, melodic loop that felt like the intro to a song I should know.

Nate walked me a little closer to the barn and the blindfold fell away, my heart nearly bursting out of my chest.

Neverland had been transformed, making the clearing look like some kind of fairytale forest with lights strung from the rafters out to some of the surrounding trees, streamers wrapped around the support beams and hanging from the ceiling, and a huge silver and blue balloon arch curved over the low, makeshift stage where the band was. Dawson's mom had an acoustic guitar slung over her shoulders next to an older, tattooed guy with a bass guitar while an attractive, black-haired guy about my age sat behind the drums.

And at the center of it all was Dawson, the man who had the power to start and stop my heart on a whim, standing under a massive banner hung on the front of the barn.

Homecoming 2025

Tears sprang to my eyes and I blinked to clear them, not wanting to miss a second of this. I was vaguely aware of a small crowd of our friends and family scattered around, parting for me as I started towards the stage, drawn in like a moth to Dawson's flame. The music slowed and faded to only Dawson and his guitar as he started singing into the mic, his eyes pinned on me.

The first lines of Alex Warren's "Carry You Home" struck me like a blow to the chest and I froze on the spot as he serenaded me. The rest of the improvised band joined in, the two guys providing backup vocals that perfectly complemented Dawson's rich, warm voice as the song kicked up.

As the song built, the people around me converged near the stage with me, whistling and cheering as though it were a real concert. When the chorus hit, everyone started clapping in time with the song and laughter burst from me at the surreality of the scene around me. Dawson's smile split his face even as he continued singing, flawless and mesmerizing as always.

His eyes never left mine for a second, every lyric and chord a love note to me in a way that was purely Dawson. His intense gaze was radiating love and desire, promise and purpose. It was more than I could ever deserve, more than my heart could bear as it pounded painfully behind my ribs.

The band and noise from our friends faded out as Dawson crooned the last lines alone, baring his heart on the stage for me and pouring every last ounce of his soul into the final notes.

Applause and shouts burst out around us as Dawson lifted his guitar off his shoulders and handed it off to his mom. A flurry of butterflies took off in my stomach as I watched him jump down from the stage and stride over to me, looking sexier than sin in his dark jeans, black button-up, and cowboy boots.

He pulled up short, leaving only a few inches between us and it took an immense willpower I didn't know I possessed not to throw myself at him, but the expression on his face told me to wait. He held a hand out and in my periphery, I saw Aly hand over a clear plastic box.

My heart lurched into my throat and those goddamn tears reappeared while Dawson carefully pulled out the white rose boutonniere and leaned in to pin it on my shirt. I opened my mouth to speak, but nothing came out. Dawson's grin widened until his eyes crinkled on the sides in that way I loved so fucking much, and he slid his hands over my jaw and into my hair.

"Happy Homecoming, baby."

I lunged forward, our mouths colliding in a desperate kiss that raced through my body like a flash fire. His taste exploded in my mouth as our tongues dueled and he swallowed my needy moan. More cheers and wolf-whistles rang out when Dawson swept his hands down to my thighs, hauling me up until I wrapped my legs around his trim waist.

I swear to fuck, that move is the hottest shit ever...

Reluctantly, we pulled back to suck in lungfuls of air, staring into each other's eyes and saying so many things that words couldn't begin to express.

"I missed you," he whispered against my lips.

"Not as much as I missed you, Mercury," I winked. He dropped me back to my feet and I finally allowed myself to look around and take it all in.

All our friends were there dressed to the nines, milling around nearby so Dawson and I could have our little reunion moment. Rhys and Cal were dancing to the music that was now playing from some big speakers while Micah, Bash, Aly, and Fin were standing around talking. Griffin, Nate and Kenji were mingling with Mr. Hayes, my dad, and Dawson's grandfather. I spotted Emilia, Uncle Don, the drummer, and the tattooed bassist over by a table of drinks that was set up. Shock ricocheted through me as it hit me how much trouble he'd gone through to put this together.

"How?...why?..." I stammered, unable to formulate a proper sentence while my brain rebooted from the enormity of what Dawson had done for me. His finger landed on my chin and gently turned me to face him, those sparkling blues holding me in place.

"The entire time you were gone, all I wanted to do was be able to show you how deep for you my love goes," he started. "We never got our Homecoming night, so I wanted a second chance to give it to you. I thought it was appropriate for the most important homecoming of all—yours."

I clamped down on my trembling bottom lip with my teeth, trying to hold in the deluge of emotion that was threatening to drown me. My hands shook where they clung to Dawson's waist and I worried if I tried to speak, I'd break down from the all-consuming happiness I felt.

"Dawson..." I choked out, my voice giving out as my throat closed up and tears flooded my eyes.

He cupped my face and stroked my cheek tenderly, his own eyes glassy and full of joy as he held my gaze.

"I need you to know I'm in this, unconditionally. Your illness will never scare me off. I'll never bail when times get hard for us. I'll be by your side for all of it. If the darkness comes, I will be your light. You can fall apart over and over and I'll pick up your pieces. Because you and me? We're unbreakable, baby. No amount of dark days can take you away from me again."

His mouth met mine again, his lips sliding over mine in a slow, deep embrace. I opened for his tongue as it flicked mine in a teasing caress, exploring me like we had all the time in the world.

Like he'd waited a lifetime to kiss me again.

Like it was the first kiss of the rest of our lives.

We broke apart and decided to join the others before our uncontrollable need won out and clothes started flying off. I only had so much self-control.

Dawson led me over to where most of the crew were circled around talking. The hot drummer walked over and clapped hands with Dawson.

"Hey, excellent job, brother. You've got some golden pipes there," he smiled. There was a faint, lilting Spanish accent to his words and I wondered why he looked so familiar.

"Thanks, man. I appreciate it," Dawson said shyly before motioning to me. "This is my boyfriend, Theo. Theo, this is Mateo."

When he stuck his hand out to shake mine, recognition smacked me in the face. "Oh shit, you were at the karaoke bar last May! That's where I've seen you. You sang "Despacito" or something, and Christ, you were swarmed with girls after that. I remember my date wouldn't shut up about you."

"We're not talking about that," Dawson growled possessively. I grinned deviously at his flare of jealousy.

"I'm surprised he didn't just steal your date," Nate muttered as he took a long pull of his drink, but it was loud enough that Mateo heard it and he turned a frosty glare at him.

"Not my thing. Even this *playboy* has his limits," Mateo sneered with a poisonous grin.

"Psh, limits my ass. I bet your safe word is 'keep going'," Nate slurred, giggling at his own joke. Bash and Dawson exchanged a worried glance, prompting Bash to drag Nate over to the drink table under the pretense of using his bartending skills.

"Dude, what's his deal?" Griffin asked quietly, but Mateo brushed it off with an easy grin.

"Eh, it's all good. Now, I don't know about you guys, but I want to hit up the dance floor." His eyes landed on Fin and Aly across the circle with a charming smirk. "Either of you two beauties care for a spin?"

Aly smirked back flirtatiously while Fin's cheeks pinkened. Before he could say anything, Griffin stepped forward and grabbed his hand.

"That's not gonna happen," he grunted, pulling a dumbstruck Fin behind him and into his arms on the "dance floor" beside Cal and Rhys.

Aly's lips rolled in and she eyed them with open amusement. "Well, okay then...I guess you're dancing with me, hottie."

She yanked Mateo out to where Griffin was dancing with a tense Fin. Kenji strolled over to join Nate, leaving me and Dawson blessedly alone. His lips curved up in a sexy smirk that made my cock twitch in my jeans, and he tugged me into him by my hips.

"Our friends have got some issues," I murmured to him.

"Do you mean Mateo and Nate, or Griffin and Fin?"

"Yes."

He laughed at my non-answer, pulling me even closer to him. I wove my fingers into his hair and brought his forehead against mine, soaking in the utter bliss of being in his arms again.

"I cannot believe you were able to do all this. This is above and beyond anything I imagined coming home to."

"I told you I'd give you anything you want as long as you come back to me," he purred in my ear.

"Mmm, anything?" I leaned back to catch his eye. "What if what I wanted was to sneak off into the woods right now and fuck that tight, sweet hole of yours?"

Dawson's sharp intake of breath and the way his hands slid down to squeeze my ass sent blood straight to my dick.

"Jesus, I've missed that dirty mouth of yours..." he groaned, nipping at my bottom lip. "Let's go."

He gripped my hand and started steering us away from the barn towards the darkened treeline, but just then the music shifted and stopped me in my tracks.

"Wait!"

Dawson turned back to me with a worried expression, but it morphed into curiosity at my watery smile. Without a word, I dragged him over to the center of the dance floor. I draped myself over him and laid my head on his shoulder as we started a slow sway to the familiar Aerosmith ballad.

I started laughing softly, tears rolling unbidden down my cheeks in a confusing blend of emotions. Dawson lifted his shoulder gently, urging me to look up at him.

"Baby, are you okay?"

My cheeks ached from the grin that I couldn't stop, even as more tears escaped and I laughed at the absurd perfection of the moment. I let the lyrics wash over me and fill my soul, just as it had that day in music therapy and I thought about what song I wanted to represent my future.

"I'm perfect," I told him honestly. "I was just thinking this is a great 'soul song', you know?"

Dawson's brows pinched together. "What's a 'soul song'?"

"I'll tell you later," I sighed, laying my head back on his shoulder as we spun around lazily. "Right now, I don't want to miss a thing."

Dawson's Epilogue

TWO WEEKS LATER

New Orleans came alive at night in a riot of colors and music along Bourbon Street as Theo and I wove our way through the dense crowd. Theo had the bright idea to take me out tonight to nurse my non-existent wounds following our loss in the College Football Playoffs earlier that day. It had sucked losing by only six points, but I had no regrets over how my football career had come to an end.

However, when my boyfriend had offered to play designated driver—or rather, designated walker—for me out on the infamous Bourbon Street, I couldn't refuse. I was already a few drinks in and walking was becoming...interesting.

Theo was committed to staying substance-free following his stint at Harbor House. It had only been a couple of weeks since he'd been discharged, but the change in him was remarkable. There was a lightness in him that I hadn't truly seen since we were teenagers before he'd been faced with the reality of his diagnosis. I didn't think it was possible, but Theo enjoyed being on his new medication combo and was diligent in taking it daily.

That wasn't to say everything would always be as good and peaceful as it was now, but he and I were ready for the bad days when they came. Along with Maggie, we had come up with a plan for if or when Theo's symptoms re-emerged and I was confident we could handle it. For now, we were going to enjoy and revel in every good day that we woke up to because we knew how precious they were. We didn't want to take a single minute for granted.

And right now, I was looking forward to the good *night* I planned to enjoy with Theo back at our hotel.

My hand was clasped tight in his as he led us in search of the bar where our group supposedly was. His sleeveless black tank showcased his toned biceps and those sexy as hell tattoos that I wanted to kiss and bite all night. I stumbled over my own feet as I ogled his ass, and Theo glanced over his shoulder at me.

"I think we're almost to the bar, and Nate said they've got seats saved for us, so you'll be able to sit down."

Several of our friends had come to support me for the game, but I also knew that New Orleans had likely been the bigger draw. But they were the last things on my mind right then.

I dug my heels into the ground, tugging on his hand. "I don't want to go to the bar," I said, hearing the booze start to leech into my voice.

Theo turned to me and cupped my cheek, furrowing his brows. "Are you okay, babe? You're not feeling sick or anything, are you?"

I slowly shook my head, gripping his ass with my free hand and stepping into him until his denim-covered cock brushed against mine. I watched his pupils dilate and the breath catch in his throat, leaning in for the kill.

I took his earlobe between my teeth, nipping it gently and sucking it into my mouth in a rhythmic pull. Theo's deep groan vibrated from his chest into mine and my cock pulsed when he thrust his hips forward.

"I need you to take me back to the room, bend me over, and wreck my hole so that I can't sit down for a week. I want to be so full of your cum that it leaks out of me all day tomorrow," I rasped in his ear.

Theo gripped my jaw and slammed our mouths together in a brutal assault on my senses. I didn't give a fuck that we were outside in a crowd of hundreds of people. If he wanted to fuck me right now, I'd eagerly drop my pants and scream his name so everyone around us knew who I belonged to. All too soon, Theo released me and spun on his heel, keeping my hand in a death grip as he hurried us in the direction of our hotel.

The seven minute walk felt like an eternity by the time we strolled through the doors and into the elevator up to our floor. Theo's fingers were tapping a rapid rhythm on his thigh while his other hand stayed latched onto mine. He glanced over at me and the heat in his eyes could have melted me alive. The air around us became intoxicating and overpowering. The instant the doors opened, Theo rushed us down the hall, stopping at our door as I shamelessly felt him up from behind.

"Christ, Dawson, you're making this hard," he grunted as he tried to get the door unlocked.

"That's the idea," I said huskily, licking the back of his neck and eliciting a growl from this throat.

We burst into the room and slammed the door behind us, coming together in a clash of mouths and hands. Clothes were torn off and tossed about carelessly as we tumbled to the bed in a frenzied tangle of naked limbs.

Theo rolled me under him and kneeled above me, the tattoos dotting his chest making me salivate. I tried to lean up to trace them with my tongue, but Theo's hand on my throat held me down. My eyes widened and precum pulsed from my dick at the hot as hell move while he smirked wickedly.

"Not now, beautiful. There'll be time for that later. Right now, I need to be deep inside your ass before I blow."

I moaned and nodded vigorously, incapable of speech. He leaned over and retrieved our lube sitting on the nightstand before shimmying down between my legs. He poured a glob of it on his fingers, bringing one to my rim and circling it teasingly as he grinned up at me. His finger pushed in just as he licked a wide stripe up the vein of my cock and I let out a savage groan. I bucked up into the sensation of him licking and kissing my swollen length while his finger pumped in and out of me.

"Theo...suck me down, please..."

My begging must have done him in because he shoved another finger in my quivering hole at the same time he took me to the back of his throat. I shouted and arched off the bed at the white hot pleasure that surged through me. I bit down on my fist, failing to muffle my sounds as he opened me up mercilessly, the filthy sounds of him devouring my cock making me dizzy with lust.

Theo finally released me with a soft pop and removed his fingers gently to lather himself in the cold gel. I was mindless with desire, needing to be filled in the most desperate, primal way. The hard planes of his body came down on mine, his tongue diving into my mouth and swallowing down all the needy sounds I fed him. I felt his cock prod at my entrance and I beared down, both of us groaning loudly as he slid in inch by inch.

"God, I'll never get tired of being inside you," Theo gasped, sliding out slowly and dragging a moan from my lips. "This hole was made to be fucked by me, wasn't it?"

"Yes...it's all yours. Now fuck me hard and fill me up."

Theo's smile was pure sin. "As you wish."

He slammed into me hard enough to shove me up the bed, setting a feral rhythm that ripped me in two. My hands flew to the headboard above me as he pounded into me, his grunts and gasps igniting me in flames and burning away everything but our carnal need.

The smell of sweat and sex swirled around us, our harsh pants and moans ringing out in the room. Theo raised up on his knees and lifted my legs over his shoulder to bend me almost in half, fucking into me even harder. A guttural cry tore from my throat, my head falling back on the pillow.

"Fucking hell, you're so deep...oh my god, I'm so close. Theo, I—"

My eyes squeezed shut as fireworks fizzed around inside me, a pressure building in my balls that threatened to tear me apart.

"Don't hold back, beautiful. Let go for me because I plan to fuck this pretty hole. *All. Night. Long.*" He punctuated his words with rough thrusts of his hips, hitting my prostate spot on.

When I felt his finger sneak in beside his cock, the extra stretch almost made me black out. I was so close to detonating, a bomb ticking down to an explosion set to raze me to the ground.

"Fffffuck, you're squeezing my cock so hard...get there for me, babe. I want to watch you come while I'm deep in your ass."

He angled his pelvis up, pegging that soft button just right. I felt a tingling heat bloom behind my dick, my balls drawing up tight.

"Oh shit, I'm gonna come...I'm—oh *fuck...*"

Theo and I looked down between us as my orgasm tore through me, cum shooting from my tip in long arcs, covering my chest in a sticky, white mess. My mouth dropped open as I came untouched, the blinding pleasure almost too much to handle.

"Holy shit, that's hot. Yeah, give me that cum," Theo ground out. "You ready for me, beautiful? You're milking me so damn good...fuck, I'm about to come..."

I groaned as his dirty words sent shudders down my body. He thrust into me harder, impaling me on his dick as he chased his own release. Suddenly, he threw his head back on a shout, flooding my insides with hot, pulsing heat. My ass fluttered around him as aftershocks ripped through me and he choked out a broken groan, pumping his seed deeper as he shook above me.

Theo collapsed on my chest, his weight sinking me into the mattress as we gasped for breath and my cum cooled between us. We stayed like that until we came down from the intense high, eventually making our way to the shower to clean up before crawling back in bed and curling around each other.

I rested my head on Theo's chest as his fingers sifted through my hair gently, both of us lost in the hazy afterglow.

"Does it feel weird to be done with football for good?"

I sighed, measuring exactly how I felt knowing that I'd played my last game and I was moving on to the next part of my life.

"Honestly, I thought it would, but right now I just feel...relief. I'm excited for what comes next. I'm sure it'll hit me later on and I'll miss it, but for now, I'm happy."

Theo hummed in acknowledgement, but didn't say anything else. I was about to ask him what was on his mind when he spoke again.

"I think I want to become a substance abuse counselor."

My head snapped up and I gaped at him, not expecting that reveal. "Are you serious?"

Theo chewed on his lip and gave me a wary glance. "Yeah. I thought about it on and off while I was in rehab, but lately the idea keeps coming to me. I really want to become a therapist ultimately, but I think getting my license for substance abuse and chemical dependency counseling first would be smart. It would give me some good experience and since I struggled with that, I feel like I could help others like me."

"What do you want to do with that specifically?"

"Actually...I've been thinking about working in a facility like Harbor House, but for teenagers," he admitted quietly. "I had such shitty experiences during rehab when I was younger, but I've seen the difference a *good* treatment center can make. Fuck, I'm living it! I want to try to give kids like me a chance at getting real help...give them hope and show them that it does get better."

My eyes stung as I saw the passion spark in his own, the determination there unmistakable. "Baby, I think that's an incredible idea."

"Yeah?" The shy grin on his face made my heart stutter.

"Absolutely. It seems like a perfect fit for you."

He pecked a kiss to my lips and squeezed me to him, looking pleased with himself. I was so fucking proud of him for not giving up and finding a goal to work towards, especially after all that he'd gone through the last several months. Hell, the last several *years*. When Theo took a short mental health leave of absence from UT for his rehab stay, I was worried it would derail his progress and he wouldn't have the drive to complete his degree, but I could see just how much this idea meant to him. He was finding his way.

"What about you, babe? Have any ideas of what you want to do after graduation?"

I untangled myself from his arms to sit up beside him, taking his hand in mine and fiddling with his fingers.

"You remember the bassist that helped me out with your Homecoming? Dante?" I asked and he bobbed his head. "Well, he's one of Mom's friends who owns this record label in Austin. He started it up a few years ago and it's doing really well lately. He called me a couple of days ago and asked if I wanted to start interning with him soon and if all goes well, I would transition to assistant creative producer within a year."

"Woah, are you serious?"

"Yep," I beamed. "He wants to expand eventually and needs a second creative producer to come on board, so he's willing to train me until I can fully take over the position. I mean, Mom definitely had a big hand in him even considering me, but I'm not going to knock it. This is exactly what I want to do and getting a foot in the door is the hardest part, so I'm really excited."

"Babe, that's fucking huge!" he exclaimed, slapping me lightly on the bicep. "How did you sit on that news for two days and not tell me?"

"Well, I was a little busy preparing for the playoff game," I smirked dryly, "but I also wanted to wait and tell you when we were on this mini vacation. I figured if the team lost and we were going to be here anyway, I might as well go big and give us something to celebrate at least."

Theo snorted and slung his arm around my shoulder, pressing a kiss to my temple.

"No offense babe, us talking about our career plans is great and all, but it's not exactly 'big'. Now, when I get my license and you get that promotion to producer, *then* we'll have something to celebrate."

"Oh, I wasn't talking about that." He cocked his head at me curiously, but I continued before he could say anything. "You know, I have a ring to give to you. Hold on."

Theo had given me my old class ring yesterday before the playoff game. He thought that since I wore it when we won the championship back in December, it could be my good luck charm. Obviously, it hadn't worked for the game, but it did work out perfectly for my plan. He let out a sound of protest when I slid off the bed.

"Hey, where do you think you're going? You can give it back to me later. Get your sexy ass back here so we can go for round two."

I tossed a smirk over my shoulder before digging in my bag for what I needed, hiding it behind my back as I sauntered over to him. I came over to his side and threw my leg over him to straddle his lap. I smoothed my fingers over his jaw as he gazed at me, taking in every inch of his gorgeous face...the one I wanted to look at for the rest of my life.

He leaned in to kiss me, but I held out the ring box that was in my hand, freezing him in place. His wide eyes were pinned on the box and he stopped breathing.

"I thought after all these years of carrying around that old thing, you deserved a bit of an upgrade," I murmured, slowly opening the box to reveal the ring inside.

Theo inhaled sharply, his fingertips sinking into my waist as if trying to ground himself. He gingerly pulled the band free, studying the intricate Damascus pattern of the dark silver steel. He looked up at me with glassy eyes and I cradled his face, swiping at the lone tear that escaped.

"We can wait until you're ready, but I can't wait another second to have my ring on your finger. I know that no day is guaranteed to us and we've already lost so much time. You are the one constant in my life, the one person I can never be without. My heart has been yours since the day I met you. My life, my very existence doesn't make sense without you, and I don't want another day to go by where I'm not by your side."

"Dawson..." Theo choked out, gripping my wrists and leaning into my touch.

“I had all your firsts and I’ll be damned if I don’t get all your lasts too, baby. Will you marry me, Theo Bishop?”

Theo flipped us so fast my head spun, his lips coming down on mine in a blistering kiss. He was the first to break for air, his warm breaths puffing over my swollen lips.

“Yes. It’s always ‘yes’ with you. There’s no one else for me but you, Mercury.”

He held up the ring for me to slip on his finger before skimming his lips over mine, but a loud buzzing pierced the silence, interrupting us. Theo’s brows furrowed in annoyance as he reached for my phone on the nightstand.

“Huh. Looks like we missed a shit ton of texts and calls from the group.”

I yanked my phone out of his hand and tossed it to the floor, dragging his face back down to mine and feathering my mouth over his.

“They can wait. We can’t.”

A wide grin broke out on his face before his lips collided with mine in a deep, possessive kiss that stole all the breath from my lungs. I was still amazed we’d ended up here after everything, but some part of me never doubted that we would. Theo was the missing piece of me that I would never let go of again.

He was the music in my soul and every beat of my heart. A second chance symphony I’d devote myself to perfecting and playing each day we were given. And as Theo slid back inside me for the second time that night, the sweetest music filled my head.

The End

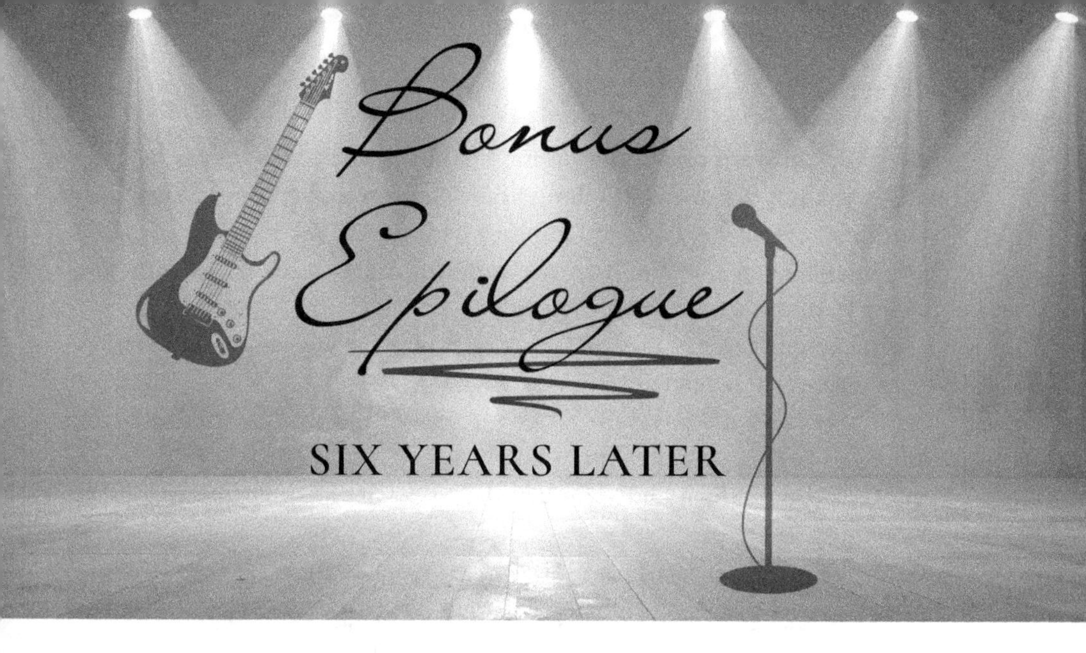

Theo

I rubbed at my exhausted eyes, blinking repeatedly at the computer screen that had started to blur in front of me. Fuck, I had been staring at the damn thing for most of the day and I was no closer to being done with my to-do list for The Lighthouse than when I had started early this morning.

The Lighthouse was my and Meryl's brainchild, our pet project that we'd spent almost two years trying to get off the ground. We had stayed close after I left Harbor House years ago, and she and Beau quickly became part of the family. When I'd started working at Harbor's adolescent wing after my master's program, Meryl had followed me there. Now we were partners in a non-profit venture to open a mental health center for at-risk youth, especially those who couldn't afford high quality mental health care.

Meryl had warned me to go home two hours ago and not get sucked into my seemingly never-ending list, but a quick glance at the clock told me I'd missed dinner. Again.

Fuck my life, Dawson's going to kill me...or deny me sexy times. Ah hell, killing me might be kinder after all.

With a muttered curse, I shut down my computer and gathered my things to head home. This was becoming a bad habit of mine, especially now that we were only three months from opening the center. More often than not, I came home long after Dawson had eaten dinner and sometimes when he'd already gone to bed, which left him in…not the best mood. Even our sex life was suffering because of it, leaving us feeling that much more disconnected.

I fucking hated it. I was just grateful it was the weekend and I could spend some much needed time with my man.

The house was dark when I got home with only the small lights under the kitchen cabinets on to help me see. I set my bag down on the countertop, noticing a folded note in Dawson's neat handwriting.

> I left a plate of lasagna and a slice of cheesecake for you in the fridge. I hope work went well today. See you in the morning, baby.
>
> I love you.

Guilt swamped me as I read it, feeling like a shitty husband for not getting home on time like I promised him I would. I didn't really have an appetite, but for some reason the thought of not eating the food Dawson had prepared for me twisted my stomach. After a quick, sad meal standing over the kitchen sink, I made my way into our bedroom and paused at the doorway, watching Dawson sleep peacefully.

I still couldn't believe he was mine sometimes, that he'd actually married me and we got to have this life. The six years we'd been back together had been a dream. There were moments of stress and arguments just like with any couple, but for the most part, we were exceedingly happy. So far, I had only had one "mood flare", as I called them, during an extremely difficult period in my master's program. But some med readjustment and a few extra sessions with Maggie put me back on track within two months, and our lives continued on as happily as they had been.

However, I could feel things starting to shift slightly in my head. I had been uncharacteristically irritable and hyper-fixated on my work, all compounded by my lack of sleep and the stress of the project. I'd already reached out to Maggie and Dr. Kay to address it before it got any worse, but until I leveled out, I was walking a razor thin line that left me and Dawson on shaky ground for the first time in our marriage.

I climbed onto the bed behind Dawson and curled myself around his solid frame, melting into the warmth of his skin. I nosed at the back of his neck and greedily breathed in his freshly showered scent. He squirmed and my name slipped out in a sleepy grumble.

"It's just me, Mercury," I murmured in his ear, placing a kiss there. "Go back to sleep. I've got you."

"Mmm...the concert...don't forget," he mumbled before burrowing deeper into his pillow.

I huffed in annoyance because I had, in fact, completely forgotten. That was par for the course lately with how occupied my brain had been. The new band Dawson and Dante had signed that summer, Brave New World, had agreed to host a fundraising concert with all proceeds going towards The Lighthouse. It was an incredible deal to help us get the remaining funds we needed and I was fucking ecstatic.

At least I should have been, if it weren't for the lead singer douchebag who constantly flirted with my husband every fucking chance he got. The rest of the band members had been chill to talk to the couple of times I'd met them, but Creed Parrish was pushing his fucking luck. Dawson said I was overreacting since the guy was apparently just a flirty dude, but I swear he was one more wink or suggestive word away from me ripping off his dick and gifting it to Dawson for our anniversary next week.

What can I say? I'm a romantic fucker like that.

I SLOWLY BECAME aware of the smell of bacon and the bright wash of sunlight against my eyelids. I rolled over and reached for Dawson, but felt nothing but cold sheets. Groaning, I gingerly got up and shuffled into our bathroom to shower real fast before following the glorious aroma of breakfast and fresh coffee.

"Morning, beautiful," I hummed as I waltzed into the kitchen, drinking in the sight of my hubby in his gray sweats and tight white t-shirt plating up a stack of pancakes. When he turned and flashed me a soft smile with those hot as fuck glasses perched on his face, I had to grip the wall so I wouldn't fall to my knees and present my ass to him in invitation.

"Morning. How did you sleep?"

"I think I got about five hours worth, so a little better than recently. How about you?" I sidled up behind him and nuzzled his neck, rubbing slow circles over his hipbones. "I hated waking up without you."

Dawson tilted his head to give me better access as I licked and nipped at his throat, eliciting a sexy little groan. "I figured you'd want breakfast ready when you got up."

"More than I want you? Impossible."

I sucked gently at the junction of his neck and shoulder, and Dawson's hands dropped to the counter to steady himself. Just as my fingers wandered down to his waistband, Dawson's phone chimed loudly from the island. I dropped my head back on a growl when he pulled away to check it. I went to grab the orange juice out of the fridge when Dawson's smile caught my attention.

"Who is that, babe?"

His head snapped up, smile falling away as he pocketed his phone rather than put it back down. "It was just Creed confirming a couple things for tonight's show."

"He has your number? Why is he texting you instead of the event coordinator?"

"I only gave it to him for the event, and he was asking about some adjustments to the set list. It's not a big deal," he said, but he seemed to be avoiding eye contact.

Jealousy filtered through my veins like a poisonous vapor and my head flickered with images that made me feel sick. I knew that Maggie would tell me this paranoia was a part of the mania brewing in my stressed out brain and not to give it any power, but that was much easier said than done when all I could focus on was that asshole making my husband smile.

"Is there something going on that I need to know about?" I heard the words escape before I could shove them down. Dawson whirled around with a startled look.

"Like what, baby?"

I opened my mouth to let it all spill out, every horrible, anxious thought that spun through my head when he'd told me Creed texted him. Instead, I took a deep breath, reminding myself that I trusted Dawson.

"Nothing. I was being a jealous ass...forgive me."

His brows pinched slightly as he came closer, running his thumb over my cheek as he studied my face. "You never have anything to be jealous about, baby. You own me, heart and soul."

His mouth met mine in a sweet, firm kiss that chased away all the doubt that clouded my thoughts. Our lips and tongues moved together seamlessly, a sensual dance I never tired of even after all these years. When my hands dropped to cup his length, Dawson pulled back before my hands could make contact.

"Alright, let's eat. The food's getting cold and there's some things I need to take care of before we leave later."

I blew out a frustrated breath, adjusting my hardening cock in my sleep pants and trying not to read anything into his quick dismissal. This was going to be an interesting night.

THE CONCERT WAS BEING HELD at The Concourse Project, an indoor music venue that was large enough to host the crowd the band had managed to draw for us. We had picked up Bash and Micah on the way, so we got there a little later than intended. Being late to events was evidently a recurring problem with them, and with the way Dawson refused to hear their explanation when they'd gotten in the car, I guessed it was for naughty reasons.

The place was packed by the time we got there, but we were lucky enough to have designated parking around back. Dawson let us all in through the backdoor, making our way into the green room where the band was getting ready. My muscles went rigid when Creed's eyes went to Dawson and he broke out in a bright grin, his pierced brow quirking up and his lip ring catching the light. Stupid, gorgeous bastard.

"What's up, you two? Theo, pleasure to see you again," he said charmingly, holding out his hand that I reluctantly shook. "Dawson, mind coming with me real fast? The sound tech needed to ask us both a quick question."

My hand tightened around Dawson's and he shot me a curious look before answering Creed and releasing me to follow him out of the room. My gaze stayed fixed to the door before Rogue, the drummer, came over to talk. I introduced the other members to Micah and Bash, noting with amusement that Bash looped his arm tightly around Micah's waist when the guitarist Joby said something that made his husband laugh out loud.

Guess I'm not the only possessive one around here...

We all settled into easy conversation for a little bit before Dante came in, alerting the band that they went on in ten minutes. Bash, Micah, and I wished them all luck and headed down the hall, but I stopped short when I saw Dawson out of the corner of my eye, laughing and smiling with Creed over in the corner. When Creed laid a hand on Dawson's shoulder before pulling him into a hug, red drenched my vision and my heart pounded with adrenaline.

I didn't remember making a conscious decision to stomp over, but in the blink of an eye, I had Creed shoved up against the wall, my forearm pinned to his chest.

"What the *fuck* do you think you're doing touching my husband?" I growled venomously. Creed, stupid fucker he was, just smirked at me, not recognizing that I was a second away from tearing his throat out with my teeth.

"Theo, what the hell are you doing? Get off him!" Dawson asked in a panic, latching onto my arm to pull me off.

"He's over here flirting with you and *I'm* the one who's in the wrong? Seriously?"

"He wasn't flirting with me!"

"Your hubs is cute when he gets all growly and jealous. Just curious, you two aren't into sharing, are you?" Creed teased.

"Shut up before I break your dick off and shoot it from the t-shirt cannon," I snapped.

"Theo!"

Dawson was cut off by a flurry of activity around us as the other band members grabbed their instruments and the backstage techs rushed around for the final checks. Creed chuckled, carefully removing my arm that had loosened slightly as I stared furiously at Dawson.

"Well, I've got a concert to put on, so I'm gonna leave you to it. Dawson, good luck."

I lunged for him again, but Dawson pushed me back roughly until we were hidden in a small alcove away from prying eyes.

"Why did you attack him like that? What the hell is the matter with you?"

“Me? What about you? Why are you over here laughing and feeling each other up in a dark corner?”

He gaped incredulously at me. “Oh my god, we were not feeling each other up. He’s helping me with something and I was thanking him, you dumbass!”

“Oh yeah? What exactly is he helping you with? Adultery?”

Dawson’s eyes flared with anger, crossing his corded arms over his chest. “You’re being a complete dick right now. I know what you’ve been going through recently is making you paranoid and irrational, and I’m trying really hard not to take it personally. I have never given you a reason to doubt me, Theo. Never.”

“Yeah, well there’s a first time for everything,” I bit out. I spun on my heel and headed for the green room, anger and hurt building in my chest as the band’s first song started up loudly. Two seconds later, Dawson stormed in behind me and slammed the door, barely muffling the music.

“You don’t get to walk away from me in the middle of an argument, especially after accusing me of cheating on you.”

“What am I supposed to think when another guy is texting you, making you smile, and has his hands all over you backstage? Fuck, the dude practically lit up when he saw you walk in! What would you think?”

“I would trust that you’re innocent and I must be missing something important, like you are right now. Christ, I would never jeopardize what we have for anything, Theo! You should know that.”

The pained desperation in his voice had me faltering, rational sense rushing in and trying to drown out the dark paranoia and distrust that my latent mania had bred. I knew one of the only ways to combat my symptoms was to not feed into them, to work through the intrusive thoughts and remember the facts. And the fact was Dawson was as loyal as they came, endlessly devoted to me and our marriage and he proved it daily.

“Then tell me what I’m missing,” I begged. “Please help me understand because I…I hate feeling this way.”

Dawson’s furrowed brows softened slightly. He pulled out his phone and clicked around before handing it to me, showing me his text thread with Creed. I quickly scanned them and though they were absent of any flirting, my eyes widened at what I *did* see.

"You—you were asking him to play onstage with them? For me?"

"Yep," he answered tersely. "It was supposed to be a surprise..."

I felt like the world's biggest tool. Dawson was calmer now, but still staring me down like I was in for a night on the couch. *Shit.*

"I'm really sorry, Mercury...that wasn't fair of me," I apologized, handing the phone back. "But I swear, Creed still has a thing for you."

His eyes widened in disbelief, his lips curling up in a challenging smirk. "Should we put your theory to the test? I think they have a break after the fifth—"

I crossed the short distance and grabbed his face, bringing my mouth down on his in a hard, possessive kiss. My tongue thrust between his lips, moaning at the way his own tongue tangled with mine. I ravaged his mouth as I walked us backwards until Dawson's knees hit the couch against the wall. I roughly spun him around and pressed on his back, bending him over the arm.

"I think you need a reminder of who you belong to, beautiful," I growled, rucking up his shirt enough to press hot kisses down his spine. "It's been way too long since I've filled this slutty hole of yours, hasn't it?"

"Oh my god, yes...please, fuck me," Dawson panted, raising his hips so I could undo his jeans and tug them down his thick thighs.

Without warning, I dove between his crease and tongued around his pink puckered flesh. Dawson cried out harshly, the sound drowned out by the band's fast-paced, drum-heavy number. I licked and sucked at his entrance, shoving my tongue inside when it had loosened under my attention. He began thrusting back on my face, pushing me deeper and babbling incoherently as I tongue-fucked his hole.

"B-baby....oh fuck, I can't wait. I need you inside me."

I licked a long stripe up his crease, bringing my hand down in a hard smack on his cheek. His shout morphed into a moan, hips rutting into the sofa arm in search of friction. I laid another loud smack to his skin, watching it redden and halting his movements.

"You don't get to come until I'm balls deep inside you," I demanded. Dawson whimpered and nodded frantically, looking back at me with blown out pupils and his bottom lip trapped between his teeth. Fuck, he looked so gorgeous like this, desperate and needy for me.

I glanced around until I spotted baby oil on one of the dressing room tables the artists used, grabbing it and slicking up my fingers. I brought them to Dawson's hole, smearing it around before pushing one finger in. His loud moan urged me on as I worked to open him up, stretching him as fast as I could without hurting him. I lubed up my dripping cock, tapping it against him and watching his hole flutter enticingly.

"You ready, baby? This is gonna be hard and fast," I warned, dragging my length up and down his crease. Dawson looked at me over his shoulder, hooded eyes blazing with desire.

"Do it. Fuck me hard. Don't hold back."

I slammed into him in one go, groaning at the exquisite pressure and heat that surrounded my aching cock. I gave him a few seconds to adjust, but when he started to squirm, I drew back and drilled into him hard. I fucked into him ruthlessly, burying myself as deep as I could go.

"Yes yes yes," he pleaded breathlessly, clawing at the couch. "Oh shit, oh god...give it to me, baby. Fill me up."

A feral snarl escaped me at Dawson's filthy demands and I pistoned into him harder, my orgasm so damn close I could taste it.

"Fuck yes...I'm going to stuff you full and send you back out there with my scent all over you and my cum deep in your ass."

Dawson let out another low whimper and his body tightened, his hole clamping down on my cock. He was close, but I didn't want his own cum spilled on the sofa and going to waste. I searched out what I wanted and saw it was conveniently thrown across the nearest table.

Thank you for your cooperation, Creed. Hats off to you, motherfucker.

I reached for the black microfiber cleaning cloth with Creed's name embroidered across the corner...the one I'd seen him cleaning his guitar with last time we met. My hand curved around Dawson's neck and I pulled him up, holding him against my chest. I brought the cloth to his red, leaking cock and started stroking him in time with my hips, and Dawson's knees almost buckled.

"Oh shit, what the—fuck, I'm gonna come," he gasped out, his left arm looping around the back of my neck.

"Come for me, beautiful. Shoot into my hand like the perfect boy you are," I purred, twisting my palm over the head of his dick just right.

Dawson cried out and stiffened as his cock jerked, spurting out ropes of hot cum into the waiting cloth. His ass was a vice around me, almost pushing me out of his body as I surged forward, fucking him through his release. When he was wrung dry and collapsed forward, I rammed into him a few more times before my orgasm barreled down my spine and I erupted deep inside his clenching channel.

I fell forward on top of Dawson, both of us catching our breath. He turned his head slightly, giving me a weird look.

"Was that Creed's guitar towel I just came into?"

"Yep," I grinned. "And that's as much of you as he'll ever get, babe."

He looked both horrified and aroused, but luckily he only smiled and let it go. We both cleaned ourselves up and righted our clothes. Leaving Creed's cloth strategically placed so he'd find it later, I hummed to myself and gripped Dawson's hand as we made our way back out to the show.

The rest of the concert was actually pretty kickass. The band was amazing and despite my dislike for the guy, Creed had a killer set of pipes and an easy charisma on the stage. I would apologize to him after the show like the semi-mature adult I was. I'd gotten my kicks in tonight anyway, so to speak.

"How you doing out there, Austin, Texas?" Creed shouted into the mic as they wrapped up one of their last songs. The sizable crowd roared happily and Creed beamed at their enthusiasm. "The band and I wanted to personally thank you for coming out to help support this incredible organization, The Lighthouse. You being here tonight is going to help turn on the lights at the center and give our kids access to the best fucking mental health care around because *no* child should ever have to suffer alone. And thanks to all of you, we have passed our fundraising goal!"

Cheers and whistles sounded around the room, and Micah knocked me on the shoulder with a wide grin, mouthing silently that he was proud of me. I smiled in thanks and turned to Dawson, but he had disappeared from my side. I was trying to search him out when Creed spoke up again.

"Alright, before we get to our last song, I have a good friend who wanted to come up here and ask a very special someone a question. Dawson, you out there?"

My head whipped around as Dawson walked on stage from the wings, strutting out there with a hint of nerves on his face. He clapped hands with Creed and was brought a guitar that he settled around his shoulders before coming up to the mic.

"Hey y'all, I'm hoping you don't mind if I change things up for a minute before Brave New World closes us out. Theo Hayes?"

Déjà vu hit me hard as I was thrown back to that night long ago when Dawson had gotten on a very different stage to sing to me. My eyes connected with his and my heart beat double-time at the hope shining out of his stunning blues.

"These last two years being married to you have been the best of my life. I am damn thankful every day that we found our way back to each other and that I get to call you mine. We have a near perfect life together...but I think we're ready to add that special piece we've been missing."

Blood pounded in my ears and tears lined my lashes as I stared up at him, trying hard not to lose my shit in front of this damn crowd. My hand went up to his ring hanging around my neck, but this time it was a silent thank you to the universe that I had survived to be here right now, to be given this moment with my husband, my best friend, my Dawson. My fucking everything.

"What do you say, baby? You ready to start a family with me?"

I nodded vigorously, feeling the tears starting to escape.

"I'm sorry, I didn't catch that," he teased with pinched brows.

"Hell yes!" I shouted as loud as I could and the cheer that exploded behind me was deafening.

Dawson laughed and I could see the shimmery glaze of tears in his own eyes as he motioned to the band to start playing. The intro chords for the Foo Fighters "Times Like These" flooded the arena and my smile grew so big that I worried it would crack my face.

Dawson sang his heart out and I hated to admit it, but he and Creed sounded awesome together, their voices blending effortlessly and harmonizing in a way that had the crowd going insane for them. And through it all, Dawson's eyes never left mine, just like always.

All the lights and noise faded away until there was nothing but us, lost in the unbreakable connection we shared as our hearts beat as one. We would struggle and stumble, falter and fail at times, but we'd do it together. Just two men who found the love of their lives at nine-years-old in Neverland and were building a beautiful, messy life. And I realized with a smile, it was more than enough for me.

Acknowledgements

THANK YOU!

As always, my first thank you goes out to my favorite person in the world: my mom. You are my biggest cheerleader and I cannot thank you enough for all you've done for me!

To my editor and platonic soulmate, Amy, thank you so much for everything you have done to help make this book a reality. I genuinely could not have finished Theo and Dawson's story without you, and my heart goes out to you for being such a huge freaking blessing in my life! I love you dearly!

To Margo, my bestie for the restie. I love you with every piece of me! I am so grateful for you every day and am so thankful to have you by my side for this crazy, chaotic journey the last few years. I would not want to do this life without you—you're stuck with me!

To my sensitivity reader, Dee, you are the best of the best! Thank you for every loving message, every phone call, every bit of support and friendship you've given me the last couple of years. My gratitude to you and for you is endless, my lovely! Hugs and kisses to you!

To my sweetest and dearest friends, both new and old: Anja, Cassie, Charlotte, Sundae, Mikaela, Chelsea, Bee, Amanda, Danielle, and Tee. You ladies are such a huge chunk of my heart and I am so humbled by the love and unwavering support you've shown me! Words cannot express how thankful I am for each and every one of you!

A massive thank you to my ARC readers and my street team! You all are amazing!! Thank you for every comment, suggestion, piece of advice, and word of love you've sent me this year!

And last but not least, thank you to all my lovely readers who waited so long for Dawson and Theo to be finished and shared with the world! This was an intense year full of fear, grief, and change and I am beyond thankful to you for hanging in there with me and sending me so much love! None of this would be possible without all of you! I would love to thank you personally if you connect with me on social media!

All my love and thanks,

Erin

ABOUT THE AUTHOR

Erin Rose is a Texas native who is constantly escaping to the world of queer romance; never far from her emotional support Kindle, she spends her days reading, writing, and guzzling coffee in amounts considered dangerous and irresponsible. She is a licensed therapist working as a school counselor while moonlighting as an MM romance author. She loves to write realistically flawed, beautiful characters who serve all the humor, spice, and emotional gut punches on their way to the most satisfying HEAs.

Visit www.erinroseromance.org to stay up-to-date with the *Texas Hearts* series.

Happy reading!

www.ingramcontent.com/pod-product-compliance
Lightning Source LLC
LaVergne TN
LVHW010558100826
845148LV00014B/2754